THE TABERNACLE OF

Kevin Schillo

The Tabernacle of Legion

Acknowledgements

I would first like to thank my graduate advisor Dr. Jason Cassibry for providing me with the incredible opportunity to research fusion propulsion for my Master's and PhD at the Propulsion Research Center (PRC) at the University of Alabama in Huntsville. I am so appreciative to have had such an opportunity that I will donate twenty percent of whatever royalties I may make from this novel to fund future research endeavors at the PRC.

I am also thankful to Dr. Steven Howe for providing me with summer research fellowships at the Center for Space Nuclear Research (CSNR), giving me my first real exposure to nuclear engineering.

Some of the technologies I researched at the CSNR and the PRC feature prominently in this novel, and I hope that they will one day become a reality and help create the future I envision.

I am especially indebted to Steve McCarter, who reviewed an earlier version of my manuscript, and provided me with invaluable editing and feedback that helped yield the far better version of my novel that you now have before you.

Special thanks is given to Mark de Rijk, Adam Hernandez, Miles Gilster, and Jedediah Storey, who supported an endeavor I pursued in a somewhat trying period of my life. As appreciation for their support, four of this novel's dramatis personae bear their namesakes, and I hope that they enjoy these characters and the adventure they have.

Dedicated to my uncle Edward Schillo, who understand the importance of what I do, and left the world all too soon.

The Tabernacle of Legion

Chapter 1

"ATMOSPHERIC REENTRY BEGINNING," reported Mark de Rijk. "See you on the other side." Loud bangs reverberated through the capsule as it shook violently during the descent. Mark gripped the sides of his acceleration couch, and breathed calmly as he looked through the window of the capsule, at the fiery red plasma that enveloped the spacecraft as it plunged through the upper reaches of the Earth's atmosphere.

This was the fourth lunar mission that Mark had commanded. The voyage to the Moon had taken three days, just as it had for the ancient Apollo missions. The veteran astronaut and his crew of five space tourists had spent a week on the lunar surface at the Interplanetary Enterprises (IE) base and exploring the terrain around it. After an additional three days of travel time, the capsule was about to make landfall back on Earth.

There was little for the commander to do in the final phase of the voyage other than wait it out. It had been like that for the overwhelming majority of the mission. The flight computer did nearly all of the work in guiding the capsule on its voyage through cislunar space.

But Mark had still had plenty to do during the past two weeks, primarily ensuring that the five passengers traveling with him were safe and enjoying themselves. They had each paid in excess of one hundred million dollars for the most expensive vacation offered by any company in the world. They deserved to get as much out of the experience as possible.

Mark was always prepared to offer them aid if they developed space sickness during the voyage, assisting them in donning their spacesuits properly for extravehicular activity, and subdue them in the unlikely event they happened to suffer a psychological breakdown. IE required all of its potential space tourists to be physically and mentally fit and undergo extensive training to ensure they were capable of making a voyage to low Earth orbit or the Moon. IE's manned spaceflight operations may have become routine, but nonetheless, Mark had to be prepared to act in the event of if an emergency happened. Such incidents could arise from things such as an impact with debris or meteoroid, a solar flare, or a failure of any of the spacecraft's myriad of interconnected systems.

Sometimes Mark thought of himself as a glorified babysitter, but that was a small price to pay for being paid to travel to the Moon on a fairly regular basis. Not to mention that it helped achieve both his and IE's long-term goals.

Good reviews from space tourists for IE and Mark's services ensured a continued influx of customers for his employer and his continued status as the commander of choice for future missions. This would open another door for him. Because, while Mark greatly enjoyed the lunar missions, he was now eying the next great opportunity on the horizon once IE began its own manned Mars missions.

It was almost a given that he would be the commander of the *Intrepid*'s maiden voyage. That incredible vehicle was still under construction, but would be the crown jewel of IE once it was operational. It would be the first spacecraft to use a fusion propulsion system, and would be capable of running circles around the Cyclers that NASA used.

But all that lay in the future, and would only come to pass if Mark safely returned from this mission.

As the capsule fell into the thicker layers of the atmosphere, the parachutes deployed, slowing the descent. When the capsule was within a few hundred feet of the ground, the hypergolic propellant liquid rocket engines on the side of the vehicle fired, providing a soft propulsive landing.

"Welcome home everyone," Mark said once the capsule had come to a rest.

Technicians helped Mark and the others out of the capsule and into foldup chairs that had been set up around the spacecraft. After spending a week in lunar gravity and a total of six days in microgravity, it required quite a bit of effort for them to stand in the heavy gravity of Earth. Nevertheless, he found it incredibly welcoming to be back on his home planet again. While the lunar surface offered more than its fair share of majesty that he greatly enjoyed, Mark always felt far more welcome on Earth whenever he returned to the planet that had given birth to his species. A world in which the most inhospitable location was still far more welcoming than anywhere on the lunar surface, or in the void separating the Earth and Moon from each other.

He enjoyed breathing fresh air that had not been endlessly circulated and recycled through a spacecraft's life support system. To feel the sun's warmth on his skin again was a blissful sensation that he always missed when he was in space.

Looking around the desert where the capsule had landed, Mark recalled the large crowd that had gathered around the landing site when he had returned from his first voyage to the Moon. That had been the first manned lunar mission since the Apollo program, and it had reignited the public's interest in space travel, but now that such missions had become more or less commonplace, the crowd was considerably smaller, and composed primarily of the friends and family of the returning tourists.

Also present was Miles Gilster, the founder and president of IE, and one of the wealthiest and most powerful men in the world.

Mustering up his strength, Mark rose to his feet to greet his boss.

"You've done an excellent job as always," Miles said to the astronaut with a wide smile.

"Thank you Miles," Mark replied. "It's always a pleasure flying for you."

"Well I hope you never get tired of it because I certainly plan on getting more mileage out of you."

"You can count on that," Mark agreed. "I never plan on retiring."

Miles smiled broadly. "That's exactly what I want to hear."

While Miles stepped over to welcome back the tourists, a younger man approached and greeted Mark.

"Welcome home big brother," said David. Like Miles, Mark's younger brother was always present at every spacecraft launch and landing during the astronaut's career.

"Thank you for being here," Mark replied as he hugged his younger brother.

***

Niflheim Research Station
Antarctica

Niflheim was the primordial realm of ice in Norse mythology, and a fitting name for this research station.

Anna Landes sat in the mess hall, eating a small breakfast of eggs, fruit, and sausages. There were others there, but she sat by herself, as she often did. Landes was the chief physician and biochemist at Niflheim. She had been stationed here for eight months and she missed the warm California sun. But there was much to enjoy about being here, and she was confident that her work here had great merit. In a time when humans were finally beginning to branch out into the solar system, it seemed appropriate to have a thriving base of operations at the bottom of the planet. Despite its extreme environment, Antarctica was still far more hospitable than any other location off Earth. The southernmost continent also harbored extremophiles that thrived in these harsh environmental conditions. Studying these lifeforms aided in ongoing efforts to find alien organisms that might exist in extreme environments throughout the solar system.

Anna would never forget the moment she stepped off the aircraft and set foot onto this frozen continent. The bitter cold air had hit her like a sledgehammer as it filled her lungs. The silence had been eerie. There were no motor vehicles, no human voices, not even the sound of animals. It was the kind of tranquility that astronauts said they experienced on the Moon and Mars. Experiencing that on Earth made her realize just how much noise pollution there was in civilized settings.

Despite the work that kept her busy, Anna had still been able to enjoy many of the incredible sites that Antarctica had to offer. She had been to the McMurdo Dry Valleys, an area of Antarctica so cold and dry that it was considered to be the terrestrial environment most similar to Mars. She had gone there accompanying a team of astrobiologists who were studying the anaerobic bacteria under the Taylor Glacier. This had provided her with an opportunity to see the Blood Falls. The high concentration of iron in the hypersaline lake lying beneath Taylor Glacier gave the outflow its eerie appearance when the iron in the saltwater oxidized upon reaching the surface of the glacier. The valleys also hosted a large number of mummified seal and penguin carcasses that were hundreds, possibly thousands of years old.

Even though Anna had always imagined that Antarctica was teeming with penguins, she had only seen a single penguin colony in all her time here. It had been equally amazing and disgusting, for the teeming masses of penguins she beheld had been accompanied by rivers of sewage the colony produced, along with thousands of corpses of the flightless birds.

The sun had been above the horizon for the past two months, ever since the onset of the Antarctic summer, but the perpetual sunlight of summer was a blessing compared to the winter. The winter months brought storms with the full fury of hurricanes. During the long, sunless nights of winter, there was little to do other than stay indoors and work, although the undulating lights of the aurora australis provided an amazing sight to enjoy in the otherwise perpetual darkness.

Anna and the other scientists at Niflheim were not the only ones that cherished the sights. A multimillionaire, whose name she had since forgotten, had come to Niflheim last year. He was touring all around Antarctica. He was the kind of person that spent more on a vacation to the Moon then Anna would earn in her lifetime. Anna could scarcely imagine what she would do if she had that kind of money, but she understood the importance that people like that had for her research and to other researchers that worked at the frontiers of human civilization.

Money from wealthy tourists seeking a vacation in exotic locations was as important to the projects in Antarctica as the funding from government agencies that supported fundamental scientific research and that from corporations hoping to cash in on new materials or biomedical technologies. It was the same on the stations in orbit over the Earth and on the lunar surface. The first lunar base had been established by a private aerospace company to function primarily as an exotic vacation locale for multibillionaires. If private enterprises like IE had their way, Mars would become the next place for the absurdly wealthy to spend their vacations.

Anna hardly ever went outside, because there wasn't much reason to. There were no penguin colonies or other concentrations of fauna nearby. She did all of her research in her lab. It was always abysmally cold outside, a cold that

7

she knew she would never be able to get used to. Although the millionaire tourist that had come to Niflheim had done nothing to disrupt Anna's or anyone else's research, her life at Niflheim was rather mundane and part of her would have welcomed it.

"Mind if I join you?"

Anna looked up to see Paul Kivi sit down on the opposite side of the table. He was Niflheim's leading climatologist. He and his team had been out collecting ice core samples, and had returned the previous night.

"Knock yourself out," Anna replied.

Paul sat down next to her, and a grin began to spread across his face.

"What are you smiling about?" Anna inquired.

"I wanted to tell you that you should come down to the ice core storage. We found something quite interesting."

"Ice core research is a bit outside my department."

He chuckled. "I'm well aware of that. But trust me; you'll definitely want to see this."

"What is it?"

"It's best if you see for yourself." Paul got up from the table.

Her interest piqued, Anna followed him.

Paul led her to the large walk-in freezer where the ice core samples were stored. They both donned heavy jackets before entering the freezer. The frigid air sapped her body heat. The freezer had to be kept as cold as the outside environment to preserve the ice core samples that occupied the shelves. These cores were vital for studying what the climate of Antarctica and the rest of the world had been like over a span of tens of thousands of years.

At the center of the freezer was a large metallic table and lying on the table was a block of ice about seven feet long encasing something dark. She walked closer to the table to get a better look at the frozen object. The translucent ice made it difficult to see the form with complete clarity, but it was obvious that it was a human body. A man. His skin was as dark as obsidian, in stark contrast to the white world in which he had been found.

"Holy shit," Anna said, almost whispering.

"We dug him up last night," Paul said.

"How did you find him?" Anna asked.

"Serendipity. We were using ground-penetrating radar to look for a good place to take some ice core samples, and the readings we got indicated that something was buried under the ice, and that it wasn't rock. We figured that we may have found something of potential significance, so we decided to dig it up."

"It's a good thing you did." She walked closer to get a better look, and was able to see the man's dark face underneath the translucent ice. She reached out and touched the top of the ice slab, directly above the man's face. The cold from the ice bit at her hand like the fangs of a vampire, siphoning thermal energy from her body, and she quickly withdrew her hand.

"Did you date the age of the ice?" she asked Paul.

"Yes. It's over seventy thousand years old."

Anna almost jumped upon hearing that. "Are you sure?" her voice trembled.

"We took twenty different samples. They all gave consistent results."

She did not say anything, and turned back to look at the body in awe.

"I don't know that much about ancient human migration," Paul mused, "but I think it's safe to say that an ancient caveman shouldn't have been able to get here. That's why we checked the age of the ice so many times."

"You were right to be skeptical," said Anna. "Seventy thousand years ago, modern humans were barely even beginning to spread beyond Africa. Not only that, but that

9

was also around the time that the Toba eruption occurred, and that reduced the entire human species to just a few thousand individuals."

"Jesus. And you think he was able to build a boat and just drifted here all the way from Africa?"

"He must have, because I don't see any other possible way he could have gotten here. You should feel honored for having found him; this is one of the greatest anthropological discoveries in history."

Anna leaned closer in an attempt to see the ancient face, but it remained obscured by the ice. One thing that did stand out to her was his pose. The man seemed to be lying flat on his back. Almost as if he had died peacefully. Either that or someone had placed him in this position post mortem.

She wondered who the man was, what kind of life he had lived. Had he been a bold explorer, bravely crossing the ocean with no idea of what he might find? Or had he been a social outcast, rejected by his people and forced to flee, and hoping to find a new and better life somewhere across the untraversed sea?

"How do you think he got here?" Paul asked, pulling Anna from her thoughts. "We're over two hundred miles from the coast. Don't you think he would've dropped dead long before he was able to walk this far?"

"He must have had some clothing that kept him warm enough to fend off hypothermia for a while," Anna speculated. "Once he reached the coast, he probably broke down his raft and used it to fuel a fire to keep warm. He must have realized that he had no hope of surviving at the coast, and then decided to walk farther inland in hope of finding food and someplace a little warmer. He might have rationed the wood as he walked, not knowing how long it would be until he found a new source of wood to burn. But he had no way of knowing how barren Antarctica is, or

10

how hopeless his chances of survival were."

"How do you think he died? Hypothermia?"

Anna shook her head. "I don't think so. If he had died of hypothermia, he likely would have curled up into a fetal position. The fact that he's in a supine position indicates that that was unlikely to be the cause. Or if he had died of hypothermia, he must have been repositioned into a supine position by someone else after he had died. Because to be honest, I can't think of any cause of death that would have led to him lying flat on his back like this if he had been alone."

"So you do think there was someone else with him that buried him?"

"If I had to propose a hypothesis, I'd say that yes, there must have been at least one other person with him, and whoever that was must have buried him. That other person or persons might have also taken this guy's clothes before they buried him. They probably figured that his clothes would have aided them in their survival, and it's not as though he would have needed them after he died anyway."

"We've been searching for other bodies, but haven't found any indication of there being more, at least not in the area we found this guy."

"Did you find any artifacts near him?"

Paul shook his head. "I'm afraid not."

Anna looked back at the iceman. "That's unfortunate."

She again peered through the ice, trying to get a better look at the iceman's face.

"It's highly unlikely he would have gotten this far without any supplies," Anna continued. "Whatever clothing he might have once worn could have told us even more about him. Where he may have originated from, what skills he may have possessed, how advanced the society was that he came from. How skilled he was in crafting things."

Anna broke her gaze away from the iceman and looked

at Paul. "I need to do a very thorough examination of him," she said. "Hopefully that will reveal a few of his secrets."

"What are you going to do?" Paul asked.

"First, I'll take a biopsy. I really want to see what condition his tissue is in after being in the ice so long. I'll also sequence his DNA so that we'll know to what ethnic group he's most closely related.

"And I think that we should give him a name," she said.

"Alright," said Paul. "What do you want to call him? Adam?"

Anna shook her head. "Too cliché." She thought back to when she had first learned about Niflheim when she was searching for employment in Antarctica. She had been somewhat confused over the name choice, and after a quick internet search, she had learned that the research facility was named after one of the nine worlds of Norse mythology. Her interest galvanized, Anna went on to read more about Norse mythology, and looking down at the iceman made her think of Ask and Embla, the first humans created by the god Odin and his brothers.

"How about Ask?" Anna suggested.

Paul chuckled. "Fine by me. Too bad we can't find Embla for him."

Anna looked back at the iceman once again. "Yeah, too bad indeed."

Chapter 2

Interplanetary Enterprises Headquarters
Hawthorne, California

DESMOND BERENS WATCHED THE STREAM OF DATA that was being displayed on the computer, monitoring the health of spacecraft as it approached the asteroid. No matter how many times he had done this, he still found himself incredibly nervous whenever he directed a miner to rendezvous with a new asteroid. It had been like this ever since Interplanetary Enterprise's first asteroid mission fifteen years earlier.

Desmond had started working with IE right after he graduated from college. Having always held a great passion for space travel, Desmond dreamed of working for a company like IE, and was overjoyed when he got the job offer.

Miles Gilster, the founder of IE, had started his company with the intention of revolutionizing commercial space activity. At the time, the greatest development in commercial space endeavors was a single commercial space station in low Earth orbit that had been established by a rival space company. Wealthy individuals paid several million dollars to spend a few days onboard. But Miles dreamed of something far more ambitious.

What Miles wanted was nothing less than to jump-start an industrial revolution in space. IE's first endeavor was to send two robotic miners to a near-Earth asteroid, where they would extract precious metals and ship them back to Earth. No aerospace company had even attempted to send a spacecraft beyond the Moon, far less try to land on an asteroid. But what truly seemed daunting about the enterprise was that it was intended to be fully self-sustaining. The robotic miners did more than just mine metals; they could also process them and build new miners.

The hope was that these miners would make asteroid mining so self-sustaining that IE would never have to launch any more robotic miners from Earth. So, while the investment to build and launch the first pair of spacecraft was very large, the long-term operational costs would be very small.

The sheer complexity of the project seemed overwhelming at first, but Desmond realized the immense benefit that it would bring to IE, and so he was fully committed to making it a reality. Desmond had worked on 3D printers while he was in college, so he had a bit of experience working on machines that could produce other working machinery. Because of this, he was assigned to work on the systems that produced the transports and new miners. To meet tight design review deadlines imposed by the company, he often worked long hours, sometimes going sleepless for days.

Naturally, there was great skepticism that IE could successfully pull such an undertaking Experts from rival aerospace companies, as well as NASA, openly criticized IE's mission plan. In the entire history of space exploration, there had been only a handful of asteroid missions that returned samples to Earth. Collectively, these missions had returned only a few kilograms of material for research purposes.

The only way asteroid mining could succeed commercially would be if the miners were successful in replicating themselves to expand operations and replace damaged or worn out machines. In addition, they had to be programmed to build tugs to transport mined material. And that was something that few believed was possible. While self-replicating machines had been utilized in many different industries on Earth, many people doubted that they could be used to establish a self-sustaining operation in space without any assistance from astronauts. If any part failed before the transports were fully assembled, then there would be no hope for self-sustaining mining operations.

This was what Desmond had been assigned to work on when he was hired by IE. At first, he was somewhat offended by what the critics were saying about his work, but he told himself that the best way to silence the critics once and for all was by conducting a successful mission. He also knew that if the mission failed, the company would be driven to bankruptcy. And if that did happen, he would blame himself, even if the failure was due to a subsystem for which he was not responsible.

Desmond was there on the day that the miners were launched from Cape Canaveral. He had seen many rocket launches in his life, carrying both manned and unmanned spacecraft, but this was the first time one had carried a spacecraft that he had worked on. He could not help but hold his breath as it lifted off, propelled by a thunderous and powerful exhaust.

It took nearly a month for the two miners to reach the target asteroid. Desmond was as nervous during the rendezvous as he had been during the launch. But like the launch, the rendezvous had been a complete success, and the two miners went right to work at extracting the asteroid's metals.

He spent most of his time monitoring the status of the miners, making sure that nothing was wrong. Sometimes he had to make small but necessary changes to their activities, but not very often. The hardest decisions he had to make were when to sacrifice one of the spacecraft.

Like all parts of the mission, the atmospheric entry of the transports was a nerve-racking experience for Desmond and everyone with whom he worked. Thankfully, like all other crucial moments of the operation, it was a complete success, and the transports landed successfully, carrying billions of dollars' worth of gold, silver, platinum, cobalt, nickel, iridium and other minerals.

The revenue that IE generated from selling the metals was sufficient to cover the cost of the mission, and it was not long before the company was profitable. By the time the asteroid's resources had been depleted, IE had generated more than two trillion dollars in profits. Several new operational miners had also been produced, and they were sent off to continue mining other asteroids.

Using the vast amount of revenue generated by asteroid mining, IE began to branch out into other space endeavors, establishing space stations in low Earth orbit, lunar orbit, and the lunar surface. While IE had not been founded as a space tourism company, Miles Gilster recognized the potential for space tourism and exploited the market to the fullest extent practicable. Several billion dollars were generated annually from people that spent days, weeks, or months on IE's stations. Some people were even choosing to live on the Moon permanently.

To help support these new operations, some of the miner spacecraft were sent to carbonaceous asteroids. These asteroids, deficient in precious metals, contained a valuable resource, water ice that was sent to space stations in Earth orbit. Some of it was electrolyzed, to provide hydrogen and oxygen for use as propellant. Some of the oxygen was used in life support systems. Some was used as drinking water. In addition, these chondrites contained nitrogen, ammonia, and other substances useful for the life-support systems in spacecraft.

This helped to reduce the cost of space operations even more, so much so that future deep space operations suddenly became very economical. IE became the single most profitable company in history, generating tens of trillions of dollars from asteroid mining and tens of millions more from space tourism.

Because of the huge profits IE reaped, other aerospace

companies scrambled to make inroads into asteroid mining and break the monopoly IE held. Some were more successful than others were. Governments funded some, fearing that the stranglehold IE held on these resources would choke their economies.

In a span of a few years, several companies had succeeded in asteroid mining, rendering mining operations on Earth obsolete and unprofitable.

As IE's operations expanded, Desmond was eventually promoted to the position of Mission Director. In the years since then, he still felt a sort of emotional connection with the robotic miners that he directed. He felt great pride when they began their work, and felt great sadness when they died. Desmond had invested a lot of pride, work and emotion into them and it was heartbreaking when a miner died or was retired. For him, it was like losing a child, a mechanical child to be sure, but a child nonetheless. He still felt connected to each miner, old or new. It was no different with this miner, which was making its final preparations for rendezvousing with the target asteroid.

This was the most delicate part of the operation. Descending under the influence of the asteroid's low gravity was more like executing a rendezvous with another spacecraft. Everyone in the control room was glued to their screens as the miner began its descent to the surface. The asteroid was so far away that data transmissions took about ninety-three seconds to travel from the miner to Mission Control. So by the time the transmission was received, the miner had already succeeded or failed to rendezvous. They were just waiting to find out. If it had failed, it would not necessarily spell the end of the mission, since there was still sufficient propellant to make several more attempts.

Desmond hoped that it would not come to that. He watched in silence as the miner unceremoniously touched down on the surface of the target asteroid. All systems were operating nominally. Everyone in Mission Control cheered.

Only then did Desmond relax. "Good work, everyone,"

The miner immediately went to work at drilling through the rock, spewing, dust and small pebbles. Some of this debris would eventually fall back to the surface, but some gained enough momentum to escape the asteroid's shallow gravity well. It was something that Desmond had seen many times before, but one that he never grew tired of, for it meant that he and his team had done their jobs well. Feeling triumphant, Desmond leaned back in his chair and resumed monitoring the robot's operations.

***

Mark de Rijk breathed a sigh of relief as he executed the final maneuver that put the *Intrepid* into orbit over Mars. He had spent the past three hours in the simulator, rehearsing each of the maneuvers the *Intrepid* would have to perform during its voyage to Mars. Despite having returned to Earth from the Moon just four days earlier, Mark had wasted no time getting back to work in the *Intrepid* simulator's command seat.

Mark could not recall the number of times he had been killed in the simulator. Micrometeorite impacts, mechanical failures of the spacecraft's interconnected systems, and sudden intense bursts of radiation from solar flares were just a few of the simulated disasters that befell him. Whenever such a disaster occurred, Mark did everything he possibly could to save the spacecraft. But there were cases where he simply had no chance of saving the mission, or even managing to survive. Those were the circumstances he feared the most, and knew that he was extremely fortunate to never have experienced such a disaster. He figured that that was one of the reasons why he was a top contender for command of the *Intrepid*.

Having commanded many missions carrying people, food, and equipment to IE's space stations, Mark took great pride in flying and fully believed in IE's objectives. Six years after commanding the first orbital mission, Mark felt honored when he was given command of IE's first manned lunar landing. As with the orbital facilities, IE's long-term goal was to create a thriving industry on the Moon. A habitat module had been sent to the lunar surface a month before the manned landing. Mark's mission was to help establish the first commercial lunar base by delivering sufficient supplies and personnel to enable permanent lunar operations. That first mission had afforded him the opportunity to walk on the Moon, one of Mark's lifelong dreams. To see Earth reduced to such a tiny sphere gave him a newfound sense of his place in the universe.

What really set the Moon apart from IE's other operations was the mining of helium-three (He-3), which quickly became a mainstay of the lunar economy. With fusion reactors now providing a significant portion of the world's energy, He-3 was a valuable resource that helped spur the development of a thriving mining industry on the Moon.

Even with all of the missions he had commanded, Mark believed that command of the *Intrepid* would dwarf everything he had done before. Like so many of his previous missions, the fusion spacecraft was intended to push the boundaries of commercial manned spaceflight. This time, the target would be Mars.

With all the advancements that IE and other private space companies had made on the Moon and in Earth orbit, government space agencies had been pressured into pooling resources and making their own advances in manned space exploration. This resulted in an internationally funded effort for the first manned mission to Mars and culminated in the establishment of a permanent manned base on Mars using mission architecture that first had been envisioned by the legendary Apollo moonwalker Buzz Aldrin. Crews were rotated between Earth and Mars on a regular basis using two Cycler spacecraft, the *Armstrong* and the *Aldrin*. Like the robotic miners that IE used, the Cyclers used nuclear thermal rocket engines that had been developed at the Center for Space Nuclear Research under the leadership of Dr. Steven Howe.

The *Aldrin* carried outbound astronauts from Earth to Mars, and the Armstrong carried them from Mars back to Earth. It took five months for the *Aldrin* to ferry astronauts from Earth to Mars. For eighteen months, the two crews shared the Collins base until the Armstrong arrived to take the earlier crew back to Earth. An entire crew mission lasted five years.

Despite the success of the Cyclers, Miles was not content to let Mars remain as a frontier solely controlled by government space agencies. With the founding of IE, Miles had made one of his goals to open Mars up to commercial development, and now he finally had the financial and technological resources to make that happen.

The *Intrepid* would be the very first spacecraft to utilize fusion propulsion, its development having been funded entirely by IE. The spacecraft was still in the process of being assembled in low Earth orbit, but once operational, it would be capable of traveling from Earth to Mars in as few as six weeks, far faster than the Cyclers. It would also be capable of carrying massive payloads, which could ferry equipment and supplies to expand the Collins base or help establish new bases.

There were plenty of millionaires and billionaires who had expressed interest in going to Mars. It was the same tourism impetus that had driven the development of so much of the commercial space industry. The opportunity to explore a whole new world and walk where no human ever had before was alluring enough for people to spend millions of dollars to spend months traversing the vast distance between Earth and Mars while living inside cramped habitat modules.

Miles had even spoken of finding the Sojourner, Spirit, Opportunity, and Curiosity rovers. He said that if he were able to bring them back to Earth he would donate them to the Smithsonian.

As was the case with the development of many spacecraft, a series of setbacks had pushed back the launch of the *Intrepid*. Originally intended to be launched the previous year, the anticipated completion date was now about two years away. Regardless of how long it took, Mark was convinced that the wait to walk on the red sands of Mars would be worth it.

After spending two hours in the simulator, Mark felt he had earned a short break.

"You did a great job there," he heard someone say as soon as he stepped out of the simulator.

Mark instinctively identified the source of the voice, and turned to see Ning Wu standing nearby. She had made a major breakthrough in fusion technology doing research in her PhD program under Dr. Jason Cassibry, one of the world's leading experts in pulsed fusion propulsion systems. Ning had used her advisor's Z-pinch fusion machine to design a prototype fusion propulsion system that was economical and could be with available technology. She went on to work on several advanced propulsion concepts for NASA before joining IE as a fusion engineer. In her years of working for the company, she had played an integral role in the development of the fusion propulsion system that would be used on the *Intrepid*.

"How many times have you been killed in there?" Ning asked.

There wasn't much of a reason for her to have asked him this. As part of the design team, she had access to the

21

files from each of Mark's simulated missions. But Mark played along anyway.

"I've long since lost count," he replied.

"How do the simulated mission failures make you feel?" she asked. "You'll know damn near every possible way you could die once you actually are aboard the real spacecraft. Knowing how your life will end was once regarded as being in the realm of divine prophecy."

In addition to her expertise in fusion propulsion engineering, Ning could be quite philosophical at times. Mark always enjoyed having philosophical conversations with her.

Ning had spent much of her time in the testing facility where the prototype engine had been built and tested. Mark had met her when she came to IE headquarters. Here, she was directing the construction of the *Intrepid*'s engine.

"Knowing the myriad of ways in which life may come to a cataclysmic end and what I need to do in those scenarios is what I need to survive," Mark said. "The fact that we can die in ways our ancestors couldn't even begin to imagine and know in advance how such catastrophes can happen is a testament to how far we've come as a civilization. Having this capability only makes me appreciate life more."

"I agree completely," said Ning. "But I wouldn't want you to go onboard it if I thought there was a serious chance you wouldn't come back alive. And I'd blame myself if you ended up dying because of something going wrong with the reactor."

"Well, I have full confidence in what you've built for us. And never sell yourself short. We wouldn't be going to Mars at all if it wasn't for you."

Ning smiled. "Doing anything after work?"

"Can't say that I am."

"Why don't you come by my place then?"

"I'll happily oblige," Mark said with a happy grin.

Chapter 3

DESPITE HAVING BEEN ON THE ASTEROID for nearly twenty-four hours, the miner had yet to find any deposits of precious metals or volatiles. But that wasn't what was disturbing Desmond when he sat down at his work station. What was unnerving to him was that the miner had not been able to penetrate through an inch of rock in more than three hours. The only other person present in the control room was Alexis Razol. She worked night shifts. Desmond had never seen her here this early in the morning, and she looked more than a little worried.

All of this told Desmond that something must be wrong with the miner. There had been occasions where drills had gotten stuck for a protracted period of time. That usually meant that any hope for extracting the asteroid's resources was gone.

"Why isn't the drill getting any deeper?" Desmond finally asked Alexis. "Is there a problem with it?"

"No," said Alexis. "Everything is working perfectly fine. It's just not able to get through the material that it's encountered."

That was very peculiar. A miner could get worn down after repeated uses, but this was a newly manufactured piece of hardware. Although there had been hardware failure on numerous miners over the years, there had never been one that suffered a drill failure immediately after commencing digging.

"What kind of material is it?" Desmond asked.

"That's just it: I don't know. From what I've been able to gather, it's harder than any substance that's ever been encountered by one of our miners before."

"And you're positive there's nothing wrong with the drills?"

"Yes."

"Have you done a spectroscopic analysis on this unknown material?"

"I tried, but I've gotten nothing back."

"What? Why not? Are the sensors not working?"

"No. There's nothing wrong with any of the miner's systems. I just can't identify whatever the miner is trying to get through."

"Why the hell is that?"

Alexis looked completely bewildered, as if she couldn't even believe what she was saying. "You may want to take a look for yourself."

"Okay, let me see it," said Desmond.

Alexis pulled up a video feed, showing the miner at the bottom of the shaft it had dug in the asteroid. The miner illuminated the shaft's walls consisting of rough, irregular, grayish asteroid rock. It was nothing that Desmond hadn't seen before.

Desmond watched as Alexis panned the camera down to the bottom of the shaft, and was a little perplexed at what he saw. At first, he thought that the miner had drilled right through the asteroid, and that he was looking out at the blackness of space. But no stars were visible. It just appeared to be an infinite darkness that seemed to absorb all light.

"What the hell am I looking at?" Desmond asked, not taking his eyes off of the monitor.

Alexis shrugged. "Like I said, I don't really know. But the drills can't make a dent in it. And I'm not getting any readings on the spectrometer. In fact, it doesn't seem to be emitting or reflecting any detectable electromagnetic radiation."

"Is that why it looks so…" his voice trailed off.

"Black?"

"Yeah. I mean, cripes, that's the eeriest thing I've ever seen."

"I don't disagree with you on that."

Desmond found himself unable to pry his eyes from the monitor. The strange material held his gaze almost hypnotically. "What kind of material could absorb radiation so effectively?"

"An ideal blackbody," said Alexis.

"Hmm." Hearing her say that somehow underscored the otherworldliness of the surface. "And what kind of material does an ideal blackbody usually consist of?"

"Well...the closest thing anyone's ever come to making an ideal blackbody material has been a special kind of arrangement of carbon nanotubes, and it was able to absorb about ninety-nine percent of electromagnetic radiation. But like I said, I haven't been able to detect the slightest bit of radiation from this thing. All indications are that it is absorbing one hundred percent of incoming radiation."

"Interesting," said Desmond. He knew what he wanted to say, but he was afraid to say it.

Alexis looked at him, and seemed to know what was on his mind.

Finally, Desmond said, "So we have something that's harder than any natural substance has a right to be and can absorb radiation as effectively as a black hole." He looked at Alexis intently. "Are you willing to say that this thing is an artificial construct?"

Alexis nodded. "Yes," she said. "I think it's safe to say it's artificial."

"Okay," Desmond said slowly. "So it's artificial. The question is: who put it there? And why?"

"There are no records of any operations on or near this asteroid by any other corporation, or by NASA. There's also no record of the Russian, Japanese, Chinese, or European space agencies doing anything on this asteroid. Not only that, but I'm willing to bet that no one on Earth

26

has this kind of material, much less the capability to secretly send it to an asteroid and burry it underneath the surface for no apparent reason."

"Then who the hell put it there?"

She did not respond, and only looked at him with deep concern.

"You don't actually think…" Desmond turned from his workstation to look at Alexis, who was looking bewildered, and even a little terrified. It was obvious that they were all thinking the same thing, but were too afraid to say it.

Desmond slumped back into his chair, took a deep breath, and let it out slowly. "Get Miles," he said. "He needs to see this."

***

David stood patiently by the front door of his brother's house. Mark was always busy at IE, and David had fully expected him to show up late. Sometimes Mark had to cancel it altogether. David knew full well how demanding Mark's job was, and never held it against his brother when last-minute scheduling conflicts happened.

Nonetheless, David had felt compelled to be here at they had time they had scheduled to meet. He was always grateful anytime when his brother was able to take time off from work to join him for a game of pool.

At least it was a decent day with only a handful of clouds in the sky with little humidity.

Around noon, Mark pulled up into the driveway. This was one of those rare occasions where Mark showed up on time.

David greeted his brother with a firm handshake and a warm smile.

"Hey David," Mark grinned as he took his brother's hand in his own, and wrapped his left arm around his back. "How are you doing?"

"Pretty good," replied David. "How has work been

27

treating you?"

"Okay, for the most part. How about you?"

"Same as usual."

"Well that's good, I suppose."

The two of them walked up to the house, and Mark unlocked the door.

"You don't have to wait for me, you know," Mark said as he walked inside. "You have a key, and you're always welcome to come in here anytime you want."

"I know," David said as he followed his brother. "But I just never feel right doing that."

The two of them walked down into the basement, which Mark had refurbished into a lounge shortly after he had bought this house. At the center was a pool table, where Mark and David had played many games together over the years.

"So," David said, as his brother set up the balls on the table, "is there a new secret project you're working on?"

"If there was, I wouldn't be able to tell you about it."

"Right, of course."

Mark finished racking the balls, and picked up a cue stick.

"Do you want to break, or should I?" David asked as he picked up another cue stick

"I did it last time," said Mark. "You go ahead."

"All right." David lined his cue stick up with the cue ball, and hit it sharply, sending the cue ball head on into the numbered balls. The impact sent them caroming wildly over the table, but none dropped into any of the pockets.

David eyed the table ruefully and grunted, "Your turn."

Mark surveyed the table, lined up his shot carefully, and sent the cue ball to kiss a green solid on the right side. The six ball rolled into the far left pocket. "Trajectory," he grinned, "it's all about trajectory. Guess I'm solids."

Mark lined up on the three ball, and made a perfect combination shot, dropping the one ball into another pocket. As he lined up a third shot, he looked up and asked, "So how have things been going at church?"

"Okay," said David. "Attendance has been more or less constant for the past couple of months."

"Better than nothing, right?"

"Yeah, I suppose."

David was pretty sure that being Mark's brother had played a significant role in his appointment as Parish priest at the local Catholic Church. Maybe they thought that with him being the brother of one of the top astronaut's in the world would help boost attendance. But the fact of the matter was that there had been no real improvement in attendance since David had been named to the position.

Mark missed his next shot. "Too much English," he growled. "Your turn."

David sized up his options with a jaundiced eye. The only shot open to him was a three-fourteen combination He needed a little divine intervention for that to work, and he didn't get it. He watched as the cue ball brushed the left side of the three ball and roll lazily into the side pocket. Letting the tapered cue slide to the floor, bouncing its rubber butt beside his foot, he shrugged, "Guess it's your turn again."

David could not remember the last time he had beaten Mark in a game of pool, but he didn't care about that. He just enjoyed having the opportunity to spend some time with his brother.

For a long time, the two brothers had drifted apart. It began when they were in school. They had gone to the same private Catholic school from kindergarten to high school. During that time, Mark grew increasingly disillusioned with Christianity as he learned about the different denominations and other religions. His studies in

29

philosophy and the sciences further challenged his beliefs in God. His faith continued to wane until he utterly abandoned his religious beliefs.

David was completely baffled when Mark embraced atheism. It sparked numerous and intense arguments between them over the years on religion, science, and philosophy. By the time the two of them entered college, David felt like they were going to different planets. Mark had gone on to study aeronautical engineering at a prestigious university while David went to a small, but excellent Catholic college to pursue studies in religion and theology. David was ordained as a priest ten years after he graduated from college, having attended Seminary where he earned a Masters in Divinity, and serving a brief time as a Deacon. Around that same time Mark became one of IE's top pilots.

Mark retrieved the cue ball and lined it up for an easy shot on the three. Making the shot, he found the cue ball surrounded by solids, leaving him no shot. He tried a bank shot at the ten to avoid scratching, but missed it. The cue ball, however, wound up resting against the cushion, leaving David with no shot at all. He smirked as David lined up his cue again. "Why don't you ask your lord and savior for help?"

"Sorry, but it doesn't work like that." David took a shot, and again failed to sink any of the striped balls.

"Oh really?" said Mark. "I'm afraid I've never really understood how that works. I mean, if he really cared about what you and what you're doing, wouldn't he help you?"

"Yes," said David, "but it is not my place to hold the Almighty God to whatever arbitrary standards humans set."

"How convenient," Mark retorted. He methodically knocked in the five ball. "You believe that your god performed miraculous acts thousands of years ago and now he just doesn't feel like doing that kind of thing anymore.

And yet you regard his current inactivity as further evidence of his existence."

"I don't claim to understand the actions of an all-powerful, all-knowing God. It would be inappropriate for anyone to make that claim. But I do believe that he interacts with us in our day-to-day lives. And I believe that the will of God is behind everything."

"Really? Well I can damn well tell you that no god brought me here. I've gotten as far as I have due to my hard work and that of all of the brilliant men and women that I work with. And I don't think your god deserves any credit for that."

David sighed. "You're entitled to your beliefs, but every time you go up, I pray for you."

"And no matter how hard you pray, it never does any good whatsoever."

"You may say that, but I know that God still watches over you. And like it or not, He is the reason why you've always come back alive."

"Right, of course he does."

Mark's cell phone rang. It was Desmond. Even with IE's rapid growth, Mark still made an effort to get to know each of his co-workers even if they worked in completely different departments. It was a mentality that Miles shared as well; he conducted his own interviews with each new potential IE employee during the hiring process. This had proven critical in maintaining morale and ensuring that every worker at IE shared Miles's grand vision for the future.

"Yes?" Mark answered.

"You need get back to the office," Desmond said urgently. "We found something you'll really want to see."

"What is it?"

"I'd rather not say over the phone. Just get over here."

Mark had never heard Desmond speak so frantically,

which, in and of itself, meant that whatever was going on was something that warranted his immediate attention.

"All right. Be there soon." Mark hung up. "Looks like I'm going to have to cut this short," he said to David.

"That's okay, I understand completely," his brother replied.

Mark took David's right hand in his own and wrapped his left arm around his brother's shoulder.

"Thanks for coming." David's voice was tinged with sadness.

"I always enjoy seeing you," Mark replied compassionately. "Keep in touch." He turned and walked out of the basement.

***

Miles stood beside Alexis' control station, his eyes transfixed upon the video feed that was being displayed on the monitor. His eyes were wide with astonishment, and a triumphant smile spread across his face. He turned away from the monitor to look at Desmond, Alexis, and all other employees in Mission Control, his eyes and smile radiating with the brilliance of a star.

"Everything that I've done in my entire life utterly pales in comparison to this discovery you've made," Miles said, almost giddily. It now looked like there were tears in his eyes. "I never thought I would live to see anything like this. This means far more to me than all of my wealth and prior achievements. Thank you all so much for having done this."

"Excuse me Miles," said Desmond, "but don't you think that you're being a little premature? We don't even know what this thing is."

Miles laughed. "Are you really so afraid of the unknown that you refuse to acknowledge what's right in front of your eyes?"

Desmond was a bit taken aback by Miles's choice of

32

words, and it was clear that everyone else in Mission Control felt the same.

"Fine," Miles continued, "I'll come right out and say it." He looked around Mission Control, continuing to smile broadly. "You found a fucking alien artifact!" he exclaimed triumphantly.

What he said was painfully obvious, but hearing it verbalized still shocked everyone into stunned silence.

"Make no mistake," said Miles, "this is an historic day unlike any other! Human history will be divided into two sections: before and after this artifact was discovered. And this has been made thanks to your hard work and dedication! You should all take pride in having made the single greatest discovery in all of human history!"

Miles turned to Alexis. "What have you found out about it?"

"Not much," replied the engineer. "All we do know is that it seems to be a perfect blackbody, absorbing all of the electromagnetic radiation that bombards it, and that we can't seem to make the slightest dent in it. Oh, and there's one other thing." She paused briefly. "We've obtained a date on the surrounding rock from the miner's spectral analyzer, so whatever this thing is, it's at least as old as what it was buried under."

"So how old is it?"

"At least three billion years."

Hearing that was almost as astonishing as Miles stating that the artifact was of alien origin. Whatever this thing was, it had been sitting there for more than half of the age of the Earth. Desmond thought of everything that the artifact would have seen over the eons. It could have borne witness to the emergence and extinction of countless species and the drifting of continents with the same perspective that a human would have towards events that happened annually or monthly. All of human history, from the births, reigns, and deaths of history's greatest figures, to the rise and fall of empires, to the origin, spread, and decline of major religions, would have all seemed to be the briefest and most fleeting of events to an artifact as old as this, assuming it had the ability to perceive such things.

A stunned look swept across Miles's face, and his smile briefly subsided, superseded by awe. "Incredible," he murmured. "Truly incredible."

"Assuming this is a machine of some sort, do you think it's possible that it could still be functional?" Alexis said. "That it's still blindly following whatever it's been programed to do long after its creators sent it there?"

"Anything is possible," Desmond said. Now that Miles had openly stated that the artifact was an alien construct, the Mission Director found surprisingly easy to talk more openly about the possibilities. "It could be that whoever built this thing is long gone. This artifact might be nothing more than a relic from a long extinct civilization."

"Enough," Miles snapped. His voice was suddenly guarded. "As you've pointed out, we know precious little about this thing. That means any theories are pure speculation at this point. I don't want speculation. I want answers. Your top priority, therefore, is to obtain as much information about it as you can." He turned to face Desmond. "Have the miner remove as much of the surrounding rock as possible. Let's see if we can get a look at the entire object."

"Yes sir," said Desmond. "Although that's probably going to take a while."

"I don't care how long it takes."

"Yes sir."

Turning his attention to Alexis, Miles said. "I want you to focus on the object itself. See what you can find. Measure its mass, volume, temperature, everything. See how it reacts to external stimuli. Do whatever it takes. And report everything. Nothing is to be considered irrelevant. Every data point will be invaluable, and I want to know everything you discover. Maybe if we're lucky, we'll find out if it has a purpose and what that purpose is. And that could tell us something about who built the thing."

"I'm on it," she said. "Do you plan to make a public announcement?"

"Of course not!" Miles exclaimed. "Not now, anyway. There's too much we don't know about this thing. Someday, yes, we will reveal this to the world. Everyone on the planet deserves to know about this, but not until after we've learned everything that we possibly can.

"And who knows?" he said with a sly grin. "We might even crack a few secrets about the aliens' technology. Imagine having all the patents on the next couple thousand years' worth of technology."

Hearing Miles say that made Desmond feel a little uneasy, as he began to think of the implications this discovery held, and what would happen if his boss did end up getting his hands on the technology behind the alien object.

"But again," Miles said, "let me stress how much I don't want any of you jumping to any conclusions. Try to avoid speculation. I have complete confidence that all of you will be able to do your jobs with the skill and professionalism you have demonstrated time and again."

The IE president looked at Desmond and Alexis, and smiled broadly again. "I realized that we don't have a name for this thing," he said to them. "And since the two of you discovered it, you should be the ones to name it.

"Some might argue that that's a pointless thing to do for an artifact that someone else built. After all, I'm sure the beings who built this thing have their own designation for it, even if it's nothing more than a serial number. We may never even make formal contact with them, and even if we do, I want something to call it by until that day comes. I think just about everyone else would prefer the same."

Desmond suddenly became aware of the historical value of what was happening. Whatever name they gave this artifact might very well be remembered for the rest of human history, a name as immortalized as that of humanity's greatest works of art, architecture, and technological achievements.

"How about the Bastion?" Alexis suggested.

"The Bastion," Miles said, thinking it over. "I like it."

"What do you think Desmond?" Alexis asked.

"I like it too," he said. He was a bit relieved she had thought it up. It took the burden off his shoulders. And his mind was still reeling from what Miles had said.

Miles nodded. "All right then. The Bastion it is."

It seemed to take Miles a bit of effort to turn away from the monitor. It truly was difficult for him to turn his eyes away from the greatest thing he had ever seen in his life. But he managed to do so, and he looked at his employees with the same passion and determination he always exhibited at the height of any of IE's groundbreaking missions.

"Get to work people," he said, and walked out of the Mission Control room.

Chapter 4

Paul was eating lunch in the mess hall when Anna walked in and sat down at the table with him, setting a loaded lunch tray down in front of her. She had the same look of bewilderment on her face that she had had when she had first seen Ask.

"To what do I owe this pleasure?" Paul asked with a grin.

"I'm just taking a little break from my investigation," she said, and took a large bite of her sandwich. Anna had been in her lab for more than four hours, obtaining and analyzing tissue samples from Ask.

"Did you find out anything new about our guest?" he asked.

"A bit," Anna said "But I'm afraid that what I found raises more questions than it provides answers."

"Why is that? What did you find?"

Anna finished her sandwich, and took a quick drink of fruit juice. "I took a blood sample, and put it in the DNA sequencer to determine where he fits on the human family tree."

DNA sequencers had become so cheap, powerful, and readily available in recent years that they were now owned by millions of people around the world. This was a valuable asset for several fields of study. After sequencing their own DNA, people would upload some of their genetic information onto a vast online database that offered many useful services. Among them, algorithms could determine potential disorders or diseases a person might be susceptible to due to their genetic heritage.

This had also led to a major boom in genealogy research. The algorithms that parsed a person's DNA could be compared to the DNA of others to determine when they had diverged from a common ancestor. This in turn led to the construction of a vast family tree for a large amount of the population that dated back tens of thousands of years. Anyone with an internet connection and a DNA sequencer was now able to determine how closely related they were to major historical figures, celebrities, or their close friends, as well as how long ago their common ancestor had lived.

"As I suspected," Anna continued, "he most likely came directly from Africa, and was born before the population bottleneck that resulted from the Toba catastrophe. That alone makes him one of the greatest anthropological discoveries ever. But I also found something incredible and completely unexpected when I performed a biopsy."

"And what would that be?"

"There's no trace of ice crystals anywhere in the tissue sample that I took. His cells are completely intact."

"What makes that so incredible?"

"When human tissue is frozen, ice crystals form within the cells and destroy the cells' integrity."

"So how has Ask managed to get around that?"

Anna took a deep breath, as if she was afraid to confide her discovery. "He seems to possess antifreeze proteins. Various species of fish and insects have such proteins that allow them to survive in frigid environments without having ice crystals form in their cells. Seeing this in a human is the most amazing thing I've ever observed."

"So does that mean this guy is part fish? Or bug?"

"No, not at all. The results from the DNA sequencer show that he's definitely a member of Homo sapiens. But it goes without saying that he's far from being an ordinary human."

There was a moment of stunned silence.

"So how do you plan on proceeding from here?"

"I'm going to perform an autopsy. And judging by what I've found already, I don't think I'll be too surprised if that reveals a few more unexpected things."

"Have fun doing that."

"Thanks."

Chapter 5

As Desmond continued to look over the data that the miner was gathering on the alien artifact, his mind churned with thoughts about what this discovery meant, his part in it, and what he should do. The more he thought about it, the harder he found it to be to abide by Miles' order to keep the Bastion a secret.

But could he really bring himself to go against his boss?

Desmond had signed nondisclosure agreements when he had first joined IE, and he had fully understood why that was necessary. In order for IE to grow and prosper, it was important for the company to keep its technological developments and industrial activities secret from its competitors. Even now, with IE dominating the space industry, Desmond would never think of disclosing any of the company's secrets to a rival firm or national space agency.

But this was different. The Bastion was the greatest discovery in human history, and the entire world deserved to know it. Not only that, but Desmond also thought endlessly about Miles' suggestion about keeping the artifact a secret in the hope that IE would learn the secrets of the alien technology.

It was impossible to know the likelihood of unlocking its secrets. Maybe the Bastion was just a piece of alien junk, with its material properties the only thing of interest. And the material the alien artifact was made of could be so advanced that it would take decades or centuries for humanity to develop comparable material engineering capabilities.

Or maybe the Bastion was a treasure trove of information, containing all of the knowledge of whatever civilization had built it, and would bestow its gift upon whoever discovered it first. Perhaps the Bastion was now analyzing the IE miner to determine how best to feed data to it, and any moment now the computers would be flooded with information about the ancient alien civilization.

Desmond was somewhat unnerved about the possibility of that happening, as it would give IE and Miles a monopoly on what could be centuries or millennia worth of technological advancements. The potential was frightening.

The media often jokingly called Miles an aspiring supervillain due to the vast wealth he had accumulated from IE's operations and his investments in constant pursuit of even more riches in space. Miles even humorously embraced this role when he made occasional appearances on sketch comedy shows or cameoed as a fictionalized version of himself in Hollywood movies. All of this was part of the effort by the IE president to build a positive public image of that people would enjoy, and to show that he was not some elite and ruthless industrial tycoon.

But Desmond had never feared that his employer had anything so absurd as megalomaniacal aspirations of world domination. Never in Miles' career had there had been indication that the IE president did anything sinister or corrupt. In fact, it was quite the opposite. Miles was as much of a philanthropist as he was an entrepreneur. In addition to funding IE's activities, he donated sizable amounts of his personal fortune to fund scholarships, fellowships, and other educational programs. He frequently spoke to students at every level from kindergarten to universities, encouraging them to pursue careers in science and engineering.

Even so, Desmond found himself thinking of a quote from John Dalberg-Acton: *"Power tends to corrupt, and absolute power corrupts absolutely."*

So while Miles was considered to be a patron saint by millions of people, Desmond still had misgivings that even such a man as he should possess sole access to whatever advanced technology the aliens may have stored in the Bastion. Power like that should be entrusted to all of humanity. Being held accountable by millions of people was what prevented national and corporate leaders from abusing their power.

But while Desmond believed with every fiber of his being that the world should know about the Bastion, he also feared what the reaction would be. Religious fanatics would likely proclaim that the alien artifact an instrument of evil, or that it would bring about the last days. There might be riots in cities all over the planet. Rioters might even direct acts of violence against IE and its employees. Even if the Bastion continued to do nothing, some people would still see it as something evil that needed to be destroyed, and if that could not be done, then the ones who discovered it should be made to suffer.

There had to be a way to disseminate news of this discovery without instigating social chaos, or at least some way to mitigate it.

Desmond then thought of the many NASA engineers and project managers that he worked with as part of IE's many collaborations with the national space agency. If he were to send news about the Bastion to them, it would quickly work its way up to Alan Prater, the NASA administrator, and from there to the President of the United States himself. President Ortega and his administration would have to have a better idea on how to handle the public reaction to this historic discovery.

Desmond knew it was a cowardly act to pass the responsibility off to NASA and the White House rather than posting information about the Bastion online where the entire world could instantly see it. But the social ramifications of unilaterally making it public plagued him and he knew he would blame himself for any resulting death and destruction that might follow.

He also knew that he was taking a major risk. Miles could very easily fire him for doing this, but he believed that this was worth the risk. And maybe Miles would be merciful.

Desmond opened his email account, and quickly compiled an email containing some of the data that had been obtained about the Bastion, as well as a live feed to the miner on the surface of the alien artifact. Whoever looked at this would initially be very skeptical, but would quickly be able to determine that it was not a hoax.

He took in a deep breath, and sent the email to his NASA contacts. He knew it would not be long before Miles brought his wrath down on him.

***

"This is the single most incredible thing I've ever seen," Mark said as he stared at the image on the main monitor at Mission Control. "And it's really billions of years old?"

"That's what the data indicates," said Alexis.

"Holy shit."

Here was definitive proof that there existed, or had existed, an intelligent civilization that had emerged elsewhere in the universe. This changed everything. No longer could humanity look upon itself as superior to all other forms of life. Such hubris could not be supported when this artifact was left by a civilization that had had the capability to traverse the stars at a time when only single-celled organisms populated the Earth.

"Think of everything they may have seen throughout the eons," said Mark, still in awe. "And who knows what kind of technology they might possess."

"That's assuming that whoever built this is still

43

around," Alexis mused aloud. "Personally, I find it a little hard to wrap my mind around the idea of a civilization that's able to survive for billions of years. Just two hundred years ago people had no way of knowing or imagining that things like the internet and spacecraft would be invented one day. I don't think anyone can imagine how drastically things will change in another two hundred years. And these aliens possibly could have had billions of years of technological development. Just try to imagine the technological advances that could be made over such a time period."

"Miles doesn't want us speculating," Desmond interjected. "He thinks it's a waste of time and it could distract us from doing our jobs properly."

"Oh come on, I don't think it's going to hurt all that much," said Mark. "And I think that we have to formulate some theories about this thing. I mean, why do you think the aliens covered this thing with rock? Would they have done it to conceal it from us?"

"I don't think so," said Alexis. "Whatever that thing is, it's been hanging around the solar system for billions of years, long before humans evolved. It's possible that it was put here even before life emerged on Earth. So if they did mean to hide it from someone, that someone isn't us."

"It could be that the layer of rock is there purely by accident," Desmond added, abandoning his objection to taking part in the speculation.

"How could it have been buried by accident?" Mark asked.

"Well, if it really has been just hanging out in the Solar System for billions of years, then that would have been more than enough time for rock and debris to accumulate around the artifact. Since the miner hasn't been able to make a single dent in this thing, it's probably safe to assume that the object can withstand impacts from rock and

44

debris without suffering any damage."

"That's some pretty impressive material," said Mark. "Do you think we might be able to figure out how to make it?"

"If you're thinking about reverse engineering the aliens' technology," said Alexis, "I don't think that's very likely to happen."

"Why is that?"

"Because we know for a fact that the artifact is three billion years old, give or take, so it's logical to assume the civilization that built it is older than that. While it's certainly possible that civilization has long since collapsed, their technology would still be billions of years more advanced than ours. If that's the case, then I don't think it's even remotely possible that we can hope to understand how to reverse engineer their technology. And even if the aliens were just a few centuries or millennia more advanced than us at the time that their civilization collapsed, I'd still be willing to bet that their technology would be too advanced for us to learn all of its secrets."

Mark smiled slightly. "Well I'm a little bit more optimistic," he said. "I'm hoping that we'll be able to learn something from them, no matter how advanced they might be."

He heard the door to the control room open, and turned to see Ning walk inside. Her eyes immediately locked on the monitor displaying the alien artifact.

"Can you believe this is happening?" he said to her.

Ning turned to look at him, and she was clearly overwhelmed. "I must believe it's happening," she said. "We all have to, for the only alternative is to deny the reality as we are capable of perceiving it, and that path will only lead to madness."

Mark chuckled slightly. "I can't disagree with you on that."

Ning turned to Desmond and asked, "Can you show me the data that's been gathered about this artifact so far?"

"I'm afraid there isn't a whole hell of a lot," he replied.

"Can I see it anyway?"

"Sure thing." Desmond gestured to an unoccupied workstation. "You can view all the data over there," he said, indicating an unoccupied station.

"Thank you." Ning sat down at the workstation, and pulled up the data stream from the miner on the computer. She stared at the computer screen for a while before speaking again. "This reminds me of the monolith," she remarked as she continued to peruse the data.

"The what?" Mark asked.

"You know: the big black monolith from 2001: A Space Odyssey."

"Oh, that thing." Mark looked at the image of the artifact displayed on the Control Center's main monitor. "Yeah, I guess I can see how you can draw similarities between the two. They're both black, were discovered in space, and were put there by mysterious aliens in the distant past."

"That is true, but there could be more to it than that."

"Really? Like what?"

"Well for one, I think it would be pretty wild if it turns out to have the same purpose as the monolith in the movie."

"What purpose is that?" Desmond asked. "I don't recall the movie being very clear about what that thing was or what it did."

"I'm talking about the novel that the movie was based on," Ning explained. "The book was nowhere near as ambiguous or trippy as the movie was. In the book, Arthur C. Clarke actually did explain what the monolith was and what its purpose was."

"Oh, okay," Desmond said. "See, I wouldn't know that, because I never got around to reading the book. So what was the monolith supposed to be?"

"Basically an observer of Earth that occasionally aided human evolution," explained Ning. "The one that the aliens dropped in Africa millions of years earlier helped the ancestors of humanity develop the ability to create tools. The one that the aliens buried underneath the lunar surface was a way to determine when humanity had achieved the technology needed to reach the Moon, and then alert them to a pathway for an even greater evolutionary development. And that was what the monolith at Jupiter did, although in the book it was located on the surface of Iapetus."

"And you think that's what this thing is?" said Alexis, gesturing toward the screen. "You think it's an observer that's been watching Earth for millions of years and intervening with human evolution? And now it's going to initiate some profound evolutionary leap for us?"

"I have no idea; I simply said wouldn't it be wild if that were the case," Ning replied forcefully. "Based on the data that we've obtained thus far, it's safe to say we don't have a clue. But since we seemed to be engaged in speculating, I threw in my two cents. There was a reason Miles told us to avoid speculation, and this kind of proves the point."

"Fair enough," Mark nodded. "Still, if the artifact really does play a similar role as the monolith from 2001, then Arthur C. Clarke made some pretty eerily accurate predictions."

"Well then that gives us yet another reason to uncover this thing's secrets: to find out just how close to reality Clarke's fiction really is."

Mark chuckled and sat down in an empty chair, his eyes still locked on the image of the artifact.

***

Miles sat at his desk in his office, looking over progress reports submitted to him by Ning and other engineers who were working on the *Intrepid*. Finishing the fusion spacecraft was now the single most important thing to the IE president. To hell with Mars! Nothing was more important than getting a crew of IE astronauts out to the Bastion as soon as possible. And he was ready and willing to commit any resources necessary to make that happen.

The phone on his desk suddenly rang, jarring Miles from his work. That was a bit surprising to him. Phone screening programs vetted all calls to the IE headquarters, and only a handful of people could make it through to reach all the way to Miles' office phone. He was also somewhat perplexed when his phone identified the caller as being the White House.

"Hello?" he said carefully upon picking up the phone.

"Hello, is this Miles Gilster?" came a familiar voice.

"Yes," Miles said in the friendly disposition he always showcased for people of importance. He recognized the voice, but could not bring himself to believe who it was. For in that instant, he knew there could only be one reason why he was receiving this call.

The caller laughed. "Well I just thought I should call and congratulate you on having made the greatest discovery in human history."

Miles felt the air go out of his lungs.

"Thank you Mr. President," Miles said, guarding his tone as best he could. There was no point in dancing around the issue and pretend he did not know to what the President was referring. It was immediately apparent that someone had leaked information about the Bastion.

"I thought you guys were amazing before, but this just blows everything else out of the water!"

The President must not have been told that the information had gotten to him through an employee's leak. Either that or he felt it best not to mention such a thing.

"Thank you. That means a lot to hear you say that,"

48

Miles said, continuing to do as bet he could to stop himself from expressing the growing rage he was feeling.

Betrayal! Unforgivable!

"I'll be meeting with my science adviser and other staff members in just a little while," Ortega continued, "and I trust that they'll be able to explain this thing to me more and what we should do about it. Anyway, I'll let you guys continue on with what you're doing. Really looking forward to seeing what else you guys find."

"Thank you again, Mr. President."

The President hung up.

Miles slammed the phone down on his desk, and stormed out of his office.

***

The door to the Mission Control room burst open loudly, and everyone turned to see Miles storm in. Mark wanted to run up to his boss and congratulate him, but knew better than to do that upon seeing how angry Miles was. The IE president was burning with rage the likes of which none of them had ever seen in him before.

Desmond swallowed hard and sat up straight as his boss walked up to him.

"Just what in the living hell do you think you've done?!" Miles demanded, his voice threatening to rupture eardrums.

"I...I did what I felt needed to do," Desmond said, his voice trembling. "The world deserves to know this."

"You fucking betrayed me is what you did!" Miles screamed.

"I'm...I'm sorry."

"No you're not. If you were really sorry you wouldn't have done this. You knew exactly what you were doing, and you did it anyway." Miles laughed bitterly. "You could have at least done something to cover your tracks. It took the IT guys no more than two minutes to find out you were

49

behind the leak."

"I didn't want to," Desmond said. "I knew that you would find out anyway, and I was fully prepared to accept the consequences of my actions."

"Well congratulations, because that's exactly what you're getting. You have five minutes to gather your shit and get out of the building. You're fired."

"Miles, please," Desmond pleaded. "I've been here since the beginning. You know that."

"And you forgot all about that when you stabbed me in the back! Now get the living fuck out of here! I won't tell you again! And if you come anywhere near me or any IE facility again, I will make you regret this day even more!"

Desmond looked around the control room. But no one offered him any look of sympathy, and said nothing while avoiding eye contact with him. He got up from his workstation and walked out of the room, fighting hard to hold back tears.

"Let this be a warning to all of you," Miles said. He was speaking into a camera that was at an empty work station. He had turned it on remotely as soon as he had entered Mission Control to record what he did to Desmond.

But by speaking into the camera now, Miles was addressing all of his employees at IE. His intention was to show the recording of the conversation he had just had with those in the control room, along with the announcement he was now making.

"I don't care how long you've worked for me," Miles said sternly, "or what you've done for me and IE in the past. I always welcome dissenting opinions. You all know this. But I will not tolerate betrayal. And I will not hesitate to fire any of you like I did Desmond if you think about pulling the kind of shit that he just did. Now get back to work!"

Miles stormed out of the control room.

50

Chapter 6

Anna stood in the infirmary, looking down at Ask's body that was lying on top of an operating table. Paul had removed the block of ice containing Ask's body from the ice core freezer as soon as Anna had asked him to, and brought the body to the infirmary as soon as the ice had melted.

Alone in the infirmary, Anna carefully examined Ask's body. There was no visible sign of decay; he looked as if he just died. He showed no sign of malnutrition, so Anna knew that the cold had gotten to him before starvation had. His eyes were open; they were as dark as his skin, and as cold as the ice that had preserved them.

Anna placed her index and middle finger on Ask's right wrist, and felt no pulse. Well of course he had no pulse. Had she actually been expecting otherwise?

She felt a slight stab of pity at what she was about to do. Ask was the most well-preserved ancient body ever found. On top of that, he had an incredible physique rarely, if ever, observed in a human before. And now she was about to dissect him. It seemed almost criminal to do this to such a unique specimen. Still, she knew that it was something that she needed to do. Every piece of information obtained about him would help to unlock one of the greatest anthropological mysteries in history. Dissecting Ask would undoubtedly contribute greatly the body of knowledge about human evolution, thus justifying in her mind the desecration that she was about to commit. Anna picked up a scalpel and brought it down to his chest, cutting the skin to make the first incision.

At the very instant that the scalpel pierced Ask's flesh, his hand shot up like a rocket and grabbed Anna by the wrist. His grip was bone-crushing, forcing Anna to drop the scalpel. Excruciating pain permeated her body, and Anna could not even strike out in defense, so overwhelming was her shock. She found herself unable to tear her eyes away from Ask's, for they were no longer cold and lifeless. Rather, they burned with a malevolent ferocity that seemed powerful enough to liberate Lucifer from the ice of Judecca at the bottommost circle of hell.

In deathly silence, Ask lowered his feet to the floor and rose from the operating table. His frame towered over Anna, who remained paralyzed with fear. Without loosening his savage grip on Anna's wrist with his left hand, Ask reached out his right hand and placed it against Anna's forehead. He then commanded thousands of submicroscopic nanomachines to exit his body through his fingers.

In just moments, Ask's tiny minions penetrated Anna's skin, flesh, and bone, flooding into her bloodstream. As they advanced, the nanomachines consumed Anna's cells to fuel their own replication, multiplying exponentially. Within seconds, they had rushed to Anna's brain where they connected to the neurons, forming a neural link between Anna's and their master's brains. Once the link was established, a one-way flow of data was established from Anna's brain to Ask's.

Ask relived every moment of Anna's life; her earliest memory of walking along the California beach with her father and gazing up at the night sky, reading her first biology book when she was five, her defense of her doctoral dissertation, and the shock and fear she had felt at his sudden touch, all with the same clarity that she had.

Like all baselines whose minds Ask had probed, Anna's memories were incredibly crude compared to his. Whereas he was able to relive his memories on a whim, baselines could only remember past events with terrible imprecision that only worsened with the passage of time.

Nevertheless, Anna provided Ask with a wealth of

information unlike any he had ever sampled from a baseline in his past life. Her knowledge of science, technology, and mathematics that the baselines had developed over the millennia was incredible. She also had a general overview of the history of the planet and the human species, providing him the background of some of the major events that had happened both before and after his imprisonment in the ice.

But the information she had that was of most immediate value was what she knew regarding this facility, the baselines within it, the threat that they might pose to him, and the reservoirs of knowledge that they had to offer.

***

Paul did not want to bother Anna when she was in the middle of the autopsy, but he felt a sudden urge to check up on her. He was not even sure if he would be able to stand the sight of the body cut open and the organs pulled out. He might just gaze in briefly and then leave.

Peering into the infirmary through a glass window, Paul saw the iceman standing right in front of Anna, gripping her head. He did not stop to think of the insanity of the situation; all he knew was that she was in danger, and he had to help her.

He barged into the infirmary, screaming, "Hey! Get away from her you fucker!"

Ask did not even seem to register another's presence. All of his attention was transfixed on Anna, who seemed to be in a trancelike state.

Paul, driven by the rush of adrenalin, picked up a bone saw and ran at Ask without thinking. Not even the buzzing of the saw and Paul's reckless dash broke Ask's concentration.

Paul plunged the buzzing saw into Ask's right arm, sending a fountain of blood spouting as it sliced through muscle and bone. Only then did Ask break his

53

concentration with Anna. He neither flinched nor gave any indication that he was experiencing any pain; he simply turned his head to look directly at Paul, his eyes burning with the flames of the inferno, locking them with Paul's horrified gaze.

Letting go of Anna's head, Ask ripped the bone saw from Paul's grip with his left hand, and thrust the spinning blade into the neck of his assailant. Paul fell to the floor, clawing at his neck and gurgling as a pool of blood formed around him.

Ask knelt down and grabbed Paul by the sides of his head with both hands. Though his right arm was coated with his own blood, the injury the climatologist had inflicted on him had already healed. As he had done with Anna, Ask extracted all of Paul's knowledge as the climatologist died.

As he did this, Ask commanded his nanomachines inhabiting Anna's brain to destroy all the neurons, and she fell to the floor dead. Because of the pain Paul had caused him, Ask decided not to give him a quick and painless death he had given Anna. Instead, he calmly walked out of the infirmary, completely indifferent to Paul's agonized moans as the climatologist bled to death.

Among other data Ask had obtained from the minds of Anna and Paul, he had learned that thirteen other baselines were still present in the facility. Were any of them to learn what had just transpired, they might escape and inform other humans that the man they had found in the ice had somehow come back to life. He could not allow that.

Ask moved with lightning speed through Niflheim, bursting forth into the mess hall where half a dozen researchers were present. Four of them were so shocked and bewildered upon seeing him that they were unable to even rise from their seats, while the other two bolted for the exit to the mess hall as fast as they could. But they had no hope of outrunning Ask, who overtook them easily.

He did not attack the staff so much as touch them briefly to inject them with his nanomachines, extract information from their brains, and kill them, all within the span of a few seconds. From each person he killed, he learned where the other baselines in Niflheim were located or likely to be.

He quickly disposed of the baselines in the mess hall and quickly made his way through the rest of the facility, and continued to kill each baseline he came across. None had any chance to escape from him or kill him. There were no firearms in Niflheim. There had never been any reason for the staff to brandish such weapons. Not that they would have done any good at stopping Ask; he knew he would be able to survive any gunshot wound.

If multiple baselines were present in the same room, he moved fast enough to probe their minds and kill them before any could escape.

Once the last of the baselines had been dispatched, Ask returned to the mess hall, tore open the refrigerator and food cabinets, and began to devour all the food within. It had been so long since he had eaten that the food that the staff of Niflheim considered to be bland was like ambrosia to Ask.

As he ate, he began to formulate his next course of action. Throughout his life nothing had been more important to him than knowledge... learning as much as he possibly could about the universe and the laws that governed it. From the minds of Niflheim's staff, he had gleaned more about mathematics, engineering, biology, and physics than he had in the entirety of his life prior to being trapped in the Antarctic ice. The baselines offered him a Pierian Spring, and drinking from it had only intensified his unquenchable thirst for knowledge. From them he had also learned that there were universities, government research facilities, and technology companies filled with brilliant scientists and engineers that knew far more than even the Niflheim staff experts, all offering access to data about the world on a silver platter. But this frozen continent had been mostly forsaken by the baselines, and Ask knew he had to leave, for it was crucial to reach the strongholds of civilization to gain ready access to the baselines' treasure trove of information.

From Niflheim's personnel, Ask had learned of a coastal settlement called Larsen. Acting primarily as a port for ships, it was where personnel and cargo were brought for distribution to stations all across Antarctica. The population of Larsen was far greater than that of Niflheim, with more than two thousand permanent and semi-permanent residents. Reaching Larsen would provide him with an opportunity to leave this frozen continent and travel to the sanctuaries of baseline civilization.

But he could not leave just yet. Niflheim was supported by a consortium of universities, government agencies, and corporations from all around the world. The staff had communicated with these organizations on a daily basis, providing updates on their projects via emails, radio transmissions, and other communiques. Fortunately, no one outside of the base had been informed of the researchers' discovery of Ask. The sudden cessation of communication with Niflheim, however, would prompt the consortium to send a team of investigators to determine the cause.

Also, if Ask were to leave Antarctica immediately and reach the citadels of baseline civilization, he would not be entirely safe. Surveillance systems equipped with facial recognition software had become ubiquitous in nearly every major city all across the world and were utilized by law enforcement and national intelligence organizations.

Multiple digital photographs had been taken of Ask before and after he had been freed from the ice.

Furthermore, cameras had been present in the examination room that had undoubtedly captured footage of Ask's revival and regenerative capability. This did not mean that the baselines would be able to find him; he planned to assume the identity of someone at Larsen so that he could leave Antarctica. But Ask did not want the baselines to know that a being like him existed, for if they did, they would never stop searching for him.

Were he a normal baseline, he would be tried as a murderer for the killings of the staff members, and sentenced to either death or life imprisonment. But if the baselines were to find the information that the Niflheim staff had obtained about him, there would be an all-out effort to capture him and lock him up as a laboratory specimen to learn all of his secrets. Baseline scientists would scrutinize the data that Anna had obtained about Ask's antifreeze proteins, as well the camera footage from the infirmary that had likely obtained footage of Ask's arm rapidly healing after the injury Paul had inflicted.

After he had eaten as much as he could, Ask walked through Niflheim again, this time destroying all of the information that had been obtained about him. This consisted of DNA analyses, biopsy results, ice core samples, photographs and camera footage. Nearly all of this information was stored on computers, and he would have to destroy every computer at Niflheim to ensure that no data on him would reach the baseline's general population.

He would have been able to find and destroy these systems even if he had not probed the minds of Niflheim's baselines, for he could feel different magnetic fields and the flow of electrical current through the myriad of devices that were throughout the facility. Electromagnetic waves were constantly pushing and pulling at his body, a force as palpable to him as the bombardment of raindrops upon his skin. The fields were far stronger and generated more diverse sensations than anything he had felt at any prior time in his life. They were yet another testament to the incredible technological advances the baselines had made.

Ask had sensed this from the moment he had regained consciousness. It had been more than enough to tell him that the world in which he had awoken was drastically different from the one he had left behind.

Walking through the facility, Ask erased the data files pertaining to him, and then destroyed the computers as an additional precaution, smashing the hard drives against the walls and floor until he was satisfied with their ruin.

Once he was certain that he had obliterated all of the information on him, Ask went to the nearest crew quarters to quickly shower, cleansing himself of the blood that still covered him.

After he was clean, Ask searched the staff quarters for something to wear that would help him blend in to Larsen's populace. The tallest member of Niflheim's staff had been a climatologist named Ben Nelson, but he still had been four inches shorter than Ask. This presented no real obstacle. Ask simply commanded his nanomachines to compress his muscles and bones until he shrank by four inches, permitting him to wear Nelson's clothes.

Once dressed, Ask made his way to the garage where several snowcats were stored. Used to transport personnel and equipment across the ice and snow, these vehicles were capable of reaching Larsen in about four hours at top speed.

Ask opened the garage door, and a cold blast of Antarctic air blew in. He climbed into one of the snowcats. He had never before seen or operated a vehicle of any sort, but many of the base's personnel had been using vehicles like this for years. The knowledge he had extracted from them made him as familiar with them as they had been. He switched on the engine, engaged the gears, and sped off toward the coast.

***

Ask brought the snowcat to a halt when he was about ten miles from Larsen. This was an act of caution, for the closer he drove to the coastal settlement, the greater the risk would be that someone would see the snowcat and report it to the Larsen traffic controllers, who would attempt to contact the operator, demanding to know who he was and where he had come from. If they somehow located him, he could not claim to be from Nifhleim, or they would attempt to contact the station to verify his claim, which would spark an investigation when there was no response. On top of that, the snowcat had barcodes that identified it as belonging to Niflheim Station, which Larsen authorities could cross check with their database that cataloged all the equipment and supplies at each Antarctic facility.

It was for this reason that Ask climbed out of the snowcat and proceeded to walk the remaining distance to Larsen. This marked the first time he had walked upon the snow and ice of this frozen wasteland of his own accord. In the ancient past, he had been brought to Antarctica completely against his will and condemned to his cryonic prison. Thinking about it caused that old fury build within him, but he quickly suppressed his anger, knowing that nothing constructive would come of it. He could not allow the fires of rage to consume him. He could not change what had happened, and he knew it was virtually impossible for him to exact any sort of vengeance on those that had wronged him. All that mattered now was the future.

As the snow crunched beneath his feet, Ask examined his surroundings with a level of scrupulousness far beyond the capabilities of a mere baseline. Even without the information he had obtained from the minds of the Niflheim staff, it was still obvious to Ask that the world was a dramatically different place than it had been seventy millennia ago. He was able to smell and taste pollutants in

59

the air that had originated from industrial centers all across the planet. He could feel heightened levels of ultraviolet radiation from the sun bombarding his skin that were of far greater intensity than he had ever felt before. Some of this was due to the reflection of sunlight from the snow, but some of this was also attributed to more radiation from the sun reaching the Earth's surface due to the depletion of ozone in the upper atmosphere. All of these environmental changes were due to the relentless advancement of baseline civilization. They had initially been oblivious to the long-term environmental damage their actions would have, but even after they had learned of the harm they were causing the planetary environment, the exploitation of natural resources continued.

It was only very recently that baselines were beginning to take actions to mitigate the damage they had inflicted upon the global environment. Nuclear and renewable energy sources had brought an end to the burning of fossil fuels. The small nuclear reactors and solar power that now helped fuel the establishment of lunar and Mars habitats, offered sources of cheap and readily available energy here on Earth. Niflheim and Larsen's electrical power were provided by the same portable nuclear reactors, and the buildings had been constructed to conserve as much thermal energy as possible.

The snow around Larsen had been compacted from a steady onslaught of human feet and tires of transport vehicles. No one paid much attention to Ask as he walked throughout Larsen. The population was large enough for a person to go virtually unnoticed. It was possible, and not uncommon, for people here to live within close proximity to each other for long periods of time and never even become remotely familiar with one another.

Even so, Ask knew it would be best if he assumed the identity of a Larsen resident as quickly as possible. It was only a matter of time before someone found the snowcat he had abandoned. This, coupled with the loss of communication with Niflheim, would prompt the Larsen authorities to conduct a search for the driver of the snowcat. Ask had no doubt that they would quickly deduce that there was a connection between the abandoned snow vehicle and the cessation of communications with Niflheim. Once an investigative team was sent to Niflheim, it would immediately be obvious to them that whoever had been responsible for the massacre had also driven the snowcat to Larsen.

Many of the buildings at Larsen served as labs or residential accommodations. If Ask entered one of those buildings in his current appearance, he would risk attracting the very sort of attention that he wanted to avoid. Instead, a location where the residents of Larsen congregated for casual social engagements was more likely to offer him an opportunity to find someone to impersonate without much risk of being noticed.

From the Niflheim staff, Ask had learned that one of the buildings was an establishment that served food and alcoholic beverages to the residents of Larsen. Due to Larsen's comparatively large population, more consideration was given to providing comfort for the inhabitants and it was the reason establishments like this existed. This was where he should go to find the person whose identity he could assume.

Ascertaining the location of the establishment, Ask wasted no time in making his way to it. Even though the settlement was comparatively large, it was a short enough walk. Entering though the double set of doors, Ask was overwhelmed by the strong odors of food, tobacco, and alcohol that permeated the air. These smells were physically new to him, but, having tapped the memories of the people he had killed at Niflheim, they were as familiar to him as they were to anyone who had spent their entire life surrounded by such odors.

Ask spent more than an hour in the bar, searching for his quarry. He did this by touching the bar patrons as briefly and casually as possible. Sometimes he would stand right next to someone at one of the bar stools, where he had an opportunity to lightly brush his arm against another's, or he would reach to sample from a bowl of complimentary pretzels just as a baseline did so that their fingers would briefly touch. Ask made sure to keep these instances of physical contact as brief as possible, lasting on the order of no more than a second or two. This still provided Ask with ample time to inject the people he touched with his nanomachines, which invaded their bodies with all the subtly of a bacterial or viral infection and allow Ask to probe their minds to determine a suitable candidate.

On occasion, someone he touched took notice of his actions, and he quickly erased their memory of what had happened. If they appeared about to raise an objection, he saw their reaction within their minds and halted them before they had a chance to act. He could not afford to allow anyone to think of him as being a threat.

The majority of people whose minds Ask probed were scheduled to remain at Larsen for many more months. While Ask could impersonate any of them, he wanted to leave Antarctica as soon as possible, so he continued to search for someone who met that prerequisite.

Ask spent more than an hour investigating the bar's customers until he found a satisfactory candidate: a man named John Neil. Neil was a crewmember of the Southwestern, an oceangoing vessel scheduled to depart Larsen and travel to Australia in three days. No one else in the bar was scheduled to leave Larsen at an earlier date. This was the man whose identity Ask chose to assume.

After identifying his target, Ask sat as far from John as

he could while still maintaining contact with the nanomachines that dwelt within John's body. Ask could only operate them at a maximum distance of about two hundred feet. Beyond that range, Ask lost contact with them, and they deactivated instantly. Once they deactivated, Ask was unable to revive them, even if they came back within communication range.

Ask did not know if this was due to an insurmountable technological barrier for the nanomachines, or if it was an artificial limitation that had been imposed by Legion, although he strongly suspected it was the latter. It seemed peculiar that Legion would give him such a powerful technology and yet impose arbitrary restrictions that prevented him from using it to its full potential, but then again, very little of what Legion did made any sense to Ask. He did not even know why Legion had given him the nanomachines in the first place, or why they later betrayed him and condemned him to a state of suspended animation.

Based on what he had garnered from the baselines, they knew even less about Legion than he did. It even seemed possible the baselines knew nothing at all of Legion. From his probing, Ask had learned bits and pieces about some of the religions and mythologies in baseline cultures. Some belief systems were still practiced by baselines across the world, while others had gone extinct long ago. There was no reason to believe that any of that had resulted from the workings of Legion since much of the content in the world's myriad of religions was contradictory and nonsensical, and nothing was consistent with what Ask had witnessed millennia ago.

Ask realized that none of the people he probed were historians or scholars on this matter. He had learned, however, that there were baseline intellects that dedicated their lives to the study of ancient mythologies and religions. Their studies would offer Ask more objective sources of

63

information that would enable him to determine if Legion truly had abandoned the baselines. This made it all the more urgent that Ask use an assumed identity that would enable him reach the populated centers of baseline civilization.

When John finally left the bar, Ask followed him, maintaining as much of a distance from him as he could manage. Soon they reached the building where John resided. John cast a quick backward glance at Ask as he followed him into the building, but, failing to recognize the danger he presented, continued walking to his quarters.

The instant that John opened the door to his quarters, Ask ordered the nanomachines inhabiting John's brain to destroy their host, and John fell to the ground like a puppet whose strings had been cut. Ask rushed to drag John's body into the room, closing the door behind him before anyone could see what had happened.

Ask then stripped the clothes from John's body, and carried his lifeless form to the bathroom, laying it down in the bathtub. As he did this, Ask ordered the nanomachines within John's body to spread and multiply rapidly, causing them to immediately set about breaking down the individual cells to fuel their population explosion. Within seconds, the body had dissolved into a viscous liquid that began to flow down the bathtub drain. Ask turned on the bathtub faucet, letting the water wash the liquefied body rapidly down the drain.

As John's disintegrated body flowed to the sewer, the nanomachines within Ask began restructuring his face and body, changing his muscle tone, skin pigmentation, and other physical features. By the time John's body had completely drained away, his duplicate appraised his visage in the mirror.

Ask had not disposed of the bodies at Niflheim in this manner because that, by itself, would not have been enough to remove all evidence of the massacre. Had he wanted to be that thorough, then after destroying the bodies, he would have had to expend additional effort and time to clean up all of the blood that stained the facility's floors. It would have cost valuable time he did not have if he wished to minimize the possibility that investigators would discover him before he had time to assume a baseline's identity. Even if he had erased all evidence of his killings at Niflheim, an investigation team would find it hard to believe that the research station's cadre had simply abandoned their facility. Theories would still abound.

The baselines might have speculated that one of the staff members had suffered a mental breakdown, killed the rest of the Niflheim team, and then disposed of the bodies somewhere else. Maybe there had been a terrorist incursion. Even leaving the scene as it was would create speculation. Possibly some contagion had been released, leaving only one remaining who, rather than suffering the horror of a disease, had dispatched himself with the first weapon he could find. No matter, the investigation would be long and exhaustive.

Ask also could not have done anything about the snowcat that he had driven to Larsen. Investigators would undoubtedly conclude that whoever had driven the vehicle had been responsible for the events at Niflheim. But who would ever suspect that they had been killed by an ancient iceman they had discovered? The strangeness of the evidence would cause it to remain an unsolved mystery, with no real clue as to whom or what had been responsible for the massacre.

Ask walked out of the bathroom and into the bedroom. He strode to the computer on the desk, sat down in front of it, and turned it on. Eager to explore and sample more of what the baselines had to offer him, Ask opened a browser and began to explore the internet.

65

He was now likely as safe as he was ever to be while he remained in Antarctica. Still, he would not feel completely at ease until he vacated the wretched, frozen wasteland that had been his tomb. Until that time came, he would learn as much as he could about this new world.

Chapter 7

Alan Prater sat at the table in the White House Situation Room along with much of the presidential cabinet and the Joint Chiefs of Staff. Monitors on the wall displayed cabinet members and Joint Chiefs who were not there in person. A wall monitor at the far end of the room showed the black surface of the alien artifact surrounded by asteroid regolith.

Everyone in the room rose to their feet when President Eduardo Ortega walked in. He was a tall man of medium build, his dark hair having grayed since taking office.

"Thank you all for being here," Ortega said as he took his seat, and everyone else sat down as well. "This is an historic occasion unlike any other, which makes your advice and recommendations on how we should handle this all the more invaluable." He gestured toward Prater. "Can you please explain to us what this thing is?"

"As best I can." Prater gestured toward the wall monitor. "This is a live feed being provided to us by Interplanetary Enterprises. It is from their unmanned asteroid miner that found the alien artifact, which the discoverers have named the Bastion."

Saying that caused him to think of Desmond Berens, the IE engineer who had leaked the information about the alien artifact. IE's ongoing cooperation was due entirely to this leak. Prater had no doubt that Miles Gilster would have preferred to keep the Bastion a secret for as long as he possibly could. Perhaps the IE president had even been planning to abandon his plans to send his fusion spacecraft to Mars and instead use it to send a crew of his own astronauts to the alien artifact in the hope of learning its secrets for himself.

Prater could not blame Miles for desiring that, but was thankful that Desmond Berens had thwarted his employer's aspirations. Miles Gilster was extremely frustrated, and had immediately fired Desmond. He had even gone a step further to make the young man suffer for what he had done. The IE president had contacted everyone he knew in the aerospace community, informing them that Desmond had committed corporate espionage, and that no one should ever offer the engineer a job of any sort. The clout that Miles' word carried meant that Desmond's career was effectively over.

While Prater felt sorry for what had happened to Desmond, he did not feel that he could do anything for the young engineer. He wanted to offer Desmond a position at any NASA center of his choosing, but to do so would raise questions about why he would do such a thing for someone who had committed corporate espionage. It would also antagonize the IE president, and maintaining a cordial relationship with Miles and his company was crucial for handling the situation. And so Desmond Berens would continue to be a pariah and martyr to the cause of public transparency in the sciences.

Prater continued, "We have no idea what material the Bastion is made of, who or what made it, or what purpose it might serve. The miner has been working to remove as much of the surrounding rock as possible, but we don't yet know how much of the asteroid's volume or mass the artifact comprises. The Bastion itself appears to be an ideal blackbody, since it seems to absorb all electromagnetic radiation that bombards it. The miner has also been unable to make the slightest dent in the Bastion's surface. In addition to that, anything that impacts the surface of the alien artifact immediately loses all kinetic energy. Based on geologic determination of the asteroid's age, the object is at least three billion years old."

Prater paused briefly as he let that sink in. Ortega's eyes went wide, and his staff looked at Prater, waiting to see what else he might add.

"And that's about it," Prater said. "That's all what we've learned about it so far. We don't have any more information for you." He leaned back in his chair and studied the expressions of everyone in the situation room. Their expressions were a mixture of amazement that this alien artifact existed and frustration at the scarcity of detailed information about it.

"So what is it?" asked the President.

Prater shrugged. "There's a ton of different theories about what it could be, each one no more or less valid than any other. It could be a probe that was just sent here to collect data about our solar system. Or it could be a piece of wreckage from a starship. Maybe it's a time capsule, containing all of the knowledge from the civilization from which it originated.

"Or it could be that whatever civilization built this has the technology to transfer their consciousness into machines, and have completely abandoned their biological ancestry. If that's the case, then this artifact could very well be a representative of their civilization. Or maybe it houses a vast assortment of minds that make up their entire society.

"All of these things are possibilities that we've considered so far. But until we gather more information, it's all just speculation. At this point it's impossible for us to have any real idea of what the Bastion actually is."

"Could it be a weapon?" asked Laurence Nesbitt, the National Security Adviser.

Prater leaned forward in his chair, and glared at Nesbitt intently, clearly agitated at the suggestion. "Of all the things that it could be," Prater ground out carefully, "I honestly believe that that's the least likely."

"Oh really? And why is that?"

"For one thing, it doesn't make any sense that an

69

advanced civilization capable of navigating across the stars would put a weapon here in the first place. You need to keep in mind that multicellular life didn't even exist on Earth when the Bastion arrived in the Solar System. And if whatever civilization built this thing still exists, I can guarantee you that we're no more of a threat to them than the single-celled organisms that were on Earth when they first arrived."

"Perhaps we're not the ones against whom the weapon was intended to be used," said Nesbitt. "Maybe the Solar System was a battlefield in some ancient interstellar war. A war that may have destroyed whatever civilization built this artifact."

"More speculation," snapped Prater. "All of this is nothing but meaningless speculation."

Ortega sighed. "Okay, you're right about it being speculation," he said. "But at this point, I don't think we have any other choice but to speculate."

Prater leaned forward in his chair slightly, looking at Ortega intently. "I want to point out that with the limited information we have on the Bastion, any theories about its origin or purpose aren't even worth the oxygen needed to formulate those theories in the first place."

Ortega sighed. "Okay, if that's what you think, you're fully entitled to stand behind your opinions. But let me point something out to you. While you may want to avoid speculating about what this thing is, there are plenty of people in the Department of Defense who are doing just that. And there are some who want to launch a bunch of nuclear warheads at it right now. So the whole purpose of this meeting is to discuss what this thing could be, and how we should proceed."

Prater did not like this, but knew he had no choice but to play along. "Okay, fine. Let's assume that this thing isn't just some piece of junk, like a fragment of some large spacecraft that was destroyed long ago. Let's also assume that it's still fully operational, even after spending billions of years buried underneath asteroid rock. After all, if the Bastion is completely inert, then it won't pose a direct threat to us at all."

Nesbitt smiled slightly. "Yes, I'd say those are good assumptions we should make to conduct a proper threat analysis."

"All right then," said Prater. "If we assume all of that, then in my humble opinion, the Bastion is most likely to be one of two things: a probe, or an unmanned miner, possibly both. After all, what's the reason we've been able to expand into space the way we've been doing lately? It's because we're finally beginning to reap the economic benefits that come from developing the resources of the Solar System. Try to imagine how what we could achieve if we had the technology for interstellar travel. The resources of other star systems could fuel economic growth orders of magnitude beyond anything that we can hope to achieve if we just stay in the Solar System forever. And I think it's safe to say any advanced civilization would follow the same path."

Nesbitt said, "But the amount of time and energy that would be needed to send a single spacecraft to Alpha Centauri, mine the resources that are there, replicate itself, and then ship the metals back to the Solar System is simply mindboggling. I don't see how that could ever be economically viable, no matter how advanced your technology might be."

"You've got to keep in mind that the resources of the Solar System aren't infinite," Prater said. "Sure, there are more than enough raw materials in the asteroids and elsewhere in the Solar System to satisfy our economic demands for the next couple of centuries, if not millennia. But if a civilization were to exist and thrive for millions or billions of years, it would inevitably exhaust the resources of its home star system. At that point, it would be an economic imperative to exploit the resources of another star system. Sure, it would take decades, centuries, or millennia for a spacecraft to travel across the stars, depending on the distance needed to be traveled and the velocity the spacecraft can reach. But if a civilization is able to exist for millions of years, then they'd become accustomed to thinking on vast timescales. We know that the Bastion is billions of years old, and if it's been operating that whole time and the civilization that built it still exists, then a million years could seem as brief a time to it and its builders as a year or two is to us."

Prater paused briefly before continuing. "Unless of course they have propulsion systems far more advanced than anything we can imagine. Maybe they have faster-than-light travel, allowing them to circumvent relativity entirely."

Ortega's interest was piqued by that suggestion. "You mean wormholes?" he said, with a gleaming look in his eye. "Warp drive? Hyperspace? Is that shit even possible?"

Prater shrugged. "You said we can't rule anything out, and I'm inclined to agree with you on that. We probably can't even begin to speculate on what kind of technology they might possess."

Although there was still no solid theoretical basis for technology to circumvent relativity, it was something that Prater had dreamed would be discovered. If there was one technology he hoped the aliens possessed, it was that.

"Even if they do possess some form of faster than light technology, that wouldn't really justify the presence of this artifact in our Solar System," said Nesbitt. "If anything, I think that would only deepen the mystery."

"Why do you say that?" Prater asked.

"Because if their intention was to send unmanned

spacecraft to different star systems to exploit raw materials, then they've done a pretty piss-poor job in our Solar System. That thing has been here for billions of years, and it doesn't seem like it's done any mining or processing of local materials at all. So they're either really bad at mining, or that thing was never meant to mine asteroids."

"Maybe it's been programmed to only mine resources from star systems that are devoid of life," Prater argued. "So if it finds any form of life present in the star system that it's sent to, it refrains from exploiting any resources. And they do this so that the native life forms have an opportunity to evolve into a civilization that's advanced enough to develop spaceflight and exploit the resources of their home star system. Maybe they even invite new civilizations into a galactic community once they've reached a certain level of technological maturity."

"Fucking naïve, wishful thinking," Nesbitt snapped.

Everyone turned to look at Nesbitt, shocked by his sudden irascibility.

"Do you not believe that these aliens could be friendly?" Ortega asked his National Security Adviser.

"Of course they're not," Nesbitt said. "Quite the contrary: I can guarantee you that they're completely genocidal."

"That's a pretty drastic stance," said Prater. "What's your rationale for thinking that?"

"Because the SETI Institute still hasn't found a single shred of evidence of an alien civilization existing anywhere else in the galaxy," said Nesbitt. "They've detected no radio transmissions and seen no signs of megascale engineering projects like Dyson spheres. And that shouldn't be the case if a civilization has ever existed with the technological capability of colonizing space. Even if they don't have the capability to travel faster than light, they would still have had ample time to colonize the entire galaxy if their civilization is able to survive for billions of years.

"This artifact does prove that there exists, or has existed, at least one alien civilization with the technology to send spacecraft across interstellar distances. But it does not prove that whatever civilization which built it currently spans the entire galaxy or that a multitude of civilizations residing in a single or a handful of star systems exist."

"You're talking about the Fermi Paradox," said Prater.

"Yes," replied Nesbitt. "And this artifact may offer the solution to that paradox."

"How so?" asked the NASA administrator.

"Simple: it's a weapon that sterilizes star systems. I'm willing to bet that these aliens send doomsday devices like this all across the galaxy. They monitor the development of life in different star systems, and as soon as a new civilization arises, they extinguish it."

Prater shook his head. "As I already told you," he said carefully, "a weapon is the least likely thing that it could be. And barring any incontrovertible hostile activity from the artifact, I'll continue to argue that it's not a weapon. Even in the unlikely event it turns out to be a weapon, it's probably inoperable, or its creators never used it in our Solar System. Or, as has already been postulated, its creators may have long since disappeared, and so the artifact is forever incapable of doing whatever it was built to do. All in all, I think it's safe to say that the Bastion won't commit any belligerent actions against Earth."

"What makes you so certain of that?" asked Ortega.

"Well for one thing, it hasn't done anything remotely hostile since it was discovered. I think that if it was going to attack IE's miner, it would have done so already. So it would be insanely presumptuous to automatically assume that the Bastion or its creators are hostile when we have no evidence to support that conjecture."

"Are you sure of that?" said Nesbitt. "One could argue that we have plenty of evidence of hostile alien activity."

That caught Prater entirely off guard.

"What are you saying?" Prater demanded, disconcerted by Nesbitt's words. He turned to look at Ortega. "Do you know something about these aliens that I don't?"

The President shook his head. "Of course not," he said. Ortega almost sounded disappointed that Prater would even suggest such a thing. "Don't be ridiculous."

Nesbitt chuckled. "You misunderstand me," he said. "I only know what you know, and used this information to illuminate and better understand other evidence that is available to everybody on Earth. And I think that that evidence indicates that these aliens are very malevolent."

"And what exactly is this other evidence that you're referring to?" Prater asked.

"Well, hasn't it been generally accepted that Mars used to be a much more hospitable planet than it is now? Isn't that why the astronauts there are still looking for native organisms that are either living or extinct?"

"Yes. What's your point?"

"We need to consider the possibility that these aliens are the reason that Mars is so lifeless now. What if they attacked Mars millions or billions of years ago, and destroyed whatever life might have once been there?"

Prater chuckled. "That's just ridiculous."

"Oh? And what makes it so ridiculous?"

"Because even if Mars ever was inhabited, it's highly unlikely that it was populated by a technologically advanced civilization. And in the unlikelihood that a Martian civilization did exist, it's extremely implausible that it was advanced enough to pose a threat to whatever civilization built the Bastion."

"Perhaps, but even if you're right, that doesn't mean these aliens wouldn't attack another planet, even if it's not a threat to them. Hell, maybe these bastards get a kick out of going around nuking primitive planets just for fun."

"If they really were that hostile," Prater said, "then why would they have attacked Mars and not Earth?"

"How do you know that they didn't?" Nesbitt countered. "For all we know these aliens could've wiped out the dinosaurs."

Prater laughed. "Now you're really off in la-la-land."

"Am I? You've said time and again that we can't even begin to imagine what the aliens' motivations may be. So how can you then go on and say that they wouldn't commit acts of mass destruction?

"And don't forget that it's entirely possible that this thing has been hanging around the Solar System since before life emerged on Earth, and that it could be capable of wielding unimaginable destructive power. Doesn't that make it a contender for causing some, or maybe even all, of the mass extinction events throughout Earth's history?" Nesbitt chuckled again, but grimly this time. "It may even be some kind of sick game that the aliens play. Every few hundred million years or so, they attack Earth and wipe out the majority of life here, just for shits and giggles. And they might just decide to do that again now. They probably do this sort of thing all over the galaxy."

It was clear that Ortega and many others in attendance were being swayed by this. Prater remained steadfast, but he was now obviously on the defensive.

"But why would they do that in the first place?" said Prater. "It would make as much sense as us dropping a bunch of nuclear bombs on Antarctica to kill all the penguins."

"I'm not disputing that such attacks would be irrational," said Nesbitt. "But you're making a mistake by assuming that the aliens would act rationally in the first place. Maybe they're completely insane, at least by our definition of insanity. You said it's entirely possible that their actions may be fundamentally incomprehensible to us due to them having a completely alien way of perceiving reality. Something that seems insane to us could be fun and games for them. Or maybe committing interstellar genocide is just a cultural norm to them."

Prater was growing increasingly desperate to prevent the President and his staff from believing that the builders of the artifact were hostile, for he believed that nothing good would come if they became convinced of this.

As calmly as he could, Prater said, "I will admit that it is possible, if not likely, that the aliens' way of thinking could be fundamentally different from ours. But I also believe that there is a limit to how alien their way of thinking can be. For one, I think it's safe to assume that a civilization reckless and irrational enough to casually commit arbitrary acts of mass destruction would destroy itself long before it's developed the technology needed for interstellar travel."

"Are you sure of that?" said Nesbitt. "Do you honestly believe that there is no possibility whatsoever that such a hostile civilization could spread throughout the galaxy?"

"Well...no. I'll admit that yes, there is a possibility that you could be right."

"And that is why we cannot ignore the potentiality that these aliens are hostile. And if they are, then we have no hope of ever reasoning with them. So I think it goes without saying that we should be prepared for an armed conflict with them."

"I'm not sure that would be a smart thing to do," said Prater. "If you are right, and they are hostile, then I can guarantee you that there's not a damn thing we can do to defend ourselves if and when they do decide to attack us. After all, it's probably safe to assume that they're billions of years more advanced than us. So if we tried to stand up to them, the best we could hope for would be to annoy them a little bit. We'd be like ants biting the foot of a titan, right before they stomp us out as easily and casually as we might step on an anthill."

"So what are you saying? That we should just surrender without even bothering to put up a fight?"

"I'm just saying that trying to fight them at all would be a completely futile gesture, and you're a fool if you think otherwise."

There was a period of tense silence.

"So what can we do?" Ortega asked.

"In regards to the safety of Earth," Prater said, "all what we can do is hope that the Bastion is not hostile. But that shouldn't be a concern because those fears are unjustified. As I said earlier, there is absolutely no rational reason why such an advanced civilization would attack a planet as primitive as ours."

"That's not exactly true," said Loretta Mosdin, the President's science adviser, speaking up for the first time in the meeting. "There is a very valid reason why they would want to destroy other civilizations, even one as backwards as our own."

Everyone in the room turned their attention to her.

"What are you talking about?" Prater snapped. "What rational reason could there possibly be?"

"To safeguard their survival," she said simply.

Prater sighed. "You can't be serious. Do you seriously believe that we'd be any kind of threat to such an advanced society? Have you been listening to us at all?

"Of course I've been listening," she countered. "And you're right that we don't pose a direct threat to them now. But in the long term, we pose a very real threat to their survival and that of any other alien civilizations that might exist."

"And how the hell is that?"

"Allow me to elaborate. It could be that whatever civilization created this artifact still exists, and they're simply not interested in colonizing space in the same way that we are."

"What? That's ridiculous. Colonizing space is the only way to ensure the survival of civilization. This is plainly obvious to any sufficiently advanced civilization."

"That's not entirely true. Think about it: the universe is extremely vast, but it is not infinite. And neither are the resources it contains. If multiple civilizations were to spread throughout the universe without constraining their growth, they eventually would consume all available resources. Conflict between civilizations would be inevitable. And even if there was only one completely homogenous civilization, they might still desire to restrict their growth in order to conserve for a time when those resources would be even more precious than they are now."

"What do you mean by that?" Ortega asked.

"The Solar System, the galaxy, and the universe seem ripe for our taking, offering us scores of resources," Mosdin said. "But it won't be like that forever. Cosmological observations indicate the universe's expansion is accelerating. If this continues into the indefinite future, then eventually all galaxies will move away from each other faster than the speed of light with respect to each other. All galaxies will pass beyond a cosmic even horizon and disappear with respect to each other, as new light from each galaxy will be unable to travel the ever-increasing intergalactic distance due to the universe's accelerating rate of expansion.

"Eventually, dark energy will accelerate the expansion of space so much that stars will be pushed away from each other, destroying the galaxies. Then planets will be pushed away from their home stars, and then the planets will be pulled apart as well. And then dark energy will break down matter itself, all the way down to the atom and beyond, until a cosmic event horizon separates every subatomic particle from each other, leaving them with no way to interact."

None of what Mosin was saying was new to Prater. He often read reports from scientists who studied this very thing. But he suspected that this was the first time that Ortega was hearing of this, as well as most, if not all, of the presidential advisers who were sitting in on this meeting. Although Prater still was not entirely certain if he knew where the President's science adviser was going with this.

"If faster than light travel is impossible," Mosdin continued, "then increasingly dramatic effects of dark energy would cause a civilization that spans the entire galaxy, or multiple galaxies, to inevitably have their empire or federation torn apart into smaller and smaller islands of civilization separated from each other by an ocean of cosmic darkness that cannot be traversed. All the great riches of the galaxy and universe will become completely inaccessible to these denizens of the distant future."

"So what?" said Prater. "Even if human civilization were to expand into space at a rate far greater than what we can reasonably expect, we still wouldn't come anywhere close to consuming all resources in the galaxy, much less the observable universe, at any time soon. And dark energy won't destroy matter until long after that happens."

"Thank you for proving my point," said Mosdin. "You're simply not capable of thinking on such vast timescales. No human can. But this artifact is billions of years old, so it's entirely possible that whatever civilization built it can and does think on timescales of cosmological significance. If that's the case, then our neglecting the ramifications that our actions will have on the universe billions or trillions of years into the future could seem as ignorant and shortsighted to them as a company that neglects the effects of global warming and environmental degradation that its activities wrought in order to turn a quick profit.

"Rather than consuming all of the resources of the galaxy and the rest of the universe right after they develop the capability to do so, these aliens could be taking their time, doing the absolute minimum they must in order to stretch out their cosmic lifespan as much as possible. They could be saving all of the galaxy's resources for some distant point in the future once the effects of dark matter become more pronounced, when such resources will be even more valuable than they are now. Maybe the rate at which we've been mining the asteroids is as rapid and reckless to them as someone who sets an entire oil field on fire just to keep himself warm."

Deathly silence fell as everyone in the Situation Room contemplated this.

"If these aliens are concerned about their civilization surviving for as long as possible," Nesbitt continued, "then they might want to stamp out any possible competition before it even has a chance to fight with them on a galactic scale. Sure, we don't pose a direct threat to them right now, but that's not what they would be concerned with. They would be concerned with the long-term effect we'd have on their own survival. By destroying a civilization like ours before we have a chance to colonize the stars, they might be able to extend their own lifespan by billions or trillions of years.

"And even if faster than light travel is possible, they might still adopt this kind of policy. If many civilizations were to arise throughout the universe, then conflict would inevitably result as a result of competition for cosmic resources. And faster than light travel still wouldn't prevent dark energy from destroying matter.

"A big disadvantage of this policy is that another

civilization may not have the same regard for conserving resources, and just consume as much energy and resources as they can. War would be inevitable between civilizations with conflicting views on this matter."

"Like us," Ortega said grimly.

"Yes, like us," Mosdin said. "But as Mr. Prater has already pointed out, these aliens undoubtedly possess technology far superior to ours. So any hostile act they commit won't be a war, but extermination.

"It could be that when they discover another such a civilization, their first course of action is to destroy it. They would probably even destroy a civilization that shares their conservative philosophy about conserving energy and resources. After all, any civilization would use energy, even one that restricts its growth. So the fewer civilizations there are, the longer they'll be able to survive into the distant future.

"Maybe they send machines like this to different star systems for the same reason we send probes and expeditions to the planets in our Solar System: to learn more about the universe. And if they discover life, they monitor its development. So this thing could have been surveying us for billions of years, waiting for a civilization to arise, only to stomp us out right when we're really beginning to expand into space. And maybe the Bastion will begin to replicate and consume the resources of the Solar System at a later time that its creators deem to be more appropriate for resource development."

"There is a cold logic to all of that," said Nesbitt. "And if the aliens conform to that way of thinking, then we could all be in a world of hurt."

Prater fell silent as he contemplated this. The entire reason why he had worked for NASA his entire life was that he had always seen space exploration and colonization as a way to safeguard the future of humanity. They had always argued that they were thinking about the long-term survival of humanity. And he had dreamed of the day when intelligent extraterrestrial life would be discovered.

And yet even he could not deny the logic behind what Mosdin was saying. Could the aliens really see humanity's activities as short-sighted recklessness that it warranted their species arbitrary extermination?

It was clear that the president and his advisers were being swayed by Mosdin's words. But he didn't see this as a good enough reason to abandon IE's plans for the future. After all, there wasn't any proof that the builders of the artifact conformed to this way of thinking. At least not yet.

"So what might their civilization be like?" asked Ortega. "Would they confine themselves to their home star system?"

"It's possible," said Mosdin. "Hell, maybe they wouldn't even expand beyond their home planet. They would certainly have the technology that would be needed to protect their planet from threatening asteroids or comets, but that might be it. Beyond that, the only thing they would have to worry about would be the eventual death of their own sun. At that point, they could transplant their civilization to another star system, but they would likely maintain strict population control.

"If they do restrict their growth like that, they might not have sufficient resources to fend off an attack by a larger and more powerful civilization. One that doesn't value conserving the universe's resources, and consumes whatever it wants to fuel waves of colonization. And it would be in the interests of the conservative civilization to try to prevent a war like that from ever happening. So it would make sense for them to send probes to stars all throughout the universe, to monitor the development of intelligent life, and perhaps to stomp it out. After all, it would make the most sense for them to destroy another civilization before it has developed the technology to travel to the stars.

"Maybe a technologically inferior civilization could try overwhelming them through sheer strength of numbers. Or it could be that the conservative civilization could possess doomsday weapons of such unimaginable destructive power that an enemies' strength in numbers would be rendered completely inconsequential. After all, the population of ants exceeds that of humanity by orders of magnitude, but even if all the ants were to somehow band together and launch a highly coordinated attack on us, they couldn't possibly inflict any serious harm on our civilization."

Prater said, "But we need to think about all of the opportunities that they'd give up if they didn't exploit the resources of the universe to the fullest extent possible now. I'm willing to bet that if they have the technology to travel across the stars, then they also have the technology to upload their minds into computer systems. And given a sufficient amount of technological development, maybe they could build Matrioshka brains for their minds to inhabit, which would allow them to achieve levels of consciousness orders of magnitude beyond what can be done with biological brains. Are you telling me that they would give up all of that just so they could live long enough to be destroyed by dark energy?"

"I don't know," Mosdin admitted. "That brings up a very serious question that must be answered by any civilization that thinks on such vast times scales: is it better to grow large at the expense of a long life? Or is it better to live for an extremely long time with a somewhat smaller society and technological capability? But since there is no evidence that this artifact is exploiting the resources of the Solar System, it may be safe to say that whoever built it cares more about living for as long as possible than expanding their own civilization."

Everyone in the room was now looking very disturbed by Mosdin's words. Prater slumped back in his seat, deeply unsettled by what this conversation had revealed to him. For his entire life, Prater had casually dismissed the idea of hostile aliens invading Earth as a ridiculously absurd science fiction cliché. There was never any logical reason for aliens to invade other than having an insatiable bloodlust against other species. Real extraterrestrials could not possibly be so mindlessly destructive. The discovery of the artifact had done nothing to shake his position on this matter. But now he could not deny the callous logic that Mosdin had presented and, for the first time, he thought that there might actually be a justifiable reason to fear the aliens.

Prater had been incredibly jubilant when he had first laid eyes on the artifact, and now he felt crushed upon consideration of the horror it might represent.

"These are all very interesting theories," said the President. "But as Mr. Prater has pointed out, all this talk has amounted to little more than speculation. And unless we obtain more information, speculating is all what we'll be able to do. This, in my opinion, highlights the significance of what our next course of action should be."

After a brief pause, the President continued. "There needs to be a follow-up mission. The IE miner is ill-equipped to adequately study the artifact. If we really want to learn as much about the artifact as we possibly can, then we need to commit ourselves to doing it. I believe that we should send a manned spacecraft to the artifact."

"Do you really think that's a wise thing to do?" said Nesbitt. "Such an act could prompt the artifact to retaliate against the crew, or against Earth itself. It may not even be safe to have the miner continuing to crawl around it."

"As you've said, it's equally probable that any of our

actions in space could incite some form of retaliation. Perhaps the first retaliatory actions have already been initiated. The artifact may have sent a message to its creators as soon as it picked up our first radio transmissions. Such a signal may just now be reaching their home world, and the alien's political or military hierarchy might soon be deciding what to do about us.

"Or maybe the artifact is gathering solar energy, and won't do anything until it's obtained sufficient power to fulfill its programming. As we've heard in this meeting again and again, we simply don't know what the artifact might do. And it's precisely because of that that I believe that sending a crew to the artifact is the wisest course of action. Having a team of highly trained scientists armed with as much sophisticated equipment is probably the best hope we have of learning more about the artifact and whoever built it."

Ortega turned to look at Prater again. "Is a manned mission to the Bastion something that we could undertake?"

Here it was. The decision that could shape the future in ways they could scarcely begin to imagine.

"Yes," Prater said carefully. "It can be made to happen, and I wholeheartedly agree with you that we should make it happen."

"Excellent. How long will it take before NASA can launch a mission to the alien artifact?"

"It depends."

"On what?"

"It depends on whether or not Miles Gilster wants to turn the *Intrepid* over to NASA for such a mission. That fusion spacecraft really represents the best opportunity to reach the Bastion as rapidly as possible. The sooner we can put boots on the ground, the better our opportunity to learn more about this artifact."

Ortega grinned. "Well I'm sure Mr. Gilster won't have a problem with that. After all, his company did find this amazing thing. He'd probably love nothing more than to have his most advanced craft used for such an historic undertaking. The PR value alone will be worth a fortune."

Prater nodded, hoping that the President was right.

Chapter 8

Mark held his breath as he walked into Miles' office. This was his first time meeting with the IE president since Gilster had fired Desmond. And it dawned on Mark that he had not felt this nervous to meet with Miles since he had first interviewed for the job as an IE astronaut, all those years ago. And he knew the source of this anxiety: Desmond's leak and subsequent firing.

The mood at IE had soured dramatically over the last few days. Everyone continued to do their work as usual, but the collective mood of the staff had darkened the atmosphere since Desmond was cast out. Desmond was not the first person to be fired from IE, but he was the only one who had been fired for leaking information. The wrath and swift retribution it aroused in Miles gave them a glimpse at a side to the man that had remained hidden until that moment. It shook them to the core.

Mark understood why Miles had fired Desmond, but was not sure if he agreed with the lengths to which the IE president had gone to completely ruin the engineer's career. Of course Mark had no intention of voicing this opinion to his boss, or anyone else for that matter. Given Miles' irritable state of mine, he knew intuitively it would still be unwise to say or do anything that might agitate the man.

Miles looked up from his desk and forced a smile as Mark walked into the office. "It's good to see you," he said, but his voice was flat, a stark contrast to the vibrant exuberance that normally defined his demeanor. It almost seemed as if the flame of passion that the artifact's discovery ignited in him had been extinguished.

"Likewise," Mark said as he sat down in the chair on the opposite side of Miles' desk. He knew better than to remain standing when his boss was sitting down during a meeting. Normally, he would not think too much of it, but

88

it was crucial to show as much respect for his boss as possible at a time like this.

"I mean it when I say that I'm glad to see you," Miles said. "Hell, having people I can rely on is all the more important in light of this clusterfuck. The feds are demanding more out of me now than they ever have before. They want constant updates about everything we're doing, even though we're already giving them the live data streams from the miner, and we have yet to discover anything new.

"What's worse is that they're giving me shit for not telling them about this right away. They know I wanted to keep the Bastion secret, and they won't shut up about it. They actually have the balls to say that it was bad for me to trying keeping it secret, even though they would have done the same thing if they had found it. The fact that they haven't disclosed this to the public proves that." He slumped his head down.

Mark though that part of the reason for the lack of public announcement was because President Ortega was still weighing his options on how best to handle such a delicate matter. Or maybe he wanted to keep it under wraps for the foreseeable future. Mark thought of Desmond again, and how he had said that the world had deserved to know about the alien artifact. But it didn't seem that was going to happen anytime soon. He thought sourly of the bureaucrats Desmond had entrusted with the disclosure.

"*Put not your trust in princes,*" he muttered, quoting the Book of Psalms.

Miles looked up. "What?"

"Nothing," Mark replied a little too fast. "Is there anything I can do to help?"

Miles nodded soberly. "As a matter of fact, there is. That's why I wanted to meet with you."

The IE president had given no indication to what he

wanted to discuss with Mark in this meeting, so the astronaut listened carefully to what his boss said next.

"I've been invited to the White House," Miles said. "I'm going to have a long conversation with Ortega and his advisers about what IE will be doing to help NASA with the next phase of what they've dubbed *Operation Bastion*."

The *Intrepid*. That had to be it. NASA must want to use the *Intrepid* to send a crew of astronauts to study the Bastion. The only other manned spacecraft that might be able to make a voyage to the alien artifact were the Mars Cyclers. Even though the *Intrepid* would not be operational for more than a year, it would still make more sense to complete and use the fusion-powered spacecraft rather than one of the Cyclers. The *Intrepid* would be able to carry far more payload and crew than the *Armstrong* or the *Aldrin*. Besides, using either one of the Cyclers would effectively force NASA to abandon the Collins base on Mars.

"They want our ship... the *Intrepid*," Mark found himself saying aloud.

The IE president nodded curtly and locked eyes with Mark. "I want you to come to Washington with me," he said.

"Why?" asked Mark. He had never accompanied Miles to Washington before; and his boss had never asked him to do anything like this. "Washington and politicians aren't my forte."

"Look, this is not going to be a walk in the park," Miles growled. "And it's not going to be anything like the games I usually have to play when I go to DC. This has the potential to get very ugly. I want an ally with me when I meet with this pack of wolves. And now, more than ever, I need someone I know I can trust."

Mark quickly realized why Miles would want him. With the huge profits generated by asteroid mining operations, IE was now part of the very backbone of the global economy. This had made Miles the wealthiest man in the world, and many politicians in Washington favored him as part of their support of American businesses and ingenuity. But there were just as many who felt that Miles' wealth and command of technology made him far too powerful, and saw him as threat.

Astronauts, on the other hand, were always seen as paragons of human achievement, regardless of whether they were employed by government agencies or private companies. And as much as Mark liked to maintain a humble mindset, he also knew that many looked upon him as one of the best astronauts in the world. His name was almost always invoked when someone spoke of human ingenuity, daring and the impressive capabilities that astronaut corps represented. .

Having Mark at his side when Miles went to Washington was a way of impressing the politicians and elicit continued support of IE, as well as a bit of leverage to coax them into ceding exploration and control of the artifact to him. Besides, after Desmond's betrayal, Miles needed reassurance that he could have faith in his astronauts. If he could no longer trust his astronauts, then he could trust no one.

"I'm with you all the way," Mark said. Despite the harsh treatment of Desmond, Miles deserved his unflinching loyalty.

"Excellent," Miles said, his mood seeming to have improved somewhat. "Get back to your place and start packing. We leave tonight."

***

Mark and Miles sat at the table in the White House Situation Room along with the presidential cabinet members, as well as Alan Prater. Miles had delivered cordial, but terse greetings to each of them upon his arrival at the White House. He held what he really wanted to say

91

until all were present, including President Ortega.

When the President entered the Situation Room, a broad, friendly smile swept across Ortega's face upon seeing Miles, and he walked right up to him. "Let me congratulate you again on having made the greatest discovery in human history," he said, offering his hand to Miles.

"I'm not the one you should be congratulating," Miles replied as he shook the President's hand. "All of the credit for this belongs to the hard work and determination of the brilliant men and women I have the pleasure of of having in my employ."

"Of course." Ortega then took Mark's hand in his own, and shook it with the same affability that he had shown Miles.

"It's an honor to meet you, sir" Mark said as he shook the President's hand.

"Please, I'm just a statesman," said Ortega, releasing Mark's hand. "Men like you are what really make this country so great." Ortega had always been a strong and passionate supporter of NASA, as well as private space endeavors. "There is no limit to the benefits your work brings to America and the rest of the world, and you're willing to routinely put your life on the line to help make that happen. I can think of no nobler profession."

"Thank you. Hearing you say that means a lot to me."

"I'd love to join you on one of your missions one day. But I fear that I'm already getting too old to get onboard any rocket. By the time I leave office, I don't think I'll be able to do anything more thrilling than driving my own car."

"Well hopefully that won't be the case," said Mark. "I'd love nothing more than to take you to space myself."

"Let's hope that's true." The President gestured toward the table. "Please have a seat."

Miles and Mark returned to their seats, while Ortega sat down in the unoccupied chair at the head of the table. The President turned his attention to the wall monitor displaying the Bastion.

"Have you learned anything new about this thing in the past few days?" he said to Miles.

"No, I'm afraid not," said Miles in a guarded tone.

"That's unfortunate," Ortega said as he turned his attention back to Miles. "But hopefully it won't remain so enigmatic for much longer.

"I've informed the leaders of Russia, China, Japan, and the European Union about your discovery. They have all agreed to keep this secret and concur that a manned expedition is the next logical course of action.

"Administrator Prater and my science adviser Dr. Mosdin have informed me that the *Intrepid* is the best option we have for such an undertaking. It is capable of delivering far more resources to the Bastion than any other spacecraft currently operating or in development, and would be able to act as a long-term research station. You last projected that the *Intrepid* would be completed in about two years' time, correct?"

"That's correct," said Miles. He was refusing to make eye contact with the President, his words were calm and cold, his thoughts focused inward.

"Good. Building an entirely new spacecraft for a mission to the Bastion would likely cost tens or hundreds of billions of dollars and many years' worth of effort. And I'd greatly prefer to spend only a fraction of that time and money to learn more about the Bastion and whoever built it. I think, therefore, that it would make far more sense to help your company complete your ship. That would be far more effective in both time and cost. And I'm sure that once your vessel is completed, you'll have no qualms with letting NASA use the *Intrepid* for this endeavor."

93

Miles looked Ortega directly in the eye. "You may have assumed too much," he said sternly.

It was as if a bomb had gone off in the room.

"I beg your pardon?" said Ortega in stunned disbelief.

"Do you know what would happen if I turned the *Intrepid* over to NASA?" Miles' voice was low, but with an edge to it. He looked at the President fiercely, like he was staring down an enemy, and his tone became far more defiant. "People will wonder why we've canceled our Mars mission, not to mention that when the *Intrepid* is completed and launched, we can't keep its destination secret. With all the amateur astronomers on and off Earth, some of them will be watching the *Intrepid* wherever it goes. You'll need to be able to answer those questions, and I don't see that you can possibly hide it from the entire world. Therefore, you will have to reveal the truth.

"And don't even think about taking the *Intrepid* from me over some bullshit about national security. If you try anything like that, I'll immediately tell the world everything. I'll tell everyone about how you tried to seize my company's property because I didn't want to hand it over to you for free. How do you think that would go down?"

Miles' words shook everyone like the concussive blast from a hand grenade.

"Are you saying that you're not going to contribute to further investigation of the Bastion?" Ortega asked. He was agitated, desperately trying to quell his anger, and not succeeding very well.

"Of course not," said Miles. "There is nothing I want more than to learn as much about this artifact as we possibly can. But IE is a corporation first and foremost. We've sunk a huge investment into the *Intrepid*, but it was always intended to turn a profit. Not for a while, mind you, but we fully expected for it to be running in the black within the next few years. If we commit ourselves to sending the *Intrepid* to the artifact instead of ferrying paying customers to and from Mars, it will be nothing but a money pit for IE.

"And I'm sure you're well aware that we've filled all of the seats for the *Intrepid*'s maiden voyage. Every single one of our clients is going to be very pissed if I tell them that their Mars vacation has been cancelled. We have more than a billion dollars in deposits already, and we're going to have to refund all of that if we do what you're requesting. The bad publicity that would generate will hurt our other projects immeasurably. So from a business standpoint, there's no benefit to IE if we turn the *Intrepid* over to you without fair and just compensation."

"Okay, I can understand that," Ortega said carefully. "Rest assured that you will be compensated appropriately."

"I'm not going to be content with the kind of compensation aerospace contractors receive. A two or three percent profit off the stuff that they work on for NASA won't satisfy our needs. I want an upfront payment that's equivalent to the amount of money the *Intrepid* would have made had it flown four missions in a year's time at full capacity. And I want IE to continue receiving payments in that amount for however long the *Intrepid* is out there studying the Bastion."

Four missions in a single year? Mark knew that was a tall order. The voyages to and from Mars were going to last no more than two months, with a turnaround time for the *Intrepid* expected to last no more than a few weeks. Mark had never heard his boss say there would be four missions in one year and he had to suppress surprise from showing in his expression. Everyone had been assuming one mission per year at most, at least until the engineers felt comfortable with ramping up the *Intrepid*'s activities.

And if the *Intrepid* was going to be spending an

extended period of time at the Bastion, that would greatly reduce the expenses for IE. Roundtrip missions would require the *Intrepid* to be refitted and refueled whenever it returned to Earth orbit. All of those expenses would be eliminated if the *Intrepid* was going to spend all of its time stationed at the artifact. IE would make a far greater profit from this than by flying passengers to and from Mars. The logistical facts could not have been lost on Ortega or anyone else in the room.

The President chuckled. "You're demanding an awful lot," he said.

"I think I'm being reasonable," Miles countered. "The upfront payment will just barely make a profit for IE, and continuing to pay us at the rate I've requested will ensure that we're getting the full return on our investment. If I were feeling really ambitious, I would demand to be on the *Intrepid* myself. Seeing this artifact with my own eyes and touching it with my own hands means infinitely more to me than going to Mars. The reason why I'm not demanding that is because I'm one of the least qualified people in the world to study the artifact, and I would just be usurping an opportunity from someone far more qualified than me who has a much better chance of discovering something new about the alien technology. Properly compensating IE for handing the *Intrepid* over to NASA is the least that you can do."

Ortega sighed. "I'm not sure I can promise you all of what you're asking for."

"Well then I guess NASA won't be using the *Intrepid*." Miles' flat statement was brinksmanship at its finest.

In the stunned silence that followed, the tension in the room was palpable. In another setting, it would have taken little to ignite the powder keg of tempers bubbling just below the surface of the stony countenances of the cabinet members.

For his part, Mark was uncertain whether the threat Miles made was just a bluff or the real deal. Mark was almost certain that Miles would give up a sizeable chunk of his personal fortune for the opportunity to see the alien artifact up close and touch it himself, but he knew that Miles wasn't going to give them the satisfaction of knowing that.

Mark looked at the Cabinet members. Their eyes revealed what their expressions did not. Some seemed completely bewildered and some were angry at the turn of events. Nesbitt looked like he wanted to strangle Miles.

"Thank you again for coming," said Ortega, not even bothering to conceal his agitation. "I need to discuss our path forward with my staff. We'll let you know what the next course of action is as soon as I've come to a decision."

"Of course." Miles recognized the dismissal. He rose from the comfortable chair, motioned Mark to follow and walked to the door. "Have a lovely day," he said as politely as he could, and closed the door behind him.

***

"Are you really going to let him push you around like that?" snapped Nesbitt.

"Of course not!" Ortega declared angrily. "I'm the fucking President! He's out of his goddamned mind if he thinks he can hijack the government of the United States!"

"So don't let him get away with it. Make the bastard regret what he just did."

"What would you have me do?"

"Demand that he hand over the *Intrepid*, and charge him with treason if he refuses."

"I really don't think you should do that," said Prater. "I have no doubt that Miles meant every word he said about going public with everything. If you threaten him with charges of treason, he'll have nothing to lose. And that's not to mention that, correct me if I'm wrong," he nodded to the Attorney General, "there is no basis for a charge of treason. His lawyers would have a field day and voters would see your administration as tyrannical."

"You do realize what he's doing, don't you?" Nesbitt said, his voice still brimming with anger at what Miles had done. "He's playing you for a fool. The bastard wants the Bastion for himself! He did from the moment he first laid eyes on it! That's why he tried keeping it a secret, and the only reason we know about it is because one of his employees cared more about the safety of the country and the world than giving his megalomaniacal boss a pathway to keeping this alien technology all to himself! And now that that's no longer an option for him, he thinks he can extort you. That's treason right there!"

The Attorney General weighed in. "I'm afraid not. In the first place, the artifact isn't even in our jurisdiction. Also, as we all know... or should know," he shot a look at Nesbitt, "Article III, Section 3 of the Constitution specifically states, 'Treason against the United States, shall consist only in levying war against them, or in adhering to their enemies, giving them aid and comfort.' Doesn't fit the circumstances."

The President waved a hand at the Attorney General and groaned. "Do we even need the *Intrepid*? What about the Mars Cyclers? Could we send one of them to the alien artifact?"

"I already looked into that," said Prater. "And yes, we could send one or both of the Cyclers to the Bastion if we really wanted to. But the Cyclers could only carry a fraction of the payload that the *Intrepid* is capable of ferrying. Not only that, but the *Intrepid* can get to the artifact in a few months, whereas both of the Cyclers would take over a year to make the same voyage. And the Collins base is completely dependent on the regular rotation of personnel and supplies that the Cyclers provide. If we were to use the *Armstrong* to send a crew to the Bastion, the astronauts that are on Mars would have no way of getting back to Earth. If we were to use the *Aldrin*, we'd have no way of sending anyone else to Mars, and the Collins base would have to be abandoned.

"But that's not even the worst of it," he continued. "The Cyclers travel on orbits that optimize transits between Earth and Mars. In order for a Cycler to reach the Bastion, it would have to perform a series of propulsive maneuvers to alter its orbit and later rendezvous with the alien artifact. Those maneuvers would consume nearly all of the propellant that a Cycler is able to carry. The crew would be stranded at the Bastion with no way of returning to either Earth or Mars. Bottom line: Cyclers are the choice of last resort."

Ortega sighed and ran his hand through his hair.

Chapter 9

Mark and Miles were silent as they left the White House and got into the rental car they shared. Even with the growing prevalence of self-driving cars, Miles still preferred being in control of the wheel. There were some who argued that, in the interest of public safety, it should be made illegal for humans to drive cars anymore, and that all transportation vehicles should be completely automated. But that was something that neither Miles nor Mark supported and never would.

Mark remained profoundly awed at what had transpired in the Situation Room. Politics often clashed with the aerospace industry. That conflict had made IE's early years most difficult. Miles had fought countless bureaucratic and political battles during his company's fledgling years just to get a launch opportunity for the first asteroid miners. Once the asteroid mining paid off, bringing him immense wealth, Miles found himself more embroiled in politics, even though he considered it a necessary evil.

Like most captains of industry, Miles played both sides of the aisle, never showing a preference for any political party. He endorsed politicians that favored supporting the aerospace industry, and quietly worked against those that did not, always avoiding political partisanship. Over time, it became clear that his influence would have a major effect on the outcomes of elections. This made him either an invaluable ally or staunch enemy for those in Washington.

Seeing Miles confront the President as he had done was one of the most incredible things Mark had ever witnessed. It was one thing to speak favorably or unfavorably on an issue over the internet; it was entirely another thing to challenge the President of the United States and openly demand, what seemed to Mark, the impossible. In his estimation it verged on extortion.

Miles was in a state of deep contemplation as he drove, thinking of how things might unfold as a result of his actions, and what he should expect. Mark remained silent, knowing that beneath Miles' friendly demeanor lurked the mind of a cold, calculating tactician.

It was not until Miles pulled the car onto Pennsylvania Avenue that he finally broke the silence. "I don't know about you," he said, "but I could really go for a drink right about now."

"I couldn't agree more," Mark replied with a nod.

Miles pulled into the parking lot of a bar that he often visited when he came to Washington. Entering the bar, Mark could not help but notice the handful of people cast quick glances at them. Miles liked this place because it was a watering hold for what he referred to as *spacephiles*: industry workers, space groupies, and hangers-on. The few outsiders in the bar either looked when others did or simply ignored them. The spacephiles recognized them either from industry contacts or the media appearances they had made. Both Miles and Mark were often featured on the nightly news broadcasts, constantly highlighted on social media, and occasionally made cameo appearances in Hollywood blockbuster movies.

Those who did not have the slightest clue who Mark and Miles were could easily find out by snapping pictures of them and then uploading the pictures to an internet search engine. Every browser had facial recognition software that allowed the user to easily identify almost any individual based on their picture. The inquisitive searcher could then bring up everything from a brief synopsis or detailed online information about that person. This software was equally effective at identifying random passersby and those who posted selfies on their social networking profile as it was at identifying famous celebrities or politicians.

101

Out of the corner of his eye, Mark caught sight of a man taking a picture of them with his cell phone. Ruefully, Mark thought, 'He'll probably post it on his social media sites, bragging to his friends about being in the same bar with a famous astronaut and the richest man in the world, and never work up the courage to approach and meet the two of them. Too bad.'

Mark was always friendly to people who recognized him. He sometimes questioned his celebrity and whether he deserved the attention, but he loved meeting people who were passionate about space travel. When he was younger, Mark always got overly excited when he met astronauts that he looked up to and idolized. Yet, even now, he found it a little difficult to accept the fact that people had the same kind of admiration for him that he had for other pioneers of space travel.

The two men made their way to an empty table. TV monitors lined the walls, most showing sports, although one was turned to a news channel. Among the news highlights were the outcome of the latest Korean presidential elections, a major earthquake in Sri Lanka, and an apparent mass killing at a remote Antarctic research station. Mark instantly felt a pang of remorse for the slain scientists, and also felt a stab of personal regret over never having been to Antarctica himself. It struck him that he had walked on the Moon, but not on Earth's southernmost continent. He would have to remedy that at some point in the future.

Sitting down, Miles and Mark quickly ordered drinks from the kiosk menu on the table, and moments later a robot server brought them their drinks. Kiosks and robot servers were now ubiquitous in bars and restaurants. It was hard to imagine it being any different, and Mark remembered how he had hardly believed his dad when he had told him that his first job was flipping burgers in a fast food joint. It seemed as archaic as the printing press, like so many other jobs millions of people had toiled at until comparatively recently. Assembly line workers, farmers, clerks, chefs, waiters, waitresses, and bartenders were just a few of the occupations that had been virtually eliminated by the proliferation of affordable and reliable robot laborers.

All the people who might have worked those jobs in previous decades were now receiving the universal basic income that the government provided to people who had been rendered unemployable by the revolution of automated labor. Such a system was only sustainable by imposing large income taxes on people like Miles and Mark, who were wealthy or in highly paid occupations that required highly specialized skill sets that robots and computer programs were unable to perform or for which they were cost prohibitive.

Mark had nothing against the government taking a significant amount of his paycheck to support those who were less fortunate than he was. Hundreds of millions of people all around the world would be starving and homeless had national governments not implemented this system. Moreover, this liberated the masses unlike any other era in the entire history of human civilization. People who would have spent all of their time working mindless jobs just to provide themselves with the necessities of life were now free to write novels, play music, study science and mathematics, or pursue any other interests they held.

Those who had such passions were paramount to the continued advancement of sciences and technologies that fueled the new economy. The need for people to fill highly skilled jobs had prompted governments to invest more in science, technology, engineering, and mathematics educational programs.

Mark saw all of these government programs as being

no different than the sources of funding for scholarships and work opportunities that had benefitted him. He and so many others would never have had careers to begin with had it not been for the federal support of NASA, national research laboratories, and aerospace companies like IE.

Miles was supportive of universal basic income as well. IE's activities had contributed to mass unemployment by advancing the sophistication of replicating robots, which had eliminated the last of the manufacturing jobs. IE had driven terrestrial mining companies to bankruptcy by underselling them. That no one had to work in dangerous and toxic environments to mine ores, he viewed as a side benefit.

Mark believed that the Bastion would place an even greater emphasis on the need to invest in science and technology, but all of that depended on how the President reacted to Miles's demands.

Setting his beer down, Miles broke the silence. "So how are things going between you and Ning?" he asked.

Mark was flabbergasted. "I'm not sure I know what you mean."

Miles laughed. "Don't try to act all innocent. Any idiot can tell that the two of you are an item."

Mark sighed, trying not to feel embarrassed. "Things are going well," he said. "To be perfectly honest, it's pretty casual. We just hang out together outside of work, and sometimes sleep over at each other's place. Nothing too serious, really."

Miles laughed again. "Well whatever you do, don't think about tying the knot. Getting married was the single biggest mistake I ever made."

The statement surprised Mark. Miles never talked about his personal life at work and, in all his years at IE, Mark had never once seen Miles with a girlfriend or wife at his side. Of course, the details of Miles's personal life were largely public knowledge thanks to the constant scrutiny of the press, and it was not as if he was unwilling to discuss the subject.

To help maintain his high public persona, Miles often made guest appearances on the news and talk shows where he would discuss things his company was doing. It was inevitable that interviewers would ask him about his personal life. In all the interviews that Mark had seen Miles give, the man had never once given any indication that he was or had been married, or that he had any children. On the other hand, Miles made so many public appearances that Mark doubted that he had seen every media appearance his boss had made.

Maybe Miles wanted to keep his personal life as discrete as possible. Mark knew that he, himself, would never bring up his relationship with Ning in any interview he might give in the future, unless of course their relationship became much more serious, and Ning explicitly agreed it could be shared publicly.

Even then, Mark knew that there were people who devoted their lives to monitoring the public and personal lives of famous and influential people like Miles. These were the kind of people who would stalk anyone of even moderate fame, surreptitiously taking as many photos and videos as they could to fuel the endless gossip on internet forums and the gossip rags that still abounded.

Mark respected his boss's privacy too much to search for that sort of information, but since Miles had brought up the matter, it appeared that he actually wanted to talk about it.

"You're married?" Mark asked.

"I was for about eight months."

"What happened?"

Miles sighed deeply, and took a sip of his beer. "I was too young and stupid to know what I was doing," he said.

"I met her my senior year of college, and it was love at first sight for me. She was a beautiful, athletic nursing student. I thought that she was the greatest woman in the world and that I couldn't possibly find anyone else like her no matter how long I lived. I was overflowing with so much oxytocin that I convinced myself that my life hadn't had any meaning before I met her, and that I wouldn't be complete unless we were together. We got married immediately after graduation. Then she decided to divorce me after I used all of my life savings to start IE. She ended up taking a good chunk of the liquid assets I had at the time in the divorce settlement. My only saving grace was that I managed to avoid having to give her alimony or any IE shares."

"Holy shit. That's terrible."

"Yeah, but the really funny thing is that a few days after the first shipment of asteroid ore arrived at Earth, she had the gall to ask me if I wanted to get back together. The bitch had finally realized just how much I was going to be worth." Miles laughed again, but harshly and with a slightly bitter tone.

He took another sip from his drink before continuing. "Mind you, that was the very first time she had spoken to me since our divorce became final. And it turned out that she had gotten knocked up by some other guy not too long after we separated. She was struggling to support herself and her kid."

"What did you do?"

"I told her to pound sand and find another sugar daddy, like whoever knocked her up." Miles then burst out laughing.

Mark was momentarily stunned at Miles' bitterness, but managed a subdued laugh with his boss.

"But you really don't need to be concerned about that sort of thing," Miles shrugged after he stopped laughing. "Ning is a great woman. I wouldn't have hired her in the first place if I had any reason to think that she was a backstabbing bitch. And the two of you are still young, so there's no reason for you not to be enjoying yourselves. Jeez, saying that makes me feel like an old fart." He took another drink.

Although Mark did not seek or even want his boss's approval of his relationships, he appreciated the sentiment of Miles' words. And it was nice to see Miles in a better mood now.

Seeing an opportunity to shift the direction of the conversation, Mark broached the subject of a bothersome matter that he could not stop thinking about since the White House meeting. "So if you don't mind me asking, what are we going to do if the President rejects your proposals?"

Miles drained the beer before setting the schooner down on the table. "Let me worry about that," he said sternly and stony-faced. "Whatever happens will work to our advantage. And I swear on my life that I won't rest until we've unlocked the secrets of the Bastion."

Mark was taken aback by Miles' tone and, momentarily, at a loss for words as he grappled mentally to understand his employer's actions. 'Why had Miles issued such a threatening demand to President Ortega?'

Fighting against opposing political and public forces was something to which Miles was well accustomed. Ever since founding IE, especially in the early years, Miles had fought ceaseless battles against those who stood in the way of his company's growth. This included luddites who feared groundbreaking technologies would threaten their livelihoods, as well lobbyists with ties to corporate giants who controlled Washington politicians and Congressional members who were afraid that IE's growth and technological innovations threatened the job market in their districts.

The greatest opposition had come when IE pursued the

development of nuclear thermal rockets. For decades, the nuclear engineering community had suffered from a highly negative public image, perpetuated by those who feared that nuclear power was simply too dangerous to be used safely. That was always a nonsensical position to Miles and Mark. Nearly anything had the potential to be used by someone to harm someone else, whether it was knives, guns, social media, nuclear power, or simple rocks. But those very same things could be used to benefit just as many people. That was the entire foundation upon which civilization had been built. Knowledge and technology were neither good nor evil; it was the individuals who wielded them that determined whether they would be used benevolently or malevolently.

Extreme government regulations had severely restricted the nuclear industry's growth through the later years of the twentieth century and early twenty-first century. No one wanted to have a nuclear testing facility in their backyard, and the government was extremely reluctant and often opposed to issuing permits for such facilities.

Miles had recognized that nuclear thermal propulsion was absolutely vital for asteroid mining. Similarly, NASA found the technology to be paramount for manned missions to Mars. Even so, it had taken a lot of convincing to get the space agency to support IE as the company and its president campaigned for a renewed effort to develop nuclear capabilities in the United States.

Congressional lobbying was as frustrating and time consuming as the engineering development. The amount of paperwork and red tape they had to work through to test the engine rivaled the task of designing and building the actual hardware. But finally, both IE and NASA received the permits needed to build and test their nuclear thermal rockets. It was like a phoenix of the NERVA program from decades past, risen from the ashes of its former self and achieving the kind of success its researchers had only dreamed of seeing.

Years later, NASA had everything they needed to initiate manned Mars missions, and humans finally set foot on the Red Planet. IE in turn now had all of the technology they required to begin their asteroid mining operations.

All the while, there was still a large amount of opposition from groups who feared to what IE's success might lead. During these early years of IE's operations, there were still jobs requiring human laborers. The demand for human labor had been on the decline for decades, but people still fought passionately to protect it even as it entered its death throes. Try as they might, they could not turn the tide of technological advancement or the development of sophisticated, low cost robotic laborers by IE and other companies that finally delivered the death blow to human labor. This had fueled the implementation of the government's universal base income, which brought an end to much of the antagonism with which Miles and his company had been forced to contend.

Shortly afterward, IE grew to become one of the largest and most profitable aerospace companies in the world. Miles' accumulation of wealth and fame provided him with immense political influence. This had been incredibly useful during the development of the *Intrepid*'s fusion propulsion system. By the time that happened, political and public support had swung entirely in favor of nuclear technologies and IE had not been forced to fight nearly as many political battles as it had during the early development stage of nuclear thermal rockets.

In all the years of running IE, Miles never resorted to bribes, although he did donate to the campaigns of candidates who supported his goals. His political influence had stemmed primarily from his position as a powerful corporate leader, as well as his willingness to embrace a celebrity status in the public's eye. The media spotlight had frequently fallen on Miles as IE's star rose, and he cultivated an image that made him a major media star. He had millions of fans and followers on social media websites and that, coupled with his financial resources, gave him enormous influence over people and events. From that power, he had grown accustomed to getting whatever he pursued.

Mark believed that Miles' scientific interest in the artifact was genuine and, despite what had been said in the Situation Room, he believed that Miles was willing to send the *Intrepid* to study the artifact on his own dime. Miles had more than enough personal wealth to complete the *Intrepid* and cover the expenses needed to fund a mission to the artifact, but that was obviously not his first choice. He preferred to have someone else foot the bill to maximize IE's profits.

In the immediate aftermath of the Bastion's discovery, it seemed to Mark that Miles wanted to send the *Intrepid* to the alien artifact himself and learn the secrets behind the highly advanced extraterrestrial technology for the benefit of IE. Being denied the opportunity to do that by Desmond's leak had ignited Miles' unmitigated anger at his former employee.

Even if the possibility for achieving a monopoly on the alien technology were gone, IE would still benefit immensely by letting the government use the company's hardware for a manned expedition to the Bastion. Miles would make sure that IE would have access to whatever data might be obtained by any NASA mission that used the *Intrepid*. The monitoring and communications systems aboard the *Intrepid* would ensure the government would not be able to monopolize data obtained about the alien artifact.

President Ortega clearly had no objection to providing

financial compensation for the use of the *Intrepid*, but would he be willing to pay IE the amount Miles had requested? Why had Miles demanded so much?

Miles was correct in assuming that if the *Intrepid* were sent to the alien artifact, it would not be possible to conceal its destination, but that did not mean the *Intrepid's* mission would be disclosed. While it was true that a significant number of people in the world owned telescopes powerful enough to observe the Intrepid on an interplanetary mission, Ortega and his staff certainly would provide a cover story. And it need not be an entirely convincing story. Who would seriously suspect the real purpose of the mission was to investigate some piece of alien hardware? Conspiracy theorists, perhaps, but certainly no rational person.

IE had been a government contractor for many space projects. Is that what Miles was hoping to gain from this? Was it all just a way for him to squeeze more money from the government? Or was there more to it than that?

Mark agreed with Ortega that the amount of money Miles had requested was exorbitant. What was really peculiar was that Miles did not seem to be interested in negotiating the figure. Why?

Would Miles refuse to turn over the *Intrepid* to the government if they refused to give him the funds that he had demanded? What would happen in such a scenario? Would he still attempt to send the *Intrepid* to the Bastion at his own expense? And how would the government react were that to happen?

They might be unwilling to acquiesce to the demands out of fear that Miles' company would gain sole access to powerful alien technology. Mark wondered that if IE launched the *Intrepid* on a trajectory to the Bastion, would military leaders be inclined to launch a strike to intercept, even destroy the spacecraft? Even if the possibilities of unlocking the power of the alien technology were small, the President and his advisers might deem it too risky to give Miles free rein. But if the government were to take any military action against a private corporation, there would be a public outcry unlike any other. Mark could see people, with full support of private enterprise, revolting over such a thing happening.

Was that it? Was Miles relying on public support of him to get what he wanted?

Had Miles revealed the existence of the artifact to the world, the media would have given more attention to him than ever before. After all, what could possibly get him more worldwide attention than revealing that his company had made the greatest discovery in human history?

Miles would undoubtedly embrace the attention, using the heightened publicity to shield himself against any government action. If charges of treason were filed against him, he could portray himself as a victim of an oppressive government, persecuted for sharing the discovery with the rest of the world. This perceived martyrdom could make him untouchable.

Maybe that was what Miles was now after. Perhaps he was now seeing the artifact as a tool to exert direct influence over the President of the United States. If Miles could pull *that* off, nothing would stand in the way of any of his future endeavors.

Miles was not one to make idle threats and if Ortega refused his requests, Mark had no doubt that his boss actually would reveal the artifact to the world. He likely was prepared to release the information to every news outlet in the world with the push of a button on his phone. Employing a strategy that accused Ortega of attempting to keep the artifact's existence secret from the world would ensure public support for Miles and IE. And if Ortega revealed what Miles had requested it would likely be viewed by the public as a political ploy and have little effect on public opinion.

Nonetheless, Ortega was no fool, and neither were his advisers. They likely knew what Miles's true intentions were, and were discussing how best to respond. If Ortega agreed to Miles' conditions, he would essentially be conceding to being Miles' puppet, and that was not something that would not go over well with any sitting President.

So how would Miles react if Ortega refused? Would he be willing to negotiate further? Or would he steadfastly refuse to accept anything other than what he had demanded, even if it jeopardized a mission to the artifact, and led to a possible confrontation with the government? Did he have such overwhelming confidence that he thought President Ortega would do everything he had requested?

This was a very dangerous game Miles was playing.

Mark desperately wanted to ask his boss to elaborate on his plans, but knew that it would be to no avail. Miles kept the intricacies of his business and political maneuvering to himself. Still, Miles' willingness to confront the President like that only served to enhance Mark's awe and respect for his employer.

As Mark was contemplating all of this, Miles reached out and clasped Mark's hand. Mark locked his eyes with Miles'. Mark fleetingly thought of the other people in the bar, who could at this very moment be watching them, recording and posting the moment on the internet. Neither he nor Miles gave it the slightest thought. Mark knew right then and there that, regardless of what happened, nothing could shake his loyalty to his boss.

Chapter 10

Mark spent much of the following day wandering around DC by himself. Miles had informed him earlier that he would be spending most of his time in the private apartment he had in DC. Mark expected his boss would be locking himself in his apartment; he had many allies and enemies in DC, and by now most, if not all of them, likely knew that he was currently in the city. Mark could imagine that many of the people based in DC who interacted with Miles were likely to be bombarding the IE president with texts, emails, and phone calls. They likely wanted to know what he was doing in the nation's capital, looking to confront him, get something from him, or possibly just to meet up and confer with him. Miles was probably coordinating meetings with those he deemed important enough.

Miles adhered to the philosophy that one keeps his friends close and his enemies closer. Therefore, his correspondence and meetings would focus on power players, including his allies, enemies, and competitors.

Despite the close relationship Mark enjoyed with his boss, Miles preferred to do some things alone. One of those things was dealing with the politicians, lobbyists, and other power brokers who prowled the halls of government, not that Mark would ever complain about being excluded from those dealings. He avoided political entanglements whenever possible, and he appreciated the chance and freedom to explore the museums and monuments in the nation's capital.

He visited the Washington Monument, and then the Lincoln, Jefferson, and FDR memorials. Mark valued the legacies of these and other American presidents who had helped to make the country what it was. He thought how each of these American icons had built a country where

114

companies like IE were possible.

It was easy to point to John F. Kennedy and his push to create NASA and to send astronauts to the Moon in the 1960s. But there was far more to it than that. After all, manned spaceflight languished for many decades in the wake of the Apollo program due to waning political support. But even during those long and somewhat difficult years, NASA had found enough funding support and forged public-private partnerships to continue to develop the technologies that helped give rise to private space endeavors like IE. Perhaps more importantly, public support for space exploration never flagged. That, as much as anything, made it possible for fledgling aerospace companies to grow in the early years when profitability was nil and business models for private space ventures were almost unknown.

What if Kennedy had not been assassinated? Or what if he had never been elected president in the first place? How differently would history have unfolded then? Would the space program have been more or less robust than it was now? Would humanity still be restricted to the confines of Earth?

Mark also thought of the impact that events like this had had on his own personal history. How much of his own existence did he owe to the legacies of these men? His ancestors had immigrated to America from Germany and Ireland in the closing years of the nineteenth century. Would they have made that journey had the social, political, and economic climates in the United States and their home nations been any different?

And how much were his own actions influencing the future? It suddenly dawned on him that his role and those of the few other people who knew about the Bastion could be as influential to the people of the future as the works of the men who once governed from this city and the titans these monuments commemorated. But he would not allow thoughts of whatever historical significance he might achieve to push him into narcissism. He left it to others to judge the importance of what he accomplished.

Mark enjoyed his anonymity among the throngs of tourists crowded the sites he visited. Above the crowds, the skies of DC swarmed with surveillance drones, always watching, waiting, and ready to react in the event of a terrorist attack. Blending with the multitude, Mark thought again of the Bastion. Compared to the Bastion builders' capabilities, he felt small and insignificant indeed.

If the Bastion was eventually revealed to the world, it was highly probable that tensions and fears would rise all over the world as people strove to understand the technological and religious implications of intelligent extraterrestrial life. Questions would flourish about the consequences of one nation or governing body gaining control of such technology and that would fuel the fears of the growing number of people who already resented the intrusiveness of government in their private lives.

There was no shortage of such people. While their anger at the growing power of a central government had been largely confined to rants on Internet forums, a few had made violent attacks on government facilities and personnel over the years. Their vehement opposition to the government would grow if it gained control of advanced alien technology. That would likely spur more of them to action, making the specter of home-grown terrorism very real. Even if scientists could not unravel the secrets of that technology, conspiracy theorists would drive panic among the ignorant, much as they had with Area 51 so many years ago.

Mark imagined that President Ortega was weighing all of these things and considering his options on the Bastion just a few blocks away in the Oval Office. Mark did not believe that the threat of civil unrest fomented by violent extremists was a sufficient justification for keeping information about the Bastion classified indefinitely, but Ortega must be thinking of how such extremists' irrational hatred could be fueled by whatever action Miles might take if a satisfactory agreement could not be reached with the IE president.

These were terrifying things to consider, but Mark did not allow that to prevent him from enjoying the sites in the nation's capital. The museums in this city housed the legacies of historical figures. Some had used science, technology, and power to build, some to destroy. The Holocaust Memorial Museum was a grim memorial to how evil man could be toward his fellow man. Mark considered a visit to the museum a solemn duty to honor all of the victims of that horrific genocide each time he visited D.C.

Standing in stark contrast to that somber place was Mark's favorite haunt, the Air and Space Museum. It was especially meaningful to him now since it was home to spacecraft IE had developed and he had piloted. It meant their legacy in space exploration would live beyond their existence. As Mark walked through the museum, he stopped to look at the exhibit displaying the IE reentry capsule that had delivered the first asteroid ore to Earth. So much had depended on this capsule. No matter how successful that first miner had been at extracting metals from the asteroid, nothing would have mattered if IE had been unable to deliver those metals to Earth. Without that IE would gone bankrupt and Mark never would have had a career as an astronaut.

Mark spent a long time looking at the reentry capsule and reminiscing about the history behind it before he moved on to the manned spaceflight exhibit. One of the spacecraft on display was the Apollo 11 *Columbia* capsule that had carried Neil Armstrong, Buzz Aldrin, and Michael

Collins on their voyage to and from the Moon.

Next to the *Columbia* was the *Phaethon*, the capsule that Mark had piloted for IE's first manned lunar landing. The *Phaethon* was the first privately funded manned spacecraft to travel to the Moon and return to the Earth. Mark had gone with four billionaires that had each paid in excess of two hundred million dollars for the opportunity to walk on the lunar surface. That mission marked the first time that humans had walked on the Moon since Apollo 17 in 1972. The *Phaethon* had been designed to be reusable, like all of IE's manned spacecraft. But Miles had realized the historical significance of the capsule, and donated it to the Smithsonian after Mark and the IE lunar tourists had returned to Earth.

Mark spent a long time in the museum looking over the collection, and wondering what further contributions he might make to it. Despite the tense situation developing between Miles and the White House, Mark fully trusted the maneuvers his boss was making.

Chapter 11

Miles Gilster received a request to return to the White House at eight the following morning. When informed of this, it came as somewhat of a surprise to Mark, and he wondered if Ortega had come to a decision on accepting or rejecting Miles' conditions. Perhaps the President wanted to negotiate more. Maybe Ortega didn't like the options presented to him, which all but dictated his course of action if he surrendered to Gilster's demands, and was prepared to use the weight of his office to fight the IE president to the bitter end.

Miles had not elaborated on his plans to Mark, but this was hardly abnormal; Miles kept the intricacies of his business planning and political maneuvering to himself, crafting them with Machiavellian precision.

When Miles and Mark arrived in the Situation Room, everyone who had been at the previous day's meeting was in attendance. The atmosphere in the situation room was the polar opposite of what it had been the one day earlier. Whereas Mark and Miles initially had been viewed as harbingers of good news and invaluable allies, they were now being looked upon with the kind of anger and suspicion usually reserved for negotiations with the administration's enemies. As they took their seats at the table, Miles maintained the same cold, hard determination he had exhibited at the closing of yesterday's meeting, his face betraying no emotion.

Ortega, in his customary place at the head of the table again, looked at Mark and Miles with the eyes of an alpha male who was facing incursions into his territory by a rival that threatened his hegemony. When he spoke, his voice was hard-edged and cold as ice.

"After much discussion with my advisers," Ortega

said, "I will now make you an offer. If you agree to turn over the *Intrepid* to NASA, the international consortium will transfer the funds IE requested. Additional funding and resources will be provided to accelerate the completion of the *Intrepid* if needed. We will also provide cutting edge equipment is necessary to study the alien artifact. Since this is to be a joint effort, I have directed NASA to work directly with the Russian, European, Japanese, and Chinese space agencies to recruit and select the most highly qualified team of scientists to serve as the crew for the mission to the Bastion.

"In addition to this," Ortega continued, "I will make a public announcement about the Bastion just prior to the commencement of the *Intrepid*'s mission. Once this announcement has been made, you will be permitted to publically disclose all the information you have on the Bastion, with IE receiving full credit for having made this discovery. Is all of this acceptable for you?"

Miles nodded and allowed a subdued smile to crease his face. Internally he was jubilant, but gloating would bring repercussions somewhere down the line, and he knew it. The old saying echoed in his mind: 'Keep your friends close, and your enemies closer.'

"On behalf of IE, I accept your gracious offer," he said solemnly. "NASA's team will have our full cooperation in this undertaking."

"Very well." Ortega smiled tightly. He had convinced the other world leaders to acquiesce to IE's demands, but that did not mean he was happy about the situation. In essence, he knew the concession would be interpreted as weakness, something no world leader could afford.

But there was no way in hell that Miles could be given any chance of getting his hands on the alien technology. Ortega had been up all night thinking what he might be forced to do if Miles were bold enough to launch the

Intrepid to the Bastion himself. To take military action against an American company, especially one as powerful as IE, was something straight out of a nightmare. Better to give the IE president what he wanted rather than risk escalating the situation to the point where the nation could be torn apart. He was banking on the success of the mission to rebuild his image. In the meantime, he would take steps to strengthen his power base.

"It will take some time to select and train a crew for the mission," Ortega resumed after a brief pause. "Hopefully the *Intrepid* will be ready to launch by the time the crew has completed the necessary training, so you will need to maintain close communication with NASA. We also want you to continue removing as much of the rock surrounding the artifact as possible. Keep us advised of anything new you learn about it."

"So basically just keep doing what we've been doing?" Miles allowed just a touch of satisfaction to creep into his voice.

Ortega's glared at him. "Yes," he replied irritably.

"You've got no objection from me," said Miles. "If it's not too much trouble, I have one final request."

The entire presidential staff glared at Miles.

"What now?" Ortega snapped, barely concealing the anger that was building within him.

"It's a simple request: I want Mark de Rijk to be the mission commander, just as we had originally intended for the *Intrepid*'s maiden voyage to Mars. If we want the mission to be successful, the *Intrepid* needs to have the best possible commander. Mark is the single most experienced pilot at IE, he has been training to pilot and command the *Intrepid* longer than anyone else has, and no one is more qualified to do this than him."

Mark tried not to show how immensely pleased he was to hear Miles say this, but he was not surprised at the request. It was with some trepidation that he awaited the President's response, however.

Slowly, a small, cold smile crept across Ortega's lips. "Of course. I have no objection to that." In spite of the affirmative response, there was no mistaking the resentment in his voice.

Mark was stunned at how quickly Ortega had acted, and was flabbergasted that Miles had gotten all he demanded. Considering the tense exchanges yesterday, Mark had expected a protracted round of negotiations. Perhaps Ortega had decided the safest option was to yield to Miles' demands rather than risking a potential confrontation with IE further down the line.

Miles got up from his seat and walked over to Ortega, allowing himself to smile a bit more broadly. In part, that had to do with the White House photographer preparing to record the close of negotiations for posterity... and for release at a more opportune time.

"This is an historic day," Ortega spoke to the camera as he shook Miles's hand. "This is the day humanity made a conscious effort to initiate first contact with an extraterrestrial civilization." His presidential pose looked a bit contrived, but his words seemed genuine.

"I am honored to play a part in it," Miles replied sincerely, flashing his famous photogenic smile at the camera.

Once the photo op ended, Ortega released Miles' hand and turned to Mark, his eyes dancing like a child's. "You know, I've envied astronauts like you my whole life," he said. "Putting up with all the bullshit that comes with being elected to office made me envy you even more. Always yearning for the adventures you have...the excitement. But I don't envy this assignment you have accepted. You could end up serving as one of humanity's first ambassadors to an extraterrestrial civilization. Our survival as a species could very well depend on how you handle it. That's an awful lot of pressure."

"Thank you for your concern Mr. President," said Mark, somewhat relieved at how candid the President's words were. Ortega seemed to have none of the animosity toward him that he clearly had toward Miles. "But this is the greatest honor and privilege that I've had in my life. I cannot thank you enough for helping to make it happen. Regardless of what happens out there, it will be well worth it to me."

Ortega smiled. "Your passion and gratitude are most admirable. God willing, your mission will be a complete success, and I'll end up welcoming alien dignitaries to the White House."

Mark nodded. "I hope for that as well."

Looking around the Situation Room, however, Mark could see that the vision of such a rosy outcome was not shared by the President's staff and Ortega himself may not have truly believed it.

***

Ask stood on the deck of the Southwestern as it left port. Since assuming John's identity, he had continued to siphon information from other people at Larsen. During his time at the depot town, his actions had not betrayed his assumed identity. With all of John's memories absorbed, he performed the tasks and social obligations expected of the man. Not a shred of suspicion arose. Such pedestrian pursuits annoyed him to no end, but it was necessary in order to maintain a low profile to avoid discovery or raise unwanted questions.

A McMurdo Station repair party sent to check on the communications network had called in the news of the massacre at Niflheim. Word had reached Larsen only a few hours after Ask had assumed John's identity. An investigation commenced immediately and found the

123

snowcat that Ask had left ten miles from Larsen. As Ask had predicted, it was inevitable that the investigators would conclude that whoever had driven the snowcat was responsible for the grisly killings at the Niflheim Research Station.

Ask had continued to probe the minds of baselines at Larsen at every opportunity. It was from them that he learned the authorities had obtained digital photographs and footage of him after he arrived in Larsen and before he had assumed John's appearance. A quick crosscheck of authorized personnel and visitors confirmed that Ask was not part of the permanent staff or any ship's crew that had come to Larsen. That he was the likely murderer of the Niflheim crew was a logical deduction.

To avoid being tracked by the baselines' ubiquitous surveillance, Ask could never resume his original appearance. He might well have to change his physical appearance often, but that was a small price to pay for his newfound freedom. The Southwestern would take Ask to Australia. From there he intended to travel the world to continue learning everything he could about the baselines and absorbing whatever knowledge they had to offer.

Chapter 12

9 months later

Mark stroked his forehead as he sat through the presentation on the status of the *Intrepid*. The engineers that were presenting had been working as diligently as Mark had. Seventy-hour workweeks had been the norm for the entirety of IE's history. But Mark didn't think anyone in the company was working less than eighty hours a week since he had gotten back from DC. And it had been demanding as hell to meet the design review deadlines.

There was more pressure to finish the *Intrepid* now than ever before. Miles and the Ortega administration wanted the fusion spacecraft to be completed and launched as quickly as possible. The fear of the potential for a public leak was a major source of the motivation.

If information about the Bastion was leaked to the world, there was a high probability of a huge public backlash against Ortega, his administration, and IE for keeping it a secret. Ortega might be pressured to cancel funding that was being given to IE. The more people who knew about the alien artifact and the more time that passed, the more likely it was that information would be leaked to the public.

One factor that increased the risk of a leak were the billionaires who had signed on to be on the *Intrepid*'s maiden voyage to Mars. Miles had refunded all of their money, but not given much of an explanation as to why the mission had been shelved. It was impossible to keep such information secret from the public, but none of the would-be Mars tourists had known about the Bastion. It was bewildering to the public why Miles would cancel the voyage; the IE president had always stated that routine manned flights to Mars had always been one of the ultimate reasons he had founded his company.

But as baffling as his actions may have seemed to the public, no one suspected what the true reason behind it was. And Miles intended for it to stay that way. The IE president was confident that he had made a good enough example with Desmond to deter any of his other employees from ever doing such a thing again.

The same could not be said for NASA and other federal employees who now knew about the Bastion. Although many of them were accustomed to knowing things that needed to be kept secret in the interest of national security, some of them could still be idealistic enough to leak the information. And a recent development at NASA might make the risk of this happening even greater. The latest space observatory that the national space agency had been developing for some time now had been canceled in favor of using its sophisticated sensors to study the Bastion. That could not be going over well with the scientists involved with that project, many of whom likely did not know about the alien artifact. What would they do if they were to find out about the Bastion as well?

NASA employees might be confident enough that they could cover their tracks well enough to avoid being caught. Or maybe, as with Desmond, they did not care about that, and would accept the consequences. Everyone who knew about the Bastion also knew of Desmond's role in leaking it to the government. It was not as if they could be punished as severely as had Desmond. There were powerful federal employee unions that offered much protection, and were anyone to leak information to the rest of the world, the public would likely galvanize behind the individual, protecting him or her from any harsh disciplinary action by the government.

Desmond had forfeited this option when he leaked the information to NASA. Now that he no longer had access to any of IE's data, there was nothing he could use to prove that the company had discovered an alien artifact. Anything he posted online about the Bastion would be dismissed as being the kind of garbage that was put out by the long discredited Ufologists. This was likely the reason Desmond had remained silent for the past three months. What could he say or do that would not make him look ridiculous and bring further ridicule upon himself?

As much as Mark wanted the rest of the world to know about the Bastion, he knew it would be best if it were kept secret until the *Intrepid* was launched.

As the presentation dragged on, Mark paid as much attention as he possibly could to everything the engineers said. The last component of the *Intrepid* had been launched into orbit two days ago, and was in the process of being integrated with the rest of the vessel.

Mark's life, and the lives of his crew, depended on all of this. He could not afford to doze off during this talk. Besides, Ning was talking as well, and that was reason enough to warrant his full, undivided attention.

When the presentation finally ended, Mark got up from his seat in the conference room and returned to his workstation. There were a few things that the engineers had discussed that he wanted to look over in more detail. But no sooner that he sat down that his office phone rang. Mark groaned until he saw that the caller was Miles, so he wasted no time in answering the phone.

"Mark," his boss said in the stern voice he always had when he discussed something crucial, "come to my office right away. It looks like they've finally started to narrow down the other crewmember candidates, and I want your feedback on the people they're considering."

"Well it's about damn time," Mark said. "I'll be there right away."

***

Mark followed Ning when he saw the propulsion engineer head to the breakroom. He was rarely able to see much of the propulsion engineer since the overhauled work schedule. Ning seemed to be in the IE lab's twenty-four-seven, doing final tests for the different engine components and getting them to the launch site.

As much as she worked, Mark sometimes doubted that she ever took breaks, but was pleased to see that she was doing so now. He had just learned of Miles' decision, and wanted to inform Ning of it right away.

Mark was happy to see that no one else was in the breakroom. Ning was pouring herself a cup of coffee, and Mark cleared his throat to get her attention.

"I have some good news for you," he said.

"What is it?" Ning asked as she sipped her coffee.

"The other crewmembers for the *Intrepid* have been selected. You're going to be the systems engineer for the *Intrepid*. No one is more qualified to handle the fusion engine." Her eyes lit up, and she set the coffee cup down and walked up to Mark.

"I would have raised hell if they hadn't given this to you," Mark said as Ning stopped in front of him.

"You have no idea how much this means to me," she said. She looked like she was going to cry tears of joy.

She threw her arms around him, then pulled herself away and pulled Mark's face toward hers, kissing him deeply.

She had never done this when they were at work, and he briefly wondered if anyone was watching them, but then realized that he simply did not care one way or the other.

"How about we celebrate tonight?" Ning said when she finally pulled away from Mark.

Mark could not help but laugh. "Are you sure you have the time to do that? I didn't think you ever left this place." They had only been together once since his trip to

Washington. Part of him had feared she had lost interest in him, even though he was as swamped with work as she was.

"We're going to be spending a lot of time together anyway," Ning said. "Consider it a practice run for our voyage. Besides, I've missed being with you."

She pulled Mark's face back to hers and kissed him again.

***

Johnson Space Center
Houston, Texas

Adam Hernandez felt mildly anxious as he walked into the office of Richard Darden. The Mars Human Exploration Program director had not told the astronaut what the meeting was about, and Adam was always anxious when meeting with the higher-ups who ultimately controlled his fate as an astronaut.

Darden smiled broadly as Adam entered his office, and rose from his chair to shake hands with the astrobiologist.

"Nice to see you," Darden said as he sat back down.

"Likewise," Adam replied as he sat at the chair on the opposite side of Darden's desk.

"I'll cut right to the chase," said Darden, his smile instantly evaporating. "I was wondering if you'd reconsider your assignment on the upcoming Cycler mission."

It was exactly what Adam had feared most. He had been scheduled to travel to Mars onboard the *Aldrin* when it made a flyby of Earth in another seven months, the most coveted of astronaut missions. The possibility of going to Mars was the entire reason Adam had applied to be an astronaut in the first place. Each Cycler had included an astrobiologist among the crew since the program had begun. Even though no Martian organisms had been found in all the years of human activities on Mars, Adam wanted to believe that he would be the one to find extraterrestrial life when he explored the Red Planet for himself. He had actually wept tears of joy when he had received the offer to fly on the *Aldrin.*

But now it seemed as though that opportunity had been taken away from him, and for no apparent reason. Adam had heard nothing of any technical issue that might have crippled either of the two Cyclers or the Collins base. And he could not think of anything he might have done that would warrant any disciplinary action.

"Have I done something wrong?" Adam asked, pleadingly. "Please tell me whatever it is, and I'll remedy it."

Darden suddenly looked very guilty. "Oh, don't worry," he said reassuringly. "You haven't been removed from the crew. I apologize if you were afraid of that."

Adam breathed a mental sigh of relief.

"What I wanted to know is if you would consider an alternative mission," Darden continued.

"One that would make me to forfeit my slot on the *Aldrin*?"

"Yes."

Adam chuckled. "I think I can tell you right off the bat that I won't be doing that. Nothing means more to me than walking on Mars."

"I hear you there. But don't be so swift to write this off. Alan Prater wants to meet with you and talk to you more about this."

"Can you tell me what this other mission is?"

"I would if I knew what it was. But I don't. They haven't told me anything about it."

Everything about this was bewildering to Adam. Both Darden and Prater knew how much Adam wanted to go to Mars. It was what every astronaut dreamed of doing. If he had been ordered to give up his mission slot, he would have done so, but only because he would have had no real choice on the matter. But letting him decide what to do, they had to have known that he would choose Mars over whatever this alternative mission was. He didn't even know what he could offer any other human spaceflight endeavor.

The continued search for Martian organisms was the primary reason there were astrobiologists in the astronaut corps at all. What other mission could possibly require someone like Adam?

***

Goddard Space Flight Center
Greenbelt, Maryland

"This is bullshit!" Oksana exclaimed.

The unthinkable order had come in from NASA Headquarters earlier that morning: the Korolev Observatory was being canceled, and the hardware would be used for another project.

"I agree with you wholeheartedly on that," Shane Walker replied apologetically. "But there's nothing I can do about this."

The project director looked tired and defeated. Seeing him like this was especially disheartening to Oksana. Walker had been the spearhead and driving force behind the Korolev Array since the project's inception five years ago. If this order from Headquarters had caused him to give up, then the Korolev truly was dead.

"Shane," Oksana said pleadingly, "we can't just give up. Korolev could greatly help expand our understanding of the universe. You know that. Let's fight this. Take it to Prater himself."

"I've already tried that," Walker replied. "And Prater told me that he fully supports whatever project is replacing Korolev. And that's where all of the sensors are going to."

Hearing that was just as gut wrenching to Oksana as

131

word of Korolev's cancellation. "This is a joke, right?" she managed to say. "What the hell would they be using Korolev's sensors for?"

The Korolev was intended to host the most sophisticated sensor suite ever deployed on a spacecraft, all intended to probe the great mysteries about the cosmos and the laws of physics that governed it. Among Korolev's sensors were the most advanced gravity gradiometers, photodetectors, and magnetometers ever developed, as well as a small particle accelerator. There were also magnetic spectrometers, which were capable of detecting the presence of more exotic forms of matter, such as antimatter, dark matter, quarks, and strangelets.

Oksana had spent much of the past five years helping to develop the sensor array. Having them taken away like this for some secret project was as insulting as it was inexplicable.

"I honestly have no idea," Walker confessed. "But there does seem to be a silver lining, at least for you."

"And what would that be?"

"Apparently whatever it is that they're planning will involve a manned space flight. And Prater said that he's interested in having you as the physicist for whatever this mission is."

Oksana could not help but laugh at that. "They come in and take away what I spent over five years working on, and now they want me involved with the very thing that killed it? That only confirms that they've lost their goddamned minds."

"Maybe. But I still think you should give it some consideration. If nothing else, it might help give some closure with Korolev. And maybe you'll even want to take them up on their offer."

Oksana laughed again. "I highly doubt that."

***

Johnson Space Center
Houston, Texas

Opening the door to the conference room, Adam saw a tall, thin man standing next to the windows overlooking the parking lot. Hearing the door open, the man turned to look at Adam with intense, piercing eyes.

"I take it you're here for the same reason I am?" Adam said to the man.

The astrobiologist had been told that two other astronauts would be at this meeting with NASA administrator Alan Prater to discuss the mysterious space mission that Darden had spoken to him about.

"If you are here to meet with Administrator Prater to discuss a mission assignment, then yes," said the man as he walked up to Adam.

"That I am." Adam shook hands with the man. "Adam Hernandez," he said, introducing himself.

"Jedediah Storey."

Right as they finished shaking hands the door to the conference room opened, and Oksana Sobolev walked in.

"You're both here for a mission assignment?" said the physicist.

"That we are," Adam said. "I'm Adam Hernandez."

"Oksana Sobolev," replied the physicist as she shook Adam's hand. She then offered her hand to Jed.

"I am Jedediah Storey," he said, shaking the physicist's hand.

"So what have they told you about this?" Oksana asked as she sat down at the table in the center of the room.

"Not a whole hell of a lot," Adam replied, sitting down opposite Oksana. "They didn't tell me anything about what we might be doing."

Jed sat down next to Adam. "I have not received any

133

information pertaining to what this mission will involve," he said simply.

"Well I can tell you one thing they have done," Oksana said, agitation showing in her voice. "Whatever they're doing has ruined something I've spent the past five years of my life working on."

"Really?" Adam asked, incredulously. "What were you working on? And how did they ruin it?"

"I'm one of the leading scientists on the Korolev Observatory," Oksana explained, still sounding agitated. "Or at least I was until three days ago. Whatever this thing is, it seems to be important enough for them to cancel the Observatory and take just about all of our hardware. They're going to be using our entire sensor suite for this undertaking."

"Shit," Adam blurted. "That's terrible."

"Tell me about it," Oksana muttered.

"Please pardon my ignorance," Adam continued, "but I'm afraid I'm not very familiar with what the Korolev was."

"It was an Observatory that was going to be used to study astrophysical phenomena like dark matter, dark energy, stuff like that."

"Hmm." Adam stroked his chin.

"Can you think of a reason why they might want Kovolev's sensors?" Jed asked.

"No. We spent years planning Korolev's mission and all of the science observations and discoveries we were hoping to make, so I can safely say that there's no better use for the sensors we developed. I'm telling you, they've lost their goddamned minds!"

Adam could not help but chuckle slightly at that. "I might have to agree with you on that," he admitted. "I'm scheduled to fly on the *Aldrin* the next time it comes by Earth, and they actually had the gall to ask me to consider giving up my seat for whatever the hell this is."

"Holy shit, they really are insane!" Oksana said, and chuckled as well.

"What is your role on the upcoming Mars mission?" Jed asked.

"I'm the mission's astrobiologist," Adam replied.

"Hmm." A look of contemplation crossed Jed's face as he pondered this information.

"How about you?" Oksana asked Jed. "What endeavor of yours did they ruin or ask you to give up for this?"

"None," Jed replied simply. "This will be my first space mission, if I accept it."

"Your first?" Adam asked, somewhat surprised. "How long have you been in the astronaut corps?"

"I received the formal offer to join the corps four days ago."

Four days? And they were already offering him a flight? No one in the corps got a mission that quickly. Adam had been in the corps for two years before he was given a chance to fly on a mission. It was like a slap in the face to Adam, and he could see that Oksana felt the same way. And this was not lost on Jed.

"It is all too apparent that the two of you are dismayed that I am here," said the mathematician. "I ascertain that both of you have been in the corps much longer." Jed looked to Adam. "How long have you been in the corps?"

"Five years," he replied.

"What have you done in that time?"

"I've been to one of the space stations and walked on the Moon once."

"Hmm." Jed looked to Oksana. "What of you?"

"I've been a cosmonaut for ten years now," she replied. "I was the payload specialist on the mission to service the James Webb Space Telescope a year ago. There were plans to do servicing missions to the Korolev during

135

its operational lifetime, and I think it's safe to say that I would have been on at least one of them."

Jed nodded.

"So what's your specialty?" Adam asked Jed.

"I am a mathematician."

"Okay. So what brought you to NASA? What do you hope to do in space?"

"I do not have much of an agenda in that regard. To be perfectly honest, spaceflight has very little appeal to me."

That made Adam raise his eyebrow. "Then why are you here? Why did you apply to be an astronaut in the first place?"

"My curiosity was piqued a few months ago when NASA put out a call, saying that they were specifically looking for mathematicians for its astronaut corps. I wanted to see why the federal space agency was suddenly interested in recruiting mathematicians to be astronauts."

Oksana laughed. "Becoming an astronaut is a hell of a lot of effort to go through just to answer that question."

"It brought me here, so I would say that my time and effort were both well spent."

"Good point," Oksana admitted.

"And it would seem as though my hypothesis was correct," Jed continued.

"What hypothesis is that?" Adam inquired.

"I postulated that the space agency was looking to recruit a mathematician for one very specific mission. And it would seem as though I was right, judging by what the two of you have said, and by how rapidly I have been offered a mission to be on."

Both Adam and Oksana fell silent as they contemplated this.

"Hopefully we will get a definitive answer shortly," Jed said. The mathematician got up from the table and poured himself a cup of coffee from a pot that was sitting on a counter along the wall.

A few short minutes later, the door to the conference room opened, and the three of them rose to their feet as Alan Prater entered.

"Thank you for coming," Prater said as he shook hands with each of them. He had met with each of them before; he did not think there was any active member of the world's astronaut, cosmonaut, or taikonaut corps with whom he had not met.

He had met with both Adam and Oksana numerous times, but only had met with Jed once during the interview process of his astronaut application. The selection process had been shorter than usual in order to find a mathematician suitable for the upcoming mission to the Bastion. Many believed that mathematics was the only universal language. As such, it was felt that having an expert mathematician on the *Intrepid* would offer the best chance of establishing communication with the builders of the Bastion, or deciphering whatever message they might have left embedded in their artifact.

Of all the mathematicians that responded to the call for astronaut candidates, Jed had held the most potential, passing all of the screenings with flying colors.

It was said that the mathematician did not have much of a social life; this was even something he openly admitted to during his astronaut candidacy interviews. But he also had a very good reputation among his colleagues in the mathematical community. He was extremely dedicated to his work, and always got along well with project collaborators.

"You all know why I wanted to meet with you," Prater said as he sat down at the head of the table. "There is a specific mission that I would like you to be on. Of all currently active astronauts, cosmonauts, and taikonauts, we feel that the three of you are the most qualified for this particular mission."

"And what exactly will we be doing?" Jed asked intently.

Prater clicked a button on a remote control he was holding, and the wall monitor on the far side of the room came on. It showed a lump of gray, uneven rock, and right next to it was a deep blackness.

"This is an image obtained by an unmanned robotic mining spacecraft operated by Interplanetary Enterprises in the asteroid belt," Prater said. "Nine months ago, it discovered this object embedded within what was believed to be an otherwise ordinary asteroid. The object is perfectly smooth, is made of a material that seems to absorb all electromagnetic radiation, and is seemingly impervious to physical damage. And it is over three billion years old."

Stunned silence fell over the conference room.

"So you've discovered aliens?" Adam asked, sounding uncertain.

"We didn't," Prater replied. "IE did. And they're also the reason a manned mission to the object is going to happen. They're leasing their fusion spacecraft to NASA, and we hope to launch in just a few more months. And I want you to be part of the crew. The mission commander and spacecraft systems engineer have already been selected. The three of you will be the mission scientists, and it will be your job to learn more about this artifact and whoever built it. That is, if you agree to do this."

"What else have you learned about this artifact?" asked Jed, his eyes remaining fixed on the image displayed on the wall monitor.

"I've already told you just about everything we know," Prater said, sounding almost disappointed that he did not have more to offer. "The artifact hasn't responded to anything, although I can provide you with the raw data, if you'd like."

"I would like to see the data," said Jed.

"As would I," Oksana said, sounding excited for the first time.

"Dr. Sobolev," Prater said to the physicist, "I know that you are infuriated over the cancellation of the Korolev Observatory. But I want you to know that this artifact is what we will be studying with the Korolev's instruments. The sensors on IE's robotic miners are insufficient to study this thing in the detail that we need. There are many who believe that the alien technology may operate in realms of physics beyond our current understanding. So I am optimistic that this artifact will help us learn more about the nature of the universe than the Korolev alone could have."

Oksana nodded. "You may be right," she said. "But I would like to look over the raw data before I can definitively say whether or not I agree with that."

"Of course."

"How many know about this?" Jed asked.

"Too many for my taste," said Prater. "Don't get me wrong. We will make a public announcement in due time. But we'd like to hold off doing that until the *Intrepid* is ready to go. The more people that know about this thing, the more likely it is that something will leak, so close tabs are being kept on everyone in the know."

Adam suddenly realized the implications of what Prater had said. The intelligence agencies would likely be monitoring his every email, text message, phone call, and internet search he made now that the existence of the alien artifact had been disclosed to him. It had been well known for years that the government engaged in such Big Brother-like surveillance programs. Adam had accepted this as an inevitability resulting from society's ever-growing dependence on the internet and social media that helped integrate the world's cultures and share knowledge unlike any other era in human history. The more interconnected everything became, the easier it was for government agencies to monitor everything.

While Adam had always suspected this to be the case, hearing the NASA administrator all but confirm that this was already happening was something else entirely.

"Dr. Hernandez," Prater said, pulling Adam from his thoughts. "I know that I am asking a lot of you by requesting that you give up your chance of going to Mars. But this artifact already proves that alien life exists. And intelligent life, no less! And if there are any biological aliens at the artifact, someone with your expertise will be invaluable for this mission."

Adam swallowed hard as he thought about what the historic opportunity that he was being offered.

"How long will this mission last?" Jed asked Prater.

The NASA administrator shrugged. "We have no way of knowing for certain. But the *Intrepid* can carry enough supplies to sustain a crew for years. So this could hypothetically last longer than the duration of Mars missions. It all really depends on what you guys discover."

A look of uncertainty swept across Jed's face, the first display of emotion he had shown.

"So how about it?" Prater asked the three of them. "Do you guys want to meet some aliens?"

Chapter 13

Mark slept soundly on the plane ride to Houston. It was a welcome break from work for him, however fleeting it might have been. Although like nearly everything else he did, the entire point of this trip was work. He and Ning were traveling to Johnson Space Center to meet with a physicist, an astrobiologist, and a mathematician who had been selected as the other crewmembers for the *Intrepid*. Together, the five of them would use the facilities at JSC to train for their upcoming mission.

An unmanned shuttle car took Mark and Ning from the airport to the JSC campus. Despite many of the buildings at the space center being more than half a century old, they hardly showed signs of their age; a result of the budget increases that NASA enjoyed in these times of revitalized space exploration.

Stepping out of the cool air-conditioned car, the Texas heat and humidity felt like a sauna to Mark, and he already felt himself beginning to break out in a sweat in the time it took him to walk the brief distance from the car to the entrance of the building where they would be meeting the rest of the crew.

None of the JSC personnel accorded much notice to Mark and Ning as they made their way through the hallways. Some might have recognized Mark, but seeing commercial or government astronauts at JSC was an everyday work experience, although few, if any of them would have known what had brought Mark and Ning here today. Only those who were directly involved with the *Intrepid*'s mission knew about the Bastion.

Reaching the conference room, Mark and Ning found Adam, Jed, and Oksana already waiting for them. Both Adam and Oksana appeared friendly and welcoming, while Jed's facial expression displayed no emotion.

"So you'll be my crew," Mark said as he walked up to them and shook their hands. "It's a pleasure to meet each of you."

"Likewise," Adam said.

"As I understand it, you're turning down a chance to go to Mars for this?" Mark said to Adam.

"I am," replied the astrobiologist. "As much as I want to go to Mars, I couldn't refuse an opportunity to go to the Bastion."

Mark chuckled. "I'm in the exact same boat as you," he said. "That being said, I still intend to walk on Mars one day. And who knows: maybe we'll be doing that thanks to some fancy toys we might get from the aliens."

"I highly doubt that will happen," said Jed. "While I don't know what we will find at the Bastion, I do think it is extremely unlikely that we will establish peaceful relations with its builders."

"Why is that?" Mark asked.

"Because we have nothing of value to offer them, so there can never be a quid pro quo between us. We would be like ants offering a leaf in the hope of obtaining all of human knowledge."

"That's some interesting insight," Mark said. "So you're a spaceflight newbie?"

"You are asking me to confirm something that you already know to be true," Jed replied.

'This guy's just a bit of a smartass,' Mark thought to himself.

"The answer is yes," Jed continued, "as you already knew. Do you intend to hold that against me?"

"Not at all," Mark said with complete honesty.

Even if this mathematician was a smartass, Mark knew it was best not to say anything that might antagonize him. Doing so would serve only to sour crew relations before the mission even began. Mark understood the importance of having a mathematician on the *Intrepid* and trusted that the NASA higher-ups had made the right decision in selecting Jed for that role.

"I'm a spaceflight newbie myself," Ning said cordially. "So you're not alone in that regard."

"I am well aware of that," said Jed. "And you may all rest assured that my lack of experience with spaceflight will not in any way jeopardize my mathematical skills, or my dedication to this mission's success. And I am willing to undergo any additional training you might feel is necessary to better prepare myself for our voyage to the Bastion." His tone was somewhat apologetic.

Mark was glad that the mathematician seemed to realize the importance of having amicable crew relations. Smiling in a friendly way, Mark said, "I'm glad you brought that up, because we all have a lot of mission training ahead of us. You all need to be trained to operate the *Intrepid* in the event that I am killed or incapacitated during the mission."

"Well, hopefully that won't happen at all," Adam said.

"I hope so too. Nonetheless, you all need to be prepared for it." Mark turned his attention to Oksana. "Dr. Sobolev," he said, "as I understand it, you helped develop a lot of the sensors that we'll be using to study the Bastion. And that they were basically…appropriated, shall we say, from the project that you were working on."

"That is correct," Oksana admitted. "But I've since gotten over my initial animosity. I've been looking over the data from your company's miner, and I agree that studying the artifact may offer an even greater opportunity to expand our understanding of physics than the Korolev observatory that I was working on. I must say that I am very thankful that I have been given a chance to study the Bastion myself."

"I'm glad you're part of this. You'll be needed to help

plan our activities for when we reach the Bastion. You will be integral to determining the order in which the sensors should be deployed, where they should be positioned on the Bastion, what experiments we'll be running, that sort of thing."

"I already have a few ideas on what I'd like to do," Oksana said enthusiastically.

"Very good. I'd like to get started on that right away. We have much to do, and not much time remaining."

***

Mark sipped his beer as David lined up his cue stick up with the cue ball. He had just gotten back to Hawthorne the previous day, and had been training with Ning, Adam, Oksana, and Jed in the neutral buoyancy tank and other facilities at JSC for the past several weeks. The training hours were grueling, but Mark now felt they were as prepared as anyone possibly could be for the impending mission. Barring any major setbacks, they would board the *Intrepid* and depart Earth for the Bastion in just over a month.

Mark wanted to spend what remaining time he could with David, not knowing how long it would be until he could see him again, and David was more than eager to play pool with Mark on this rare occasion he was able to take time off work.

David took careful aim with his cue and sent the cue ball off to collide with the ten ball, which caromed into the middle right pocket of the pool table.

"Good shot," Mark said

"Thanks," David replied, and lined up for his next shot. "I really appreciate you taking the time off work to do this with me."

"It's well worth it," Mark said with complete honesty. "After all, I don't know how long it's going to be until we can do this again."

144

"You really can't tell me what you'll be doing?"

"No, I'm afraid not."

"Are you going to Mars? Last I heard, all the Mars tourists had their vacation plans canceled. But that fancy fusion ship of yours is still being built, isn't it? Are you still going to fly it to Mars?"

Mark looked at his brother intently, wanting to tell him the truth. But he could never forget that look of desperation that Miles had shown when his boss had asked him to travel to Washington to discuss the Bastion. The desperation to believe that he could still trust those closest to him.

If he told David about the Bastion, and Miles found out about it, it would destroy his boss's faith in his employees completely. Mark could easily see the entire *Intrepid* mission unraveling if there was another leak. As much as Mark loved David, he could not bring himself to risk that.

"I'm sorry David," Mark said with heartfelt regret, "but I can't confirm or deny anything that we might be doing."

"You've been able to tell me what you were doing on every other mission you've flown. Why is it different for this?"

"You'll understand when we make the public announcement, which will happen soon enough."

David nodded. "Okay, I believe you. And I'll pray especially hard for you this time. Something tells me you might need it."

"If I believed in the power of prayer, I might be tempted to say you're right about that."

***

Mark breathed calmly as the hatch to the command capsule closed, sealing him and his crew off from the terrestrial environment for what he knew would the longest trip in his life. It would be many years before any of them

145

would be able to walk freely on their home planet. This was the day; the day that the voyage to the Bastion would finally begin.

The launch vehicle they were in would carry them to the Nimbus space station in low Earth orbit, where the *Intrepid* was waiting for them. They were scheduled to give a brief press conference on Nimbus before embarking on their deep space voyage to the alien object.

Despite the historic nature of this launch, there was virtually no attention being given to it. There were still a handful of sightseers at and around the spaceport; the kind of people who never got bored with rocket launches. And they would undoubtedly be very happy to have witnessed this once they learned of the historic undertaking the crew was about to embark on.

Mark breathed carefully as the countdown progressed.

Chapter 14

MIT NanoMechanical Technology Laboratory
Cambridge, Massachusetts

Ask gazed at a computer monitor showing the most recent sample of his nanomachines. He had been in the lab for twelve hours straight. This was a typical amount of time he spent in the lab every single day since arriving at the Institute.

He had spent most of the past sixteen months traveling the world, learning much from the baselines. While the internet provided a vast wealth of data for him, he still found it useful to extract information directly from baselines' brains.

His quest for direct knowledge had cost him ten months of travel across the Earth learning as much as he could from the baselines. The method provided him with hundreds of years' worth of hands-on experience in a wide array of different technologies; skills he could not obtain simply by reading information available in books or on the internet.

He paid for all of his traveling expenses with money that he pilfered from baselines whose minds he probed. He was careful to erase the baselines' memories of their encounters with him, and took as little money as possible to avoid arousing suspicion. During his travels, Ask never once reverted to his original appearance. To do so was far too risky. As an added precaution he constantly altered his physical appearance to safeguard against the possibility of baseline authorities tracking him down.

Ask's travels had been fueled by his interest in the baselines' accumulated knowledge of physics and engineering. But what he really desired was more hard facts about Legion, and that was something for which the baselines were no help.

As he had come to suspect in Antarctica, his world travel confirmed that Legion had abandoned the baselines following their betrayal of him. There had been no sudden appearance of highly advanced technologies at any point in recorded baseline history; all of the advancements the baselines had made throughout the millennia had been the result of a more or less steady rate of scientific and technological progression.

The baselines had many myths and religions centered on deities with incredible powers, but none of them were even remotely consistent with what Ask had witnessed of Legion. The absurdities and contradictions in these mythological stories had convinced Ask that among the thousands of different deities the baselines had worshiped throughout history, none of them had been Legion. It was obvious that the baselines had developed different religions entirely by themselves to explain the mysterious nature of the world: such things as the movements of the stars and planets, the weather, the changing of seasons, the unfolding of natural disasters, and death.

Many baseline myths had the gods doing strange things to humans, sometimes imbuing select individuals with powers or abilities rivaling their own, or fathering godlike children with human women. The reasons behind these actions made very little sense to Ask, as did all of the baselines' religious beliefs. Ask was forced to concede, however, that if Legion had anything in common with the baselines' gods, it was that they often did things that seemed to be completely nonsensical.

Ask knew that Legion had directly intervened with baseline history at least once, and that had been millennia ago when they had given him his nanomachines. It was an incredible gift. In addition to enabling him to change his appearance and probe baselines' minds, the nanomachines also altered his physiology, allowing him to heal from any injury, immunized him against any disease, kept his body perpetually young, and permitted him to survive in hostile environments ranging from barren deserts to the frozen wastes of the polar ice caps. The gift effectively made Ask immortal.

Legion had instructed Ask to use this gift to guide the baselines to develop civilization. The nanomachines had given Ask a major advantage over the hunter-gatherer societies that he had been born into, and he had come to dominate them with incredible ease. And yet during all the time that he had ruled over the baselines in the past, he never truly enjoyed doing so. For Legion had also given Ask a fleeting glimpse of the extent of their power. It was awe-inspiring how mighty they were, and it had also shown Ask that the nanomachines swarming within his body were but the feeblest examples of Legion's technological prowess. This brief vision had convinced Ask that what he did on Earth utterly paled in comparison to Legion's power.

So why had Legion commanded Ask to dominate the baselines? If the objective was to civilize humanity, then why did Legion not simply share all of their great knowledge with him and the baselines alike? Why had they even given the nanomachines to him and only him? What was the point of having him lead the baselines along a path of discovery when Legion surely already had all of the solutions to the problems that a fledgling civilization faced?

All of these were questions that Legion had resolutely refused to answer, but when they had given Ask that fleeting glimpse of their true capabilities, they had also given him a goal. They had told him that if he led the baselines to travel beyond the confines of Earth, he would be bestowed with power equal to their own.

The vision they had granted him had left Ask with conflicting thoughts on the nature of Legion' intentions for him. Was there a higher purpose behind their actions, one that Ask could not even begin to fathom? Or were their acts the result of minds driven mad by the sheer vastness of their own power? Ask had contemplated the question since the moment he learned of Legion's existence. His sine qua non was to know the truth, to know all that Legion knew, and have access to the same godlike power that they wielded. He despised being their pawn, and desperately wanted to be free from the control they exerted over him.

Still, Ask knew he had no choice but to do Legion's bidding. There was no point in attempting to resist them. They could crush him like the measliest of insects any time they wanted to simply by turning his nanomachines against him.

The irony had not been lost on Ask; he knew that the only way he could escape from the power and influence of Legion was if they permitted it. And so Ask had guided the baselines in establishing the foundations of civilization, all in the hope that Legion intended to keep their word about bestowing him with their knowledge and power.

And then the cataclysm struck, destroying all of his efforts. Legion had to have known the cataclysm was coming, and yet had done nothing to warn Ask. It was possible they had even caused it; Ask had considered this terrifyingly possible because of Legion's action in the aftermath of the cataclysm. Shortly after disaster struck, Legion had betrayed Ask, entombing him in the Antarctic ice. This convinced Ask that Legion did not possess great wisdom derived from eons of intellectual advancement. Rather, they had been driven completely mad, and everything that they did was just a symptom of their madness.

Despite the destructiveness of the cataclysm, the baselines managed to survive, and their civilization had emerged like a phoenix from the ashes of the primitive hunter-gather societies that Ask had attempted to unify. Yet, even with all the advances the baselines had made over the past seventy millennia, Ask knew that their scientific progress would have proceeded far faster had he retained control over them throughout all that time. The unfolding of baseline history convinced Ask of the baselines' desperate need for an immortal leader like him throughout their bloody, chaotic history.

Over the past seventy millennia, there had been many destructive wars that vanquished prosperous, technically advanced societies. There had also been many times when civilization plunged into long periods of dark barbarism that undid much social and technological advancement, slowing or halting the rate of progress for years, decades, or centuries. All of that senseless destruction and barbarism would have been avoided if Legion had allowed Ask to retain the hegemony he had established over the baselines.

Why had Legion betrayed Ask? Why had they abandoned the baselines? Did they still exist, or had their madness escalated to the point that they had destroyed even themselves? There were so many questions and so few answers.

If Legion truly was gone, Ask would still do everything he could to learn as much as possible. After traveling across the world for ten months, Ask felt that he had gathered all the information of benefit to him that the baselines had to offer. He had focused primarily on their knowledge of physics and nanotechnology. That still left a vast repository of knowledge on a wide variety of subjects that Ask had not yet acquired. While subjects such as civil engineering, climatology, nuclear engineering, and spacecraft design intensely interested him, he decided to concentrate his efforts on learning as much as he could about the only piece of Legion' technology available to him: the nanomachines dwelling within his body.

Despite his ability to control them, Ask actually knew very little about them. He had no idea what powered them, what they were made of, how they worked, or even what they looked like. Legion had never directly shown them to him, and only described what they were in vague terms. Now the baselines had technologies that would hopefully allow him to learn more about the nanomachines than he had ever known. Even if the tiny machines within his body really were incredibly primitive compared to Legion' true technological capability, Ask still hoped to he would be able to learn more about Legion by unlocking the secrets of the nanomachines. If nothing else, it would provide him with valuable technological data that the baselines lacked.

Ask attempted to interface his nanomachines with the baselines' computers, but consistently failed to establish a connection. It seemed as though they could only form a connection with human brains. As with the limited range of control, Ask believed that this was due to an artificial limitation that Legion had integrated in their structure.

When Ask learned about computer engineering and nanotechnology from the baselines, his desire to understand Legion's nanotechnology had only been intensified. The resources and capabilities of the MIT nanotechnology lab seemed to offer the best opportunity for him to accomplish further his studies. Ask had killed and assumed the identity of the laboratory's director, Baldev Venkatesh, after he arrived at MIT. By masquerading as Venkatesh, Ask was able to devote all of his time and energy to researching his nanomachines.

Unfortunately, Venkatesh also had a wife and three children, and they would function only as a distraction for Ask. He considered killing them, but ultimately decided against it. The murder of Venkatesh's family would likely spark a criminal investigation that could compromise Ask. Although it would be simple enough to dispose of their bodies the same way he had done so to every baseline whom he had impersonated, it would be difficult to explain the sudden disappearance of Venkatesh's family members. Again, there was the probability of a long criminal investigation that would attract attention he could ill afford.

Ask also considered the possibility of causing their demise, one by one, in different public settings. He could use his nanomachines to rob Venkatash's children of muscle control while doing some strenuous physical activity, causing them to suffer possibly fatal injuries. Perhaps he could have his nanomachines induce a fatal heart attack in Venkatesh's wife while she was driving a car with their children inside, ensuring that they all died.

Still, this would give rise to questions that would attract unwanted attention. Ask ultimately decided that dispatching Venkatesh's family was too risky, and that the safest and most logical course of action was simply to bury himself in his work. With any luck, Venkateh's wife would eventually file for divorce and take the children with her.

It would have been much easier for Ask to conduct his research if he revealed the nanomachines to his colleagues at the Institute. Explaining their existence, however, would be difficult if not impossible, for even though the baselines' technology was advancing rapidly, the likelihood that they could create anything remotely comparable to Legion's technology was nil. Were he to reveal the nanomachines to the Institute, far too many questions would be raised about their origin. He could imagine whole teams being devoted to their study, not to mention the potential for government intervention. It was more of the attention that he needed to avoid. And so he had to conduct all of his research on his own, hoping he would have a breakthrough.

Even now, after all the time he had spent at MIT, Ask had learned very little about the machines that dwelt within him. This was due to another factor of which Ask had been unaware until he had begun his research efforts. Whenever Ask examined the nanomachines with laboratory equipment, they would rapidly disintegrate into their constituent molecules. It was as if they had been programmed to destroy themselves if someone or something tried to examine them closely. He surmised that it was caused by yet another limitation imposed by Legion....something internally programmed in the nanomachines.

But how could they possibly know if they were being examined by Ask, or someone else? Ask hypothesized that the nanomachines within his brain must be constantly monitoring his thoughts and perceptions, and then relaying this data to all the other nanomachines throughout his body. So whenever Ask was able to actually observe a sample, they were alerted to this, and then proceeded to destroy themselves. Ask found that this same act of self-destruction happened to any nanomachines that passed beyond his communication range.

Despite these obstacles, Ask had been able to acquire precious bits of data. He managed to obtain a few brief images of the machines on the scanning electron microscope before they disintegrated. He found that they had many different shapes; some resembled simple geometric shapes such as pyramids, spheres, and cubes, whereas others had completely amorphous and irregular configurations. They also ranged in size from being larger than bacteria to smaller than viruses.

By examining the remains of destroyed nanomachines, Ask found that they were composed of many of the same materials found in a healthy baseline's body, such as iron, carbon, magnesium, calcium, molybdenum, copper, and zinc. It was almost as if they were an extension of Ask's physiology. He attributed the abundance of ferrous metals to be the reason behind his ability to sense electromagnetic

154

fields.

Despite his lack of any major breakthrough, Ask remained undeterred. He spent nearly every waking moment in the laboratory, and vowed that he would find a way to overcome the constraints Legion had imposed.

As Ask continued his analysis, he heard a loud commotion outside of the lab. The interruption annoyed him and he left the lab to investigate. As a senior faculty member, he was required to keep himself well-informed of upcoming events that he would be required to attend, but none were scheduled for today.

Many of the people in the building were surprised to see Venkatesh/Ask emerge from his lab. He kept his encounters with other faculty members, students, and staff to an absolute minimum, never saying anything more than was required in order to curtail the length of conversations he engaged in.

Today, however, the crowd was unnervingly quiet as they were transfixed by the Presidential Address being broadcast on screens on the lobby walls.

Chapter 15

President Ortega sat at his desk in the Oval Office as he began his broadcast to the nation and the world. He maintained the calm demeanor that always projected when he made public announcements, despite the gravity and historical significance of what he was about to say.

"My fellow Americans," he said into the camera, "it is my duty and honor to reveal to you what is undoubtedly the single greatest discovery in all of human history. For centuries, philosophers and scientists all across the world have pondered mankind's place in the cosmos. One of the most profound questions ever raised across the centuries is if we are alone in the universe, or if we share it with other intelligent beings. And now that question has finally been answered.

"About sixteen months ago, a robotic miner operated by the aerospace corporation Interplanetary Enterprises rendezvoused with an asteroid. The objective of this mission was no different than any other asteroid mission that IE has undertaken; they sought to extract precious metals and ship them back to Earth, just as they have done many times in the past. But this time, they found something more incredible than anything they could have imagined. We will now show you what was discovered."

Everyone watching the President's announcement saw their screens split in half vertically, with the President on the right side, and an image of an asteroid on the left. It showed a black sphere, nearly invisible against the backdrop of space. The distinguishing feature was the complete lack of stars. Almost like a hole in the universe.

Ortega continued, "This is a live feed being provided by one of IE's unmanned miners positioned near the unknown mass that was discovered beneath the asteroid's surface. In the sixteen months since its discovery, all of the asteroid rock surrounding this object has been removed. We call the object the Bastion. It is a sphere about four miles in diameter, and has been determined to be at least three billion years old. It is made of a material with bewildering characteristics; a material that cannot be the product of any known natural phenomenon, nor one that any of our scientists or engineers are capable of creating. Therefore, the only possible explanation is that the Bastion is an artifact that was built by an ancient and highly advanced extraterrestrial civilization.

"I cannot stress enough how historic this discovery is, for it offers definitive proof that we are not alone in the universe. I must also mention that, since whatever society built this artifact predates ours by at least several billion years, we cannot even begin to imagine what technology they may possess if they still exist, but it must be extraordinary.

"I understand that this may cause many of you concern, even fear; to know that we share the cosmos with an alien civilization that is likely immensely superior to our own. But I implore you to not to let fear overwhelm you. This is not something we should fear at all, but something that we should feel grateful for discovering. Some of humanity's greatest intellects have spent their entire lives contemplating the question of whether or not extraterrestrial intelligence exists, and to be alive when that question is answered is something to cherish. The knowledge that intelligent extraterrestrials exist should be seen as a gift and a privilege. For this knowledge is the single greatest truth that humankind has ever uncovered about the cosmos and our place within it.

"All of the information that has been gathered about the Bastion thus far will be made available to the public immediately. Unfortunately, it is incredibly sparse, leaving

157

us with a great many questions that have yet to be answered. We do not know who built the artifact, what purpose it may serve, from where it originated, or if its builders even still exist. But we have every intention of finding the answers to these questions, and we have taken the necessary steps to do so.

"As you may know, Interplanetary Enterprises, the same company that discovered this artifact, has spent the past several years constructing the *Intrepid,* the first spacecraft propelled by nuclear fusion, using their own internal funding. Originally intended to ferry people and cargo to Mars, IE canceled those plans sixteen months ago, shortly after the Bastion was discovered, and redirected the *Intrepid's* maiden voyage to the alien artifact. She will carry a crew consisting of some of the brightest and most capable scientists and engineers serving in the world's space programs. The *Intrepid* also carries aboard the most advanced scientific equipment available. This will allow the crew to study the alien artifact more thoroughly. The crew of the *Intrepid* will work tirelessly to learn more about the Bastion, and, God willing, may establish contact with its creators. If peaceful relations can be established with the beings who built this artifact, the benefit to humanity would be incalculable.

"The *Intrepid* will depart from low Earth orbit and begin its voyage in just under twelve hours. I regret that it is only upon the very eve of this historic mission that this information is being shared with you, but this was done to safeguard the protection of the *Intrepid's* crew and to maximize the probability of the mission's success. I hope that you will all understand why it had to be this way. But know that from this point forward, everything shall be made public knowledge. This will include all of the data that obtained about the alien artifact thus far, as well as the exact details and specifications of the *Intrepid's* mission and her crew. Anything and everything that is discovered about the Bastion will be made public knowledge immediately. At the conclusion of my announcement, Miles Gilster, the president and CEO of Interplanetary Enterprises, will introduce the crew of the *Intrepid* to the world.

"Let us now stand together as a united planet as we venture further into the heavens than ever before to learn more of these beings who traveled to our Solar System from across the stars eons ago. And, God willing, we shall forge a mutually beneficial relationship between our cultures. Thank you and God bless America and the world."

Chapter 16

President Ortega had informed Miles of the time he would his announcement and what information he would disclose. Still, he watched Ortega's speech intently. It was Miles' habit to carefully watch speeches that, directly or indirectly, could affect aerospace companies like IE, especially those made by powerful politicians. Miles also knew that he had to begin his own broadcast as soon as the President's speech concluded. Knowing any changes to the draft he'd been given would allow him to capitalize on the transition without losing viewership once Ortega was finished.

The computer monitor that Miles used to watch the presidential address had also provided him with the number of views that Ortega was receiving on the television and internet broadcasts. The audience had started small enough at several million, but it skyrocketed once details of the speech began to spread through social media. It swelled to over one hundred million viewers by the time Ortega wrapped up.

Now all of those people were watching Miles. This would be the largest audience he had ever addressed, but he was not the least bit intimidated by that. Miles felt equally at ease speaking in any setting. His delivery to millions of viewers around the world was no different than when he addressed a small group of close colleagues.

The first image the worldwide audience saw was Miles standing next to a window filled with the blackness of space contrasted with the blue curvature of the Earth in the lower right corner. Effective imagery was everything to the media, and Miles wanted everyone watching to know where he was.

Unlike most people in his position, he was not content

with using a spokesman or hosting such an important press conference in the comfort of his corporate headquarters. Miles preferred being front and center when IE launched a new spacecraft. He did this not only to maintain the media spotlight, but because of the emotional and financial investment he had in the projects. His heart sang whenever a new IE rocket soared into the skies, and wept whenever one was lost due to a technical failure.

His role would be larger now than the one he usually played for IE's major missions. Introducing the *Intrepid*'s crew to the world was simply too important an occasion to entrust to anyone else. It warranted the ride on a rocket to Nimbus, something that would have terrified many corporate officers of his stature. Having visited the space station many times before, he also knew the view from its promenade deck would provide a stunning backdrop worthy of the occasion. But perhaps of most importance, he had come to Nimbus because he wanted to be with the crew until the very moment they closed the *Intrepid*'s hatch and began their long journey.

Miles smiled brightly into the camera as President Ortega concluded his address.

"Good evening," he said cheerfully once the camera began to broadcast his image across the world. "I'm Miles Gilster, president and CEO of Interplanetary Enterprises. I'm speaking to you from onboard the IE space station Nimbus, where the *Intrepid* has been constructed, and where her crew is making final preparations for their departure. I would like to thank President Ortega for the support he has shown for the continued investigation of the alien artifact. He has helped provide invaluable resources to accelerate the *Intrepid*'s completion, and helped muster additional aid for this effort from the international community. Without the combined efforts of President Ortega and other world leaders, we would not be where we

161

are today.

"I also want the entire world to know how thankful I am for all of my employees who made this incredible discovery. Now that we have gone public, each and every one of them will be receiving their just acknowledgement from me once I have returned to Earth. You can show your support for this as well. I urge you all to go to the IE website and read about the people who really set this ball in motion. We have listed everyone responsible for this, along with interviews conducted with each of them.

"The live feed of the artifact that President Ortega showed during his address is now available on my company's website, so that anyone who wants to will be able to watch the Bastion. As President Ortega said, there has been no detectable activity from the Bastion since we discovered it. But for all we know, that could change at any moment's notice. Maybe it has been monitoring our transmissions and has waited until we've informed the entire world about it before it does whatever it's going to do. Or maybe it's been waiting until the sun has reached a certain position in its revolution around the center of the galaxy. We have no way of knowing if or when something might happen, so it will be valuable to have extra sets of eyes available to continuously monitor the artifact.

"And as President Ortega said only a few short minutes ago, we are now about to take the next step to investigate the Bastion and see what we might learn about the aliens who built it. And I am thrilled beyond all measure that IE is helping to make this happen. However bold my original plans were for sending the *Intrepid* to Mars, investigating this alien artifact is a far more important matter. I am incredibly honored that IE discovered the Bastion and that an IE spacecraft will be used for this historic mission to the alien artifact.

"Once the *Intrepid* reaches the Bastion, it will act as a

long-term research station. We have no idea how long it may take to learn as much as we can about the artifact and its builders, but this state of the art vessel will be able to remain on station for years, and the crew is well prepared for an extended stay."

The camera panned away from Miles and came to rest on three men and two women dressed in flight suits standing at the other end of the module. "This is the crew of the *Intrepid*," Mile said as he stepped back into the camera's line of sight, careful not to obstruct its view of any of the crewmembers. "President Ortega was not exaggerating when he said that this crew represents the very best in all of the world's astronaut corps. They are arguably the most qualified people in the world to study the Bastion. And now I would now like to introduce you to each of these brave men and women who will examine the artifact, and possibly serve as humanity's first ambassadors to an extraterrestrial civilization."

Miles stepped toward the nearest man, who was about the same height as him and had a dark complexion.

"This is Jedediah Storey," said Miles into the camera. He then turned his full attention to Jed. "You're widely regarded as one of the world's most brilliant mathematicians."

"I cannot bring myself to agree or dispute that," said Jed, locking his attention on Miles and not giving the camera so much as a glance. "I leave such judgements to my peers on the matter."

"That's a very admirable quality to have," said Miles.

"Thank you."

"Can you tell the world what you plan on doing at the Bastion, and what you hope to learn about it and the beings who built it?"

"Mathematics is the only real universal language," said Jed. "It therefore represents the only hope we have of

163

communicating with the extraterrestrials. This of course assumes that there's some way to communicate with or through the artifact, whether that is with an artificial intelligence or the builders themselves. I might note that we are making a huge assumption the artifact is even capable of communicating with us. While I intend to try as hard as I can to make new discoveries, I will not be the least bit surprised if my efforts prove to be entirely in vain."

Miles smiled and said, "Well, at least you're honest."

"I'm always honest about everything. I consider it one of my greatest strengths."

"I think most people on Earth can appreciate that honesty," said Miles. "It's especially important now that there will be no more secrecy on this mission."

"Good, because it is the sharing of one's discoveries with the rest of mankind that really give meaning to what I do. That's why it has been somewhat of a burden for me to have kept this mission and my selection for it secret for these past sixteen months. I would not be here were we required to maintain that secrecy indefinitely."

"Thank you for your candor, Jed and the best of luck on your mission."

Miles walked from Jed to the slightly taller man standing next to him. "I'd now like to introduce you to Adam Hernandez. Adam is the mission's astrobiologist."

"Thank you," Adam smiled. "It's an incredible honor to be here and to serve as a member of this crew. I know the rest of my crewmates share the feeling. It is an honor and privilege and I'll never be able to express how thankful I am for the opportunity."

"It is we who should be thanking you," Miles returned. "Can you tell those who are watching what you'll be doing onboard the *Intrepid*?"

"I think my role on this mission is straightforward enough. If we find that the artifact is harboring any biological lifeforms, I'm tasked with studying and perhaps classifying them. We have some excellent equipment onboard the *Intrepid* that I will be using to perform biological tests and analyses. Of course, a lot of the analyses that I imagine myself doing are based on the assumption that the life forms will have cells and DNA, or something analogous to that."

"Is there a reason why you think that they won't have cells or DNA?"

"That's a difficult question. We are constrained by that with which we are familiar. Even with the astonishing diversity of life on Earth, and all the dramatic differences exhibited by various species, all of them evolved on the same planet, and we have a common ancestor that lived eons ago.

"In stark contrast to this, whoever built the Bastion will have had a completely separate evolutionary history, and it's entirely possible those that built the Bastion will be quite different than anything that evolved on Earth. From our study of extremophiles we have an inkling of how environment helps shape life, and we haven't a clue what kind of environment produced the builders of the Bastion. The concept of them being humanoid may be entirely erroneous."

"I always hated humanoid aliens being so prevalent in science fiction," said Miles. "I wish that the people in Hollywood had a better grasp of even basic biology."

"I actually have been a biological consultant on a few movies and TV shows," Adam nodded in agreement, "but that doesn't mean the people who produce them actually listen to what I tell them."

"I've dealt with Hollywood a bit myself," Miles said, nodding, "I know where you're coming from. We look forward to your reports from the Bastion."

The IE president turned to move on, trying to keep to

the schedule, but Adam wasn't quite done.

"You know," Adam continued before Miles could escape, "many of my scientific colleagues think these aliens might not be biological at all. They believe they may have developed the technology to transfer their consciousness to computer systems and free themselves from the limitations of biology. Regardless of how dramatically different their evolution and biology may be compared to ours, it's still safe to say that there's an upper limit to the amount of information that can be stored in their brains. But if they could transfer their consciousness into computer systems, then they could build computation nodes far larger than anything that could be supported by any kind of biological brain. It's entirely possible they've built Matrioshka brains, making it possible for them to achieve levels of consciousness orders of magnitude beyond our own."

"I've often thought about that myself," said Miles. "If they really have created Matrioshka brains and higher levels of consciousness, one wonders what would dominate their thoughts, and what projects would they pursue? I'd be lying if I said thinking about that hasn't kept me up at night sometimes."

"Those are valid questions and concerns," Adam agreed. "Hopefully we'll be able to answer those questions when we get to the Bastion."

"I hope for that as well. But if there is no biological evidence on the Bastion, aren't you worried that you won't have much to do?"

"Not in the least bit. If it turns out that the Bastion really is an artificially intelligent machine, then it likely will have information about its creators, who were surely biological in origin. Some have speculated that the artifact could be a time capsule. If that's true, it may contain a digital database with the genomes of its creators, and possibly even of their entire planet's biosphere. That's what I'm really hoping for. But even if that's not the case, there's still so much we could learn from this, and I don't think it's possible that I or any of the rest of the crew could possibly be disappointed with what we do learn."

"On that, we can agree," Miles nodded. "Again, thank you for being an integral part of the crew."

Miles smiled before taking a step to stand next to the Russian woman to Adam's left. "This is Oksana Sobolev," he said into the camera. "She is the brilliant physicist on this mission."

"Hello everyone," Oksana said into the camera with a wide smile, and turning to Miles added, "and thank you for your kind words."

"Can you tell everyone what your role will be?"

"Simply put, I'll be researching the physical aspects of the Bastion to determine what it's made of and how it works. For all we know, the technology the object operates on principles of physics that we're just on the cusp of understanding ourselves."

"I'm sure you'll be up to the challenge," said Miles. "As I understand it, you've done a lot of groundbreaking work designing sophisticated sensors to test string theory and the standard cosmological model hypotheses on dark matter and dark energy."

"That is correct," said Oksana. "Perhaps our research on the Bastion can resolve some of the great questions about our universe. If, as some posit, the artifact is a repository of knowledge, we may be able to unlock the secrets of dark matter and dark energy, or if they even exist. The evolution of our computer models has resulted in conflicting evidence. The problem is, they are all based on theory since there is no direct, only indirect evidence from which we infer their presence. The fact is, we could be completely off base."

"I'm sorry, you have lost me. I thought dark matter and dark energy were established fact."."

She smiled. "Not even close, despite what the popular science media would have you believe. But then that is the whole basis of theoretical physics, isn't it? To look at the universe, formulate hypotheses, and then test them.

"It is physics and its sister sciences that have shattered the myths that were once used to explain our existence and dispel our once held geocentric theories. Astrophysics helped us discover that there are many Earth-like exoplanets in the galaxies.

"Now we have definitive proof that life emerged elsewhere in the universe, and not only did extraterrestrial life emerge; it gave rise to intelligence far greater than our own. That is very humbling when we contemplate our place in the universe. It shows that we're not special all, and that there exist aliens who surpass us in every way technologically. As President Ortega said in his speech just a few short minutes ago, this is not something that we should fear, but something that we should embrace, for it may lead us to even greater discoveries."

"That's a wonderful mindset to have," Miles said. "It certainly is humbling, not to mention sobering to know that something…someone greater than ourselves exists."

"I've always found theoretical physics to be very humbling. Newton said that if he had seen far, it is only because he has stood on the shoulders of giants. And that's what it's been like for me. All of the contributions that I've made to the field of physics research have been made possible because of the legacy of all the great men and women who came before me, and through the collaboration of contemporary physicists. And I can never say that I deserve to be here anymore than some of the brilliant people with whom I've collaborated with throughout my career. Now the question is, if the Bastion offers us a

168

method to communicate with the alien race that built it, will they be willing to share their knowledge, and more importantly, do we have the capacity to understand it?

"Acknowledging the brilliance of someone else is absolutely vital to expand one's own knowledge base. And I'm sure that these aliens would have to have a similar collaborative effort as their society advanced and obtained the vast knowledge that I'm sure they possess. As hard as we've worked to understand the cosmos, I have no doubt that the builders of the artifact will have a greater understanding of physics and the universe. Will they be willing to share their knowledge with us? I don't know. But I hold out hope that will happen. I like to think that same hope is serving as one of the primary driving forces behind this mission. And it is my hope that we will learn things of great value from them, if they're willing to share their knowledge with us."

"I certainly hope so," Miles replied soberly. "Thank you for sharing your vision, and Godspeed on this journey."

He then stepped over to the woman standing next to Oksana, beaming with pride as the camera remained focused on him. "Now it is my very great pleasure to introduce Ning Wu," he said to the worldwide audience. "What sets her apart from the rest of the crew members I've spoken with thus far is that I have known her for many years. Ning is our chief propulsion engineer in IE's breakthrough propulsion division. And I'm not exaggerating at all when I say that she is one of the most brilliant individuals I've ever had the pleasure of knowing. She basically invented the fusion engine that powers the *Intrepid*. Without her, the *Intrepid* would never have been built, and this mission wouldn't be happening."

"Thank you for saying that," said Ning. "But I should be the one thanking you for making this happen. Without your bold vision for space exploration and willingness to invest so much of your own money in my research, the *Intrepid*'s fusion engine would only exist in the pages of my dissertation."

Miles smiled. "Please, I'm just a businessman," he said. "Brilliant minds like yours are what have always made the world work. People like you made IE what it is today, and have provided us with the means by which we may make contact with beings from across the stars. I cannot thank you enough for everything that you've done."

"Thank you again for your kind words," said Ning. "But I think it's also worth mentioning that unlike the other crewmembers you've spoken to so far, I won't be directing any of the research once we reach the artifact. My job is to make sure the fusion engine and the rest of the ship operate nominally and to fix any unexpected problems that might come up during the mission. Once we arrive at the artifact, I'll be doing whatever I can to assist Jed, Oksana, and Adam in their research efforts."

"Don't undersell yourself," said Miles. "You know more about the fusion drive than anyone else alive. It simply wouldn't be right to have anyone else here in your place."

"Thank you again," said Ning. "I've worked my entire career developing a propulsion system that will allow us to explore the solar system like never before. And the first time this engine will be used in space, it will carry us on an expedition to uncover the legacy of beings that came from across the stars. I can think of no better way to break it in."

"That's precisely the reason you're part of the crew," Miles said. "But I'm afraid that I feel compelled to bring up something regarding the aliens. Are you at all worried that they might have forms of propulsion more advanced than what we've got?"

"If they don't have anything better, then that could

mean that they're either incredibly slow at developing new propulsion technologies, or their civilization collapsed before they had an opportunity to develop something better.

"As proud as I am of the *Intrepid*'s fusion drive, I'd be very disappointed if these aliens don't have something far, far better. And like Dr. Sobolev, I hope that they're willing to share some of their knowledge and technology with us."

"Indeed," said Miles. "Thank you again, and we're all trusting you will keep the *Intrepid* purring. Safe voyage, Ning."

"Thank you."

Miles at last stopped beside Mark. "And finally, we come to Mark de Rijk, the commander of the *Intrepid*," he said proudly. "Like Dr. Wu, Commander de Rijk is another IE employee that I was fortunate enough to hire. He has never once disappointed me in all his years of working for me.

"There can be no doubt that Commander de Rijk has proven himself to be the most capable and reliable spacecraft pilot IE has ever employed, and, in my opinion, one of the greatest pilot to ever fly in space."

"You flatter me too much," Mark said, smiling into the camera.

"I only speak the truth," said Miles. "Any neutral observer who examines your flight record for themselves will see that I am in no way exaggerating. I encourage everyone viewing this to do just that and remind the viewers that biographies of each of the crew are available on IE's website." Looking back at Mark, he asked, "Commander, how do you feel about leading this mission?"

"Words can never do justice to this great privilege that I have been given," said Mark. "There truly has been no other opportunity in my life that remotely compares to it. Commanding the most advanced spacecraft ever built by humans and using it to examine the first extraterrestrial

171

artifact humanity has discovered, perhaps even serve as an ambassador to that alien civilization, is an unparalleled honor. Like the rest of the crew, I would be remiss if I failed to mention the hundreds of men and women who have worked tirelessly to make this possible. I only wish that there was enough room on the *Intrepid* for everyone who deserves to be onboard."

"And I want the world to know how fortunate we are to have you as the commander," Miles said sincerely, shaking Mark's hand warmly. "There is no one I would rather have commanding this mission."

"Thank you. That means a great deal to me."

Miles smiled at Mark again, then turned his full attention back to the camera and the nearly half billion people that were now watching.

"I regret that we must now bring this broadcast to an end," Miles said to the world. "The *Intrepid* will be departing Earth orbit in just under twelve hours. The crew will need that time to make final preparations for their departure. But there are many cameras onboard the *Intrepid* that will provide constant coverage of the mission's progress. The fusion drive will make it possible for the *Intrepid* to reach the Bastion in less than three months. During that time, the crew will transmit live updates and give you a virtual tour of this incredible ship.

"Let me again thank President Ortega and everyone else who have done everything in their power to support the *Intrepid*'s endeavor. I also want to thank all of you who are watching this broadcast. I share President Ortega's regret that it is only on the very eve of this mission's initiation that we are sharing this with you. This is the greatest venture we as a species have ever undertaken, and we must stand united as a planet if we hope to gain as much from this as possible. Thank you again and please join me in wishing the *Intrepid* and her crew a safe voyage."

Chapter 17

Ask's eyes went wide as he watched the broadcast from the White House and the Nimbus space station. Was it possible? Could the baselines have truly found the Tabernacle? If so, then this represented both a boon and a curse for him. Seeing what the baselines had found in the depths of the asteroid belt reignited a conflict within him, one that had lain dormant for most of his existence...whether he should do Legion's bidding or attempt to rebel against them.

This internal debate had been ignited when Legion first made their presence known to Ask and ended at the very moment they showed him a fleeting glimpse of the extent of their power. This brief vision had convinced Ask that he could no more hope to defy Legion than an ant could stand against the fury of a hurricane.

But Legion had also told him that if he were to reach an artifact they called the Tabernacle, he would gain all the knowledge and power that they possessed. The Tabernacle's location was another valuable piece of information that Legion had refused to share with him. All they had said was that it was beyond the confines of Earth, and that he must find and reach it entirely on his own. Seeing no other option available to him, Ask resigned himself to the task that Legion had laid out before him: guiding the baselines on the path to civilization, hoping that they would eventually develop the capability to reach the coveted Tabernacle.

After Legion had betrayed him, Ask had given up all hope that he would ever find the Tabernacle, assuming it had even existed in the first place. Since his awakening, Ask became all the more convinced that even if the Tabernacle had existed, Legion had either destroyed it or taken it with them when they abandoned the baselines. They could have left Earth immediately after they had betrayed him, or any time after that over the past seventy millennia.

This artifact the baselines had found, however, was forcing Ask to reconsider the most pressing issue he had faced in life: the dichotomy between slavery and freedom. What if this artifact truly was the Tabernacle? Should he attempt to reach it? He also had to consider what it might mean if he were to make such an attempt. For if he did endeavor to reach the Tabernacle, he would be once again conceding that he was completely powerless to resist the whims of Legion. Was there really any way for Ask to defy Legion and still attain the knowledge and power that they possessed?

He had conducted his research on his nanomachines in the hope that he could learn more of the technological secrets that Legion had refused to yield to him. But he would not allow himself to be blinded by hubris, and had to consider the possibility that these efforts were ultimately in vain. After learning as much as he could about what the baselines knew of nanotechnology, he had entertained the possibility that continuing his research would ultimately prove to be a Sisyphean endeavor.

As his research efforts were met with consistent failure, Ask now considering it to be a very real possibility that if Legion did not want him to learn anything substantial about the nanomachines, then he had no hope of circumventing the constraints that Legion had imposed. Under that assumption, it would be completely futile for him to continue his research. On the other hand, if he were to give up, he would be conceding that there was nothing he could do that Legion did not will.

But how could he know if this artifact was the Tabernacle? What if it had not even been built by Legion?

175

In the past, Ask had actually witnessed Legion performing numerous feats that were even beyond the current baselines' understanding of physics. This Bastion, as the baselines called it, could very well have been built by Legion.

The baselines had said that this Bastion was at least half as old as the Solar System, and could very well be much older. While doing the bidding of Legion millennia ago, Ask had never learned how old the universe was; that was yet another fundamental truth that Legion had chosen not to reveal to him. But Legion had claimed to be older than the sun, which seemed to be corroborated by the age of the artifact, if Legion had in fact built it.

If this artifact truly was the Tabernacle, then Legion must have been present in the Solar System for nearly its entire history. If that were the case, then why had they acted so recently in that multi-billion year time frame? They had endowed Ask with his nanomachines a mere seventy millennia ago. However, Legion had not indicated that their contact with Ask was the only time they intervened with the development of life on Earth, which left open the possibility that they had been in the Solar System much longer.

Some among the baselines already were speculating that the builders of the Bastion had been responsible for some, perhaps all, of the mass extinctions in Earth's history. That certainly seemed possible; Ask had practically witnessed one firsthand.

Others speculated that the aliens had founded many religions by assuming the roles of the gods spawning the myriad of the world's mythologies. But Ask remained reasonably certain that this was not the case. Many skeptical baselines had arrived at a similar conclusion.

So was it possible that Legion had not built this Bastion? If they were not the builders, then who was? Ask did not know if there were other extraterrestrial civilizations throughout the universe. Like so much valuable information Legion surely possessed, the answer to this question had been denied to Ask.

Perhaps other intelligent beings did exist all throughout the cosmos, and Legion intervened in the early history of their civilizations in much the same way they had with humanity. Perhaps it was Legion's policy to endow individuals of nascent civilizations with powerful nanotechnology, and then betray them for no apparent reason, as they had done to Ask. Or perhaps they betrayed some of the leaders they created, and allowed others to guide their respective civilizations to prosperity. Ask would not have been the least bit surprised if there existed no consistent pattern to Legion's actions.

Ask knew that all of these thoughts were just hypotheses that he constructed out of the very limited amount of information he had about Legion, which forced him to contemplate the most pressing matter at hand: should he attempt to reach the artifact? He had already conceded to himself that continued research of the nanomachines was likely to be futile, so why should he expect to have any more success with uncovering the secrets of the artifact? But, because Legion had explicitly stated that the Tabernacle was the key to their knowledge and power, it seemed to represent the only hope Ask had of obtaining the secrets of the universe that he so desperately longed for.

Doubts still plagued Ask. If the object was the Tabernacle, what if it did not bestow on him what he had been promised? What if the Tabernacle was just part of another inexplicable game of Legion, like their betrayal of him? What if the artifact was not the Tabernacle? Would it still be worth the risk of attempting to reach it?

Even if Ask decided he should travel to the Bastion,

there was a major obstacle that could prevent him from even making the attempt: the *Intrepid* would depart low Earth orbit and begin its voyage to the Bastion in just a few hours. No manned rocket was scheduled to launch from any spaceport to rendezvous with Nimbus Station during that time. The fear that religious fanatics, terrorist organizations, or psychotic individuals would attempt to hijack a rocket to disrupt the *Intrepid*'s mission was too great to allow the possibility for such a nightmare scenario to occur.

Ask was therefore forced to concede there was no possible way that he could get aboard the *Intrepid* before it left Earth orbit. An anger of an intensity he had not felt since Legion's betrayal built within him. It was obvious that President Ortega had waited until now to announce the *Intrepid*'s mission in order to reduce any risk of sabotage or terrorist attack directed toward the crew and spacecraft. Despite the advances in surveillance and security, violent acts motivated by ignorance stemming from religious or ideological beliefs still occurred.

Ask cursed himself for having failed to infiltrate national space agencies or private aerospace companies. He had been very interested in space travel and spacecraft engineering, but eschewed it as not being of immediate benefit to him. Now he was deeply regretting his decision.

Ask could have also probed the minds of senior politicians, but he held such figures in low esteem. Had he penetrated the halls of power of the world's most powerful nations, he might have learned of the artifact early on and would have had more than ample time to assume the identity of one of the crewmembers of the *Intrepid* before the now impending launch. That he allowed himself that level of arrogance added to his fury.

Ask, however, was a rational being, and logic quelled the flames of rage as quickly as they had built. Nothing worthwhile could come of rage, and he could not allow his anger to overwhelm him. In moments, his stoic mindset returned.

Should he then resign himself to watching the baselines uncover the secrets of the artifact? What if Legion decided to give their power to these baselines? If that were the case, then nothing he did could ever change that. But what if Legion only intended for those such as himself to be bestowed with their power? In that scenario, the baselines' expedition would accomplish nothing. But if the Bastion was not the Tabernacle, or if it was and Legion refused to give Ask its power, then any journey he attempted would be just as fruitless.

If Ask did nothing, he knew that he would be haunted by his inaction for as long as he drew breath. He would constantly think of the artifact, wondering if it was meant to be his. Even if he tried not to think of it, it would eat away at his mind like a cancer, until he was driven mad.

He had to reach the Tabernacle. It was as simple as that. And even though the *Intrepid* may have been out of his reach, he was not prepared to give up. If there were any other way to get to the Tabernacle, he would find it.

Chapter 18

"All systems remain in the green," said the CAPCOM at Mission Control.

"Roger that," replied Mark. "All systems are nominal here."

The *Intrepid* had undocked from Gulliver Station and moved to a safe distance using its maneuvering thrusters. Mark was strapped in the acceleration couch located in the front and center of the command deck, while Ning, Oksana, Jed, and Adam were in the couches behind him.

Mark wanted to hold Ning's hand at the moment he activated the engine that she had spent so many years turning into a reality, the culmination of the dream he and so many others had shared for years, but that was not possible. Instead, he reflected on all of the arduous training he had gone through to become an astronaut, the overwhelming jubilation he had felt upon his being selected as IE's first astronaut, and the thrill of his first spaceflight.

He had long since lost count of how many times he had trained for this moment in the simulator at the IE headquarters. He had gone through nearly every conceivable scenario, and he was confident that he was as prepared as anyone could possibly be in his position. He knew firsthand how real the disaster scenarios he dealt with in simulations could be on actual spaceflights.

The worst mission he had ever commanded had been a commercial lunar flight. The landing craft had suffered an engine malfunction, and he had been forced to make emergency landing more than twenty miles from the nearest habitat. But no one had died on that mission or any he had commanded since, and he had every intention of keeping that track record.

Mark's finger hovered over the switch on the control

panel that would ignite the fusion drive, eagerly waiting to receive the final go-ahead.

"You are go to ignite the fusion drive," said the CAPCOM.

"Roger that," Mark said enthusiastically. "Let's light this candle."

He flipped the switch, and a column of deuterium and helium-three gas was ejected into the Z-pinch reaction chamber. Capacitor banks discharged a powerful current along the gas, stripping it of electrons and ionizing it into plasma. The Lorentz force then compressed the plasma until fusion reactions were initiated.

As the plasma from the fusion detonation expanded, the magnetic field lines along the interior of the reaction chamber were compressed. This caused the magnetic pressure to increase and slow the plasma's expansion until the magnetic pressure was equivalent to the plasma's dynamic pressure. The magnetic field lines than rebounded like a spring to their initial configuration, ejecting the fusion plasma from the reaction chamber and propelling the *Intrepid* forward. Then, less than a tenth of a second later, another column of fuel was ejected into the reaction chamber, and the cycle was repeated.

The thrust was nowhere near as great as that offered by chemical and nuclear thermal rockets, and was so miniscule that it only felt like a series of small taps against Mark's body. Had Mark and the others not rehearsed this so many times in the simulator, the ignition of the fusion engine might have seemed anticlimactic. But the engine would burn for a full twenty days before being shut down, the longest continuous operating time for a propulsion system that had ever been used on a manned spacecraft.

"Engine operating nominally," Mark reported. The *Intrepid* had the smoothest ride of any spacecraft he had flown. Even so, he found his heart hammering, and he was fighting to control his excitement. "We are underway."

He looked away from his control console for a brief moment to gaze out the window into the darkness of space. With the engine pulsing such a small amount of acceleration, it was next to impossible to tell that the *Intrepid* was moving. But even so, Mark already felt the thrill of closing on the Bastion.

* * *

Miles watched a video feed of the *Intrepid* on a monitor. The mighty spacecraft was too far away from the Nimbus station for him to see with the naked eye; the image was being provided by a surveillance satellite. The rear of the *Intrepid* glowed brightly as the fusion plasma pushed the vehicle out of low Earth orbit, initiating its interplanetary journey.

Part of him wanted to weep. From the moment he had seen the first images of the Bastion, Miles knew that nothing IE or the rest of human civilization had accomplished could ever compare to the technological might that the aliens possessed. It didn't matter that no one knew exactly how advanced the aliens actually were; the Bastion's presence in the Solar System showed that whatever civilization responsible for building it had possessed the capability to travel across the stars. That was all the proof anyone needed to see how technological superior the extraterrestrials were to humanity. Despite the might of the *Intrepid*'s fusion engine, it was still insufficient for an interstellar voyage.

Still, Miles felt a surge of pride at watching the spacecraft begin its voyage, knowing that he had helped to make this possible. And even if the aliens possessed technology that made the *Intrepid*'s fusion drive look like a steam engine, he would always look upon this as a crowning achievement of IE and human civilization. Nothing he had ever done could compare to this moment, and he doubted that anything could possibly surpass it during his lifetime.

He would monitor the progress of the *Intrepid*'s mission with the level of meticulousness that he always allotted to IE's historic space ventures, dating back to the first asteroid miner. Whenever he managed to have free time from the myriad of obligations he had to contend with on a daily basis, he intended to devote that time to checking in on the status of the *Intrepid* and her crew. It was never easy for him to find free time: there really were not enough hours in the day to run IE, and the Bastion and *Intrepid* would only intensify his workload. Traveling to the Nimbus and seeing the *Intrepid* off was the closest he had come to a vacation in a long time. But he owed it to the men and women onboard the *Intrepid* who were putting their lives on the line to give them the attention that they deserved.

Thinking of that caused his thoughts to turn to Mark and Ning, who he viewed of as being more than just his employees: they were family.

"Godspeed, *Intrepid*," Miles said into the com link.

"Thank you," Mark replied warmly. "We'll make you and everyone on Earth proud."

"You've already done that. Just make sure that you guys get there and back safely."

"Will do, Miles."

Chapter 19

"All right everyone," Mark said to his crew, "you are now free to move about the ship."

He unbuckled himself from his acceleration couch, and the rest of the crew followed suit. Jed, Oksana, and Adam turned to leave the command deck, but Ning remained, and moved closer to Mark. The commander took a moment to relish this now that he no longer had to concern himself with the engine.

"You built one hell of an engine," he said, looking at her fondly.

"Thank you," she murmured.

He desperately wanted to kiss her, but couldn't just yet; too many eyes were focusing on them. He would have to hold off on that until later when they were in a more private setting. There was much time before they reached the Bastion; plenty of time that they could spend together.

***

Adam Hernandez went to his quarters immediately after Commander de Rijk gave permission for everyone to leave the command deck. He pushed himself out of his ouch and down the long central hub. The spacecraft was huge; it had been designed and built to carry far more than five people for the voyages to and from Mars. Miles had wanted the *Intrepid* to be a versatile spacecraft, one capable of traveling even farther than the Red Planet. The fusion engine that Ning had developed would effectively open the entire Solar System for manned exploration. After the *Intrepid* had proven itself capable of making rapid, routine voyages to Mars missions, Miles had intended to build another fusion vessel and contract it out to NASA. With such a ship, manned missions to Jupiter, Saturn, and beyond might be possible.

184

Much of the past sixteen months had been spent refurbishing the *Intrepid* to make such a long-term voyage. It had been fitted with a hydroponic garden in the outer hub that would provide the crew with a steady supply of fresh fruits and vegetables. It was a vital capability for the longer duration missions that Miles had envisioned, and all the more paramount for the voyage to the Bastion. With this and the plentiful stores of shelf-stable powdered foods and oils for the 3D food printer, they would be able to remain stationed at the Bastion for several years without any resupply.

Adam moved about a quarter of the way down the central hub before pushing himself down the shaft that led to his quarters on the rotating out hub. The crew quarters were located farthest from the center, where centripetal acceleration was greatest. The hub rotated fast enough to simulate 0.4 g; a welcome feature to the entire crew.

He and the rest of the crew had been in microgravity for the past several hours while making the final preparations for the *Intrepid*'s departure. While Adam welcomed the return of gravity as he slid down the ladder and reached the outer hub, it felt a little weird to be lighter than he did on Earth.

Even with the simulated gravity, frequent exercise was vital to the crew's health during their voyage. Lack of exercise would cause loss of muscle and bone mass, and the prolonged deterioration would be so great that they would never be able to walk on Earth again.

The other major threat to the crew's health was the solar and cosmic radiation that bombarded their spacecraft unceasingly. There was a layer of polyethylene fabric material in the hull that shielded the crew from much of this radiation, and the many water tanks positioned near the crew quarters provided additional shielding. However, even with this protection, anyone onboard the *Intrepid* would still receive far higher levels of radiation than they would have be exposed to on Earth.

If the *Intrepid*'s mission lasted for years, as many expected it would, the radiation would cause such excessive damage to the crew's DNA that it was inevitable that they would develop cancer. Fortunately, the *Intrepid* was equipped with a sophisticated robotic surgeon that could remove tumors wherever any might grow. A medical 3D printer could also create replacement tissue and organs for the crew if needed. Similar medical equipment was now in nearly every hospital around the world, and was indispensable in the lunar and Mars facilities.

The crew quarters were luxurious by spacecraft standards; Miles had them designed and built large enough to accommodate honeymooning couples and small families on their excursions to Mars. Now, they provided ample personal space for each crew member.

Adam sat down at his workstation and turned on his personal computer. As he had expected, there was a flood of messages from his friends and colleagues. He only had time to start looking through them when the screen indicated an incoming video call from Earth. Adam and the others had been told that their loved ones would be informed of the optimal times to contact the crew. Adam answered the call, and his wife Maria appeared on the computer monitor. Her eyes were wide, and she looked like she was about to hyperventilate.

"Adam," she said, almost whispering. "Are you okay?"

"Yes, baby," Adam said to his wife.

"Is this really happening? Are you really going out there to an alien machine?"

"Yes baby. As strange as all this may seem, it's not some wild fantasy."

Maria took in a few quick, sobbing breaths. She was at a loss of words. Prior to leaving, Adam, observing the veil

186

of secrecy imposed on the entire project team, had told her only that he would be gone on an extended orbital mission. Since much of what he worked on was classified, she hadn't asked questions.

"It's okay baby," Adam said comfortingly. "I love you, and I'm very glad I can see and talk to you now."

"So am I," said Maria. "But I can't say I'm happy about this. After all, you did lie to my face. You said you were only going to be in orbit for a few months. For God's sake, why didn't you tell me you were doing this?"

The official story the crew had told their family members was that they would be testing long-term deep space technologies, the sort of capability that would be needed for expeditions to Jupiter and beyond.

"I'm sorry baby," Adam said. "I really am. But if I had told you the truth, I would have been kicked off the mission, and then the feds would have taken legal action against you and me. They could have thrown both of us into prison for who knows how long. And then after they decided to let us out, we'd both be under constant surveillance for the rest of our lives. And to be honest, I can understand why they'd do that, because I would have violated the nondisclosure agreement that I signed and betrayed their trust.

"But now that everything's out in the open, we can talk about anything you want, and we can talk as much as you want to. I swear on my life that there won't be any more secrets. But as we get farther away from Earth, the time delay will become greater and greater. By the time we get to the artifact, any messages we send to each other will have a thirty-minute roundtrip because of the speed of light limitation."

Maria nodded. "I understand."

"No matter how busy I am while I'm out here, I'll always give you the full attention that you deserve."

187

Maria smiled wanly at that. "Thank you. I know you will. Although it's not like there's any shortage of attention. I've been getting phone calls every few minutes, from friends and people I barely even know. And my social media network is just blowing up. Some of the neighbors are even starting to line up outside the house. People I've never heard of are trying to talk to me now that I'm the wife of one of the most famous astronauts ever."

"You don't need to talk to anyone if you don't want to," Adam said.

"I don't mind the attention, sweetheart. I just wish you were here with me...or I with you."

"So do I baby. Are you still mad at me?"

She managed a laugh. "No, I'm not mad at you. I've never been more proud of you and I've never been prouder to be your wife."

"Thank you baby. I'm an incredibly fortunate man to have you in my life."

Her thin smile grew a little broader. "How long are you going to be out there?"

"I honestly don't know. No one does. It all depends on what we learn about the artifact, and how quickly we're able to do it. It could very well last several years, and we have all the food and oxygen we'll need to stay out there for a long time."

That really seemed to upset Maria. "You're going to be gone for years?" She looked like she was about to break out in tears.

Adam nodded. "It's very possible. You were prepared for me to spend years on Mars, remember?"

"Yes, but that's not quite as dangerous as meeting aliens. You seemed so heartbroken when you told me that you had been removed from the Mars crew. Were you lying then?"

Adam nodded sadly. "They didn't remove me from the

188

Cycler mission. I really did want to go to Mars, and I chose to give up my slot for this. But you're right; I have been lying to you for a long time. And again, I'm sorry."

Maria was fighting back tears. "Truth be told, I was happy that you weren't going to Mars, because it meant that you weren't going to be away from me for so long. And now that you really will be gone for years, I just..." Her voice trailed off, and she broke down crying.

"I'm sorry baby," Adam repeated. It was horrible to be causing his beloved wife this much emotional trauma. No matter what the justification was for lying to her, he wasn't sure he could ever forgive himself for this.

Maria took a few quick breaths. "No, you shouldn't be apologizing. Really, I do understand why you took this mission. It's just..." Her voice trailed off.

"I know, baby. I hope that I'm not out here for years on end either, but it's really out of my control. And as happy as I am to be doing this, I'm already looking forward to being with you again. I promise that I'll make up for all of this when I get back to Earth."

"You'd better. I'm holding you to that."

***

Sitting in front of her laptop in her quarters, Oksana shifted through her email account. A flood of messages inundated her inbox within a few minutes of her appearance on the broadcast at Nimbus station.

Colleagues from universities and national research laboratories with whom she had collaborated with over the years sent good wishes. Others were from those who had been rivals opposed to her theories, oftentimes for no reason other than petty rivalry or arrogance. Some had called her an idiot that unworthy to work in the physics community now found it convenient to be friendly. Some sent frantic requests for details on what experiments she intended to run, asking her if she had thought of an

189

experiment they had in mind, and offering her ground-based support.

As she sifted through the emails, the video messenger rang. It was her sister, and Oksana answered it immediately.

Anastasia's vibrant face appeared on the computer screen, and she smiled broadly when she saw her sister's image on her screen. "Is this a bad time?" she said, looking nervous. "They said I could call you anytime I wanted, but I don't want to be bothering you if you're doing something important."

"No, don't worry about it," Oksana said. "You're fine."

Anastasia smiled more brightly, and then started to laugh. "Holy shit, Oksana," she said. "I can't believe you're doing this. I mean, you're in fucking outer space!"

"I know. I can hardly believe it myself, but watch your language... this could be rebroadcast."

"I always knew you were smarter than me, but I never thought that you'd be doing anything like this."

"Neither did I."

"So you're really going to meet little green men?"

Oksana laughed. "I am going to a real alien artifact, but we have no idea if the aliens who built it are going to be there waiting for us. They probably aren't, because the Bastion seems to have been hanging around without doing much of anything for the past few billion years. But if the aliens who built it are still there, I don't know what they'll look like, but I think it's safe to say that they won't be little green men."

Anastasia laughed again. "You always were the smarter and logical one. And now you're an astronaut and ambassador to aliens! I have a hard time believing that we're in the same gene pool."

"Nonsense 'Stasia," Oksana used her sister's pet name.

190

"You're the best sister anyone could hope to have."

"Now they'll have to give you that Nobel Prize you've always deserved."

Oksana laughed. "Thanks, but I don't think I'll be getting one of those just yet. It's not like I discovered the Bastion."

"But it's safe to say you're the one who'll find out what the aliens can do. Isn't that the sort of thing they'd give a Nobel Prize for?"

Oksana chuckled. "I think you're getting a bit ahead of yourself. I have no idea what I'm going to find."

"You keep saying that. But I know you. You never were satisfied. Every time you learned something new, you just had to go on from there to see what else there was to know. I know that you'll never give up, no matter how difficult or impossible it might seem."

"Thank you. I love you. Take care of Mom while I'm gone."

"I will. And be sure to take care of yourself."

***

After the crew had completed their personal calls, Mark called everyone to the galley for the first dinner they would have onboard the *Intrepid* together. Mission planners had felt that communal meals were vital for the crew morale, and Mark agreed wholeheartedly. On such a long-duration voyage, it was paramount that no one felt excluded to prevent dissention and social cliques from forming. The team needed to remain cohesive and focused. It was Mark's job to see that happened.

There was one table in the galley large enough to accommodate all of the crewmembers. It was a roundtable, an idea that was attributable to Miles. The IE president abhorred rectangular tables in meeting rooms. In fact, Mark didn't think there was a single rectangular table in any of the meeting rooms at IE's headquarters. Miles was

191

intentionally channeling Arthurian legends by using roundtables, not wishing to project any veil of authority over his employees that might deter them from speaking with complete honesty at meetings.

That Arthurian philosophy was one that Mark shared and he intended to uphold it on this mission.

There was a small stockpile of specialty foods onboard, considered to be somewhat gourmet by spaceflight standards. This included salmon, shrimp, chicken, and pulled pork. It was reserved for special occasions, and since this was the first meal onboard the ship, Mark felt it fit that bill.

Other special circumstances included the crew's arrival at the Bastion, their final return to Earth, and a select few holidays. A small portion of the stockpile had been set aside as a celebration in the event that a particularly profound breakthrough was made regarding the Bastion. No one could really say what would constitute such a discovery, but Mark was sure he would know if and when such a situation might arise.

"This is our first meal together on this historic voyage," Mark said as he sat down at the table with a plateful of steaming chicken. "All of the cameras are off, so be yourselves."

"Why would you feel the need to act differently when the cameras are on?" asked Jed.

"As a simple act of civility," Adam interjected.

"So do you act like a barbarian when you know people aren't looking at you?"

"No. I'm just saying it's better to consider how other people will interpret your behavior, and that it's best to be scrupulous about good manners when others will be watching and scrutinizing you."

Jed laughed. "I've never understood why people like you find it necessary to act differently when you are around others, or when your words or actions are being recorded for public scrutiny. It's no different than wearing a mask, and you wear such a mask because you're afraid of people seeing what you're really like."

"That's not it at all!" snapped Adam.

"But you just admitted that you act differently when you're on camera than you otherwise would. Why are you trying to backpedal now?"

Adam's head slumped, and he said nothing.

"Are you saying the rest of us are liars and barbarians?" Oksana asked Jed.

"Not at all," replied Jed. "I'm just acknowledging it as a possibility."

"So are you a liar too?" asked Ning.

"Not at all," Jed replied simply. "I never say anything in private that I'm not willing to say in front of other people. And I'm willing to say the same thing in front of my mother as I am to you, as well as the rest of the world. I've never had to act like anyone other than myself, and I attribute my brutal honesty to part of the reason why I'm here now."

"I congratulate you on that," said Mark. "And I'm glad to have you as a member of the crew. But I don't appreciate you calling me a liar."

"I never accused you of being one," Jed replied. "You pretty much admitted it yourself. And being deceptive may have been just as effective in your having been chosen for this mission as my honesty was in my selection."

"What the hell's the matter with you?" snapped Adam. "We've barely even gotten started, and you're already trying to start something."

"Nothing is wrong with me," said Jed. "And I'm not trying to start anything. I'm just being honest, like I always am. Although I wouldn't say that being deceitful is always a bad thing. After all, it's gotten you here as well. From

193

your own perspective, it doesn't matter what path you took, so long as you arrive at your intended destination."

"Jesus," Ning muttered. "That's awfully Machiavellian."

"Call it what you will. But it works, or else you would not be here." Jed ate a spoonful of salmon, and said, "On a side note, I can easily see myself living off this stuff for the next two or three years, or however long we'll be onboard."

Mark was relieved when Jed suddenly changed the subject. While the mathematician had no problem with voicing his opinion, his empathetic side left a lot to be desired. But it was good that he obviously did not see any reason to spark an argument.

"Enjoy it while you can," Mark said. "We'll only be eating like this on special occasions. The rest of the time we'll be eating the stuff grown in the garden and what the food printer is able to churn out."

"A small price to pay for being here," Jed said. "Besides, I would not even consider the crops in the hydroponic garden to be unpleasant. At least they will be fresh. And I would gladly eat the worst foodstuffs ever created if that was a requirement to be here."

"I can agree with you on that," said Adam.

"Same here," said Ning.

Mark smiled inwardly, and raised a cup of water in a toast. "To the *Intrepid*," he said proudly. "May she ferry us valiantly into the unknown."

They all raised their cups.

"And to the Bastion," said Oksana, "may it be willing to offer its secrets to us."

They all downed their drinks.

Chapter 20

Mark went to his quarters once dinner with the crew was completed. Like the other crewmembers, he had a mountain of emails to sift through. He quickly saw that he had not received anything from David, and decided to give his brother a call.

After a few rings of the video phone, David's face appeared on his computer screen. "Hello little brother," Mark said.

"Hi Mark," said David. "I didn't want to call you because I figured you were pretty busy."

"Well thanks for the consideration, but I'm not occupied with anything pressing at the moment, and I was looking forward to chatting with you."

"I'm glad you did," David smiled. "I didn't think you could possibly step things up after you became a hotshot astronaut. And look what's happening now." He chuckled slightly. "You always said you wanted to meet aliens more than anything else, and it looks like you're finally going to do that."

"Maybe. No one really knows what we're going to find at the Bastion. They're may not be anyone or anything at the Bastion to talk to."

"Have some faith."

"Right. So tell me, what are you making of all of this?"

David's smile evaporated. "You mean what do I make of the religious implications of extraterrestrial intelligence?"

"Yeah. I figured that that would be occupying a good portion of your thoughts."

"Well you're right about that. The aliens are the only thing that people are talking about."

Almost immediately after the president's speech, the

internet had exploded with people preaching that the end of the world was imminent. Some said that the aliens were minions of evil and the Bastion would be the instrument that would bring about Armageddon. Others thought that the aliens were holy and the only hope for humankind's salvation.

"Things are a bit hectic down here," David continued, "as I'm sure you understand. And I can't stop wondering what role the aliens play in the divine plan."

"Yeah, about that," said Mark. "I want you to think about how old the Bastion is. It may very well be older than life on Earth."

"Yes, I'm well aware of that."

"What if it has been monitoring Earth all this time? Do you know what that would mean?"

David nodded grimly. "Yes, I do."

Mark knew that his brother had never believed in young Earth creationism, but he knew members of his congregation that did. Many people had left when David said that evolution was true and opted instead for congregations that believed in biblical literalism. The Bastion offered definitive proof that the biblical story of creation was nothing but a myth.

"It's not just the creation myth that this discovery demolishes," said Mark. "So much of your religion is based on what's written in your sacred texts. The Bastion has been hanging around the Solar System for a very long time, so it's entirely possible that its builders could have a much better documentation of what really happened. They could have seen exactly what Moses, Jesus, Mohammed, and all the other major religious figures actually did. They may have seen for themselves that there were no miracles. No divine intervention. They might have definitive proof that all of the religions are founded on nothing but a bunch of myths."

David smiled grimly. "It's true that these aliens are old enough to have witnessed the emergence of Christianity and other religions. I'll give you that. But now you're assuming that they've been watching Earth this whole time, and that in the brief amount of time that humanity has existed, the aliens have had both the resources and the interest to carefully monitor the everyday actions of Christ and all other biblical figures, as well as religious figures from other faiths. That's an awful lot to assume."

Mark laughed. "Are you afraid that this could be true?"

"I do not believe for one second that the aliens have any historical records or knowledge about the nature of the universe that contradict Scripture. The very idea that they could have such information is completely ridiculous. And if you do manage to make contact with the aliens and they claim to have some records about the events in the bible, I wouldn't believe it. It would be too easy for them to fabricate that sort of thing."

Mark laughed. "So you'd ignore evidence that flies in the face of your religion simply because you don't want to believe it's true. How can you trust anything? Why believe an astrophysicist who tells you that the Earth orbits the sun and not vice versa? Hell, using that same logic I could say that the entire universe was created five seconds ago, and all memories I have of earlier events are false. It's a path to solipsism."

There was no shortage of outlandish theories about the aliens being responsible for all of the alleged miracles described in the Bible. Stuff like the burning bush, the parting of the Red Sea, the virgin birth and resurrection of Jesus. All of it, some claimed, was explainable by extraterrestrial intervention.

"So is that what you think happened?" David asked. "Do you think that these aliens spoke to Moses and all the other biblical prophets? That the desert dwellers who wrote the bible saw the aliens working their amazing technology and figured that it was the power of God? And then these aliens used artificial insemination to impregnate Mary? And then they cloned Jesus and used a transporter to beam the dead body out of the cave?"

"I wouldn't go that far," said Mark. "I always just figured that the so-called miracles in the Bible started as half-assed stories that were more or less pulled out of thin air, which gradually became corrupted until they became undisputed fact by the time they were written down. Drugs may have been involved too. I don't think that the aliens are behind the myths in the bible. But I don't know what these aliens may or may not have seen or done on Earth. That's the whole reason I'm doing this: to learn as much as possible about the artifact and, if possible, the aliens who built it."

"Tests of faith are what separate the believers from the nonbelievers," said David. "The truly faithful never fear such tests. And I do not fear whatever you may discover. I hope that we learn a great deal about the aliens and their way of viewing the universe. But no matter what we might learn from them, I do not believe that it will lead to the end of Christianity. In fact, I believe that the exact opposite will happen: we will obtain a better understanding of the divine plan and humanity's place in it." David sighed. "I wish we had had the opportunity to talk about this face-to-face before you left."

"I wish we could have done that too," Mark said. "But secrecy was a necessary safety precaution. The fear of the reactions of religious fanatics is one of the main reasons we waited until now to reveal what we were really doing. There was a ton of fear that religious lunatics would launch suicide attacks against launch sites because they'd rather no one get to the Bastion."

"Not everyone who holds strong religious faith would

do such a thing," said David. "You should know that."

Mark nodded. "You're right about that. But you must understand why we needed to do it this way."

"I do."

"Good. And I can tell you right now that if we do establish contact with these aliens, you'll change your beliefs on God."

"You may very well be right. But I do not believe they will cause me to abandon my belief in the Almighty."

"We'll see about that." Mark paused.

"Your safety is what I'm really concerned about," said David. "This is unlike anything you've ever done before."

"I'm well aware of that. I'm not worried, but thanks for your concern."

"I saw the broadcast you all were in. It would've been hard not to have seen it. And I know you guys all touched on this. But I want to hear it from you, and I want you to be completely honest with me. What are you going to do if these aliens do turn out to be hostile?"

"There's not a damn thing we can do in that case," Mark said simply. "If they want us dead, then we're dead. That goes not just for us, but Earth as well. Believe me, if they have the technology to travel across the stars, extinguishing life on a planet like Earth will be child's play for them."

"I was kind of hoping you'd say something a little more uplifting."

"If I did, I'd just be lying. But if the Bastion or its builders do destroy us, then at least we'll die having learned something of great value. Because it will be proof that it's not derelict. And I would much rather be killed by the aliens than by some mechanical or software failure in the ship." He looked at his brother. "You think that's crazy?"

"No, of course not," said David. "On the contrary, I

199

think that's a very noble position to have. I've always had nothing but respect for what you do, and always recognized it as among the bravest and noblest endeavors any human has ever pursued. I just wish, above all else, that I could be there alongside you."

"Thanks. We may not see eye-to-eye on a lot of things, but I've always appreciated your concern for me. But don't think for one second that I'm going to try to convert these aliens to Christianity. If we are able to make contact with them and they want to know about our culture, I intend to tell them about the world's religions too. I'll be treating Christianity no different than any other religion."

David nodded. "Of course. I'd expect nothing less from you. And I'm going to keep you in my prayers, just as I always have whenever you've gone off into space. I know you don't think that amounts to anything, but that doesn't mean I'll stop doing it."

"Thank you," said Mark. "I do value the concern you've always shown toward me, and your unwavering support. I've always appreciated that. And yes, I do admit that at times, I can be a bit disrespectful toward your beliefs."

"Just a little bit," David said with a slight smile.

"But no matter how disrespectful I've been or may continue to be, I want you to know that I'll always love you."

"And I'll always love you unconditionally. Take care, big brother."

"You too, David."

Chapter 21

Desmond sat calmly next to Ryan Belue, his eyes darting between the host and the camera that would be broadcasting their interview live across the internet. Belue had a large following online and hosted a popular internet talk show were he discussed many social, political, and technological issues that were of central significance to the world. Astronauts and world-renowned scientists were frequent guests of his.

In the wake of the *Intrepid*'s launch, people at NASA and IE were finally able to talk about the Bastion's discovery. This inevitably led to the revelation that Desmond had leaked the discovery to NASA in direct defiance of Miles, which was the reason behind the IE president blacklisting him. Not that it did much to change the level of isolation in which Desmond found himself. The past sixteen months had been very trying on him. Nearly all of his friends in the aerospace industry had ostracized him because of his blacklisting. Even now that the full truth was finally beginning to come out, many still thought of him as a traitor who deserved Miles' wrath.

It was a bit of an adjustment having to live on the government's universal income program. Anyone living on the universal income was able to survive comfortably enough, but that was about it. Having the income from a real job had allowed Desmond to live far more luxuriously in comparison to people who were unemployable. He had built up a considerable savings from his time working at IE, but still had been forced to live rather frugally as he adapted to permanent unemployment.

Belue had invited Desmond onto his show upon learning about how the former IE employee had been responsible for NASA learning about the alien artifact. Belue's invitation was about the friendliest gesture that

201

Desmond had received in the past sixteen months. But Desmond was not here to seek sympathy, and he did not really care if people saw him as a martyr. He simply wanted to tell his side of the story.

Belue smiled broadly into the camera as the broadcast began. "A very special guest is joining me tonight," he said to his internet audience. "Desmond Berens is an engineer who formerly worked at Interplanetary Enterprises. He worked there from the company's early days until a little over a year ago."

"Thank you for having me here," Desmond said.

"As I understand it, you were one of the employees responsible for the discovery of the Bastion."

"I was just doing my job. I can't and won't take sole credit for the discovery. The Bastion was found thanks to everyone at IE doing their jobs."

"Is that why you leaked the news of the discovery against your boss's explicit orders?"

Desmond swallowed hard, and looked visibly uncomfortable.

"Sorry," Belue said, and shifted back to his friendly demeanor. "But seriously though, why did you leak it?"

Desmond took a few deep breaths before speaking. "I shared the information about the discovery with Alan Prater. I figured that he, of all people, deserved to know about the Bastion."

"But if you really wanted the world to know about the Bastion, you could have leaked it to the public. Why didn't you?"

"I…I guess because I was afraid of how people would react. I trusted that Prater would be able to handle the situation better than I ever could."

"Okay. So you trusted that the government would be able to handle the information disclosure better?"

"That's what I hoped for."

202

"Is that also why you waited until now to talk about this?"

"Yes. I vowed that I would not talk about what happened until after a public announcement about the Bastion had been made."

"Didn't want to make things worse for yourself, did you? Because as I understand it, you've been out of the workforce since you were fired from IE."

"I..." Desmond swallowed hard again as he answered. "Yes, that is true."

"And if I am not mistaken, this is due to your former boss blacklisting you?"

Desmond sighed. "Yes, that is true as well. And because of that, I have become something of a pariah in the aerospace industry."

"How angry are you about what Miles Gilster did to you? You are, after all, part of how he became as successful as he has. And then he went and did this to you. Doesn't that infuriate you?"

Desmond sighed. "In all honesty, I can't blame Miles for what he did. Like you said, I did something that he explicitly told me and everyone else not to do."

"So you knew that Miles was going to blacklist you, and yet you did it anyway?"

"Yes."

"Do you regret what you did?"

"No. Not at all."

***

Neil Armstrong Operations and Checkout Building
Kennedy Space Center

"Do we really have to do this?" Brianna Rothman grumbled.

"Yes," replied Johnathan Donner. "These kinds of public outreach efforts are vital. You know that."

203

"But no one's going to be watching this anyway," the geologist groaned. "The *Intrepid* is the only thing anyone's talking about. This is just another pointless hoop we have to jump through."

Donner fully understood how Rothman felt. Even now, weeks after the *Intrepid*'s departure, it dominated social media websites, debates among politicians, and religious gatherings. There had been more than a few riots in major cities all around the world.

"So what if it is?" said Anton Ryabkov. Anton was the astrobiologist, and had been Adam Hernandez's backup. Since moving from a backup to a prime crewmember, Anton had been a source of ceaseless jubilation, now that he would be going to the Red Planet more than two years earlier than expected.

"Hell, I'd jump through any hoop they hold in front of me," Anton continued. "That's hardly an unfair price to pay for going to Mars."

"And that's part of why I'm glad you're onboard," Donner said with complete sincerity. Looking back at Rothman, Donner continued, "The fact of the matter is that we owe it to everyone who made this mission possible to make a public outreach effort. And we're going to be giving more public interviews after we get onboard the *Aldrin* and once we're on Mars."

Donner already knew exactly what questions people would ask. What's it like to be in space? What's it like on Mars? Things like that, which he and nearly every other astronaut had explained in a public forum ad nauseam.

"And no one will care the least bit about that either," Rothman snapped.

"Those bastards on the *Intrepid* couldn't even tell us what they were doing," grunted Jun-seo Hwan.

Donner could not help but share the animosity expressed by the nuclear and propulsion engineer. The

Aldrin crew had found out about the *Intrepid*'s real mission at the same time the rest of the world had. No one else in the astronaut, cosmonaut, or taikonaut corps had known about the Bastion. Even Anton had not been told why Hernandez had given up his slot. It was not right they had all been kept in the dark like that.

"I honestly can't blame them for the secrecy," said Vera Mirnov, the mission's botanist. "Look at how insane things have gotten since they left. They would have jeopardized their safety if they had revealed it before they launched."

Donner knew how right she was. There had already been several failed terrorist attacks on the spaceport in New Mexico. The security force had been significantly increased for Kennedy Space Center and other spaceports around the world in response to the failed attacks, as well as to the growing social turmoil. He just hoped that nothing disastrous would happen in the next several days.

***

Commander Donner and the other four members of his crew looked into the camera that was broadcasting a live feed over the internet. Right next to the camera was a computer screen that was displaying videos of people asking questions that had been submitted to the NASA website.

The *Aldrin* Cycler was due to make a flyby of Earth in just a few more days. This provided a small window of opportunity for a crew of astronauts to launch from Earth and rendezvous with the spacecraft.

Donner had been in the astronaut corps for ten years, and this would be his second assignment on the Mars expeditions, and the first time as the mission commander.

In the last days before their launch, a Mars crew answered questions that had been submitted over the internet. Donner had given one of these question and answer sessions during the last days leading up to each of one of his space missions. He had never craved the public spotlight, but he understood the importance of doing things like this to maintain public and political support for NASA and the Mars corps.

By far, the majority of the questions were submitted by space fanatics. These were the kind of people that worshipped astronauts, and quivered at any chance to be able to talk to them, even if it was over the internet. He had always enjoyed speaking to people like this, since he considered himself to be one of them for as long as he could remember.

Even so, NASA managers always had to vet the questions that were submitted so that only appropriate ones would be presented to the astronauts. There were always people who would submit videos of themselves blabbering incoherently, or saying something that was sexist, racist, homophobic, or some horrible combination thereof.

The first questioner was a kid from Alberta named Zachary Eggers. He looked to be about thirteen, and nervously asked, "Why are you still studying Mars rocks? We've been exploring Mars for decades now and brought rocks back to Earth already. What more is there for you guys to learn?"

Rothman took it upon himself to answer the kid's question. "We've been studying Earth in a geological context for a very long time now," he said without the slightest hint of agitation that he had voiced only a few minutes earlier. "And yet we continue to discover new things about our home planet. By comparison, we've barely even begun to explore Mars. New crews always travel to new locations that previous crews did not go to so that we can gather more geological data. Every mission to Mars teaches us something new about the Red Planet. And even though I won't be the first person to walk on Mars, I can

206

safely say that I will walk somewhere that no one else has set foot before. And I intend to use that incredible opportunity to build upon our collective knowledge about Mars."

The second question came from Chelsea Norris, a middle-aged woman from Philadelphia.

"I was wondering if you could tell me why you're still looking for life on Mars?" Chelsea asked. "The Bastion proves that aliens exist, so what's the point of having you guys still looking to see if there are aliens on Mars?"

Donner was almost appalled to hear something so ignorant, and he knew his crew felt the same way. Still, he understood why the NASA managers had presented this question to them for this session: many people did not grasp the importance of continuous fundamental research projects. This was a question that he knew Anton should answer, so he deferred to him.

"It is true that the Bastion has already provided an answer to the age-old question of whether or not we're alone in the universe," Anton said as tactfully as possible. "And while we have not found any life on Mars yet, there is still the possibility that it exists on the Red Planet, or did exist there in the ancient past. Although we've not found signs of intelligent Martian life, if we ever do find existing or extinct Martian life, it will still be a major discovery, because it would indicate that life might be commonplace in the universe."

The next question, directed at Mirnov, was from a man from Nigeria named Isah Adegboye.

"What's the greatest challenge we face in opening up Mars for colonization, and what are you doing to overcome that?" Isah asked.

"The real limiting factor is the logistics of shuttling people between Earth and Mars," Mirnov responded. "We do this now with the *Armstrong* and *Aldrin*. The Cyclers are the best transportation system available to us that permit a sustainable and permanent human presence on Mars. Even so, the Cyclers can only carry a crew of five.

"Collins is equipped with a greenhouse that has been able to produce crops since the base became operational. Without the greenhouse and its crops, we would not be able to sustain crews there for the duration of each mission. Also, during the most recent expeditions the crews at Collins have been working to expand the base and the greenhouse to support larger crews farther down the line. Because I'm the botanist for this expedition, my task will be to continue to focus on the expansion of the greenhouse and improve the crop yield. This is crucial for the colonization of Mars.

"But as you know, any plans for sending the *Intrepid* to Mars have been put on hold for the foreseeable future because of its current mission. Even so, we cannot abandon our long-term goal of expanding the population on Mars. While we may temporarily be putting expansion of the base on the backburner, it is crucial that we continue the work that will enable that goal farther down the line once the *Intrepid* or another fusion spacecraft are available to ferry humans to and from Mars."

The next question came from a man named Chris Conroy from Waleska, Georgia.

"Do you think it makes any sense that the *Intrepid* is being used to for the mission to the artifact?" Conroy queried. "Wouldn't it make more sense to use one or even both of the Mars Cyclers, which have been operational for years and have proven track records?"

This very question had already been answered in depth. A detailed paper on the subject had been co-written by NASA engineers and the President's science adviser, and was made publicly available on the White House website less than an hour after Ortega had given his speech.

The paper explained that altering a Cycler's orbit so that it would travel to the artifact instead of Mars and then performing a rendezvous maneuver upon reaching the artifact would exhaust nearly all of the propellant that a Cycler was able to carry. This would effectively make such a voyage one-way.

By contrast, the *Intrepid*'s fusion drive was a far more versatile propulsion system. With such a high specific impulse and payload to mass fraction, the spacecraft was well suited to travel to a myriad of destinations in deep space. It was not at all difficult for the *Intrepid* to rendezvous with the artifact and return to Earth at a later point in time. Her passenger and cargo space, normally intended to ferry a large number of people and equipment to Mars, was now carrying sufficient supplies to sustain the crew for years and an abundance of advanced equipment to study the Bastion.

Even though this information was readily available to anyone with internet service, Donner had fully expected such a question to come up during this Q&A session, and he answered it as tactfully as possible.

"I'll spare you the technical details," Hwan said into the camera. "But the fact of the matter is that it's not even remotely practical to send one of the Cyclers to the alien artifact. Part of this is because the Cycler's aren't able to carry enough propellant to alter the orbits that they're on, reach the artifact, and then return to Earth. And even if it was possible to do all of that, we would be forced to abandon the Collins base. Abandoning Mars is not something that I or anyone else at NASA wants to do.

"The *Intrepid*'s fusion propulsion system significantly outperforms the Cycler's nuclear thermal propulsion system. Therefore, it only made sense for NASA to accelerate the *Intrepid*'s construction. So even though the *Intrepid* hadn't yet been completed when the Bastion was

209

first discovered, finishing it and using it for this mission was still the most practical course of action.

"The very fact that we have the option of sending one spacecraft on a deep space mission while using two others to continue supporting the Collins base on Mars is yet another testament to the great strides we have made in space travel. When I was a kid, NASA had to devote all of its manned spaceflight operations to the old space shuttle and a single space station. That utterly pales in comparison to what we're now able to do in space."

But Donner almost felt like he was being deceitful about saying that last bit. Even with all of the advances that he had just enumerated, he knew compared to the technological capabilities of the aliens who had built the artifact, we were in the stone age of space travel. That was humbling and somewhat terrifying.

President Ortega had spoken of this very thing during his announcement, and it was something the media discussed endlessly. They wondered what the point was in continuing to pour immense sums of money into scientific and space research when another civilization had already discovered everything of value.

Donner would not allow himself to be governed by such a fatalistic philosophy. Knowing that there were extraterrestrials with far superior technology gave him no reason to believe that humanity should abandon its own scientific advancements. If anything, it should give humankind a stronger incentive to better itself as a species, and to soldier on in the endless pursuit of greater knowledge.

The next question came from a woman in Taiwan named Mei-ling Liou. "Are you worried that the *Intrepid* mission is stealing all of the attention from your mission, and the Mars program in general?"

This was another question that Donner had fully

expected. He knew that IE and their hotshot astronaut, Mark de Rijk, would have stolen the spotlight had the *Intrepid* completed its original mission to Mars. After all, the whole point of the *Intrepid*'s original mission was to make the Cyclers obsolete.

"It is absolutely imperative that we do everything that we can to learn as much as possible about the artifact and its builders," Donner said, fixing a serious gaze on the camera lens. "Given the critical importance of that mission, I'm not the least bit surprised that the majority of the world's media attention has been focused on the *Intrepid* and her crew. They rightfully deserve the attention that they've been getting.

"That being said, does the *Intrepid*'s mission undermine what we're doing? Of course not. Even though it's incredibly vital that we learn more about the alien artifact, it must not be forgotten that we all have an obligation to maintain our society and uphold its values, whether that involves continuing to send your kids to school, going to work, paying your taxes, or maintaining our assets in space."

The next question was from a kid from Beijing named Yan Lee, and his question was directed towards all of them.

"If you had been given the chance, would you have given up your place on the *Aldrin* in order to be a crewmember onboard the *Intrepid*?"

Even though Donner had answered the previous questions, everyone still expected that as the mission commander, he would answer first, which he did.

"I didn't join the astronaut corps to boost my own ego," Donner said. "I did it to push the boundaries of human spaceflight. That's why it's important that we continue the Cycler program. I'm glad that I have the opportunity to go back to Mars so that I can continue contributing to building mankind's future on the Red

211

Planet. And, if for some reason I should feel the need to raise my spirits, I just need to remind myself that I'm getting a chance to go to Mars, and I'm getting paid to do it. So I really don't have anything to complain about."

This was the sort of rhetoric that Donner had repeated ad infinitum when he spoke publicly. But no matter how many times he said it, he still meant every word.

The question and answer session continued for another two hours. More questions were addressed to all, while some were addressed to specific crewmembers. Some were mundane, others not so much. But all were answered as politely as possible without condescension. It was a testament to the sophistication of NASA's public speaking training.

***

Immediately after the press conference, Donner left the Operations and Checkout Building and drove to Cocoa Beach. It was beginning to get dark, and he wanted some time to himself. Donner had always appreciated having a chance to walk along Cocoa Beach before each space mission he had flown.

There weren't many people on the beach at this hour, and no one seemed to recognize him. There was irony to this, since many of the beachgoers had come to Cocoa Beach to watch the launch. Even though manned space launches were becoming more and more routine, there was still a surge of tourists and beachgoers in the days leading up to a launch.

More tourists were at Cape Canaveral and Cocoa Beach now than there had been for any space mission since the *Tyr* that had carried Thomas Aytche and his crew on the first manned mission to Mars. This heightened public interest was undoubtedly attributable to the *Intrepid* and the Bastion.

It was amazing how quickly the public grew bored

with space endeavors. The majority of the population now viewed something as technologically challenging as sending humans across the vast void between Earth and Mars as a mundane exercise. New missions that expanded human spaceflight capabilities did revitalize a general sense of wonder, but it was always temporary.

But Donner didn't care to have people gawking at him like he was a celebrity. He enjoyed being able to get out of the public spotlight, and valued his privacy. This was especially beneficial in that it helped provide him with one last opportunity to enjoy the sights and sounds of his home planet. He always had a sense of tranquility when he walked along the beach at night. He enjoyed feeling the course sand and rough seashells against the soles of his feet, listening to the crashing of the waves, tasting the sea salt in the breeze.

He looked up at the stars, and the rusty red glow of Mars quickly drew his attention. He thought back to when he was a kid, a time when people walking on Mars was strictly the realm of science fiction. And yet now there were people living and working there, and in only a few short months, he would be there himself.

But then his thoughts again turned to the Bastion. To know that there existed, or had once existed, aliens who had come to the solar system from across the stars stirred something primal in him. Despite what he had said at the press conference, Donner truly did desire nothing more than to see the artifact and its builders with his own eye. That was why he could never blame Adam Hernandez for having left his crew and joined Mark de Rijk's. Hell, he would have given up command of the *Aldrin* in a heartbeat had it meant gaining a seat on the *Intrepid*. But he could never say that. That would be disrespectful to himself, his crew, and NASA in general.

Chapter 22

The day of the launch arrived, and the crew went to the mess hall for their final meal before their departure. Also present in the mess hall was the NASA administrator, veteran astronauts, and the directors of Marshall Space Flight Center, the Jet Propulsion Laboratory, and Johnson Space Center. Each spoke highly of every one of the crewmembers; the sort of rhetoric that had been repeated relentlessly as of late.

After they had finished eating, they quickly suited up, and walked down the hallways to the building's exit. The hallways were crammed with their family members. Among those present were Donner's wife and two young sons. The commander stopped to hug them and tell them his heartfelt goodbyes.

Donner and his crew then exited the building and climbed into the transport van, which took them the eight miles from the Operations and Checkout Building to Launch Complex 39A. There was more security at the spaceport than there had been at any other time in the history of the Mars corps. This was not unusual these days; security had been dramatically increased at all spaceports around the world in the wake of the *Intrepid*'s departure.

There was no shortage of ways that terrorists could make suicidal attempts destroy or severely damage a mission or a spacecraft. They could murder engineers and scientists, detonate propellant stores, and possibly try to hijack a spacecraft and use it as a missile against civilian or military targets. All launch vehicles had self-destruct mechanisms to destroy them in the event that someone or something outside of NASA took control of the vehicle, or in the event of software or mechanical failure.

The discovery of Bastion had greatly amplified the

fears for security breaches. Within a few minutes of President Ortega's speech disclosing the alien artifact, riots had broken out in many cities all around the world. Religious implications of extraterrestrial intelligence were a major source of fear and violence. There were many who viewed the Bastion's very existence as a form of blasphemy. Religious fanatics could not bring themselves to imagine that their deity had created other beings gifted with intelligence greater than that He had bestowed on His human children. They still refused to believe in evolution and a universe that was billions of years old. Few things were as heretical to them as highly advanced aliens that were a product of the blind forces of natural selection and had conquered interstellar distances eons ago.

To many the alien artifact was a harbinger of Armageddon. Some were even trying to take it upon themselves to hasten what they believed was the end of times, launching attacks against government facilities, schools, and rival religious organizations.

Madness, all of it. But even in the face of these threats, society was still managing to hold together. Markets continued to operate much as they had before Ortega's announcement, and people who still held jobs continued to work them as faithfully. And everyone at NASA had continued to work with the same loyalty and passion that they always had.

There was a very narrow launch window for a crewed capsule to rendezvous with the *Aldrin* as the Cycler flew passed Earth. NASA had not missed a single such window since the inception of the Cycler program, and that would not change now.

In addition to the usual supplies of food, water, and propellant, the command capsule was carrying a significant amount of advanced research equipment that was to be used on Mars. This included powerful laser scanners, gravity gradiometers, and magnetic spectrometers.

President Ortega had issued an executive order, instructing the astronauts on the Moon and Mars to actively search for other alien artifacts. Many believed that Ortega's gesture was pointless, and that if there were other alien artifacts in the Solar System, it was highly unlikely that they would ever be found. The discovery of the Bastion in the asteroid belt had been entirely serendipitous. After more than sixteen months of ceaseless observation, virtually nothing had been learned about it, certainly no telltale signs that could lead to the discovery of additional artifacts that might have been left behind by the builders of the Bastion.

Ortega's executive order did not impact any of the research that was being done at the Mars and lunar bases, so there had been no objection from the astronauts or scientists at NASA. If anything, it provided the crews on the Moon and Mars with another incentive to continue their thorough research. After the executive order had been issued, the astronauts expanded the careful inspection of every interesting geographic or magnetic phenomenon, searching for even the smallest anomalies. Anything that had the slightest trace of mystery attached to it was now being investigated in great detail, all in the hopes of discovering another alien artifact. Unfortunately, closer examination so far had revealed such phenomena to be completely natural in origin, and no additional artifacts had yet been discovered.

Nevertheless, Donner and his crew would be continuing that search, for even though the probability of finding an alien artifact on Mars may be small, the payoff could be immense.

The van brought the crew to the launch site where they stepped out of the van and into shadow of the launch vehicle. The rocket towered over them, but it was nowhere near as massive or powerful as the mighty Saturn V that had carried astronauts to the Moon decades earlier. There was no reason for it. Unlike the Saturn V, this launch vehicle merely had to deliver the astronauts and their capsule to low Earth orbit. Once there, the capsule would rendezvous with an orbiting nuclear thermal rocket, which would then push the astronauts out of low Earth orbit on a trans-Mars injection and eventual rendezvous with the *Aldrin*.

The company that built this launch vehicle also used it to ferry wealthy individuals to private space stations. NASA was simply another customer for the launch provider, and bought flights from them, saving the cost of building and maintaining their own manned rockets. With transport to low Earth orbit now the realm of private companies, NASA was able to concentrate a greater portion of its resources on the exploration of Mars and other efforts in deep space.

Donner and his crew climbed into the elevator at the base of the launch tower. The ascending elevator offered spectacular views of the subtropical greenery that blanketed Kennedy and the blue of the Atlantic toward the east.

Shortly after the technicians had strapped Donner and the others into their seats in the command capsule, the countdown began. The astronauts and flight controllers proceeded through the standard flight checklist. Everything proceeded nominally as the countdown progressed and the time for ignition arrived. The sudden thrust generated by the engines' ignition pushed the crew into their seats.

As the rocket ascended, each of the crewmembers were subjected to engine vibrations as the rocket shot over the blue waters of the Atlantic Ocean and further into the heavens. They could feel the engines' gimballing and the accompanying change in the thrust vector. The crew and the flight controllers at Mission Control carefully monitored all of the rocket's systems, ready to act in the event of an anomaly.

The flight was uneventful as the vehicle continued its ascent. After a nominal burn, the engines on the first stage shut down and the accompanying cessation of acceleration thrust the crew forward in their seats, followed by momentary freefall.

"Main engine cutoff," Donner reported.

Then the pyrotechnic bolts holding the first and second stages together blew apart, inducing further vibrations as the two stages separated from each other. The second stage engine then ignited, pushing them back into their couches as the rocket continued to accelerate into orbit.

"Second stage ignition," said the commander.

The first stage would fall for a few miles before firing its engine again for a powered landing at the same launch pad it had departed just a few minutes earlier, ready for for refitting and use on a future mission. The second stage was equipped with a heat shield that would enable it to survive atmospheric reentry, and it too would execute a powered landing at the same launch pad after descending from orbit to be used again.

Reusability had been the main factor that had dramatically lowered the cost of manned space exploration. Gone were the days of only single use rockets. The propellant had always represented a small percentage of the total cost of launch vehicles. But reusability had been deemed to be too complicated during the years and decades of space travel.

Earlier generations of rocket stages were condemned to burn up in the Earth's atmosphere after their first and only use, leading to the exorbitant costs of space activities that had held back human expansion into space for decades. Reusable launch vehicles caused a paradigm shift that changed all that.

Reusing rocket stages was now a central feature of all space mission architectures. Even the capsule launch escape tower, which had been an integral component of early generation manned space capsules, was no longer necessary. Instead of a solid fueled rocket mounted on a tower at the top of the capsule, there was an array of hypergolic propellant liquid rocket engines that was not jettisoned from the capsule. This allowed it to be used in emergency situations, as well as to provide a propulsive landing. This meant both the capsule and the rocket array could be used on multiple missions.

The second stage's engines operated nominally, and after only a few short minutes, the capsule was in orbit.

"Second stage engine cutoff," Donner said.

The pyrotechnic bolts fired, separating the capsule from the launch vehicle's second stage.

The crew looked out the windows at the curvature of the Earth below them.

"I've got to admit that I never get tired of this view," said Hwan.

"I don't think anyone can," said Donner. "I have yet to meet anyone impervious to the overview effect."

Viewing the Earth from orbit led many astronauts and cosmonauts to view their home planet as a fragile oasis of life in an otherwise barren and inhospitable cosmos. It seemed a crime to many of them how abusive their species had been to the world that had given birth to them. The lack of national boundaries made more palpable the pettiness of human conflicts in the grand scheme of the universe.

The capsule orbited the Earth three times to catch up with the Mars lander and the trans-Mars injection stage. The lander had been launched from Earth on a separate rocket two days earlier, and had rendezvoused with the Trans-Mars Injection Stage (TMIS). The TMIS had itself arrived in low Earth orbit from deep space a week earlier, and had an extensive history of use in the Cycler program.

"Preparing for docking with lander," Donner said as the autopilot guided the capsule to the conjoined spacecraft.

A slight vibration propagated through the capsule as it docked to the Mars lander.

"We have capture and hard dock," Donner reported.

"Roger that," replied the CAPCOM.

The crew worked through their Earth departure checklist in preparation for trans-Mars injection (TMI). It took a little over and hour for the crew to cycle through their Earth departure checklist and receive the go-ahead from Mission Control.

"You are go for TMI," said the CAPCOM.

"Roger that, CAPCOM" Donner responded. "Initiating TMI burn now."

The TMIS's nuclear thermal rocket engine fired, passing hydrogen through a nuclear reactor and then expelling the superheated gas to generate thrust. The crew was pressed into their couches as the vehicle accelerated at two g's.

"Engines operating nominally," Donner said calmly into the mike of his headset.

"Roger that," replied the CAPCOM. "All telemetry is looking good from our end."

A burn time of seven minutes depleted the hydrogen propellant in the TMIS, and the acceleration ceased.

"TMI burn complete," Donner reported as microgravity returned to the capsule.

The TMIS detached from the joined lander and command module. It would go on to swing past Mars and eventually return to Earth in time for the next Cycler crew. The capsule and Mars lander would continue on to the *Aldrin*.

"You guys have done an excellent job," said the CAPCOM. "We couldn't ask for a more perfect day."

"Thank you," said Donner. "Settle in people," he said to his crew. "The hard part is over."

However, the crew's survival was far from guaranteed. It would take another ten days for them to rendezvous with the Cycler. If they failed to make the rendezvous with the *Aldrin*, they would perish once they depleted the limited supplies aboard the capsule.

About an hour after the crew had completed the TMI burn, they received a message from Mark de Rijk on the *Intrepid*.

"The crew of the *Intrepid* would like to congratulate the Mars corps on their successful launch and trans-Mars injection," Mark said in his friendly demeanor. "We wish them continued success on their voyage to the Red Planet."

Similar messages of congratulations were pouring in from the stations in Earth orbit, lunar orbit, and on the lunar surface.

"It's nice of them to give us a sendoff," Mirnov said.

Donner looked like he had his mind on something else. "Yes," he said absentmindedly. "It's very thoughtful of them."

***

"Rise and shine people," said Donner, pulling his crew from their slumber.

It had taken the capsule ten days after the trans-Mars injection to catch up to where the *Aldrin* was going to be.

Ryabkov groaned. "Can't I get a little more sleep?"

"No can do," said Donner. "We've got a long checklist to go through. And you should be thankful. We're getting an upgrade in our housing today. The *Aldrin* is a goddamned castle compared to this capsule."

"What I'm looking forward to having gravity again, even if it's simulated," said Vera. Without continuous exercise and the simulated gravity offered by the *Aldrin* the crew's muscle atrophy would render them too weak to walk

221

on the surface of Mars when they arrived in another five months.

"I'll be relieved not having to sleep right next to Anton anymore," said Hwan.

"I don't know how I feel about that," Ryabkov said as he pulled himself out of his sleeping bag mounted against the wall of the capsule. "I kind of like the coziness we have in here."

"Well you could stay in here," Rothman said. "You'd have this whole luxurious capsule to yourself while the rest of us are on the *Aldrin*.

"Maybe. But I don't think I could handle being away from you guys like that. And I like to think you wouldn't want that either."

"As if," Mirnov said jokingly.

***

"I have to admit that she is a real beauty," said Hwan as the *Aldrin* came into view.

The massive vehicle loomed before the capsule as the two spacecraft approached each other. The Cycler looked like a pair of cylinders joined together by a third. One cylinder consisted of the habitat modules. The other consisted of the docking module, nuclear reactor, and rocket engine. They were connected by a smaller cylindrical module through which crewmembers could pass between the docking module and the habitat modules.

The vessel was a testament to the world's commitment to a sustained human presence on Mars. Until the *Intrepid* had been built, the *Aldrin* and its twin, the *Armstrong,* were the largest and most advanced manned spacecraft.

And after so many years of operation, the Cycler was beginning to show signs of its age. It was scarred from micrometeorite impacts. Some of these impacts had barely dented the outer hull. Others had been severe enough to warrant repairs by previous crews. Patchwork jobs that were made on spacecraft in the void between the planets.

In spite of their long years of service, the Cyclers continued on their long paths, dancing ceaselessly with the planets to the tune of Newtonian physics. Even if the *Intrepid* had been used for its original mission to rapidly ferry people to and from Mars, the Cyclers likely would have been kept in operation in one form or another.

Like the TMIS, both the *Armstrong* and *Aldrin* used nuclear thermal rockets for propulsion. The *Armstrong* was refueled while it was in orbit over Mars. A propellant station on the Martian surface produced the hydrogen used by the *Armstrong* and the landers that ferried astronauts to and from the Martian surface.

Because the *Aldrin* Cycler did not enter into a parking orbit over Earth or Mars, it did not have to execute nearly as many maneuvers as the *Armstrong* did. However, the *Aldrin* had to perform a series of propulsive maneuvers on each cycle in order to maintain its optimal Earth-Mars trajectory. Unmanned freighters resupplied the two Cyclers with food, water, and propellant periodically throughout their voyages between Earth and Mars. To conserve propellant, the freighters used low-thrust ion drives, which sometimes took years to rendezvous with a Cycler.

"She's our home for the next five months, so you better like her," Donner said.

As the Cycler loomed closer, the commander said, "Separating from lander now."

The command capsule and lander detached from one other; each spacecraft needed its own docking port on the *Aldrin*. As the distance closed between them and the *Aldrin,* the each executed preprogrammed maneuvers to position for docking.

"Lander separation complete," said Donner. "Preparing for docking with *Aldrin*."

The autopilot onboard the lander and capsule guided

223

the two spacecraft to the *Aldrin*'s airlocks. The commander would only take command if an emergency arose, which had yet to happen.

There was a slight popping noise as the docking latches of the capsule engaged with the docking port of the *Aldrin*, and mated the ships together.

"We're locked on," reported Donner. A few seconds later, the lander docked at the other airlock.

Donner focused his eyes on the airlock hatch like a laser, and waited patiently as the pressure in the capsule and Cycler equalized. At the instant the hatch opened, the time to act had come.

The charade ended, and Ask/Donner ordered the nanomachines inhabiting the crew to terminate their hosts. The four crewmembers died instantly, and Ask pushed himself through the hatch and into the *Aldrin*, making his way to the Cycler's command module as quickly as he could.

***

Johnson Space Center
Houston, Texas

The personnel in the Mission Control Center were a mixture of veterans and novices. Some had worked on dozens of space missions, and others were fresh out of college. All were sitting at computer consoles, analyzing data from the crew capsule and the *Aldrin*. A large screen dominated the wall at the far end of the control room, showing the crew in the interior of the capsule.

Everything had been going by the book since launch, but the Mission Control team was trained to respond quickly to emergencies. William Balch had been the flight director of more missions than he could count, and tried not to let himself grow complacent when things were going well. That did not make it any less shocking when the disaster began to unfold.

"Flight, Surgeon!" came a cry from the trenches of computer terminals. It was Rahul Senapati, the flight surgeon. "We have an emergency!"

"Surgeon, Flight," Balch replied, maintaining a calm demeanor. "What is it?"

"I've lost vital signs on four of the crew."

"What? How the hell..." His voice trailed off when he saw the crew on the large screen that was on the wall of the Mission Control Center. Their bodies were bumping into each other, clearly lifeless.

"Holy shit," he whispered. "Surgeon, Flight. What the hell happened to them?"

"I...I don't know. Their heart and respiratory rates just came to a sudden stop."

Balch looked at the large screen at the far wall of the control room, which showed the interior of the *Aldrin*, and Commander John Donner was rapidly making his way through the Cycler.

"Surgeon, Flight. How is Donner doing?" asked the flight director.

"His vitals are still going strong," reported the flight surgeon.

"*Aldrin*, Houston," said Josh Baban, the CAPCOM. "Commander Donner, please report. What has happened to the rest of the crew? They seem to have suffered some sort of medical emergency."

Balch waited anxiously for the commander's response, fighting to maintain his calm demeanor. In an unfolding emergency like this, it was crucial that he stay in control of both himself and the control room.

There was a time delay of five seconds between the *Aldrin* and Mission Control due to the vast distance separating Earth from the Cycler. Balch counted down those seconds. They felt like an eternity. His eyes kept

225

darting back and forth between the camera feed that was showing the seemingly dead crewmembers, and Donner, who was moving from one camera's field of view to another as he continued to traverse the *Aldrin*'s corridors.

Then the five seconds passed, and Donner continued to move through the *Aldrin*'s modules and refusing to respond. That was when Balch knew that there was something very wrong.

"Donner, please reply," said Baban.

The commander remained unresponsive.

"Donner, what the hell's going on?" Balch demanded, taking over the CAPCOM from Baban. "Respond, god damn it!"

***

Of all the baselines whose identities Ask had assumed since his awakening, he found impersonating Donner to be the most demanding. Ask had always conformed to the baselines' social norms for the sake of avoiding attracting unwanted attention, but always kept to himself, and never did anything more than what was necessary. Ask was able to remove memories that he did not desire. Whenever he obtained information from a baseline, he would purge all of their memories of family and friends, and only retain what he valued, which was their knowledge of mathematics, science, or engineering.

In order for Ask to get aboard the *Aldrin*, it was crucial for him to perfectly emulate all of the commander's interests and mannerisms with the utmost conviction, although there was no real risk of discovery if he failed to do this. If Ask acted any differently than Donner normally behaved, none of the baselines would ever suspect that Donner had been killed and his identity assumed by one with Ask's ability to alter his features and behavior to match his host.

The Cycler mission directors, however, might fear that

he was suffering from some sort of psychological episode, and be compelled to replace him with a backup. This made it prudent for Ask to retain all of Donner's memories and mimic him in every way. By now used to identity assumption, it was an annoyance he longed to be free of so he could return to his true self.

On the day prior to the launch, Ask's perfect charade even fooled those who knew the commander best, including Donner's family. None of this elicited even the slightest trace of remorse within his mind. He had never been very empathetic as a ruler of people, and Legion's betrayal that left him icebound for millennia removed any vestiges of it that he once might have had. All what mattered to him was getting to the Tabernacle, and he was willing to do anything that it took to reach that objective.

Retaining all of Donner's memories caused Ask to experience the emotions that the commander felt. And while Donner's emotions were powerful, Ask controlled them, never surrendering to them, such was his mental strength.

Prior to the betrayal, Ask had walked the Earth for centuries, experiencing more pain, hardship, and mental anguish than Donner or any other baseline whose mind he had absorbed. This was the wellspring of his indomitable willpower that no baseline thoughts could ever penetrate. If anything, controlling his response to Donner's emotions made Ask feel stronger. It was the mental equivalent of rigorous physical exercise to maintain muscle tone.

Using one of the Mars Cyclers to reach the Tabernacle was something Ask conceived once he realized that he would be unable to get onboard the *Intrepid*. All of the pertinent data about the Cyclers' trajectories, propulsion capabilities, and life support systems was publicly available on the internet. What he read made it abundantly clear that, even if he was able to seize control of the *Aldrin* to travel to

227

the Tabernacle, it would be a one-way voyage.

If the artifact were not the Tabernacle, then Ask would likely be condemning himself to certain death. Even with the nanomachines, Ask would die without the necessities of life: food, water, and breathable air. With careful rationing, Ask could live onboard the *Aldrin* for years. But with no hope of returning to Earth, these consumables inevitably would be exhausted. His only hopes of survival would be if the Bastion was the Tabernacle or if he could commandeer the *Intrepid*.

And there was another issue he had to face. Even if Ask managed to get onboard the *Aldrin* and alter its trajectory to rendezvous with the Tabernacle, the journey would take nearly sixteen months. The *Intrepid* would get there more than ten months earlier. But if Legion intended to share their power with these baselines rather than him, then it would not matter if he reached the Tabernacle before or after the crew of the *Intrepid*.

Despite the risks, Ask still believed that this was the proper course, the *only* course of action available to him in his quest to learn more of the truth behind Legion.

Ask moved through the *Aldrin*'s modules as quickly as he could. With the rest of the crew now dead, he would have to act quickly before Mission Control seized control of the Cycler. There were cameras on the capsule and the *Aldrin*, providing Mission Control with live video feeds. The time delay between Mission Control and the Cycler was only a few seconds, and by now Mission Control realized that something inexplicable had caused the deaths of the rest of the crew.

"Donner, what the hell's going on?" said a voice over the ship's intercom. The voice belonged to William Balch, the flight director. It had gone from a command to a desperate plea for him to respond.

"Respond, god damn it!"

Ask did not think the flight controllers at Mission Control would act quickly enough to stop him. Even though he was the only one still alive, they would not immediately assume that he had been responsible for the deaths of the other crewmembers, much less that he would attempt to alter the *Aldrin*'s orbit. Still, he had to hurry, for they would inevitably surmise that he was suffering a psychological breakdown and would lock out manual control as a safety precaution.

As soon as he reached the *Aldrin*'s command deck, Ask shut down the comm link between the Cycler and Earth, denying Mission Control video feed and telemetry. It also would prevent them from overriding manual controls and remotely operating the *Aldrin*'s systems. He then hurried back to the capsule, pushing aside the dead bodies of the slain crewmembers, and shut down the capsule's comm systems as well. He then moved back down the *Aldrin*'s corridors to the Mars lander and shut down its communication systems. As Ask anticipated, he was able to do all of this before Mission Control had a chance to react.

There was just enough propellant on the *Aldrin* for him to alter the Cycler's trajectory to rendezvous with the Tabernacle, and Ask knew it would be best if he burned as little of the Cycler's propellant as possible. To conserve some of the *Aldrin*'s precious propellant, he intended to fire the engines on the capsule and the Mars lander to provide additional thrust, and then discard them after their propellant was exhausted.

As he prepared to make these propulsive maneuvers, Ask was able to revert to his original appearance, the first time he had done so since leaving Antarctica. He had crossed the Rubicon, and now nothing would stop him from reaching the Tabernacle.

***

When the feed from the *Aldrin* ceased, chaos erupted

229

in the control room.

"Everybody shut the fuck up!" Balch screamed.

Never once had he lost a crew, and if this was to be the first time, the least he could do was find out exactly what had happened.

"GC, Flight. Lock the doors!" Balch barked.

His command brought a veil of silence down onto the control room. Everyone turned their full attention to him, waiting for him to give his next order.

Balch took a few deep breaths before continuing. "I know this is hard for you all to hear," his voice subdued, "and it's painful for me to say it, but we have to declare the crew is lost. And as for the commander..." His voice trailed off. What he had witnessed was simply too horrifying, too unbelievable, and he fought to maintain his composure. It was crucial that he prevent panic from taking hold of the MC staff. This was an unfolding disaster, but panicking would only make things worse.

***

"Do you have any explanation of what's happened?" Alan Prater asked.

"I really wish I did," said Balch. "I've been trying to wrap my head around this, but it doesn't make any damn sense at all."

"But if you had to make an educated guess, what would it be?"

"I...I don't know. Either Donner had a psychotic episode or he planned to do this. Either way that means we have a failure in our screening process. The only other explanation is we sent an imposter into space, and there's no way in hell that happened."

Prater nodded grimly. "You need to be prepared for damn near everyone to ask you the question I just did for the foreseeable future. The President is demanding answers, and so is everyone else."

Balch nodded. "I know."

"People aren't going to be content with not knowing what the hell's going on," said Prater. "They're demanding that we explain this, and when we can't, they'll make up shit and start another damn conspiracy theory. People are already saying that the aliens are behind this."

"Do...do you think it's possible this incident could be connected to the Bastion in some way?"

Prater looked at Balch with disappointment on his face.

"You can't be serious," the NASA administrator said sadly. "You think that the Bastion was able to take possession of Donner? That the aliens decided to only do this to him and kill the rest of the crew? And that for some reason they didn't do this with the *Intrepid*? Does any of that make any sense to you?"

"No," Balch admitted. "But nothing about this situation makes any sense. And the more I think about this, the less sense it all seems to make. It all seems like something straight out of a goddamn nightmare."

Prater sighed. "You're right about that... this is a goddamn nightmare. But we can't put stuff like that out because then we'd be feeding into people's fears. When we're faced with inexplicable circumstances like this, the most important thing we can do is keep digging and do our jobs."

"You're right," said Balch, nodding. "Our team is doing everything humanly possible and even that isn't enough. We're going to need help on this one."

"Already in progress."

The first thing the NASA administrator had done after learning what had happened onboard the *Aldrin* was order every available telescope the space agency controlled to be pointed at the Cycler. Without telemetry, getting a visual was the only way to get any idea of what was happening to the spacecraft.

Balch sighed. "I'm still just in shock about the whole thing," he said. "I mean, I was with Donner just a few days ago, right before the launch. Nothing seemed wrong with him. He seemed entirely normal."

"I was with him too," said Prater. "And I won't pretend to understand this either. But—"

He was interrupted by a knock at the door. The two of them turned to see Basant Kumar, the *Aldrin*'s flight dynamics officer.

"Umm…sorry to interrupt," Kumar sputtered nervously, "but we've learned a few things that you'll probably want to know about."

"What is it?" asked Prater.

Kumar stepped into the office, looking like the bearer of bad news.

"We have managed to obtain images of the *Aldrin* with several of the space telescopes," he said. "The command capsule and the Mars lander have been jettisoned, and we've also been able to determine that the *Aldrin*'s course has been altered. It's not going to Mars anymore."

"Do you know where it is going?" Prater asked.

Kumar nodded. "Based on our revised projections, yes."

Chapter 23

Mark was lifting weights in the *Intrepid*'s exercise room when his wristband buzzed. He wore it at all times, and had programmed it to go off whenever a message arrived for either him personally or as crew commander. Looking at the wristband, Mark saw that it was a message that the entire crew needed to see.

Mark went to the wall terminal and turned on the ship's intercom.

"Everybody report to the galley," he said. "We've just received a high priority message."

The commander swiftly made his way to the galley, where Ning and Oksana were already waiting for him.

"Do you know what's going on?" Ning asked Mark.

"No idea," Mark replied. He went to wall terminal and opened the message that had come in, but waited for Jed and Adam to arrive.

"So what's going on?" Adam asked upon entering the galley and taking his seat at the table.

"We're about to find out," Mark said and activated the communications link, bringing up the image of Miles Gilster. The IE president had an extremely grim expression on his face. That was all Mark needed to know that something dreadful had happened.

"There are a lot of people at NASA who will be mad at me for telling you this," said Miles. "But you were going to find out about it eventually, so I figured I might as well be the one to break the news to you. NASA is in crisis mode right now, so it might have been a while before the guys in Houston even thought about informing you of this."

Miles closed his eyes momentarily and took in a deep breath before continuing.

"This is as insane as it gets, so please bear with me as I

233

tell you what's going on." He paused, and took another deep breath. "As you know, the *Aldrin* made a flyby of Earth not too long after you guys left, and a Mars corps team was sent to rendezvous with it. The crew rendezvoused with the *Aldrin* earlier today. And once they did...the entire crew died, with the sole exception of Commander Donner."

Stunned silence fell upon the crew. Ning's eyes seemed to light up. A look of horror swept across the faces of Oksana and Adam, whiles Jed's face remained completely impassive.

This could not possibly be happening. Mark had met Donner before. Like just about everyone else in the astronaut corps, Donner had possessed a burning passion for space and fierce loyalty to those that served on crews with him. The loss of his crew must have devastated him.

"This has to be a joke," said Oksana, almost whispering.

"Miles would never joke about something like this," said Ning. "This shit is real."

"How did he the crew die?" Mark asked Miles.

The time delay between Earth and the *Intrepid* was now at two minutes, and would become more pronounced as the mission continued to progress.

"No one seems to know," his boss replied after the frustrating time delay. "The mission was going by the book until the command capsule docked with the *Aldrin*. And then...they just seemed to die without any cause. After that happened, Commander Donner shut down communications."

"Holy shit," Mark said.

"As much as I want to learn more about the Bastion, your safety is and always will be the top priority," Miles continued. "So if you guys think it's too dangerous to keep going, or if you'd rather help the Collins crew, I'll back you up one hundred percent. You're the ones putting your lives on the line, so you should be calling the shots. And I'll fight NASA to make them understand whatever you decide to do."

"Thank you very much for informing us," Mark said. "It's good to know that we can always count on your unwavering support. *Intrepid* out."

Mark sucked in a deep breath before turning away from the terminal to look at his crew.

"You're not seriously considering what he suggested, are you?" said Ning. "I mean about aborting our mission and going to Mars instead?"

Mark looked at Ning intently, and then to the rest of his crew, who were anxiously awaiting his answer.

"First things first," Mark said. "We need to jumpstart a conversation with Mission Control." He went to the comm link and opened the channel to the control room in Houston.

"Houston, *Intrepid*," said the commander. "Is it true that there has been a disaster on the *Aldrin* Mars Cycler? That her crew has been killed?"

It felt like an eternity before a response came. Benjamin Gonzalez, the flight director, appeared on the monitor. He looked as grim as Miles had.

"Miles just told us what he did," said Gonzalez. "I can't say I'm all that surprised he was the one to break it to you. He thought you guys needed to know about it right away. And I can't say I blame him either. Although for what it's worth, I would have told you myself, if I wasn't so caught up with all of the shit that's going on because of this." He paused momentarily. "Yes, everything that he told you is true. The *Aldrin* crew has died, with the sole exception of Commander Donner. We have no idea how they died.

"But there's one piece of information that I know

Miles didn't share with you guys, because we just figured this out for ourselves. Although everyone has been speculating about it since the incident occurred, and I'm sure that you guys have considered the possibility as well by now." He took in a deep breath. "The *Aldrin* has been inserted onto a new trajectory that will take it to the Bastion." He paused to let them all digest that.

"Is anyone here even remotely surprised to hear that?" asked Jed.

"I'm not," said Oksana.

"That being said," Gonzalez continued, "it is worth noting that the *Aldrin* won't reach the Bastion until about ten months after you guys get there. But after that, everything's up for grabs. We have to assume that Donner has suffered some sort of mental breakdown. So it's possible that he wants to ram the *Aldrin* into the Bastion in a suicidal attempt to destroy it. Or maybe he wants to rendezvous with the Bastion. Given the low amount of propellant he has, it's also entirely possible that he'll miss his target completely and sail off into oblivion. There's also the possibility the *Intrepid* could be his intended target. Some are saying that we should have you abort the mission and return to Earth. But he poses no threat to you right now, and won't for quite a while, if at all. So we've decided that your mission should proceed as planned."

"Thank you for keeping us in the loop," Mark said. "*Intrepid* over and out."

There was a period of tense silence after the transmission from Gonzalez ended.

"What about the Collins crew?" Adam asked, breaking the silence. "Should we help them like Miles suggested?"

Ning and Oksana looked horrified by Adam's words.

"What do you propose we do?" Jed said. "Take them back to Earth?"

"I think that goes without saying."

236

"We'd be abandoning our own mission," said Jed sternly.

Hearing Jed say that made Mark feel uneasy. They had barely begun their mission; to end it now, and to do so voluntarily, seemed absurd. It was all too obvious that Ning and Oksana felt the same way.

"We wouldn't be aborting," said Adam. "We would only be postponing it for a while. I don't see why we can't help the Collins crew and then go to the Bastion. We have plenty of room onboard to accommodate them for a voyage home. We could resupply in Earth orbit, and then go to the Bastion. That thing has been hanging around the Solar System for billions of years. It can wait a few more months or years, but the Collins crew doesn't have that option. I'm more than willing to put our mission on the backburner if that's what it takes to save them. And all of you should too."

"Mission Control thinks we should continue on to the Bastion," said Jed. "We'd be mutinying if we do what you're suggesting."

"I'm willing to do that if that's what it takes to save the lives of the Collins crew. And I'd like to think you all would be willing to do the same thing."

"If we do that," Jed said, "then the *Aldrin* and Donner will reach the Bastion before we do. And when we get back to Earth, they're not going to let us back into space ever again. A different crew will be sent to the Bastion, if it's even still there."

Jed's words caused a moral conflict in Mark. He wanted to get to the Bastion more than anything else. But he would forfeit that historic opportunity if they were to the Collins crew. But could he allow his fellow astronauts to die if he could save them?

"So what?" Adam snapped at Jed. "The lives of our fellow human beings are far more important than getting to the Bastion first."

"You heard what Gonzalez said," Jed argued. "Donner's intention may be to crash the *Aldrin* into the Bastion. If that is his intention and we abandon our mission, we may be giving up the chance of being able to study the artifact in its current state."

"I don't think that we should be concerned with that," Adam said. "The miners haven't made a dent in the Bastion after all this time. And don't forget that it's been getting pummeled by asteroid rock for billions of years anyway. So I'm willing to bet that the Bastion is either indestructible, or any serious damage that could be inflicted on it has already been done. Perhaps most importantly, if Donner does try to take out the Bastion in a kamikaze strike, then there's not a damn thing we can do about it. We have nothing onboard that we could use as a weapon to destroy the *Aldrin*. And if we go back to Earth to pick up any kind of arsenal, the *Aldrin* would end up getting to the Bastion before us. So like it or not, there's not a damn thing we can do to protect the Bastion from the *Aldrin*. All we can do now is hope that striking the Bastion isn't his intention."

"Which makes it all the more prudent that we get to the Bastion first and learn as much as we can about it in the event that it can be damaged or destroyed by the *Aldrin*," Jed insisted. "Having a narrow window of opportunity with which to study the aliens' technology makes it even more imperative that we fulfill our mission objective."

"If I had to choose between that and saving the lives of our fellow human beings, I'd choose the latter without a second thought," Adam retorted.

"The Collins crew is not in any danger of dying," said Jed. "They grow most of their own food, so it's unlikely they'll starve. The supplies that the *Aldrin* was carrying weren't vital for their survival. And it's not as though they're trapped on Mars forever. Hell, they weren't even going to use the *Aldrin* to get home. You know that. They weren't going to go back to Earth until the *Armstrong* returns to Mars in another eighteen months, and nothing about this situation has changed that. Barring an accident with the *Armstrong*, they will be going back to Earth just as they were scheduled to. If we abandon our mission to help them, we wouldn't be saving their lives. All we'd be doing is needlessly aborting both of our missions."

"Enough!" Mark snapped, ending the debate. "We at least need to talk to Collins about this."

He turned back to the computer terminal and opened a channel to the Mars facility.

"Collins, this is Commander Mark de Rijk of the *Intrepid*," Mark said. "We have just been informed of the situation regarding the *Aldrin* Cycler, and we felt compelled to check in on you and see how you're doing."

This was not the first time he had spoken to the Collins base commander. Since the objective of the *Intrepid*'s mission had been made public, Mark did not think there was a single person in the world's space programs from whom he had not received a message.

An image came up of Zhangyong Hou, the current commander of Collins base. Standing on either side of him were his four crewmembers. There was no visible window, leaving no indication that they were actually on the Red Planet. Not that a window would serve much purpose. The modules that made up Collins were buried underneath a layer of regolith to shield the crew from the high levels of radiation constantly bombarding the Martian surface.

Hou smiled broadly. "It's nice to hear from you guys. How's that fancy ship of yours holding up?"

"Pretty well, if I do say so myself," Mark said. "How about you guys? How are things going on your end, given the recent events?"

"We're as shocked as everyone else is about what's

239

happened with the *Aldrin*," Hou said following the time delay. "Her crew was among the bravest and most intelligent men and women I've had the pleasure of knowing, and I was looking forward to seeing them here. It breaks my heart that they perished and Donner has lost his mind. I can't believe it happened. It's horrible tragedy." He paused momentarily.

"But you must also be aware that our immediate situation hasn't been affected by this," Hou continued. "There haven't been any catastrophic equipment failures, and we've got plenty of food and water. And considering what's happened to the *Aldrin* crew, I don't think we have any right to complain about anything."

Mark felt his heart hammer as he thought again of the victims of the *Aldrin*. They had been brave men and women with a burning passion to explore the unknown. Now they had paid the ultimate price for that.

His own glory be damned! Mark would never allow more of his fellow astronauts to die, not when it was within his capability to prevent further tragedies.

"You know, we might be able to help you guys out," Mark offered. "We're not even halfway to Mars's orbit, and the *Intrepid* still has plenty of propellant remaining. We could probably alter our trajectory and arrive in Mars orbit rather than continue to the asteroid belt. Then you guys could evacuate, and we'd ferry you back to Earth. There's plenty of room onboard to accommodate you for the voyage home."

Adam was the only one who seemed to approve of Mark's offer. Even Ning glared at the commander angrily.

"Your offer is greatly appreciated," Hou replied, "but I really don't think you should do that. Like I said, we're not in any dire situation. Our greenhouse produces enough food to make Collins self-sufficient, and there's more than enough water in our stockpile. Plus there's even more water underneath the regolith we can tap into if need be. So all of our food and water needs are met for the foreseeable future. We should be able to get by easily enough without the resupply the *Aldrin* would have provided. So the fact of the matter is that we shouldn't have any trouble surviving until the *Armstrong* comes back. And it's not just that." He paused briefly. "The truth is that we don't want to interfere with your mission. We want you to get to the Bastion as soon as possible. Learn as much as you can about it and the aliens who built it. Your mission is vitally important to all of humankind. We'll be just fine here. Your assistance, while appreciated, is not required."

It did not surprise Mark to hear Hou say this. The astronaut corps was filled with people willing to put their lives at risk for the sake of space exploration. Still, Mark had felt all but obliged to make the offer and if Hou had accepted, he would not have hesitated to alter the *Intrepid*'s course to reach Mars.

"Roger that, Collins," Mark replied. "Please keep us updated on your status."

"Will do," Hou replied. "Take care *Intrepid*."

"You too Collins. *Intrepid* out."

Mark turned off the transmitter, and turned around to look at his crew. The conversation with Collins seemed to have alleviated their moods somewhat.

"Well congratulations, we're doing things your way," Mark nodded to Jed.

"You need not congratulate me," replied the mathematician drolly. "I raised my objection to rendering aid to the Collins crew solely due to my commitment to the success of this mission."

Mark looked at the rest of his crew. "So, we maintain our current trajectory. Let's continue with our preparations. There's a lot to be done before we get there."

As the crew dispersed, Mark considered the effect this

would have on the long-term exploration of Mars. During the long battles in NASA centers and Congress to fund the Cycler program, proponents had touted how the Red Planet would be permanently occupied by humans. Brian Trossel, the commander of the first crew that had traveled to Mars on the *Aldrin*, had been a particularly vocal advocate. Stepping onto the Martian regolith for the first time at the site that became the Collins base, Trossel had proclaimed that from that day forth, there would always be a human presence on Mars. It was the first step to establish humanity as a truly multi-planetary species.

The events of today, however, put all of that in jeopardy, at least temporarily. Once the Collins crew was evacuated on the *Armstrong*, Mars would be devoid of human life, just as it had been for its entire multi-billion year history before Thomas Aytche and the crew of the Tyr first set foot there. Now Trossel's vow of a permanent human presence on the Red Planet would be broken.

Soon the *Intrepid*, bearing Mark and his crew, would be passing beyond the orbit of Mars to travel farther than any humans had before. As that boundary was crossed, Mark still felt that the likely abandonment of Collins would be a terrible setback for the space program.

***

Sitting at his desk in the Oval Office, President Ortega prepared to address the nation and the world on the unfolding situation with the *Aldrin*. He could not afford to let anyone see him appear weak. It was in times of great crisis when it was most vital that he show strength and leadership.

During his time in office, Ortega had given speeches in the wake of tragedies such as school shootings, natural disasters, terrorist attacks, and military coups in other nations. Those had been the sort of crises that he had fully expected to deal with after he had obtained the presidency.

242

When calamity struck other nations, he carried on the United States' legacy by calling on his countrymen to offer humanitarian aid to those unfortunate enough to be affected. When tragedy befell America, he stressed the importance of national unity, and the need to work together as a country to support the victims of the disaster. While prepared for the inevitable natural or man-caused disaster, he fervently hoped they would be infrequent.

Tragedies in manned spaceflight programs were something that Ortega had hoped he would never have to face while in office. Despite the risks, redundant systems and careful preflight inspections had made accidents and fatalities extremely rare occurrences.

The years that Ortega's presidential predecessor had served had been marked by a huge upsurge in space activities. This had included the booming industries of asteroid mining, space tourism, and the establishment of the Collins base on Mars. Ortega's continued support of space programs was partly personal, but mostly political. The current operations in space generated trillions of dollars for the global economy. Disasters in the space industry could severely impact the revenue flow, not to mention damage him politically.

Still, he knew all too well that fatal disasters could strike manned spacecraft. He thought back to his time in elementary school when the space shuttle Columbia had been lost, and when he was in college a four-manned capsule that had burned up during reentry during its return from the International Space Station.

But this was different. This was the kind of tragedy that no one could have possibly expected or been prepared for. Everything about the situation defied what seemed possible. And that made it all the more terrifying.

"My fellow Americans," Ortega said into the camera, "I am sure that by now, most if not all of you are aware of the tragedy that has unfolded in space.

"I offer my condolences to the families of the *Aldrin*'s fallen crewmembers. All of them knew the danger that their loved ones faced when they first climbed into their spacecraft, but that does not make their loss any less of a burden to bear. I wish for all of you to join with me in mourning the loss of the *Aldrin* crew. Their deaths and the loss of the *Aldrin* constitute the worst disaster in the history of the space program.

"In addition, it appears that the lone survivor, Commander Donner, has altered the trajectory of the *Aldrin*. NASA experts now project the spacecraft has been rerouted to a path that will intercept the Bastion. If true, the *Aldrin* will arrive at the alien artifact in about sixteen months. Why the commander would put the *Aldrin* on this new trajectory is something that we cannot currently explain. But despite what many have speculated, there is no direct evidence suggesting that a connection exists between the Bastion and the disaster that has befallen the *Aldrin*. We still have no reason to believe that the extraterrestrials or their enigmatic device have any malevolent intentions toward our species. NASA is continuing to investigate this situation, and we must hope that answers are forthcoming.

"That brings us to the matter of what we can do, and unfortunately our options are very limited. No spacecraft will be able to rendezvous with the *Aldrin* while it remains on its current trajectory. Its loss, however, is entirely another matter when it comes to the Mars program.

"As of now, the crew of the Collins base on Mars is in no immediate danger. They have sufficient supplies to survive until the *Armstrong* arrives at the Red Planet again and can return them to Earth. Once they have vacated Mars, however, I am afraid that the Collins base may be abandoned for a time. NASA administrator Alan Prater has informed me that he and everyone else at NASA will work

244

tirelessly to ensure the continued safety of the Collins crew and determine how to continue the exploration of Mars after they have returned to Earth. The inception of the Cycler program came with the commitment to make the Red Planet the next frontier into which human civilization would expand. We cannot allow ourselves to abandon that endeavor. To do so would serve only besmirch the memory of the brave men and women who died today so far from their home planet.

"You may rest assured that, despite the severity of this tragedy, we will not allow it to curtail our ambitions in space. The loss of the *Aldrin* will not in any way disrupt the *Intrepid*'s mission to the Bastion. Commander Mark de Rijk and his crew are continuing on their mission of discovery. If anything, the loss of the *Aldrin* and her crew makes the mission of the *Intrepid* and all our other activities in space all the more meaningful, for there is no better way to honor the memories of fallen astronauts than by continuing our exploration of the cosmos. No matter how dark days like this are, our perseverance is vital to building a brighter tomorrow.

"Thank you and may God bless America and the world."

Chapter 24

Ashley Donner's eyes kept darting between the camera and Ryan Belue. She had thought that the only thing worse than having her husband leave her for five years on a voyage into space would be if he were to die on that voyage. But what was happening now was more terrifying than her worst nightmare. The entire world was speculating endlessly about John and whether the incident with the *Aldrin* was a horrifying crime that he had committed, or if it was just some terrible accident that no one could have prevented.

Ashley had never given an interview like this before; always eschewing the attention that could be focused on an astronaut's wife. But she had to forgo her disdain for the limelight now. She had to defend John now that the entire world questioned his competence and his loyalty.

"I'm joined by a very special guest today," Belue said, facing the camera. "Ashley Donner, wife of John Donner, the commander and only survivor of the *Aldrin* Mars Cycler. Thank you for taking the time to talk to us."

"I'm only here because I owe it to my husband," she said grimly. "I'm here to defend John's good name. It's just plain wrong for people to question his loyalty to his crew and the Mars program. John is most certainly not a murderer or a terrorist."

"I'm sorry about what you're going through," Belue said, trying to sound comforting. "I understand that this must be very difficult for you to talk about. We've spoken to the families of the other crew members, and they're as devastated by this as you are."

Ashely felt herself go cold at hearing him mention that. After the selection of the *Aldrin* crew, she had met with the other crewmembers' parents, siblings, children, spouses, nieces and nephews on numerous occasions, and kept in regular contact with them. But she had not spoken to any of them since the disaster had occurred. That would be far too emotionally draining. It had taken all of her strength to appear on this talk show, and she was not sure how much more of this she would be able to tolerate

"I know that you're as baffled as everyone else is on how John killed his crew, but—"

"Don't you dare say that my husband is responsible for this!" Ashley blurted, momentarily losing her composure. "John would never do this! You, of all people, should know that! You've interviewed him numerous times."

"I'm sorry Mrs. Donner. But with all due respect, you've seen the footage. Everyone has. Commander Donner can clearly be seen moving from camera to camera in the *Aldrin* turning them off and then to the capsule and lander to do the same. It's logical to assume..."

"Don't you dare say it!" Ashley's fingernails dug into her palms. "It's an insult to my husband and the space program! That kind of unfounded talk is disgraceful! John would never do anything to harm his crew. He couldn't. As you say, you've all seen the footage. Tell me what he did. One minute his crew was alive and the next they were dead. Did you ever stop to think that he turned off the cameras to keep the families from seeing it? Well did you?"

Belue dropped the sympathetic facade and assumed the confrontational demeanor he was known for. "That, Mrs. Donner, does not account for him hijacking the *Aldrin*!"

At that, Ashley lost it. "It's the goddamned aliens! They're behind this! You're all a bunch of fucking idiots if you can't see that!"

She broke down into tears.

***

Mark stood in his quarters, gazing out the window. There was nothing spectacular to see; the Earth had faded to a miniscule point of light, no more or less significant

247

than any of the other stars that filled their field of view.

He remembered the first time he had seen the Milky Way on a clear, moonless night at Craters of the Moon. Seeing that vast collection of stars and knowing that many of them were hosts to planets provided more fuel for Mark's desire to travel beyond the confines of Earth one day.

And now he wondered if any of the stars he saw had been the parent to the planet from which the builders of the Bastion originated. Or had that star long since been extinguished, and all of its photons passed beyond Earth eons ago? Was it possible they had even originated from another galaxy? These were but the most immediate questions he had regarding the aliens. What if these questions could not be answered by examining the Bastion, no matter how thorough their efforts were? And how far was he willing to go to get those answers? A high price had already been paid.

Mark thought of the demise of the *Aldrin* crew. He did not know how many times he had watched the chilling footage of Donner pushing aside the bodies of his crewmates as though they were bags of garbage, and his lack of response to the pleas of Mission Control.

It would have been wrong to keep the existence of the Bastion classified. But what if they had waited longer to reveal it to the world? Could they have waited until after the *Intrepid* had reached the alien artifact? Would Donner's crew have survived in that scenario?

No one could have possibly anticipated that *Aldrin* incident would be a consequence of the Bastion being public knowledge. But Mark still could not shake the uneasy feeling that the two might be connected.

"What are you looking at?"

Mark turned to see Ning standing next to him. Even when she was wearing the ordinary mission flight suit, she

248

was still extremely alluring. She always had been. She often invited herself into his quarters, something to which he had never objected.

"I'm not looking at anything in particular," he confessed. "I'm just thinking about what we've done. We've crossed a major point: we've gone beyond the orbit of Mars. We've now traveled farther from Earth than any other humans ever have before. And we owe that to you and your wonderful fusion drive."

Ning laughed. "You never seem to get tired of showering me with praise over that, although I do have to admit that I never get tired of hearing it."

"And you deserve every bit of it," said Mark. He looked down at the floor briefly, and his voice then took on a depressing tone. "But it also makes me think about what that means in relation to whoever built the Bastion."

Ning nodded. "I know what you mean," she said. "The aliens were able to traverse the stars, and they did it billions of years ago, quite possibly before life even emerged on Earth. And here we are just beginning to travel across our own solar system with our most advanced technology. Everything that we've accomplished as a civilization is completely insignificant compared to what they did in the distant past. And if the aliens' civilization still exists, they must be nothing short of godlike by now."

Mark laughed slightly. "Yes, that's it exactly," he said. "Great minds think alike."

"I concur. But it makes me wonder if they'll be willing to give us anything. If they do, it will be done entirely out of philanthropy, and not because they hope to gain anything of value from us. Or it could be done out of curiosity: they want to see how a species as primitive as ours will use or misuse it."

"If they made that kind of offer, would you turn it down?"

"No. But that could still be interpreted as being damaging for our culture. Because if they do offer us their knowledge and technology, that might destroy our impetus for innovation. We'd probably just read through their databases, knowing that we're so far behind that we can never make advancements beyond that technology."

"How is that any different than how we were educated?" Ning asked. "Did you develop calculus, or did you learn it because Newton had already developed it? Did you derive the Navier-Stokes equations from scratch, or did you learn them from books that other people wrote on fluid dynamics in a school that was built with someone else's money and resources? We stand on the mountains of knowledge left behind by all of those who came before us."

"I know that. But part of what motivated me all the years of life has been the hope that I could help to build upon the collective mountain of knowledge. And I like to think that I've succeeded, at least partly, by helping to design and test out different spacecraft systems. But I still fear that that won't amount to a tinker's dam compared to the aliens."

"You need to remember that they're not gods, no matter how advanced they may be," Ning said. "And it doesn't mean that human civilization as a whole is completely irrelevant. Neither is our mission. Sure, we may not be at the top of the galactic social pyramid, but we've done things that these aliens haven't done. The stuff that our culture has produced makes us unique."

"So if nothing else, we should take pride in the knowledge that our society has spawned things like Mozart, comic books, and cartoons?"

Ning smiled. "I'm already proud of those cultural achievements. And you should be too."

"And what if they have music so beautiful that it makes Mozart sound like nails on a chalkboard in comparison?"

Ning laughed briefly. "I don't think we need to worry about that too much," she said. "If they do have music, they would have developed it based on whatever they find to be most appealing to their range of hearing and what they perceive to be an engaging form of melody, harmony, and all other music structures. All of their arts will undoubtedly be far different than what we find pleasing. Everything about these aliens should make us more humble, but at the same time, we can't allow ourselves to be trapped in some sort of inferiority complex."

Mark sighed. "You're right, you're absolutely right." He looked out the window again. "I think it's just easy to think of one as being miniscule when we're out here."

"Well I might be able to help take your mind off of that."

"Oh?" Mark arched one eyebrow.

Ning grabbed Mark by the waist and pulled him toward her, and pressed her lips against his.

Mark smiled. "That'll do it."

He wrapped his arms around her, and they embraced passionately.

***

"To everyone tuning in now, I'm joined by one of the most notable men in history," Belue said into the camera. "Thomas Aytche."

"Thank you for inviting me," said Aytche.

The talk show host looked at the retired astronaut in awe. The elderly man was sitting directly at eye level with him. Even at his advanced age, Aytche still commanded respect, with eyes as sharp and clear as the day he had stepped onto Mars, and a mind that was razor sharp.

"It's always a privilege for me when you come on my show," said Belue. "Just being in your presence is an incredible honor that I'll always appreciate. For our viewers who don't know, and I'm sure that's very few, Thomas Aytche was the first man to walk on Mars."

"Thank you, John. While I will always be extremely proud and grateful for the honor to be the first human to set foot on Mars, it's important to remember that my mission was never just about me. It was always about making the Red Planet a second home for humanity. I never wanted my mission to be the only time that humans walked on Mars. That's why I've always done everything I can to support the Cycler program.

"And it's never been more important to support the program than now, when it's been struck by such a horrible tragedy. Just as President Ortega said, it's crucial that we not abandon our investment on Mars. It's also important that we learn the facts and the reasons behind this occurrence."

"That's something I've really wanted to ask you," said Belue. "I'm sure you saw my recent interview with Ashley Donner."

"Of course I did...and I agree with everything that she said."

"Really? You believe that the aliens took possession of the *Aldrin* and perhaps Donner himself and they are responsible for the deaths of his crewmates?"

"Of course. There really is no other way to explain it. I've known Donner for years, and I'd trust him with my life. If I were offered the chance to go back to Mars under his command, I'd take that offer in a heartbeat. He would never harm his crew, and there's no way in hell he suffered a breakdown. And even if he did, that still wouldn't explain what's happened.

"I know a lot of people will think it's crazy for me to say this, but the aliens are in control of Donner's body and mind. I have no idea why they've done this, but I know for a fact that they're behind it. I just hope that the same thing doesn't happen to the *Intrepid*."

Chapter 25

"Are you absolutely sure that you're okay?" Maria asked plaintively.

"Yes, I promise baby," Adam said. He always responded to Maria's messages as promptly as he could. He felt he had to, for it was now taking nearly fifteen minutes just for a communique to reach the *Intrepid* from Earth. "Things are fairly monotonous here. That's arguably one of the defining characteristics of long-term deep space missions."

They had spoken to each other every day since the *Intrepid*'s mission had begun. It was becoming more difficult and frustrating to carry on conversations with the time delay growing increasingly more pronounced. But they still enjoyed talking to each other, and made it part of their daily lives.

"I figured as much," Maria said when her response came after the time delay. "But I've been worrying about you more ever since what happened to the *Aldrin*. And now everyone is saying that the aliens are responsible for it. I know how crazy all of this sounds, but I can't stop thinking about it. And I can't help but feel that you're in even more danger now. I've lost so much sleep thinking about you. Oh God Adam, I just want you to come home."

Maria looked like she was ready to cry again, and Adam felt terrible for putting his wife through this emotional turmoil.

Prior to the *Aldrin* incident, there had not been a single manned space mission derailed due to one or multiple crewmembers suffering a debilitating mental breakdown. The astronaut selection process included rigid psychological screenings to weed out candidates who might be susceptible to them. Testing had subjected astronaut

254

candidates to intense physical and mental challenges to ensure that they could stand up to whatever challenges they might face on long-term, deep space missions. The Mars corps had the most demanding and selective of all the manned programs.

It was unthinkable that anyone selected for a nearly five year-long mission would suffer a breakdown only a few days into the voyage. To countenance a commander of such a mission to plan to murder his crew and hijack the Cycler was beyond insane.

Many people involved with manned spaceflight operations, from engineers to flight directors and astronauts, both active and retired, were refusing to speculate on if, far less how and why Donner might have committed this atrocity. Some with high public profiles, including Thomas Aytche, were now speaking out in support of what Ashley Donner had said: that John Donner had not been responsible for the disaster on the *Aldrin* at all, but rather the builders of the Bastion were behind it.

This served only to increase public fear. If the aliens could take possession of an astronaut, what was to stop them from controlling those on Earth? Maybe they would turn a president or prime minister into their puppet, and make them launch nuclear arsenals and annihilate the world's population.

"You really shouldn't worry about that, baby," Adam said as comfortingly as he could. "No one at NASA really believes that the aliens are behind what happened to the *Aldrin*. The current thinking is that Donner suffered a mental breakdown. Granted, they still don't have a clue how the crew died. But that doesn't mean that the aliens are behind it, and we shouldn't think that they are.

"You need to remember that really paranoid and imaginative people have been blaming aliens for just about everything, even before the Bastion was discovered. You know what I'm talking about: the wild conspiracy theories that the government has been hiding aliens for decades, or that every politician is an alien. These lunatics are convinced that every war, every economic downturn, every natural disaster, every one of the world's problems are part of some enormous conspiracy orchestrated by aliens. All of that is just crazy thinking, and you can't allow yourself to believe it."

There had always been a significant number of people who believed in such conspiracy theories. Some of the most ignorant were arguing that it would be best to ignore the Bastion and pretend that it simply did not exist. Fortunately, few voiced these opinions outside of internet forums, and the ones that were willing to speak more openly about it were almost always ignored. But their voices had grown louder in the wake of the *Aldrin* incident.

Even some politicians were using that rhetoric in their attempts to rally support from the populace in their bids for power. If powerful legislators and heads of state were to hold such opinions, it could pose a threat to the *Intrepid*'s mission and other ongoing deep space research projects. It was common sense and sound reasoning that kept people like that from gaining any significant amount of power. Despite a collective distaste for this fringe element, disasters like the *Aldrin* catastrophe gave them the attention they craved.

Still, Adam had to admit that not everyone who believed in alien conspiracy theories was completely ignorant or irrational. The fact that someone as intelligent as Aytche spoke out in support of Ashley Donner's claims about the Bastion builders being responsible for what happened on the *Aldrin* was enough to convince many people to believe that it was, at the very least, possible.

When Maria replied to Adam's last message, she looked somewhat less distressed. "Okay baby," she said

256

calmly. "I trust you. But I still worry about you, and I won't be able to put that fear aside until you're in my arms again.

"I'll defend you and your crew against any high-profile asshole that says something bad about you or what you're doing. It's the absolute least I can do for you. Another thing, I..." Her voice trailed off briefly. "I promise that if you don't come back, I won't have a breakdown like Donner's wife. I will be devastated if you die, but I promise that I'll be as strong as I possibly can be."

That made Adam smile inwardly. "I know you would, baby, but I don't intend to put you to that test. I promised you that I'd come back, and I fully intend to keep that promise."

***

Jed had been keeping to himself, even more than he had before the *Aldrin* incident. He never spoke to anyone except at the occasional crew gathering, and even then only when spoken to. He spent most of his time in his quarters, immersed in his own thoughts.

He continued to do the tasks that he was assigned on the ship. He ran routine tests on all of the equipment they were carrying to ensure everything was in proper working order and ready for use upon their arrival at the Bastion. Unlocking the Bastion's secrets was still of the utmost importance to him. He knew how crucial it was that he did his own part for this mission. Even with these responsibilities, he was still able to make time to continue working on new mathematical theorems that had constituted the bulk of his career.

An electronic buzz at the entrance to his quarters pulled Jed from his thoughts, and he looked up to see Oksana standing in the doorway.

"Can I help you with something?" he asked the physicist.

"I was just wondering what you were up to," she replied.

"Working on a number of things, like I usually am," he said simply.

Oksana smirked as she walked closer to the mathematician. "Sounds like fun."

"Your sarcastic tone does nothing to detract from the importance of what I do."

Oksana giggled girlishly. "I wasn't trying to talk down about you or your work."

"Intentions are irrelevant," Jed snapped. "What matters are the ramifications brought about by your words and actions. It is abundantly clear that you don't think what I'm doing is worth the time I devote to it."

"That's not it at all! I'm just saying that there are other things you can do with your time other than work incessantly," Oksana demurred.

"We exist for only the briefest moments in the lifespan of the universe. Time is one of the greatest commodities we are given. I can think of no better way to spend that invaluable resource than by expanding one's knowledge. That is why I have never strayed from my path of pursuing knowledge, not to mention that it's the entire reason why I am on this mission."

"Okay, I respect that. But you don't need to lock yourself in here all the time."

"Solitude often helps me concentrate. The mind is where all great discoveries are made, especially in pure mathematics."

"I've always felt that mathematics is only meaningful if it describes something in the physical universe."

"That is a very limited perception. The universe is finite. Mathematics is not. What better intellectual exercise is there than to construct mathematical systems and concepts that transcend the physical reality that otherwise

258

confines us? Furthermore, it may affect the motivations of whoever built the Bastion and how successful our mission is."

"What do you mean by that?" Oksana asked curiously.

"Are you familiar with the works of Kurt Gödel?"

"Yes. Didn't his theorems prove that it's impossible for mathematics to ever be fully completed?"

"Yes. Any mathematical formulation developed will contain statements that cannot be proven or disproven. This necessitates a larger formulation to prove or disprove those statements, but that formulation will have its own unprovable statements that require an even larger formulation to be proven or disproven. This branches off into an infinite tree of mathematical logic.

"I do not like speculating about what purpose the Bastion may serve. But it is safe to assume that they would have discovered the incompleteness theorems long ago, and have been exploring the infinite limbs and branches of that logic tree ever since."

"So you think the aliens just sit around developing new mathematical systems?"

"That's what I do. And I find it to be very fulfilling. It goes without saying that any advanced society that continues to thrive will devote at least some of its resources to the eternal pursuit of mathematical formulation."

"Okay, you're probably right about that. But that doesn't mean you need to be so cold all the time. There are things to enjoy in life other than studying mathematics."

"I beg to differ. I feel that there is no greater way to spend that limited time we have than by learning as much as possible. I'm putting my life at risk now, and that is something I do as part of my lifelong striving in the pursuit of knowledge."

Oksana walked closer, and took his hand in hers. "There are other things we can enjoy during our short

259

period of existence. For one thing, we can enjoy each other."

Jed looked at her with bewilderment. "Are you making a proposition?"

She laughed. "Nothing gets past you, does it?"

Now it was Jed who laughed. "You're wasting your time," he said. "I have no interest in copulating with you."

Oksana released her hand from Jed's in utter shock. "What? Are you serious?"

"I always am."

She cocked an eyebrow. "Are you not interested in women? I can't think of any other reason why you'd turn me down."

"It's not just women that I'm not interested in. I have no interest in any form of sexual activity."

Oksana was dumbfounded. "What the hell is wrong with you?"

"Nothing is wrong with me. I just happen to be asexual. Do you really find that to be so unusual?"

"Quite frankly, yes, I do."

"Have you never known an asexual individual? Or is it that you've never been turned down before?"

"Both," Oksana snapped.

Jed chuckled. "Then you should at least be thankful that I've provided you with a new experience by being the first asexual individual you've met."

"You're insane."

"Accusing someone else of madness is often the first thing they resort to when confronted with a profoundly different way of perceiving things. This is almost always the reaction one feels when they meet someone with a sexual orientation they find to be disturbing or unusual for whatever reasons they may have. And it speaks volumes to your character that you accuse me of being mentally ill because of my asexuality."

"I wasn't accusing you of that."

"Oh, but you did, only a scant few seconds ago. Your fear at being accused of having a bigoted mindset and your need to convince yourself otherwise is so overwhelming that it causes you to contradict yourself without even realizing it."

"I'm not afraid of anything of the sort. You see things that aren't there."

"I see perfectly well. And I'm able to do so because I do not allow my emotions to blind me."

"So I'm blind. But at least I'm not a narcissist like you."

"Now you resort to the fallacy of moral equivalence." Jed laughed before continuing. "And you really think I'm so petty as to warrant being called a narcissist? I'm afraid you've got me all wrong."

Now Oksana laughed. "I doubt that. You're about as narcissistic as they get."

"Not at all. I'm just here to learn more about the Bastion. I like to think that I'll see something that anyone else in my position would otherwise have missed in the data that's gathered, and that I'll have a better idea of where to direct our research efforts. But don't think I'm narcissistic enough to believe that I'm the only one who could do this task.

"The Bastion is a great representation of just how little we know about the cosmos. It shows us that there's someone else out there who knows a shitload more than we do about damn near everything. And there is no doubt in my mind that I'm as dumb as a mentally retarded monkey compared to them. So whatever your opinion of me may be, do not think for one second that I'm a narcissist."

Oksana stared at Jed in silence for a brief moment. Then she turned and walked out of his quarters, leaving him alone with his thoughts again.

***

Sitting in front of his computer in his quarters, Adam checked the status of the program that was comparing the genomes of ten different cephalopod species, which continued to progress at a snail's pace. His laptop was incredibly puny compared to the supercomputers he used for this research back on Earth. But even if his laptop couldn't do a whole hell of a lot, it was still contributing to this research endeavor. Reconstructing the genomes of ancient, extinct species was one of the most computational intensive undertakings ever pursued, and every computer that could provide additional computing power was a valuable asset. Adam would transmit his results back to his colleagues on Earth once his laptop completed its computations, knowing he would have made a small but worthwhile contribution to the ongoing research into the genetic history of evolution.

Millions of personal computers all around the world contributed to this effort by running a much less sophisticated version of the program Adam was using. People were free to download the program from the internet, taking advantage of the processing power of a personal computer that would otherwise sit idle. Distributed computing had been in use for decades, and was a valuable tool for research projects that required huge amounts of computational power.

Research efforts like the one Adam was engaged in were a natural byproduct of the explosion in genome sequencing of both species and individuals and the ever expanding global genetic database. By comparing the genomes of different species, it was possible to reconstruct the DNA sequences of the ancestral species from which they had evolved.

The genome for the common ancestor of humans and chimps was the first to be reconstructed. Soon afterward

262

came the reconstructing of the genomes belonging to the progenitor species of all the primates. Then there came the genomes to the so-called father species of horses, cats, whales, and other placental mammals. By comparing the genomes of all known living species of placental mammals, it had been possible to construct the genome for the progenitor of them all, an unassuming opossum-like creature that had lived tens of millions of years ago.

Adam found it to be one of the most beautiful and elegant techniques to explore the unity of life that had ever been developed. Because by carefully examining the DNA of all living organisms, it would inevitably show the convergence of animals, plants, fungi, bacteria, and all other forms of life.

For the time being, he was focused on constructing the genome of the common ancestor of cephalopods. It was a long, complicated process that would likely take years to complete.

There was talk of using artificial wombs to grow specimens of the ancestral species whose genomes had been reconstructed. Resurrecting extinct species had already been done before with passenger pigeons, woolly mammoths, and thylacines, a process that had been called de-extinction.

Adam had contributed to those de-extinction projects earlier in his career, and had been motivated both by his fierce passion for genetic research, and as a way to atone for past wrongs committed by the human species. Throughout his life, Adam had felt somewhat ashamed for the damage that humanity had done to the environment and all the species that had been driven to extinction by mankind. He was pleased that he could do his part in reversing that damage by helping to restore lost biodiversity.

Bringing back the mammoth and thylacine had been

comparatively easier than what would be required to resurrect ancestral species. For one, the complete genomes for those species had been obtained from fossils and museum specimens, which ensured that the specimens that were created through de-extinction efforts actually were authentic members of the original species.

If a creature was grown from a reconstructed ancient genome, however, there could be no guarantee that it was identical to the ancestral species in question. Even if the reassembled ancient genome was ninety-eight percent identical to that of the organism in question, that two percent error would likely result in nihilistic medical flaws. Even if there were no medical issues with the specimen, the two percent difference was enough to make the specimen grown in a lab an entirely different species from the actual ancestral species. A two percent genetic difference is all that separates humans from chimpanzees. Without a living specimen of the ancestral species with which to compare it, there would be no way to determine with complete certainty if the genome that was constructed was identical to that of an actual species that existed in the distant past. Any organism produced this way could very well be the first of an entirely new species outside of the evolutionary chain.

Even so, Adam knew this fact would not deter people with the finances and resources to create such organisms. There was a growing market for creating, breeding, and selling grotesque genetic chimeras. The first and most popular of such genetically engineered creatures were genetically engineered chickens whose ancient, dormant genes had been activated, giving them limited dinosaur features like long tails, claws at the end of their wings, and snouts loaded with sharp teeth.

There were still the dreamers who hoped to clone dinosaurs. This presented many challenges, not the least of which was the fact that dinosaurs disappeared so long ago that any DNA from fossilized specimens had long since fully degraded. Since well-known species like the tyrannosaurus and triceratops had no living genetic descendants, it would be impossible to reconstruct their genomes with the accuracy that was expected to be in the genomes of reconstructed species like the ancestors of mammals and the cephalopods. Still, the fascination with dinosaurs would likely create a demand that someone would try to fill.

Adam wasn't sure how he felt about an entire species being created whose sole purpose might be little more than an exotic collectible to showcase some eccentric multi-billionaire's prodigious wealth.

There was still great debate about what to do with species that had been resurrected. The successful efforts at de-extinction had resulted in only a handful of specimens, and they all lived in zoos, research facilities, or on private estates owned by the wealthy.

Many hoped that as artificial wombs and other related technologies advanced and the costs associated with them went down, it would lead to the production of enough individuals of formerly extinct species to sustain a breeding population. But if that were to happen, then releasing a breeding population into the wild would be a highly controversial issue. Some believed it would restore ecological balance that had been lost as a result of the extinctions. Others thought it would disrupt whatever new ecological balance may have been achieved since the species' demise.

But that was an issue for the future. For the time being, Adam would continue his research as best he could. Continuing his genome work during voyage kept Adam's skills toned. This was as vital to his mental acuity as the rigorous physical exercises he subjected himself to in the gym each day was to muscle maintenance. And he was somewhat fearful that this was the only biological research he would be doing while he was onboard the *Intrepid*.

Adam seriously doubted that there would be any biological aliens housed within the Bastion. If there were, it would be because the aliens had some sort of a suspended animation system that could preserve biological tissue for billions of years. That seemed unlikely to him, but then again he could not rule it out. Or maybe the Bastion held a microcosm of the alien's home planet. By now it would have evolved into drastically different organisms utterly unlike anything that might have existed on their ancestral home world.

But even if there were no biological aliens waiting for them at the Bastion, Adam still would have come onboard the *Intrepid*. This was the opportunity of a lifetime, and if it meant having to give up a few years of devoting all his energy to the research he did on Earth, then so be it. He could still collaborate with his colleagues on Earth on this and the other projects he was involved with, so it was not as if he was committing career suicide.

Adam's ability and expertise to sequence and compare so many different genomes was a vital capability in the event that there were biological aliens at the Bastion. If they found biologicals there and were able to obtain genetic samples, one of Adam's first tasks would be to determine if they had DNA and if it shared similarities with DNA from Earth organisms. This would help answer the lingering question of whether or not the beings who had built the Bastion were truly alien in origin.

Many had wondered if the builders of the Bastion had seeded Earth with life from their home planet eons ago. It might have been little more than bacteria, which had then gone on to evolve into the vast tree of life that had taken root on Earth. If that were the case, then the builders of the

Bastion were distant genetic cousins of Earth life as opposed to truly biological aliens.

Adam thought that was unlikely. If the aliens had intended to propagate the Solar System with life from their home planet, then they could have terraformed Earth, Venus, and Mars, and built gargantuan space habitats using the asteroids and comets. And yet there was no evidence that anything of the sort had happened in the entire history of the Solar System. Why the builders of the Bastion had not exploited the resources of the Solar System was one of only many questions that this expedition sought to answer.

Adam hoped that the Bastion builders were not genetic cousins of Earth life. For if they were, then they would not answer the question of whether or not a second genesis had occurred elsewhere in the cosmos. It would still be incredible that another intelligent species to which all Earth life owed its lineage had evolved on another world and traveled across the stars billions of years ago. But he would always wonder if true aliens existed somewhere else in the vastness of the universe.

He also wondered how a dramatically different evolutionary history would impact human attempts at communication with the builders of the Bastion. It had been known for decades that dolphins and whales had complicated forms of communication, but cetologists still had no idea what they were saying to each other, or if what they were saying was as remotely complicated as human languages. That inability for interspecies communication existed even though they originated on the same planet and shared a common ancient ancestor.

In contrast, human beings shared no kinship whatsoever with the Bastion builders if they were truly biological aliens. They might simply be far too different for any meaningful dialogue to occur between the two cultures.

Jed and Oksana, on the other hand, seemed fairly

confident that communication with the aliens was possible through the shared understanding of the fundamentals of physics and mathematics. Adam hoped that they were right.

As he continued to watch the program run, he was interrupted by the buzzing at the door announcing a visitor, and turned from his computer to see Oksana standing at the entrance of his quarters.

"Oh hey," he said to the physicist. "What's up?"

Oksana looked a little upset. "Nothing much," she said as she walked toward him. "I was just wondering what you were up to."

"I'm just continuing to work on the projects I'm involved with back on Earth. Same old stuff."

"Which is what exactly, if you don't mind me asking?"

"I'm reconstructing the genome of the progenitor species of cephalopods."

"Ah, a Lazarus project. So what are you trying to grow? An ammonite?"

"It's only a gene mapping program. We're not trying to grow it in a vat. We're nowhere near ready to attempt that anyway. I'm just trying to put its genome together. And with the error margins I have to deal with, I'm afraid that if it ever was grown in a lab, it would be less Lazarus and more Frankenstein's monster."

Oksana nodded. "Right. Of course." She walked around Adam's quarters and groaned.

"Something wrong?" Adam asked.

The physicist took in a deep breath. "The truth is that I was wondering if you might like some company."

"I see." Adam got up from his computer. "Am I the first one you've propositioned?"

She hesitated for a moment that dragged. "No."

Adam nodded. "I can't say I'm all that flattered at being your silver medal choice. Or am I the bronze?"

Oksana groaned loudly. "Are you really going to bitch

about that?"

"I'm not bitching. I'm just curious. So, what's your rationale for propositioning me?"

"Well if you really want to know, I'm a human being with urges, and keep in mind that there aren't that many options available on this ship."

Adam laughed sardonically. "You continue to flatter me."

Oksana groaned again. "Look, if you're going to give me that attitude, I can always just entertain myself without needing you or anyone else."

"Now why would you do that? It's always a lot more fun and enjoyable when you have a partner."

Oksana smiled slightly and walked closer to him. "I concur."

Adam got up from his seat and walked right up to Oksana.

"Why the sudden aggressiveness?" he asked her.

"Something unforeseen could happen to us at any time. A mishap, mechanical failure, or maybe we could get attacked by the Bastion when we get there, or sometime before then. So we don't know how much longer we're going to be alive. Why not make the most of the time that we have to be alive?"

"Carpe diem."

"Exactly."

"May I ask why you didn't come to me first?"

"I wasn't sure you'd be interested. And I thought that you might get offended if I did approach you. After all, aren't you married?"

"I am. But my wife and I have an open relationship." Adam grinned widely before continuing. "We're both allowed to play with whomever we want whenever we want."

Oksana returned Adam's grin. "Lucky you."

"You're not the first one who's told me that."

Oksana walked closer to Adam. "It's too bad your wife isn't here to join us."

"I agree. She would enjoy you immensely, and I know for a fact that you'd love her."

Oksana continued to smile. "Maybe when we get back to Earth, we can all have some fun together."

"I'd like that very much."

Adam placed his hands on Oksana's cheeks and kissed her deeply.

Chapter 26

Six months after leaving Earth orbit, the *Intrepid* began its final approach to the Bastion. The entire crew was on the command deck, the first time they had all been here together since they had departed Earth.

The absence of stars was the only thing that enabled them to see the artifact.

Everywhere Mark looked, there were stars, except of this single completely black patch. It wasn't that it was simply devoid of stars; it seemed as though all light was falling into this pit of darkness, as if it was a hole in the very fabric of the universe.

Mark had seen countless pictures and hours of footage on the Bastion that IE's miners had transmitted. Still, it was unnerving to actually see it in person, even from this distance. And that unnerving feeling seemed to grow increasingly larger as the *Intrepid* drew closer to cold darkness that marked the position of the artifact.

As the spacecraft continued its approach, Mark could that the infinite blackness of the alien artifact was broken in a few places by faint glimmering from the IE robotic miners that had removed the asteroid rock that had encased the Bastion for until billions of years.

Ordinarily, IE would direct its miners to a new target once they depleted the resources of any asteroid they had been mining, but Miles had refused to redirect even one of them away from the Bastion. Instead, he had ordered propellant shipments to be delivered to them on a regular enough basis to keep them fully operational. He didn't care that this reduced the amount of valuable minerals that otherwise would have been shipped back to Earth. He thought of it as an investment; if there were even a slight chance that they could discover something new about the Bastion, it would be well worth keeping the machines

271

positioned here. Maybe one of them would record something that the others missed, or incite some kind of reaction from the alien artifact. Perhaps they would be able to assist the crew of the *Intrepid* in some way. Regardless, Miles felt that it was worth a slight drop in IE's profits.

Mark kept his hand on the joystick, ready to shut down the autopilot and take control were some emergency to arise at this crucial phase. Some theorized that the Bastion had some sort of detection system, and would surely retaliate in response to the arrival of a spacecraft as large as the *Intrepid*. If it did, Mark did not think there was much he would be able to do to save his spacecraft and his crew. Nevertheless, he was prepared to act.

The tension on the command deck was wasted. Nothing happened as the *Intrepid* completed its rendezvous. The Bastion's mass was too small to offer useful orbits, and Mark brought the *Intrepid* to within one hundred meters of the Bastion's surface until their relative velocities were zero. The attitude control thrusters would make periodic adjustments to maintain position during their stay here.

"Mission Control, this is *Intrepid*," Mark said. "We have successfully rendezvoused with the Bastion. All systems continue to operate nominally. We will now begin preparations for extravehicular activity."

He then undid his straps and pushed himself out of his control seat. The vast distance between Earth and the Bastion meant there was a twenty-minute delay before Mission Control would hear Mark's radio transmission. Since their response would take an additional twenty minutes, waiting to hear back from them would just be a waste of time.

The team had been trained to operate as independently as possible from Mission Control, so Mark opted not to delay the EVA. Even though they were going to be here for

272

months and possibly years on end, Mark wanted to begin the examination of the Bastion right away.

"All right, we're here," Mark said to his crew. "Let's get to work people."

They all got out of their acceleration couches and left the command deck, each of them as eager as Mark was to begin their research efforts.

***

Mark, Jed, and Ning donned their spacesuits and made their way into the *Intrepid*'s airlock. Adam and Oksana would stay onboard the *Intrepid*. Mission parameters dictated that a minimum of two crewmembers remain aboard the spacecraft at all times.

When the airlock depressurized and the hatch opened, Mark confirmed the maneuver with the two ship-bound crewmembers. "We are exiting the airlock now," the commander reported, and pushed himself out of the *Intrepid* and into the black void.

The cameras in the airlock and on the exterior of the *Intrepid* documented their every move. Still, Mark knew that it was important to describe the away team's actions as explicitly as he could during the exploratory excursion. He had done this for EVAs (Extravehicular Activity) on every mission he had commanded and his descriptions were precise and detailed.

The unique circumstances of this mission rendered this this all the more prudent. Nearly everything they were doing was an historical first. This spacewalk was the farthest from the Earth ever undertaken, and soon, he and his team would be the first humans to make physical contact with an artifact built by an extraterrestrial civilization.

Mark gazed into the light-swallowing darkness before him. Even though he was scarcely closer to the Bastion than he had been to it on the *Intrepid*'s command deck, the alien artifact seemed stranger...even eerie. Mark knew logically that was absurd. If the Bastion did represent some sort of threat, it was highly unlikely that being aboard the *Intrepid* offered much, if any more protection than spacesuits did.

Still, Mark could not shake the eerie feeling growing within him. He mentally suppressed it and fired the thrusters on his Manned Maneuvering Unit (MMU) that propelled him toward the Bastion with Ning and Jed, slightly to his left and right, following close behind. There was a slight crackle on the receiver on *Intrepid's* observation deck as Mark's voice activated the VOX.

"We are making our approach to the surface of the Bastion now."

"Roger that," came Adam's reply as he watched the trio's progress on multiple high-resolution screens.

The *Intrepid's* crew had trained extensively for this, with nearly every action during the first extravehicular activity preplanned. During the initial excursion, the primary goal was to set up the sensor suite on the Bastion's surface. Subsequent EVAs would be planned around the data those sensors gathered.

Although Mark and his crew had never doubted the importance of physically inspecting the Bastion, many involved with mission planning had vehemently opposed it. There were those who thought that the aliens might take offense to the trespass, triggering a retaliatory action. Others argued that a human the crew crawling around the Bastion would be comparable to having the aliens crawling on the Statue of Liberty, the Great Pyramid, or the Taj Mahal. Such arguments were shared by those who simply could not control their fear and those who worried that the aliens very well might consider human existence as offensive.

The simple fact was that there was no way of knowing

what might be considered culturally taboo by the aliens. Logic seemed to dictate that having a crew of astronauts probe the Bastion with sensors and explore its surface presented no more or less risk of offending the aliens than any other action.

Given that IE's miners had scraped away much of the accreted asteroid rock and even attempted to probe the artifact with their drills and elicited no detectable reaction, this argument seemed to be the most credible. If the Bastion contained some form of artificial intelligence, then it would surely was capable of recognizing that such sophisticated robotic machines were the product of intelligent life. Of course it was entirely possible this AI chose not to react to them as a way to entice the miners' creators to come to it.

So many possibilities, so very few concrete answers.

That was their purpose in for traveling all this distance: to unlock the secrets of the Bastion and its builders if possible. And now Mark, Jed, and Ning were about to conduct their very first experiment on the Bastion: determining if it exhibited any response to organic lifeforms.

"Wu, Storey, hold this position," Mark ordered once the trio was within fifty meters from the Bastion.

"Roger," Jed acknowledged.

"Decelerating," Ning said.

Ning and Jed fired the thrusters on their suits, bringing their relative velocities to zero while Mark continued on to the Bastion's surface.

Since Mark was the mission commander, no one had doubted that he would be the first to touch down on the surface of the alien artifact. It was for the protection of the crew that he was the first. Had there been solid data that the artifact was benign, it would have mattered little to Mark who went first. He would not countenance risking one of their lives, however, when there was no way of knowing how or if the Bastion would react. The thought that being first to set foot on the artifact was in itself an historic moment was secondary in importance.

The ethereal blackness of the Bastion loomed before Mark as he neared the surface. Part of him feared the darkness would swallow him up like it did every photon that bombarded it. And that feeling of unease, that there was something very wrong about the alien artifact, only grew the closer he came to the surface.

Thoughts crowded his mind. Was he experiencing the same kind of bewilderment that a dog or chimpanzee might have felt when they examined a machine manufactured by humans? How baffled would an ant be at a nuclear reactor? Or what if, like the ant, he simply lacked the capability to understand its function and the purpose it served? But he would not turn back now, not when he was so close after having come so far.

"I'm about to make contact with the Bastion," Mark reported.

As he descended to the black surface, he thought of the sheer number of people back on Earth that must be viewing this unfolding historical event. More than half a billion people had watched Neil Armstrong take the first steps onto the lunar surface. Six decades later, four billion people had watched Thomas Aytche step off the ladder of his lander and become the first human to set foot on Mars. Aytche's first steps had attracted the single largest audience for a televised event in world history, and Mark had been among them. At the time he doubted there would ever be a future space mission that would garner anywhere near that level of public interest.

Once the *Intrepid* left Earth, however, the public's attention had been transfixed on their mission in a way unparalleled by any other space mission. That attention was likely to be at its highest level now that Mark was about to actually touch the alien artifact. He could not help feeling the pride that came with the accomplishment, and no matter how hard he tried to suppress it, the thought of the billions of eyes back on Earth watching him now was thrilling. Then it struck him that audience would not see the event until twenty minutes after it occurred. A single thought jolted him back to reality; he could be dead by then if the Bastion reacted hostilely to him.

Mark also considered that the eyes belonging to the ones who had built the Bastion might be watching, assuming they had optical sensory organs similar in function to human eyes. Would they react to his presence? Could they differentiate between a mechanical object like the miner and an animate object like himself? After all, the suit was not biological. It was an articulated hard suit made of carbon fiber composites that made it light and agile as well as resistant to micrometeoroids and radiation. Would the Bastion have some way of determining the organic lifeform it contained?

Unceremoniously, he touched down chest first onto the surface. He instinctively tried to grip the surface, but he immediately found it was pointless; the instant his body made contact with the Bastion, he lost all momentum, just as the robotic miners had. It was the strangest sensation he had ever experienced.

He took a few deep breaths. While it was a relief that the Bastion had not exploded or displayed any other undesirable reaction to his landing, Mark felt disappointed and somewhat disconcerted that the artifact had not reacted at all.

Mark righted himself slightly. Face to face with the utter blackness of the artifact, he could not help thinking of the incredible places he had visited in his lifetime. Extraordinary places on Earth like Yellowstone, Mount

Everest, the Great Barrier Reef, the Grand Canyon, and countless others, not to mention the surface of the Moon. No photograph or footage of any of those places could ever compare to the experience of actually being there. In many ways, it was no different now, yet there was also something dramatically different about this. All of the remarkable places Mark had been to on Earth and the Moon had been filled with a majestic beauty forged over millions of years by geologic forces, or by life's drive to adapt and thrive in different environments.

The Bastion stood in stark contrast to all of that. Mark did not feel like he was looking at the surface of a physical object. It was almost nothingness, like he was looking into a hole in space-time itself. It did not seem possible that this was actually an artifact that had been forged by a civilization, no matter how advanced it may have been. The Bastion seemed out of place, like it did not belong in the same universe as life, planets, stars, galaxies, or matter itself.

He recognized the feeling for what it was: an irrational, primitive fear that arose from confronting something far beyond that found in the environment for which humans were adapted. But it was a fear that Mark could control.

He thought again of the historical significance of this moment, and that historically significant words were expected from each human who first set foot upon a new celestial body.

The first words that Neil Armstrong had spoken upon stepping off the *Eagle* had become one of the most famous lines spoken in all of human history. *"That's one small step for man, one giant leap for mankind."*

Aytche had echoed that same spirit when he stepped off his lander and onto the surface of the Red Planet. The words he uttered taking those steps had become as immortal as those of the Apollo 11 commander.

278

"Armstrong took a small step. We have made a giant leap."
So many people on Earth were saying that the *Intrepid*'s mission would be remembered for all of human history with even greater regard than the Apollo 11 and Ares missions. So for better or worse, Mark knew the words he spoke when he touched down on the Bastion could very well be remembered long after the words of Armstrong and Aytche had faded into obscurity. Mark knew he would be expected to say something profound. He hoped what he had rehearsed would measure up.

Mark took a deep breath before speaking. "We have come here in the hope of learning more of our brethren from across the stars. We do so in the spirit of peace and, should we meet those who built this artifact, we extend to them our hands in friendship on behalf of all humankind."

None of his crew said anything; they all understood and respected their commander's mark in history. Having played his mandatory role for the history books and realizing that he should be the one to break the silence, Mark resumed standard mission communique.

"There are no imperfections in the surface that I can feel," he said as he cautiously moved his right hand along the smooth surface. "I seemed to have lost all of my kinetic energy as soon as I hit the surface. This confirms the data we received from the sensors on the miners.

"I'm also feeling no vibrations or anything that indicates a reaction to my presence," Mark continued. "Oksana, are you seeing any changes in the data from the miners?"

"That's a negative," reported the physicist from onboard the *Intrepid*. "Everything looks the same as it's always been. Nothing has changed. At least nothing that we're able to detect."

Oksana remained open to the possibility that the alien artifact operated in a realm of wholly unknown physics.

279

Maybe all of the important things the Bastion did could not be detected by any of the sensors they had brought with them; perhaps not by any technology that humans had invented.

"That's good, I suppose," said Mark. "I'd rather get no response than a hostile response."

"Roger that!" Adam exclaimed.

"I concur," Oksana chimed in.

Mark pushed himself up as slowly as he could and carefully stood on his feet. He had to do this with great care. So low was the Bastion's mass that any sudden or forceful movement could propel him to escape velocity.

Once he was upright, Mark took a few moments to survey his relative position. The Bastion was so small that there was scarcely a horizon that he was able to perceive; the black horizon just seemed to drop off, blending with the surrounding universe. Looking into the black surface once more, Mark found himself thinking of something that Nietzsche had said. *"When you gaze long into the abyss, the abyss also gazes into you."*

Here on the Bastion, Nietzsche's words rang true. Mark could not shake the feeling that the Bastion was watching and studying them just as they were watching and studying it. If that were true, it probably already knew more about them then they would ever know about it.

At the same time, he knew that he could not trust that instinctive feeling. Yes, it was possible that he the Bastion was watching him, but he also knew it was entirely possible that the artifact was completely inert, no more functional or self-aware than a discarded booster from one of the old Saturn V rockets that continued to drift aimlessly across the Solar System as they had done for decades.

That was what the logical side of his brain told him, but it was not what he wanted. He desperately wanted the eerie feeling he had to be justified. He wanted there to be a

280

mind, an intelligence behind this enigmatic blackness. And if there was some form of consciousness that resided within or beyond this black surface, he wanted to communicate with it, to learn of its builders. To know all that it had seen during its multi-billion year lifespan. To unlock the mysteries.

The commander looked up and saw his two crewmates just a few dozen feet above him.

"Ning, do you feel like joining me?"

"I thought you'd never ask," she said jokingly.

Mark watched as she descended, he felt his heartrate quicken. Even though he was already standing on the Bastion and it had yet to act in a hostile manner, he could not help but worry that the artifact would do something to harm Ning. He breathed more easily only when she touched down on the surface less than twenty feet from him and nothing happened.

"I've touched down on the surface," Ning reported.

Mark thought that he detected a hint of disappointment in her voice. "What do you make of this Ning?" Mark asked.

"There's nothing spectacular going on where I'm at." Again, there was that hint of disappointment.

"Nothing's changed on my end either," said Mark. "Oksana, what are you seeing?"

"There's still no change in the data from the miners' sensors," replied the physicist

"Understood."

Ning stood up and began to walk slowly toward Mark.

"Jed, you are go to come down here as well," Mark said.

"Roger that," said the mathematician.

Mark watched Jed descend, and the mathematician made the same unceremonious landing that he and Ning had just made.

"I've touched down on the Bastion," Jed reported.

"Third time the charm?" Adam said.

"Doesn't seem so," Jed replied. "The surface feels exactly the way Commander de Rijk and Ning have reported. There doesn't seem to be any response to my presence."

"Same here," Mark said. "Nothing's changed."

"Likewise," Ning said in agreement.

The team proceeded to deploy the small sensors they had brought with them. In little over a half hour they were up and running. Oksana monitored the data feeds as soon as they began coming in from their directional transmitters that were pointed away from the Bastion and toward the *Intrepid*. This prevented the signals from being absorbed by the Bastion.

"There's no change in the readings from any of the miners or the instruments you guys have deployed," reported Oksana.

"Understood," said Mark.

The commander could not help but feel a little disappointed. He had held onto some hope that touching it would elicit some sort of reaction.

"It doesn't seem to notice that we're here," said Oksana. "Or if it is, it's not giving any indication."

"Well, I think it's safe to say that the Bastion isn't responsive to life, human or otherwise" said Jed.

"Yeah, I'm thinking that you're right," Mark said.

"I'm inclined to agree with you," Oksana added.

"At least that's one possibility that we can put to rest," the mathematician said as he slowly stood, mimicking Mark's earlier moves.

"Let's start setting Oksana's array up," Mark instructed. He moved to the sensor package contained in a gray cylinder packed with as many sensors as it could carry, most of them from the canceled Korolev

282

Observatory. It had been deployed from the *Intrepid* and landed on the Bastion just prior to the team's EVA.

Even though the miners indicated that the artifact absorbed all forms of radiation, some attributed it to the miner's sensors lacking the sensitivity to detect the range of particles and radiation actually present. The array would address that. It had extremely sensitive receptors.

Two identical array packages were onboard the *Intrepid*. They were scheduled for deployment prior to the next EVA to different locations on the Bastion's surface. In the event deployment or space debris damaged them, there were sophisticated 3D printers onboard to print replacement components. If needed, IE's asteroid miners could deliver needed raw materials to the *Intrepid*.

In addition to the sensor arrays, microsatellites had been deployed above the surface of the Bastion to measure at a variety of distances any change in particles or radiation emitted by the artifact. They also functioned as relay stations, allowing continuous communication between EVA crews and hardware on the Bastion.

***

Mark, Jed, and Oksana returned to the *Intrepid* after four hours spent setting up equipment on the surface of the Bastion. They doffed their suits once through the airlock and proceeded to the galley, where Adam and Oksana were waiting for them.

"How are we doing?" Mark asked Oksana. Even though there had been no reaction within the past four hours, he held onto a glimmer of hope that something would happen once they retreated from the Bastion.

"All sensors are continuing to perform nominally, and the data is pouring in," reported the physicist. She kept throwing glances at her wristband, which was displaying some of the raw data from the sensors.

"Very well," Mark said as he grabbed a pack of the

specialty food from the storage unit. Moving all that equipment on the spacewalk had depleted his reserves and stimulated his appetite. He had available only freeze-dried rations on his previous space missions, and that made the fresh produce from the *Intrepid*'s hydroponic garden a welcome delicacy. The success of their EVA was cause to indulge in one more of their gourmet meals. The mood was festive as the crew took their seats at the round table.

"Is this like Christmas for you?" Adam asked Oksana as he dug into roasted duck.

"I suppose," she said. "But it's going to take a while to comb through all of the data and see what exactly it is we've got here."

"That's fine," Mark remarked as he began to dig into his sweet and sour chicken. "We can stay here as long as necessary. I don't know about the rest of you, but I don't plan on going back to Earth empty handed."

There was a chorus of agreement from the others. Jed, as was his habit, had to throw a bit of a wet blanket on the celebration.

Looking up from his meal the mathematician noted dourly, "We might as well get comfy here because I don't think the answers are going to come to us very easily."

"You're not saying anything you haven't already said before." Ning sounded peeved. "Not that I disagree with you, per se. I'd be surprised if we're able to crack all of this thing's secrets all at once."

"I'm glad you all have patience," Mark said, heading off what might have been another Jed-sparked spat.

"We got a shitload of messages while you guys were outside," Adam interjected.

"Of course we have," said Mark, not the least bit surprised. "Play one that's meant for us all."

Adam rapped out a command on the keyboard and an image of President Ortega appeared on the monitor.

"As I understand it, you won't be receiving this message for some twenty minutes after I send it," said the President. "I wanted to wait until you had completed your extravehicular activities before I messaged you. What you're doing right now is beyond all measure of importance, and the last thing I'd want to do is distract you from your duties.

"I can't even begin to tell you how proud I am of what you've already accomplished. The *Intrepid* is the crown jewel of human spacecraft engineering, and with it you have traveled farther than any humans ever have before. Regardless of how successful you are in learning more about the alien artifact, you have already achieved a great triumph for humanity.

"Even as we continue to reel from the tragic loss of the *Aldrin*'s crew and contend with a myriad of challenges here on Earth, the continued success of your mission is made all the more paramount, for it doing exemplifies our determination to pursue our destiny among the stars despite the tragedies that may befall us.

"Supporting your mission is the most important and, I hope, the best decision I've made since taking office. You can be assured of my continued support and enthusiasm as long as I am President. Everyone on Earth eagerly anticipates the discoveries that you will make. Godspeed *Intrepid*."

"We've gotten similar praise and encouragement from the other world leaders that supported our mission," said Oksana.

"Pull them up," Mark said. "We owe our thanks to all of them."

"You might want to see this first," Adam said, and played another message. Miles appeared on the monitor, beaming with pride.

"It would be an understatement to say that I'm proud

285

of what you guys have done," said the IE president. "When IE launched our first asteroid miner, I was just hoping that it wasn't a one-way ticket to bankruptcy for me. Never in a billion years did I think it would lead to where you guys are now. There is nothing in my life more meaningful than having done all that I can to help get you to where you are now."

Miles laughed merrily. "I know you guys don't have anything to drink," he continued, "so I guess you could say I've been doing the drinking for all of you."

Mark had to smile at that. Miles was very good at keeping himself composed, even after consuming copious amounts of alcohol. The IE president always drank somewhat excessively in celebration of any great achievement his company made. He had drunk nearly an entire bottle of champagne himself, along with many other drinks, on the day when the first shipments of asteroid ore had landed on Earth.

While Mark was sure that Miles had done the same thing when the *Intrepid* had rendezvoused with the Bastion, his boss did not appear the least bit intoxicated in the recording, but that was not at all surprising. Miles was always careful never to appear inebriated when cameras were present. So he must have compiled his message before he opened the champagne bottle, or at least before he drank enough of it to affect his on-screen persona.

"You'll probably also like to know that your EVA is the single most-viewed event in human history," the IE president continued. "'Over six billion people watched you walking on the Bastion."

Mark could see the intense emotion that his boss sometimes had to fight to keep from overwhelming him on occasions like this.

"My only regret is that I'm not there with you," Miles said, "and I wish more than anything else that I had

286

something of value to offer your mission that would justify my being there. You are beyond a doubt the finest crew ever. I don't want to take up any more of your time. I wouldn't blame you if you don't listen to this message for a while. You must be exhausted after everything you've done today. I know I don't need to tell you to keep up the good work, because I already know you will."

Chapter 27

Ask floated by the window of the *Aldrin*'s habitat module, staring out into the void of space. Ordinarily when the Cycler carried a crew of astronauts, it would be spun about its center of mass to generate simulated gravity. Even when the Cycler was rotating, astronauts had to devote more than two hours each day to strenuous exercise to maintain muscle and bone mass that otherwise would occurred during the five-month voyage between Earth and Mars in microgravity

While exercise consumed a significant amount of astronauts' time on long duration space missions, Ask had no need to subject himself to such physical exertions. His nanomachines prevented muscle atrophy and bone loss, and repaired any damage inflicted on his cells by solar and cosmic radiation. This left him with no reason to rotate the *Aldrin*, and so he would remain in microgravity for the full duration of his voyage to the Tabernacle.

Ask had to constantly monitor the Cycler's systems for malfunctions and failures. With the accumulated knowledge of dozens of astronauts and spacecraft engineers, he was reasonably confident that he could resolve any technical crisis that might arise. As yet no issues had yet arisen that warranted his attention. This left him with little to do other than contemplate what was happening at the Tabernacle, and what he would do upon reaching it.

He thought of the circumstances that had led to his awakening. It seemed peculiar that the baselines had found him in the Antarctic ice and revived him at the same time another group had discovered the Tabernacle. Was it merely serendipity? Perhaps, but it was hard for Ask to accept that possibility wholeheartedly.

Could Legion have arranged for the baselines to discover him at the time when they did? Even if it seemed that Legion had abandoned humanity, this did not at all prove that they had. Ask knew that it was certainly possible, if not likely, that Legion was monitoring him through his nanomachines. Or perhaps they had a far more sophisticated means of observation of which he knew nothing.

Legion may very well have been closely monitoring baseline activities throughout the past seventy millennia, and they could have compelled the baselines to find Ask at the same time they found the Tabernacle. It would have been easy for Legion to make the baselines' discovery of him inevitable. They may have moved the ice formation in which Ask had been trapped so that the baselines would be likely to find it once they began to explore Antarctica in earnest. From what Ask had witnessed in the past, it would have been a trivial task for Legion to manipulate the position of a glacier without the baselines having any perception of it.

Even if Legion was behind these events, the question remained as to what purpose it served. What value did Ask have to Legion? Why imprison him in the ice and then allow the baselines to revive him millennia later? Why had they not simply destroyed him?

He had so many questions. He had to know if there was a higher purpose behind it, or if it was all just madness. The Tabernacle was his only means of finding answers. The status of the *Intrepid*'s mission gave him yet more to contemplate.

He knew that the *Intrepid* should have rendezvoused with the Tabernacle by now. The crew had probably deployed the plethora of scientific equipment they had brought along to monitor the Tabernacle and probe its mysteries. Despite having known from the onset that there

289

was no way he could avoid it, Ask was still infuriated that it would take many more months before he reached the Tabernacle.

With the *Aldrin*'s communication system shut down, Ask had no way of knowing what discoveries the crew of the *Intrepid* might have made. Even though he did not know how their mission was progressing, Ask was reasonably certain that the baselines had not yet unlocked the power of Legion.

Ask believed that if the Tabernacle were to grant the baselines with even a fraction of the power he had witnessed Legion wield, they would be able to reach out across the interplanetary void to seize him and the *Aldrin*. The fact that nothing of the sort had happened convinced Ask that the baselines had been unable to unlock the Tabernacle's power.

What would he do if his own efforts proved equally fruitless? What if Legion did not intend to give their power to the baselines or him? Most importantly, what if the Bastion was not even the Tabernacle?

In that eventuality, Ask refused to resign himself to die by remaining onboard the *Aldrin*. Before Ask decided to attempt to hijack the Cycler, he formulated a contingency plan that could enable him to return to Earth.

His first thought was to seize control of the *Intrepid* and pilot it back to Earth, but the obstacles and challenges made success unlikely.

The mission directors were probably anticipating that he might make a suicidal attempt to destroy the *Intrepid* by crashing the *Aldrin* into it. As a precaution, they no doubt would order the *Intrepid* to move a considerable distance away from the Tabernacle once the *Aldrin* was on the cusp of reaching it.

The journey to rendezvous with the Tabernacle would exhaust nearly all of the *Aldrin*'s remaining propellant.

With little maneuvering capability left, the Cycler would no longer pose a threat to the *Intrepid*. It was, therefore, reasonable to assume that the *Intrepid* would eventually return to the Tabernacle to complete its mission.

If the baselines still believed that Ask was Donner, he might be able to use that to his advantage. Ask had considered resuming his original appearance before he had shut down communications with Mission Control, but if he did that, the crew of the *Intrepid*, along with the rest of humanity, would know the deceit he had perpetrated.

Knowing that there existed a being that could perfectly imitate the physical appearance and personality of someone else would terrify the baselines. Paranoia would spread among the *Intrepid*'s crew, making them dangerous adversaries. Although it was unlikely that the crew would become so paranoid that they would turn against each other. Every astronaut whose mind he had probed had revealed just how physically and mentally prepared they were for the rigors of their missions. Although they could not have possibly anticipated Ask's ability to assume so perfectly another's identity, or his capability to kill so easily, they would not allow it to jeopardize their mission.

Ask intended to resume the appearance of Donner for the inevitable confrontation with the *Intrepid*'s crew. He could use their faith in a fellow astronaut to convince them that the loss of the *Aldrin's* crew had been an inexplicable accident... something beyond his control. He could explain his subsequent actions as a grief induced break from a reality so horrible it was beyond his ability to cope, but he had gradually regained his mental balance on the long journey. It suddenly struck him that they would still question why he had altered the Cycler's trajectory for this destination. That would be harder to explain.

Alternatively, Ask considered feigning surrender and allowing the crew of the *Intrepid* to subdue him, and then killing all of them after they brought him onboard their vessel. However, given the demise of the *Aldrin*'s crew, such an attempt would be met with skepticism. If they were that wary, it was possible, even likely, that they would not allow Ask onboard the *Intrepid*, fearing a similar fate. It would be a simple matter to lock out manual control of the airlock. If that happened, would it be possible for Ask could to force his way onboard? He doubted it.

Ask quickly realized that all of that may very well be irrelevant. For even if he was able to get onto the *Intrepid*, kill the crew, and pilot the vessel back to Earth, there was still a major obstacle that he would be forced to confront. The *Intrepid* had been designed and built to operate entirely in the vacuum of space and could never survive atmospheric reentry. The only way that Ask would be able to walk on Earth again would be if a shuttle were to dock with the *Intrepid* while it was in Earth orbit and then ferry him to the planet's surface.

If Ask were to kill the *Intrepid*'s crew, it would be impossible to hide and no other crew would ever be allowed onboard the vessel while he was still alive. Even if the baselines could not identify how he had been able to kill both crews, they doubtless would decide it was far too dangerous for another crew to come into contact with him.

The baselines would never destroy the *Intrepid*; it was far too valuable, and they would desire to salvage it and use it for future missions. However, they would have no reservations about blowing the hull open in order to kill Ask. That would not be a difficult thing for them to do. They could launch a small missile to impact the *Intrepid*, shoot it with a laser, or simply direct one of the many thousands of small and inexpensive satellites that orbited the Earth to collide with the spacecraft. Any such object would be small enough to pierce the hull and de-pressurize the spacecraft without causing any irreparable damage to the mighty vessel.

A team of baseline astronauts could then wait until Ask had exhausted all of the available spacesuit oxygen tanks before boarding the *Intrepid*. Even though the baseline authorities likely would prefer to capture him alive, he had no doubt they would ultimately conclude that it would be safer for the general population if he were to be killed.

After carefully considering all of these scenarios, Ask realized that if he did not obtain the power that Legion had promised him, there was only one practical option that would be available to him. He would have no choice but to surrender the *Aldrin* and himself to the crew of the *Intrepid*, and disclose to them everything that he knew.

Ask knew that baseline politicians and scientists alike would demand to know how he had been able to kill the crew of the *Aldrin* and alter his appearance. Once he revealed his nanomachines to them, they would never execute him as to enact justice for all of his killings; he would be too valuable to them. Ask had no doubt that the baseline authorities would keep him alive, but in all likelihood isolate him from any direct human contact. Perhaps with the combined efforts of many baseline scientists, some actual progress could be made in determining the secrets of Ask's nanomachines. Ask felt revulsion at the very idea of having to tell the baselines everything and become their lab rat in order to safeguard his survival.

If the baselines had made a public announcement about the Bastion shortly after its discovery, he would not have needed commandeer the *Aldrin* at all. He could have assumed the identity of one of the *Intrepid*'s crewmembers. He would have done all of the duties that were required of the baseline crewmember he impersonated, and would never have even considered killing the rest of the crew. If the Tabernacle did not respond to Ask, he would have still desired to know if it responded to the baselines if Legion intended it to be theirs.

Of course, there had been another option available to him. He could have simply waited until the *Intrepid*'s mission ended, and the spacecraft and her crew returned to Earth. If they suffered a catastrophic failure at any point during their voyage, it could be years or even decades before another expedition was sent to the Tabernacle, but it would surely be done eventually. Even if the baselines did not learn as much about the Tabernacle as they hoped to, it would still be the central focus of all space research for the foreseeable future.

Ask was biologically immortal, after all. He could have simply waited however long it would take for a second expedition to be sent to the Tabernacle, and assume the identity of one of the crewmembers of that future mission.

So why did he have to get to the Tabernacle now, especially if doing so involved risking his own life and exposing himself to the baselines? Because time was another factor that he had to take into consideration. If Legion was monitoring him, as he feared, then they could step in and betray him at a moment's notice, just as they had done before.

In addition, there was always the potential for an environmental disaster or devastating global conflict that could devastate Earth, and destroy the baselines' capability to build infrastructure in space. The facilities on the Moon and Mars would struggle to survive, and would inevitably perish. That would delay the space program by years, if not decades, and sending further expeditions to the Tabernacle would be completely out of the question.

Perhaps Legion had intended for the baselines to revive Ask right when they discovered the Tabernacle. Did they desire him to reveal himself to the baselines? It was impossible to know what Legion wanted. Perhaps there were rival factions within Legion that had opposing philosophies. Maybe one faction had supported imbuing Ask with his nanomachines, and then an opposing faction had prevailed, and it was they who had condemned him to a state of living death.

More speculation that had no answers.

Ask still desperately wanted to believe Legion had told him the truth about the Tabernacle. It had been extremely difficult for him to make the decision to commandeer the *Aldrin,* as this forced him to concede to himself that he was nothing but a pawn of Legion. If all of this proved to have been wasted effort, he would plunge into a well of despair even deeper than the one into which he had fallen in the distant past in the wake of the cataclysm. Even if that happened, Ask knew it was a well would pull himself from, just as he had done after his awakening.

Until he had answers to these questions, he had nothing to do but wait, immersed in his own thoughts.

Chapter 28

"Ning," Oksana said, "can you move that sensor package right in front of you about ten centimeters to the right?"

Oksana's helmet display showed her the exact positions of Ning, herself, and all of the sensors she was relocating on this EVA.

"I'm on it," replied the engineer. A brief moment later, she had repositioned it exactly where Oksana wanted it.

The physicist smiled at her colleague's prompt response. She, along with the rest of the crew, had noted Ning's willingness to volunteer for spacewalk duty on the Bastion. Perhaps it was out of boredom. There had been no major issues with the *Intrepid*'s reactor or other critical systems in all the time that they had been at the Bastion. None of the crew had failed to notice that the propulsion engineer seemed to have limitless stamina.

Oksana looked back down at the eternal blackness beneath her. She would never forget the first time she had set foot upon it; that feeling of unease they all had they first made contact with the Bastion. Now walking here was just another day on the job. Amazing how one could actually grow bored with walking on the surface of an alien artifact.

Amazing, too, was the Bastion's refusal to yield its secrets to the complex array of sensors now scattered on its surface. Among those secrets was the artifact's apparent violation of some physics fundamentals.

Hopefully this latest experiment would help provide confirmation of one of the most blatant physics violations this artifact seemed to exhibit. Oksana had requested that all of the IE miners be returned to the surface of the Bastion, the first time they had been on the artifact since the *Intrepid*'s crew had begun their research.

The miners were integral to this research endeavor. All of them were positioned on the exact opposite side of the Bastion from Oksana and Ning. If what Oksana had suspected were true, this experiment would prove it beyond a shadow of a doubt. She almost feared that confirmation because of its implications, and she knew that many of her colleagues back on Earth felt the same.

"That's it for today," Oksana said. "Let's head back to the ship."

"Roger that."

Oksana pushed herself off the surface of the Bastion toward the *Intrepid*. Ning followed close behind her.

***

Oksana stared glossy-eyed at her computer monitor. A ceaseless stream of data had been pouring into the *Intrepid*'s computers from the sensor arrays clustered on and around the Bastion. She constantly ran analysis software to interpret the incoming data from the sensors. She sometimes found herself staring at the raw data herself, but that served only to amplify her building anxiety. Very little of what she was seeing in the data stream and analyses seemed to make any sense. So much of what she was seeing was impossible according to her understanding of physics.

They checked and rechecked all the sensors on the surface of the Bastion, along with the coding in the sensor and analysis software. Everything was functioning as it should. They checked for interference from the artifact, but if that was occurring, it was so effective as to be beyond detection. None of it made any sense. For the first time in her career, Oksana was stymied.

She constantly exchanged theories with her colleagues on Earth. She sent them video from the sensors and the satellites monitoring the Bastion. She live streamed data feeds to all of the world's leading physicists who fed it into their own analysis software and physics models, and yet none had come up with a practical solution. They all seemed to be as perplexed by it as Oksana. That only contributed to the growing fear she now felt toward the Bastion and its makers.

"How are you holding up?" said a voice.

Oksana looked to see Ning at the entrance to her quarters.

"I'm doing well," Oksana replied, and immediately turned her attention back to her computer monitor. "Everything's going well."

"You don't come out of your quarters very often," Ning said as she walked closer to the physicist.

"Can't afford to," Oksana said into her computer. "Nothing about the Bastion fits our theories, but I have to hold onto the hope that I'll make sense of it eventually. I keep praying for a Eureka moment."

Ning was now standing right by Oksana's workstation. She lightly drew her hand across the computer and then across the physicist's hand. Oksana didn't pay the slightest amount of attention to this.

"What is it that you're struggling with?" Ning asked.

"Damn near everything. The Bastion is challenging our entire perception of reality. It's fucking nuts."

Ning retained a calm, inquisitive expression. "Are you really that surprised?" she asked. "I remember you saying that you expected the aliens to have a much better grasp of the true underpinnings of the universe. It sounds like your research is confirming that."

"Pretty much," Oksana nodded in agreement. "But I'm still desperate to learn whatever went into making the Bastion. Because right now it's just…I don't even know. It doesn't even seem to belong in the same reality as us."

"Maybe we just haven't been able to perceive reality as it really is," Ning mused. "We could be chained to the

298

walls inside of Plato's cave. And maybe the aliens have broken free from those chains, and can perceive and interact with the world beyond the cave. The Bastion may not break our chains, but maybe it could help lengthen them. Or maybe it will allow us to see the source of light that's casting the shadows on the cave wall. And maybe, just maybe, in due time, we'll find a way to break the chains ourselves."

"Maybe. I keep hoping for that, but I just don't know anymore."

***

Strapped into his seat on the command deck, Mark gazed out the window at the Bastion. He came here sometimes to think, even though the view had remained unchanged in all the time since they had arrived.

Faint glitters of light were emanating from the sensors and miners scattered along the artifact's surface. No major issues had arisen in all that time. All of the equipment continued to operate nominally and no conflicts or drama had arisen among the crew. No major crises had erupted on Earth, as fear about the Bastion, its creators, and the *Aldrin* seemed to have substantially subsided from the public's attention.

Mark was aware the *Aldrin* was drawing closer to the Bastion with each passing day. The mission directors back on Earth had yet to decide what the *Intrepid* should do once the Cycler finally did arrive. The mission was explicit; learn as much about the Bastion as possible before the *Aldrin* arrived. Unfortunately, they had learned next to nothing. It had been an exercise in sensor placement and monitoring, little else.

As time continued to pass, Mark found himself growing increasingly frustrated. He attributed this mostly to the fact that his crew had yet to make any earthshattering discoveries about the Bastion or its builders. They had failed to penetrate the surface of the artifact, and found no message hidden among the data they had gathered.

On a few occasions, Mark found himself looking at the raw data that the sensors were feeding into the *Intrepid*'s computers. Unfortunately, he did not understand what any of it actually meant. For all he knew he could be looking at the aliens' version of the Rosetta Stone with no key to unlocking its mysteries. He did expect that Jed or Oksana would be able to identity some valuable gem of knowledge in the mountain of data and that they would inform him when they made such a discovery.

Mark endeavored to assist Jed and Oksana in their research efforts, which typically involved moving equipment to and from the ship. In many ways, they were directing this mission more than Mark, not that that bothered him in the slightest. He had similar experiences on previous missions he had commanded.

He had ferried astronomers, astrophysicists, geologists, and other scientists to the Moon on nearly every mission he had flown. They studied phenomena such as cosmic rays or lunar geology, and were the people who were truly pushing the boundaries of human knowledge. Mark respected and fully supported what they did, even if their research did not particularly interest him, but this was different. The Bastion and its builders were things in which Mark had a burning and abiding interest. The lack of answers was a major factor in Mark's growing frustration.

There was another factor Mark had to consider was contributing to his frustration. This was the longest space mission he had ever been on. Mark knew that there was always the possibility that being here and overseeing the project was extremely stressful to his psyche. It put him at risk for a psychotic episode.

Mark was a consummate professional, however, and nothing he said caused Mission Control any concern. He kept these fears to himself, certain that he would never suffer such a breakdown. But part of him wondered if a break with reality was inevitable. Maybe it started small before spreading uncontrollably, like a single cancer cell that propagated until it had given rise to a fatal tumor. And maybe that was what had happened to Donner.

Mark thought of the astronauts and cosmonauts who had spent months or years orbiting Earth in the cramped space stations of decades past. The low rate of rocket launches of that bygone era had only offered them a handful of spaceflights during their entire careers. They just circled the Earth endlessly, in the long years following the Apollo program and before the revolution in private space travel, but at least they were treated to multiple sunrises and sunsets every day. Most importantly, they were free to look down at the beauty and majesty of Earth.

Crews on the Moon and Mars had the option of stepping outside of their habitats and were free to walk on new ground where no human had set foot before and explore the empty, alien worlds on which they resided. This relieved the monotony of their missions, reducing the sense of isolation that led to psychotic breaks.

While the *Intrepid* was the first manned spacecraft to go to a new destination in years, it had been to a place that lacked any of the visual majesty offered by other locations. It had a profound effect on the crew that was unlike that encountered by any other space mission in history. Perhaps there was just too much time to think.

Mark reflected on the situation back on Earth. Tensions between nations were still high, and many old UFO conspiracy theories had resurfaced, sparking fears that national leaders were just puppets of aliens. It had even become the focus of some intelligence agencies. It was crazy, but it was fueled by the mystery of the *Aldrin*. An explanation for how the crew had died and the subsequent actions by Donner still eluded investigators.

The lack of information naturally led to rampant rumors on the internet. It bred a fear that *Intrepid's* crew would suffer a similar fate. The commander of the *Aldrin* had turned on his crew, so why should the same fate not befall the *Intrepid?*

None of the crew had given the slightest indication that they were wary or fearful of their commander. They may have been too focused on their tasks to devote time to rumor, or they simply dismissed it as unfounded speculation. Mark suspected that his crew was as frustrated by the lack of progress as was he. That their every waking moment was programmed with time allotted for tasks, exercise, meals, recreation, personal matters, and sleep helped maintain mental stability and kept conflict low key and at a minimum. As commander, Mark had a more flexible schedule. That was both a boon and a curse.

Mark rose from his couch and made his way from the command deck. Sometimes it was nice just to be able to move around. He never failed to appreciate how large and luxurious the *Intrepid* was compared to the tin cans in which most astronauts were accustomed to spending long duration missions. It was amazing and a testament to the astronaut training program that any of them had been able to retain their sanity.

He propelled himself down the *Intrepid*'s central hub, then down to the habitat ring and down its corridor until he came to the hydroponic garden. Racks lined the walls that teemed with growing crops. Banks of LED and UV lights above the racks bombarded the crops with light to enhance photosynthesis. It was far hotter and more humid in here than in the rest of the ship. A strong odor of thriving and flowering plants perfumed the air.

Mark was not the least bit surprised to find Adam in the garden, tending to the crops. The biologist had taken it

302

upon himself to manage the garden, and tackling the many tasks required to keep the garden in optimal production provided him with steady work. Adam periodically replaced the nozzles that irrigated the plants and replaced depleted growth media. Among the crops growing under his watchful eye were potatoes, wheat, rice, soybeans, and peanuts. This supplied the crew with all of the protein, carbohydrates, starch, amino acids, vitamins, and minerals that were needed for a healthy diet.

Mark watched as the biologist exhaled a deep breath onto the plants he was tending at the moment. Adam liked to think he was feeding the plants more directly even if the amount of carbon dioxide he expelled was much smaller than that provided by the air conditioning system.

"How goes it?" Mark asked.

Adam looked up, turned his attention from the crops to the commander, and smiled a bit sheepishly.

"Sorry... I was kind of focused. All systems are nominal, Commander," he grinned, tossing Mark an irreverent salute.

"Well that's good." Mark looked at the crops that fed his crew, and stared at the rows of crops in silence for a brief moment.

"Is there something wrong?" Adam asked.

"I suppose."

"What is it?"

Mark sighed and let his guard down for just a minute. "I don't know. I guess I'm just getting a little bit discontented."

"About what?"

"Our situation. I mean, think about it: we've been out here for months now and we've learned virtually nothing about the Bastion or whoever built it."

Adam nodded. "I understand why that frustrates you," he said. "But I never thought that the answers were going to come to us all that easily. Were you really expecting anything different?"

"No. But that doesn't make the reality of our situation any easier for me to accept."

"I understand where you're coming from. Hell, I'd be lying if I said that I don't share your dissatisfaction. And I'll bet everyone else here and back on Earth shares the same frustration."

"Thank you for understanding."

"It's the least I can do." Adam chuckled. "It's not like my expertise is any in way helping me to do my job onboard this ship. I'm just a source of manual labor, and a gardener."

"Don't be ridiculous. You were able to confirm no organisms live on the Bastion. And without you, all these crops would have died long ago and we'd have nothing to eat."

Adam laughed again. "Trust me, there's nothing I do in here that the rest of you wouldn't be able to do yourselves. I'm just lightening your workload."

"Nonsense. You're a valuable member of my crew."

"Not like you are. You're the commander. We need you to operate the ship and provide a functional command structure."

"I'm not indispensable," Mark replied ruefully. "If I'm killed or incapacitated, Mission Control will be able to direct the rest of you on how to get the *Intrepid* back to Earth. Hell, they can fly the ship remotely if need be."

Adam laughed again. "If something happened to you, I don't think the rest of us would last very long."

"Don't say that. Besides, I intend to stick around for the duration."

"Good to know. There's no one I'd rather have commanding this great vessel."

"I appreciate that."

"I must admit that I am a little envious of Jed and Oksana. After all, they're the ones who are really keeping themselves busy with the Bastion."

"True. But I'll bet that if you told them that, they'd probably tell you that they're just feeding the data to their colleagues back on Earth."

Adam smiled at that. "Well, it's nice that there's no shortage of humility among us, given the historical significance the mission, and the extreme level of selectivity that went into choosing this crew."

"That kind of mentality is vital for any crew to operate nominally. The fact that everyone here exhibits that humility is proof that the mission planners made the correct selections."

"Perhaps," Adam mused, "but a harsh truth is always better than a reassuring lie, and the truth is that this mission hasn't benefitted much from my knowledge of biology. In a way, I anticipated this when I first signed up for this mission. But even now, when it's safe to say that there's no trace of life, living or extinct, on the Bastion, I still wouldn't trade being here for anything else. I know the significance of this mission, and that my presence helping in any way I can, is the greatest thing that's ever happened to me."

"All of you are the finest crew I've ever had the honor of commanding," Mark said. "And you are an invaluable member of that crew. Don't ever think otherwise."

***

When Mark finished talking with Adam, he went to his quarters, where Ning was waiting for him.

"You're always a welcome sight," he smiled.

"And you never cease to flatter me," Ning replied. She walked over to the commander and kissed him. "I listened in on some of what you and Adam were talking about."

Mark was not all that surprised to hear this. Ning was

often discrete. He never worried that she would say anything out of turn and he was never concerned if someone overheard his conversations. He had no reason to conceal anything from his crew, least of all a somewhat philosophical discussion with the ship's astrobiologist.

"Why didn't you join us?" he asked. "Your thoughts and opinions are always more than welcome in any discussion."

Ning shook her head. "I think it's worthwhile to hear what others can come up with on their own accord without any input from me. Knowing what happens in the absence of certain stimuli is just as important as knowing what transpires when that stimuli is present."

Mark nodded and smiled. "I love the way you think," he said.

"Ah, more words of flattery." She grabbed him by the waist, and pressed her lips against his.

Afterward, they lay together in the small bed. Mark had his arm around Ning, holding her like he was afraid she would disappear.

"I'm going to call a crew meeting tomorrow," he said.

"Any particular reason?" Ning asked.

"I want to get a better idea about where we stand in our progress with the Bastion."

"But you said earlier you fully trust that Jed and Oksana would tell you right away if they made a major discovery."

"Yes, I did say that, and I meant what I said. I haven't been pestering either of them because of the trust I have in them."

"So what exactly are you hoping to get out of this?"

"I just want to get it out in the open. I mean, we don't even talk about it at communal meals."

Ning looked deeply into Mark's eyes. "I think everyone's getting anxious. That's why we need your guidance."

Mark touched her cheek. "I'll do the best I can. Right now I'm just glad I have you."

Ning was the best thing about being so far from Earth. Mark felt closer to her now than he ever had on Earth. Perhaps that was inevitable, given how long they had been living in such close proximity to each other.

Would they have gotten this close if they had never gone on this mission together? Perhaps. Still, Mark appreciated this. Had it not been for Ning, he might have gone stir crazy.

Chapter 29

The next day, the crew gathered in the galley for the meeting Mark had called. They all sat at the roundtable together, just as they always had for meals and other special conferences.

When they had departed Earth, they were all optimistic; that was to be expected of any great explorers venturing out into the unknown. Now the atmosphere was dramatically different. Their time at the Bastion seemed to have eroded their spirits like waves crashing against the rocks on the shore. Oksana, particularly, looked battle-weary.

"This is just going to be among us," Mark said. "I'm not recording what is said today for Mission Control to scrutinize at some later date, unless you'd rather I did."

"It makes no difference to me," Jed said simply.

Mark smiled slightly. "I'm not the least bit surprised you feel that way. Your honesty has always been greatly appreciated." He looked at the rest of the crew. "Does anyone else share Jed's feelings on this matter? Or would anyone prefer it if we record our conversation and then transmit it to Earth?"

The lack of response told Mark the crew was in agreement.

"All right then. Let's proceed." Mark looked intently at Jed and Oksana. "I want to hear everything that you've found and any theories you might have about what the Bastion is and what purpose it serves."

Oksana looked at him with pleading eyes. "We're still gathering data," she said. "So I don't think we can really give you a proper idea at all of what the artifact really is."

"Just tell him," snapped Jed. "Don't hide behind silence like those back on Earth." The mathematician looked at Mark intently. "Mission Control has seen all of the data we've sent them, and so have all of the world's most brilliant minds. And everyone is too scared shitless to talk to us about what we've found."

", "What's he talking about?" Mark asked Oksana.

The physicist looked visibly shaken. "We're still trying to make sense of the data we've gathered," she said. "It's just so bizarre that I don't think we can form a coherent theory to explain it as of yet."

"Please just explain to us what data shows that you're struggling with. Give us your best explanation."

"Okay, fine." Oksana took a deep breath. "I was never fully convinced that the Bastion was able to absorb all electromagnetic radiation, as was originally postulated. The radiation monitors used by IE's miners are nowhere near sensitive enough to say with complete certainty that the Bastion was an ideal blackbody. So I've been conducting experiments with the lasers and particle accelerators we brought with us."

There had been a considerable amount of objection to bombarding the Bastion with lasers and accelerated particles. Many feared that the beings who had built the Bastion, or the possible artificial intelligence within it, would interpret such actions as hostile, and would retaliate. But when all efforts to obtain a sample from the Bastion were met with consistent failure, Oksana, as the crew's senior physicist, made a unilateral decision to use both the lasers and particle accelerators.

"The accelerated electrons and ions that I bombarded the Bastion with seem to behave the same way everything else has when they make physical contact with the surface," Oksana explained. "They immediately lost all of their kinetic energy once they struck the artifact. And the lasers seem to just disappear when they hit the surface, just like all other forms of radiation. The sensors that I've been

309

using for these experiments are among the most sophisticated ever developed. Based on the data that I've gotten from those sensors, I think we can now definitely confirm the initial findings: the Bastion does not reflect any form of electromagnetic radiation. Every single photon that strikes it is absorbed with one hundred percent efficiency. It acts like, for lack of a better comparison, a black hole in that respect."

Oksana's eyes seemed to light up right after she said that, as if she was afraid of her own suggestion.

"Okay, but it obviously can't be a black hole," said Mark. "Otherwise we wouldn't be able to walk around on it the way that we have. We'd disappear behind its event horizon and be crushed by its gravity. Right?"

"I…" Oksana's voice trailed off.

"It can't be a black hole," Mark said again, sounding like he was trying to convince himself of this. "Can it?"

Oksana glanced furtively at everyone sitting at the table, and then refocused her attention on the commander. "No, I don't think it is," she said. "Like you said, it doesn't absorb matter like a black hole would. And as you know, it has an escape velocity comparable to an asteroid of similar size, rather than the speed of light. Additionally, the sensors haven't detected any Hawking radiation. Those are properties a black hole has that the Bastion lacks. But there are a few things about it that completely defy explanation."

"Like what?"

"I've been using atomic clocks to try to get a better understanding of the Bastion's mass distribution. These clocks are so precise that one such clock that's placed within a millimeter from a pebble will have a measurable amount of time dilation compared to another clock that's a millimeter farther away due to the effects of general relativity. I put these clocks at different positions on and above the Bastion's surface. If there were even the slightest amount of variation in the mass distribution in the artifact, the clocks would be able to measure it."

"And what did you find?"

"Clocks positioned on the surface of the Bastion have measurable amount of time dilation compared to clocks that are not on the surface. And that time dilation is consistent with previously measured values for the mass of the Bastion. But what's weird is that there's no time dilation for clocks that are the same distance from the Bastion's center of mass. All of the clocks that I placed on the surface are reporting the exact same time, with no measurable time dilation at all. It's the same thing for clocks that are positioned the same distance from the surface. This indicates that the mass distribution in the artifact is completely uniform everywhere. As far as our instruments can determine, there is not a single pit or bump anywhere on the surface of the Bastion or change of density within it."

"Okay, I think that tells us something useful," said Mark. "So we know that the aliens must have cared an awful lot about precision and uniformity when they built the Bastion. Could it be that they just really hate asymmetry, and wanted to make a perfectly round sphere for some cultural reason?"

"I don't think so," said Oksana, "because the data from the clocks revealed something else about the Bastion. And this is the weirdest thing of all."

Everyone had their full attention on Oksana, eagerly anticipating what she would reveal, with the exception of Jed, who looked like he already knew what she was going to say.

"There has been no measureable change in the momentum of the Bastion," the physicist said in a quiet voice.

There was a brief moment of silence among the crew.

311

"You're joking, right?" said Mark.

"No, I'm not. You're well aware of the fact that anything that impacts the Bastion immediately loses all of its kinetic energy. We assumed that this was because all of the impacts were perfectly inelastic. But there has been no accompanying change in the momentum of the Bastion. Our instruments are sensitive enough to detect changes in the Bastion's momentum that should have resulted from all of our activities."

"You're absolutely certain of this?"

"I didn't believe this at first, and neither did anyone else back on Earth. I've been taking as many measurements as possible with everything available to me. I even directed the robotic miners that were on the surface to fire their engines at full thrust along the same vector because I had to impart as much momentum as possible to verify that what I've been seeing is real. And even then, there was no change in the Bastion's momentum whatsoever."

Mark leaned toward Oksana, and very carefully said, "Are you seriously saying that this thing is violating Newton's First Law?"

Oksana took a few quick breaths. "Yes. Based on what I've been observing, that's the only explanation."

"How is that possible?"

"I don't know. This thing completely violates one of our most fundamental understandings of how the universe works. There's no way that I or anyone else back on Earth can explain this shit."

Hearing Oksana say these impossible things seemed to reaffirm that eerie feeling that Mark had gotten when he had first laid eyes on the Bastion that had been reinforced when he had seen it up close and then touched it himself: that the Bastion was not an object in the same sense that the *Intrepid* was. This *thing* had not just come from beyond the stars, but it did not seem to belong in this universe.

"So why, and how would someone build something like this?" Mark asked. "What purpose could it serve?"

Oksana shrugged. "I have no idea. I don't think we can even begin to speculate on that. This is completely beyond our scientific and technological capabilities to understand."

There was a hint of terror in her voice. There was just something so unnerving about the thought of beings that seemed to have established complete mastery over space and time.

Mark ran his hand through his hair. He now understood why Oksana and Mission Control had not been talking about this.

Ning appeared stoic. Adam looked like he was struggling to make sense of this...exactly the way Mark felt.

The commander turned his attention to Jed.

"Jed, what do you make of the data that Oksana has gathered?" Mark said. "Have you found anything that you consider to be of particular significance or interest in your data review? Something that could be a message?"

Unlike Oksana, Jed did not seem unnerved at all. He had the same stoic expression that he wore all the time.

"I've been combing through all of the data that we've collected," said the mathematician, "looking for anything that could be used to convey an intelligent message. I held onto a slim hope that I would be able to find some patterns that could be a message, or anything at all that could help us find what could be the builders' language. Some had hypothesized that the aliens might have encoded a message into the structure or material of the Bastion. And now I can safely say that my first hypothesis was correct. There is no message in the Bastion waiting for us to discover. No message that's intended for us, anyway."

"How can you be so certain of that?" Adam asked.

"Because you just listened to Oksana explain how incredibly advanced the technology behind the Bastion

313

must be. And all we've really been able to do is get a slightly better idea of just how far beyond us these aliens are. Oksana just said understanding it is beyond out capabilities. Quite frankly we are as dumb as monkeys compared to the aliens, and I'd wager that's a generous assessment. Because you need to remember that monkeys are not just incapable of understanding how something as complicated as a fusion reactor works: they have no hope of ever understanding what it is, how it works, or what its purpose is.

"The only possible way we could learn anything from the aliens is if they choose to reveal it to us, and even then they'd have to dumb it down extensively for us to understand it. And it seems pretty obvious that they don't want to do that. We're so insignificant to them that we don't matter to them in the slightest. We are motes of dust in the eyes of gods. We may be at the foot of Olympus, but Prometheus is not going to bestow us with fire."

"That's a pretty fatalistic outlook so have," said Ning.

"Call it that if you want, but it's the only way to explain what we've been able to learn so far. The Bastion and the technology behind it are simply too advanced for us to understand. And our fortune isn't going to improve anytime soon. And it's delusion to think that we're going to find an alien Rosetta Stone, Encyclopedia Galactica, or Wikipedia server."

"We've only been here for a few months," said Adam. "Why do you think we'd get the answers in that time? And how can you say that all our future research here is entirely futile? You don't know anything of the sort. You're just being absurdly fatalistic."

"No I'm not," Jed countered. "Think about the golden records that are on the Voyager probes. There are simple instructions on them, so that if any extraterrestrials happen to pick up the probes millions or billions of years in the future, they'll be able to figure out how to play the records. That's because the people who made the Voyagers' records wanted whatever hypothetical aliens might find the probes to be able to easily access the information contained in the records. If the Bastion contains any meaningful information, and its builders wanted someone else to learn that information, it would only make sense for them to have included easy to find and easy to understand instructions on how to access that information. The fact that we've found nothing of the sort on the Bastion makes it pretty damn obvious that the builders don't want to share their knowledge with anybody, at least not anybody as primitive as we are to them."

"Okay, but that doesn't mean we'll never learn anything of value from the Bastion," Adam insisted. "Oksana has explained how it's a major challenge to our understanding of the laws of physics. I say that's a good thing, because it gives us an insight into how the universe really works. So maybe sometime in the near or distant future, you guys or someone back on Earth could make a breakthrough and figure out what makes the Bastion tick and how it really works."

Jed laughed. "I don't think we have reason to be that optimistic."

"So what would you have us do?" said Ning. "Should we just give up and go home?"

"Not at all. I'm just saying that we need to be honest and realistic about what we can hope to accomplish, which isn't a whole hell of a lot. Understanding the futility of an endeavor such as this is the only way we can hope to learn anything of real value. I fully intend to spend the rest of my life studying this artifact and all of the data that we have gathered and continue to gather about it. But the information that we really want to know: the aliens' history and culture, the secrets of the technology they used to build

315

the Bastion, their motivation for placing it here in our Solar System, whether or not their civilization still exists…none of that is stuff we have any chance of learning in our lifetimes. Everything that we have learned thus far is only a fraction of a fraction of the truth about the artifact. And I have no doubt that things will be no different in another ten thousand years."

Silence fell amongst the crew again.

Mark let out a long, disappointed sigh. "Well I suppose it could be worse," he said. "The President's science adviser speculated that the Bastion was a weapon that sterilizes star systems so that other species can't colonize the stars."

Jed smiled thinly. "I think it might be safe to put that fear to rest. The Bastion definitely would have destroyed us all by now if it was an operational weapon."

"I guess I can sleep better now," Mark replied sourly.

He did not want to admit it, but he was beginning to see the logic in what Jed was saying. Maybe there really was nothing more they could do out here, and they would never learn more about the Bastion until humanity reached the technological maturity commensurate with the artifact's builders.

"So is this it?" Ning said to Mark. "On the day we first got here, you said that you didn't want to go home empty-handed. Have you lost that conviction?"

"Of course not," Mark replied. "But I'm not a fool. Whenever I've learned what my own limits are, I've never had any problem admitting it to myself or anyone else. And I have to admit that what Jed said made a lot of sense."

Mark looked at his crew. "Thank you all for your honesty and your unceasing commitment to scientific inquiry," he said. "I do wish that we had made more progress by now, but I greatly appreciate your willingness to continue on to the bitter end. Even if Jed is right about the unlikelihood of making major breakthroughs, it is the effort to carry on which matters the most. And we're not going home anytime soon. I intend to stand by our mission objective, and stay out here for as long as we can and learn as much as we can, no matter how dismally slow that process may be."

Mark thought again of Donner on the *Aldrin* that was getting closer to them with each passing day. He had always dismissed the notion that the Bastion builders were controlling Donner. But if the aliens had total sway over time and space, then warping a human mind would have been a trivial thing to do.

Yet he still could not bring himself to believe that was the reason behind the Cycler disaster, for the simple fact was that there seemed to be no logical reason for them to do so. At the same time, the function and purpose of the Bastion now seemed to completely defy explanation. Maybe that held true for all of the aliens' actions.

Chapter 30

Life onboard the *Intrepid* continued as it had since their arrival at the Bastion. The crew continued to gather data and share it with their colleagues on Earth.

Ning now spent every night with Mark. He needed her to comfort him even more in the wake of the roundtable discussion about the Bastion. She was vital for mitigating the commander's growing sense of isolation and fear of the potential futility of their mission.

Three weeks after the roundtable meeting, Mission Control contacted the *Intrepid* with a new set of orders. Everyone gathered in the galley for the high priority message.

"We're all very proud of what you guys have done," said the CAPCOM. "We understand your frustration about not having cracked the artifact's secrets, or being able to make contact with the aliens. It's not for lack of trying. You've done everything that anyone in your situation could do. And ee have some of the most brilliant minds on the planet working on the data you send to us. It's going to keep them all busy for the rest of their careers.

"But I'm afraid we also have some bad news to report to you. As you know, we've been keeping a close eye on the *Aldrin*, and it will arrive at the Bastion in just four more days. And it's still within the realm of possibility that Donner intends to crash the *Aldrin* into the Bastion in a suicidal attempt to damage or destroy it. Given what you have found about the nature of the artifact, we're not very worried about it being damaged by the *Aldrin*.

"What we are concerned with is your safety. We want you to move the *Intrepid* to a safe distance from the *Aldrin's* projected terminus. The *Aldrin* doesn't have enough remaining propellant for Donner to chase after you if you are his intended target.

"So we feel that it's best if you recover your equipment and start moving the *Intrepid* away from the Bastion as soon as possible. We want you to put a distance of at least five thousand kilometers between yourselves and the Bastion. Once the *Aldrin* has crashed into the Bastion, rendezvoused with it, or flown off into the void, you can return and resume your research. So please start gathering up all the equipment immediately, and be prepared to start moving the *Intrepid* to a safe distance within the next thirty-six hours. Mission Control out."

"I'm calling bullshit on this," snapped Ning angrily as soon as the transmission ended.

"I agree," said Oksana. "Are we really just going to turn tail and run?"

"There's no need for us to put ourselves in unnecessary danger," reasoned Mark. "Mission Control is right that we need to think of our own safety. Personally, I'm hoping that Donner does plan on rendezvousing with the Bastion." He had turned on the comm link camera as soon as he received the message from Mission Control, and was addressing Houston as well as his crew.

"We still have to assume that he's dangerous," Mark continued, "and that he could pose a real threat to us. If he does rendezvous the *Aldrin* with Bastion and comes outside for an EVA, he'll be at the mercy of Newton, and we'll have an opportunity to neutralize him. If, on the other hand, he decides to stay inside the *Aldrin* with his thumb up his ass, then we can board it and subdue him.

"Afterwards we can fly the *Intrepid* back to Earth and pick up propellant and a new crew for the *Aldrin*. Then we could come back here, refuel the *Aldrin*, and let the *Aldrin*'s new crew get the Cycler back onto its regular orbit between Earth and Mars. Normal operations could then resume at the Collins base, and we can resume our study of

319

the Bastion. That's probably the best outcome we can hope for."

Mark then turned away from his crew and to the control console, looked directly into the comm link camera, and spoke directly to NASA. "Mission Control, we've received your instructions and will immediately proceed to recover all of the research equipment and get it back onboard. Then we'll move the *Intrepid* away from the Bastion. Over and out."

The commander turned back to face his crew. "Start packing everything up," he said. "We need to get out of here, and we don't have a whole lot of time."

Adam, Jed, and Oksana immediately walked out of the galley. Mark started to follow them, but stopped when Ning suddenly grabbed his wrist.

"We can't leave," she said. Her grip was like an iron vise and the look in her eyes was ominous.

The commander looked at his wrist, and then up to Ning. "I know exactly how you feel," he said, feeling very confused. "I don't want to abandon the Bastion either. But I agree with Mission Control that our first priority needs to be our own safety. Besides, we'll probably be coming back here in a few days anyway."

"You don't understand," Ning said. Her eyes were pleading as she moved closer to Mark until their faces were only inches apart, and she continued to hold his wrist in her bone-crushing grip. "It would be far more dangerous if we allowed the one who commandeered the *Aldrin* to reach the Bastion. If he gets to it, all hope is lost."

Mark looked at her inquisitively, and felt a cold sweat on his palms. Ning still did not release his wrist from her grip. "What do you mean, 'the one who commandeered the *Aldrin*'? It's John Donner. We all know—"

"He is not Donner," Ning said sternly. "And he poses a grave threat to all."

Mark was beginning to lose circulation in his wrist, but barely noticed it as fear began to grip him. "What the hell are you talking about?"

Ning had helped keep the sense of dread from overwhelming him for so long, and it seemed as though she was about to open the floodgates.

She released Mark's wrist. She then quickly placed her hands on either side of his head, and sent swarms of nanomachines probing through his skin, skull, and into his brain, and began to share with him what she really knew.

Chapter 31

It took only a few seconds for the data transfer to complete. And when it was over, Mark looked at Ning with knowing, angry eyes. The dread was gone. In its place was anger unlike any he had felt before in his life.

He wanted to yell at her, to tear her apart for having deceived him and everyone else. But there was no need for either of them to say anything; they had shared minds, and everything that needed to be said between them had already been said.

Mark moved to the control console and turned on the ship wide intercom. "Everyone needs to get back to the galley immediately," he said. "There's been a change of plans."

Ning and Mark stood in silence until the rest of the crew returned. Adam was the first to notice the tension between Mark and Ning.

"Uh...is everything okay with the two of you?" Adam asked nervously.

"Share with them what you shared with me," Mark snapped at Ning.

Without saying a word, Ning walked up to Adam, and placed her hands on either side of his head. When she was done, Adam looked at her, astonishment registering on his face, but said nothing. Ning then went to Oksana and Jed, and shared with them the same information. A long period of tense silence then followed.

Then Jed began to laugh. "This is all so fitting," he said. "It's beautiful, really. All so fucking beautiful."

Adam glared at Ning, and then looked to Mark. "So what do we do now?" he asked the commander.

"We have to stop him," Mark said grimly. "It is as simple as that."

"And how the hell do you plan on doing that?"

Mark did not reply. He only looked at his crew with solemn remorse.

"Holy shit," Adam whispered. "You're going to ram the *Intrepid* into the *Aldrin*, aren't you?"

Mark remained silent.

"Are you fucking insane?"

"Probably," Mark said. "But if that bastard is able to use the Bastion's power, we're all as good as dead anyway. And so is everyone else back on Earth. I have to stop him, and this is the only option available to us." He breathed deeply. "But you're not going to die with me. I want you all to get down to the Bastion. We have two days to make our preparations. That will give us time to move all the spare oxygen tanks to the surface."

Oksana said, "If you destroy the *Intrepid*, you'll effectively be killing the rest of us. We'll die once the oxygen runs out. So why don't we just stay onboard? Since we'll end up dying regardless of what we do, we all might as well go down with the ship alongside you."

Mark sighed. "No, none of you are going to stay here with me," he said. "This may be a bit of a long shot, but I still think it's possible that the Bastion is monitoring us. And if the *Intrepid* is destroyed defending the Bastion from that asshole, maybe that will finally show it that we're worth something after all. And maybe, just maybe, it will rescue you guys."

Jed laughed. "This is the worst kind of wishful thinking. You're going to try appeasing the gods with a human sacrifice."

"It's all we can do!" Mark yelled. "Your deaths will be sealed if you stay onboard with me. At least if you go back down to the Bastion, you might just have a slim chance of surviving this. And no matter how slim of a chance that may be, it's still worth taking."

323

"It's still a completely futile gesture," said Jed. He looked at Ning. "This little bitch has been trying to turn the damn thing on this whole fucking time. And you haven't had much luck, have you? What makes you think that's going to change now? I think she's already proven that the aliens don't give a damn about her or the rest of us. Postponing our deaths for a few more hours isn't going to make this any less futile." He chuckled. "Hell, they probably don't care about the other guy either, and he'll have no more luck at making that goddamned thing work when he gets here. So why are we bothering to do this?"

"Because the risk is too fucking great!" Mark shouted. "It could be that the ones who built the Bastion really did intend for him to use it. And he'll destroy everything if he can wield that power! We must err on the side of caution for the sake of Earth. And if that means we all die, then so be it!

"You may be right that nothing will come from this, that it's all just a postponement of the inevitable. But if there's even a slight possibility that this could save the billions of lives on Earth, and maybe yours as well, then it's worth doing. It's our only possible hope."

"Nietzsche said that hope is the worst of all evils, for it prolongs the torments of man."

"I don't give a fuck what Nietzsche said! I gave you a goddamned order! Now shut the fuck up and get going now!"

A brief glimmer of anger and defiance seemed to wash over Jed, and he locked eyes with Mark. The mathematician clenched his fists, and looked like he was about ready to fight the commander. But he restrained himself, and turned to leave the galley.

Mark and Ning stared at each other for one final, intense moment. They said nothing, and Ning left the galley. Adam and Oksana followed suit, with Mark right

324

behind them.

***

The atmosphere among the crew was extremely sour for the rest of the day and into the next. They worked tirelessly to move all of the reserve oxygen tanks to the surface of the Bastion. As they did this, they also moved research equipment back into the *Intrepid* in order to avoid arousing suspicion in Mission Control about what they were planning.

Ning was involved with every spacewalk; there was no point anymore in concealing her enhanced physical capability. In addition, she now offered the same enhancement to her fellow crewmembers during spacewalks, providing nearly inexhaustible stamina needed to complete their tasks in the little time remaining.

They rarely spoke to each other during this time; their full attention devoted to their work. No one wanted to talk to Ning at all, and spoke to her only when it was absolutely necessary to do so when transporting equipment. Mark managed to avoid speaking a single word to her altogether since the revelation in the galley.

Then it was time to for Adam, Jed, Ning, and Oksana to leave as Mark had ordered. Their goodbyes to the commander were terse and solemn. But he continued to meet Ning with only silence. He knew this was likely to be the last time he would see her, but the anger he felt toward her was simply too great.

Mark waited until everyone was gone, and then moved up the ladder to the central hub, reaching the command deck as quickly as he could. He strapped himself into the commander's seat for what he knew would be the last time. He felt a modicum of pride in knowing that he would die piloting the mightiest spacecraft ever built by man. At the same time, it hurt to know that his death would also destroy this wonder of engineering and most likely lead to the

325

deaths of his crew.

Ning's manipulation and concealment of the truth exacerbated the pain that Mark felt. She had made preparations for this confrontation, which Mark interpreted as being both good and bad.

He logged onto the *Intrepid*'s main computer, overriding the privacy protection so that he could gain access to all of the crew's personal files. He navigated to Ning's files, and quickly found what he was looking for. Ning had written a program that would deny Mission Control the option of overriding manual controls and left a simple executable for the commander to use in this exact situation. All Mark had to do was click *"Run"* on the exec file and the program would initiate. The program would allow the crew to continue communicating with Earth without giving Mission Control an opportunity to interfere or seize control of the *Intrepid* remotely.

This made Mark realize that Ning truly did care for the crew. If all she cared about was stopping the *Aldrin* hijacker, she could have killed them all just as Mark now knew the *other* had done to the Cycler's crew. It would have been possible for her to program the *Intrepid*'s flight computer to intercept the *Aldrin* once the Cycler was too close to avoid collision, giving her just enough time to escape to the Bastion. Mark smiled ruefully. He was not about to let the *Aldrin* get that close.

At least this program would permit the crew to say their final goodbyes to their loved ones. Mark, for his part, could not bring himself to bid Ning farewell... he would never forgive her deceit. He had grown closer to her than he had to anyone. How much of it was a lie? If she had not cared for him, why had she continued the masquerade or the relationship during their time onboard the *Intrepid*? There was no reason for it.

Still, he was not entirely convinced that Ning had

shared everything with him. He thought back to when he had first learned of the *Aldrin* hijacking, when he had considered abandoning their mission to lend aid to Collins. What if the Collins crew had needed and requested their help? Would Ning have killed Mark and the rest of the crew just as the *Aldrin* hijacker had done? She had not revealed what she would have done in that eventuality, but Mark believed that she would have done everything she could to reach the Bastion at all costs.

He activated Ning's program, and then opened the comm link to Mission Control.

"Mission Control, this is *Intrepid*," Mark said. "I'm afraid that we cannot comply with your orders to vacate the vicinity of the Bastion. We are not doing this lightly. We are disobeying because we have just obtained crucial information about the Bastion and the *Aldrin* hijacking. The Bastion contains a power unlike anything you can envision, and the one who commandeered the *Aldrin* is not Donner at all. It would take too much time to explain to you exactly who and what he is, so I will not take the time to do so in this transmission. What you need to know right now is that he may be capable of wielding the vast power of the Bastion. If we allow him to rendezvous with the Bastion and he does unlock its power for himself, then he will pose a great danger to the Earth. I know how insane all of this sounds, but I promise you that it is the truth.

"I am therefore preparing to crash the *Intrepid* into the *Aldrin* in order to destroy the hijacker before he can rendezvous with the alien artifact. I have ordered the rest of the crew to evacuate and return to the surface of the Bastion so that they will not immediately perish when the *Intrepid* and *Aldrin* are destroyed. You may think of it as being naïve, but I hope that the Bastion will save my crew once it sees the sacrifice I am willing to make to protect it. It is all that I have left to hope for, and I will hold onto that

327

hope until my final breath.

"Time is something that has become a precious commodity for us, and one that must be used carefully. So please do not question why I am doing this, or how I obtained this information about the Bastion. You cannot dissuade me in my purpose, or persuade the rest of the crew to turn against me. They all understand what is at stake, and are just as willing as I am to make this sacrifice. We will remain steadfast, and will not deviate from what we plan to do. I am leaving personal comm channels open so that my crew may say their goodbyes to their families.

"Furthermore, do not try to lock out manual controls. Any attempt to do so will be in vain.

"I'm going to make a recording in the intervals between our sending and receiving of communiques, and during these intervals I will describe in more detail why I am doing this and how I acquired this information. I will transmit that recording to you right before I crash the *Intrepid* into the *Aldrin*. That is all for now. *Intrepid* out."

As soon as Mark had completed the transmission, he turned the video recorder on, and began to describe everything that Ning had shared with him. He could never do justice to the experience, but he owed it to everyone on Earth to tell them all he had learned as best he could.

***

Adam, Ning, Oksana, and Jed moved in silence as they made their way to the main airlock. Reaching it, they solemnly began to suit up for what they knew most likely would be the last time.

"We're exiting the airlock now," Oksana said over the comm. As the quartet activated their MMUs she added, "Making our way to the Bastion now."

"Understood," replied Mark.

***

Mission Control

Houston, Texas

Flight Director Ian Bertoch watched the message from Mark de Rijk in stunned silence and horror. No one in the control room said anything as the commander described his intentions.

What made this even worse was that the commander sent his transmission not only to Mission Control, but to all of the public channels as well. So now everyone in the world knew of the impending disaster. Things were going to be as chaotic as the aftermath of the *Aldrin* tragedy, if not worse.

Bertoch could not think that now... not when there was still something that could be done to save the crew.

When Mark's transmission came to an end, chaos erupted in the control room.

"Everybody calm the fuck down!" Bertoch screamed. "We have to take charge of the situation ASAP! GNC, Flight. Override the manual controls. Do it right now!"

"Copy that Flight!" replied Mihir Hasar, and he began to frantically pound at his keyboard, sending the command from his terminal.

"Mark said we shouldn't bother trying to do that," said Philip Caillo, the Flight Activities Officer.

"I am aware of that," Bertoch returned, "but that sure as shit doesn't mean we shouldn't try." He looked to Ryan Boghossian, the flight surgeon. "Surgeon, Flight. How are they holding up?"

"Flight, Surgeon," Boghossian said in response to Bertoch. "They all seem to be perfectly healthy."

Bertoch breathed a sigh of relief. "Well at least that's a silver lining," he said. He had feared that the rest of the *Intrepid*'s crewmembers could have suddenly and inexplicably perished, just like the crew of the *Aldrin*. But even if that had not happened, the wanton destruction of the

Intrepid would effectively condemn them.

Bertoch looked at the monitors on the far wall of the control room that displayed feeds from various locations on the *Intrepid*. Mark was on the command deck, and the rest of the crew was already suited up and preparing to exit the main airlock.

"Holy shit!" the Public Affairs Officer declared, staring at the same image. "They really think that the Bastion is going to save them. They've got to be as crazy as Mark."

"Or maybe they're too afraid to try to stop him," said Bertoch. "I'm not sure which possibility I find more terrifying. But after we've taken control of the *Intrepid*, that might make them get back onboard. So all the more reason we need to get control. GNC, Flight. How's that manual override coming?"

"Flight, GNC," Hassar replied. "I've sent the override command. Now it's just a matter of waiting."

"Good. Hopefully we can stop Mark before he wrecks the *Intrepid*."

He could hardly believe he had said that. Mark de Rijk was one of the greatest astronauts ever. Then again, the same thing could be said about Donner. Why would he be doing this? Would Mark turn on his crew once NASA took control of the vessel?

Bertoch thought of the endless speculation that the Bastion and its creators were behind the loss of the *Aldrin*. Yet, if Mark had not suffered a mental breakdown, then it might be possible the Bastion, or some other force tied to the Bastion's makers, had somehow made contact with the commander.

The flight director dared not speak of this now. He could not fuel the fire of panic that was threatening to reduce the Center to chaos.

***

330

"We are touching down on the Bastion now," reported Oksana as the four crewmembers came to rest on the surface of the alien artifact for what could well be the last time.

"Roger that," replied the commander.

Adam, Jed, and Oksana carefully rose to their feet, but Ning lay sprawled on the surface, and did not make the slightest amount of effort to stand up.

'Please hear me,' she said within her mind. The Tabernacle had to hear her thoughts. It must have been aware of her presence. Despite Legion's millennia-long silence, she did not believe they had abandoned her, Earth, or the baselines. They saw everything. Why were they ignoring her? It was their prerogative, but why?

'I have done all that you have commanded,' she said to the Tabernacle. *'He who would destroy everything approaches. You must know this! If you find me to be undeserving of your power, please at least stop him! Humanity does not deserve to suffer under his yoke again! I know that I am not fit to question your judgement. If you deem me unworthy of your power, then you are right to do so. But you surely cannot mean to bestow him with the power that you wield!'*

She was commanding scores of nanomachines to leave her body and move across the surface of the Tabernacle, crawling as far as they could until they passed beyond the range of communication and died. She had made similar pleas to the Tabernacle since first she had touched it. It had taken a great amount of self-restraint to allow Commander de Rijk to touch down on the surface of the Tabernacle before her.

She had considered enticing the commander to allow her to touch the Tabernacle first. While she was reasonably confident that her powers of persuasion were sufficient enough to sway the commander, she knew that the mission

331

planners back on Earth would not have allowed it. Of course, she could have easily ignored what they said. It was not as if they would be able to stop her. But the rest of the crew likely would have found it unusual for her to attempt to sway the commander's mind in such a manner. They might have grown suspicious of her, especially in light of the circumstances surrounding the incident with the *Aldrin*.

She knew it was certainly possible that the Tabernacle would bestow its power to whoever was the first one to touch it. After all the millennia she had waited, it would have been crushing if Legion decided to give their power to one of the baselines and not to her. But she was not willing to harm Mark or her crewmates just so that she could touch the Tabernacle first.

When the commander's touchdown on the Tabernacle did not unleash Legion's power, Ning had breathed a sigh of relief. She was confused and uneasy when she too failed to unlock the Tabernacle's power. Her pleas for a response from the Tabernacle since she had made that first contact had gone unanswered. She had gone to the Tabernacle more often than any of the other crewmembers always pleading for a response and getting none.

She began to question if it were possible that the Bastion was not the Tabernacle. Could another ancient starfaring civilization whose might rivaled that of Legion have built the Bastion?

Ning had considered this possibility, but ultimately dismissed it as absurd. The power of Legion extended throughout the entire universe.

Still, the failure to unlock the Tabernacle's power did not give her reason to believe it was forever beyond her reach. Perhaps it was only through her unrelenting resolve and persistence that Legion would deem her to be worthy of her power. Her consistent failure to unlock the power that the Tabernacle supposedly contained caused her to fear that Legion had, in fact intended to give their power to the *other* all along.

Impossible! She obeyed every order given to her, never once questioning the will of Legion. They had ordered her to trap the *other* in the ice in Antarctica, and she had done so. They had promised her that the power of the Tabernacle would be hers one day...promised!

She had not flinched when she had been instructed to remain in the shadows rather than guiding the baselines on a path to prosperity. Never again could she allow the baselines to know of her powers. When wars, plagues, famines, and other disasters befell humanity, she was forbidden from using her power to resolve them. Once the *other* was imprisoned, Legion decreed that the baselines would now have to do everything themselves, with no one to give them the guidance they so desperately needed.

She had never questioned Legion as to why they had reversed their policy for the baselines. Never once had she hesitated to obey whatever they commanded of her.

She had betrayed her male counterpart without a moment's hesitation when Legion commanded her to do so. She did wonder why they had not killed him, or ordered her to kill him. At the same time, she knew it was not her place to question. When Legion ordered her to bring him to the frozen wastes of Antarctica, she again obeyed without hesitation, even though they intimated the *other* might be liberated some distant day in the future.

She could not fathom why they wanted to preserve him after all that he had done. They had never explicitly stated that the *other* would be denied the power of the Tabernacle and she had always feared that Legion had always intended it to be this way.

For the longest time, she feared that a natural event would melt the ice on the frozen continent and free the *other* from his cryonic prison. Then after more than seventy millennia of wondering the Earth alone, it appeared baselines would be responsible for the *other*'s liberation due to a warming climate resulting from excess carbon dioxide produced by the baselines' industrial activities.

During those tumultuous years of rapid industrialization and callous disregard for the environment, Ning had been tempted to assume the identities of CEOs of fossil fuel companies or leaders of developed nations in order to force a halt their wanton destruction of the planet's climate and environment. But that was precisely the sort of activity Legion had forbidden. She was condemned to remain in the shadows. It was no less a prison than the ice was for the *other*.

If she began to accrue too much influence, she abandoned her position and assumed a new identity. It was frustrating, but she dare not risk incurring the wrath of Legion.

She had breathed a sigh of relief when the baselines stopped climate change entirely on their own by embracing renewable sources of energy. With climate change averted, it seemed that the Antarctic ice would remain intact, and continue to keep the *other* trapped. But the extreme environment could not keep the baselines from establishing a presence on the ice-bound continent of Antarctica. And Ning feared that their relentless drive to explore would inevitably lead to them discovering the *other*.

Then there came the massacre at the Niflheim Antarctic station. Intuitively, she knew the baseline scientists at Niflheim had found and awoken the *other*. Pursuit was out of the question. He, just as she, could easily disguise himself as any baseline he desired. Furthermore, it was only by Legion's intervention that she had been able to overpower the *other* all those millennia ago.

Ultimately, she knew that the *other* would find his way to someone who knew about the Tabernacle, and then find a way to travel to it. It was the reason she fought as hard as she could to join the *Intrepid*'s crew. She had allowed herself to believe she was safe once they left Earth. That it did not matter if the *other* had awoken, because no other ship could take him to the Tabernacle. Then her greatest fear was realized when the *Aldrin* was commandeered, for only the *other* could have done such a thing.

'*I have exposed myself to the baselines,*' Ning said to the Tabernacle. '*Please forgive me for breaking your commandment. But I did not believe that I had any other choice. I could not prevent the other from reaching you without their aid. Please stop him for the sake of us all.*'

Still no response came from the Tabernacle.

***

"If you're going to do anything, you best do it now!" Mark yelled.

"I've been trying," said Ning. She did not even try to mask the feeling of defeat that was in her voice. "I've been pleading for them to help us, and there's just no response. This is exactly what I've been doing all this time. I don't know what else I can do."

There was a long, horrifying silence. Mark had pinned his hopes for his crew on Ning's connection to Legion. With that hope gone, it left him with one remaining, drastic course of action.

Breaking the silence Mark finally said, "I'm going to stop him. I'm sorry, but you all know this has to be done. I want you to know that you are the finest crew I've ever served with and had the privilege of commanding."

No one said anything.

Mark wanted to tell them to go to the other side of the Bastion so that the alien artifact would shield them from the radiation generated by the *Intrepid*'s fusion drive, but he knew that that was probably unnecessary. Ning's shared nanomachines could counteract all of the harm that radiation poisoning would do to their bodies, and Mark did not believe she would allow any of her crewmates to die needlessly.

If Legion had abandoned Ning, or if they no longer existed, it would not matter anyway. The crew's oxygen would run out long before radiation poisoning could kill them. The crew would likely want to watch the spacecraft that had brought them here for as long as possible. Still, it disturbed Mark to know that the exhaust from his ship would bombard his crew with high-energy neutrons and bremsstrahlung X-rays. But time was of the essence, and he could afford to wait no longer.

"Firing engine now," Mark said

He had hoped that the next time he fired the engine it would be to return to Earth with whatever treasures they had gleaned from the Bastion. Now, no matter how noble the cause, he was turning his beautiful *Intrepid* into a powered battering ram.

He flipped the switch that activated the engine, and felt the slight push against him as fusion pulses pushed the *Intrepid* forward. It had been so long since the engine was used that Mark had almost forgotten what the drive's acceleration felt like.

"Engine is operating nominally," the commander reported. Then he sighed sadly. "I'll relay to you any messages that your families might send," he said to his crew. "And I promise that I won't eavesdrop on them," and to himself, 'I don't have the time.'

***

Jed, Oksana, and Adam looked up at the bright engine of the *Intrepid* as the spacecraft began to move away from the Bastion.

"Looks like your attempt to get their attention is as futile now as it's ever been," said Jed, breaking the silence.

"You're not doing anything to help!" Adam shouted.

"I'm not claiming to," Jed said. "I'm just being the voice of reason. Make no mistake: we will all be dead in just a few hours. Hoping for a miracle isn't going to change that, so don't waste your time futilely praying to false gods. Don't be one of those who can only take solace with their impending demise by believing that salvation or a blissful afterlife awaits those who pray to nonexistent deities."

***

Mission Control
Houston, Texas

"What's the status of the ship?" Alan Prater asked Bertoch. The NASA administrator had raced to the control room upon hearing Commander de Rijk's suicidal declaration.

"We'll know soon enough if the manual override was successful," Bertoch replied. He had feared that Mark would shut down communications just as Donner had done on the *Aldrin*. Fortunately, he had done nothing of the sort.

"Flight, GNC," said Hassar from his computer console. He looked afraid to speak.

"Please give me some good news," Bertoch said desperately.

Hassar grimaced. "I'm afraid I have none to give," he said. "The manual override didn't work."

Bertoch groaned. With all of the shit that had gone wrong, he almost did not even find this to be surprising. "Why the hell not?"

"A program executed by *Intrepid's* nav computer has locked out the manual override."

"Jesus Christ. You mean he had something already written that he was planning on using for this?"

"He must have, because I don't think he could have written a program like this in the time between when he informed us of his decision to ram the *Aldrin* and receiving our response."

337

Bertoch ran his hand through his hair, and let out a long, exasperated sigh.

***

"Commander Mark de Rijk," said Bertoch on the console. He spoke carefully, trying as best he could to talk the commander out of committing suicide. "I know that you told us not to waste our breath telling you abandon your plan, but that is simply beyond my capability. Please. I beg you with every fiber of my being not to do this." He took a few deep breaths, desperation registering on his face.

"Mark, please don't do this!" the flight director begged. "I don't pretend to understand what's happening right now, and I can't imagine what you've learned. But you can't kill yourself. Think of your crew. You owe it to them and their families to bring them home safely. Whatever you think you've learned, it can't be worth all of your lives!"

Mark laughed grimly once Bertoch's message ended. "I know that you tried locking out manual control," he said, "despite my warning not to waste your time trying. Now you're trying to talk me out of doing this, even though I told you not to do that either. You obviously don't believe me when I say that I'm doing this to protect Earth.

"So let me spell this out for you again as plainly as I can: no words can persuade me to abandon that which needs to be done. You know that the rest of the crew has made their decision committing to this, and their resolve is as strong as mine is.

"I know that you probably still won't believe me after you receive the recording I've made where I describe in depth what's happening and why. Trust me when I say that I don't want to do this. I'm doing it because I have no choice. Our lives are a worthy sacrifice to save everyone on Earth. I don't know if you'll ever be convinced of this, but I swear on my life and the lives of my crew that it's the truth.

338

Intrepid out."

Mark turned off the radio and sat in silence for a few moments. Then he resumed recording his account of what he had learned from Ning.

A scant few minutes after the first transmission from Mission Control, there came a message from Miles.

"Mark, I'm in the minority here when I say that I don't believe you've suffered any sort of mental breakdown," said the IE president. His voice was soft and sad. Mark had never heard him speak like this. "I believe what you've said about the danger that the Bastion and the *Aldrin* hijacker pose. I don't know how you've learned this, but I have always trusted you. And it would be a betrayal of that trust if I did not believe you now, in these most extenuating of circumstances. Mark, I..." His voice trailed off, and tears were swelling in his eyes. "I can't bear the thought of you dying. Every time you flew on one of our spacecraft, I had complete faith that you'd be coming back. You mean so much to me. And I don't know what I'm going to do after you're gone."

Mark fought hard to keep himself from crying as Miles was at this moment.

"I'm sorry Miles," he said, practically choking on his words, "but this has to be done. The man that commandeered the *Aldrin* is far more dangerous than you can imagine. He must be stopped from reaching the Bastion, no matter what the price."

He wanted to tell Miles just how much he meant to him. But he had gotten closer to Ning than he thought he would, only to find just how much she had lied. Even after she had shared her mind with his, he could not be certain if the feelings she seemed to have toward him were genuine. And even in the last hours of his life, Mark felt powerless to express how he felt toward Miles, and he hated himself for that.

"Miles, I can't thank you enough for everything that you've done for me," Mark continued. You've done more for me than anyone else ever has or ever could. And I'm beyond honored to have helped you with your goals, and for being your friend.

"Please do not feel bad that it has led to my death, for there is no other death I could ever have that could be more honorable than the one I am facing. No words can ever do justice to the level of gratitude I have for you. Thank you again for everything that you've done for me Miles. Goodbye."

Mark turned off the comm console, and wiped tears from his eyes before resuming his recording.

***

Adam heard the voice of his wife on his suit's radio.

"Adam, please...I," Maria stammered. "Honey, I...oh God, I don't even know what to say."

Adam could hear her crying hysterically.

"You can't do this," Maria said, struggling to gain composure. "You promised me that you'd come back. I'm still holding you to your word! You can't leave me alone forever! You've got to come back!"

"Baby, I'm sorry that I'm going to break that promise I made to you," Adam said, choking back tears. Damn the time delay! What he'd give to have his last conversation with his wife occur in real time.

"I'm sorry that I will soon be leaving you forever," Adam said. "All of the best years of my life were spent with you, and I wouldn't trade that for anything. It was only after I met you that I realized just how empty and devoid of meaning my life had been before our glorious meeting. If I could do everything all over again, the only thing I'd change is that I would have married you earlier than I did.

"My biggest regret is that I won't be able to hold you

in my arms ever again. And I know that my passing will greatly hurt you. But please don't mourn me forever. I want you to continue enjoying life after I'm gone. The best way that you can remember me is by living your own life to the fullest.

"I love you Maria, and nothing has made me happier than being able to call you my wife."

***

"Oksana, please tell me you aren't doing this," Anastasia said over her sister's radio channel. "You can't be doing this. You're smarter than me and at least ninety-nine percent of the population. You can't seriously believe that something evil is about to spring forth. And...oh sweet Jesus, please don't let this happen! Please don't kill yourself!

Oksana breathed deeply and steadily before replying to her sister's message. "We have not suffered mental breakdowns," she said as calmly as she could in spite of her racing heart. "I wish I could tell you how we know this, but it transcends speech. But I trust that Commander de Rijk is explaining the extenuating circumstances that we are facing as best anyone can. It is not easy to accept my impending death, but I am trying to be as brave as I can be. Even if I completely lost all of my courage, I wouldn't be able to come back. My death here is all but set in stone. But I'm not going to cave under this. I'm standing with my crewmates until the bitter end. I will not allow panic to overwhelm my capability for rational thought.

"But please understand why this is being done. You're in danger. Everyone is. You, Mom, everybody. We're doing this to protect everyone on Earth.

"I don't regret coming here. I've learned more about how little we actually understand the universe in my brief time here than I have in my entire life. And I feel a surge of pride knowing that I'm dying so that the rest of humanity may live.

"I am sorry for the grief that my death will cause for you and Mom. I wish that this didn't have to happen, but I'm afraid that there is no alternative. Thank you both for always being there for me, always supporting the endeavors that I pursued. I love you very much. Goodbye."

***

"Daddy."

That single word, spoken in that small, innocent, familiar voice was all that it took to shatter the illusion that Jed was alone in the universe, for the mathematician immediately identified the voice as belonging to the one thing that mattered more to him than discovering the truth about the Bastion.

"Daddy, please," Karen said. "Please come home. You've been gone too long. Please don't die. You have to come home. Please. You can't die. I love you Daddy!"

"Karen," Jed said somberly, fighting hard to hold back tears. "Listen very carefully to what I say, because this is very likely to be the last time I am able to speak to you. I have never lied to you about anything. Before I even considered having you conceived, I knew that I would never deceive any you or any other offspring I might have. I wanted you to be as intelligent and inquisitive as possible, and the best way to encourage that was by always explaining the truth to you, no matter how grim those truths may be. This is why I explained the nature of human reproduction to you when you inquired about it, rather than tell you a falsehood as a way to preserve childlike naiveté. It is why I explained the concept of death to you when your grandparents perished. And it is why I never wanted you to believe in such foolish folkloric figures such as Santa Claus or false gods, for such beliefs poison the intellect. I have nurtured your curiosity in the hope that you would follow in my footsteps to expand humankind's knowledge.

342

"The most deceptive thing I ever did was not tell you what I would be doing when I left Earth. Doing that and leaving you was the hardest decision I have ever made, but I did so because I believed this would allow me to bequeath you with greater knowledge of the Bastion and its makers, the greatest gift that I can conceive.

"And I will not deviate from my practice of always disclosing the realities of life, death, and the nature of the universe to you, least of all with what will be the last words you ever hear me utter.

"You have undoubtedly heard the words of my commander, who believes that we are sacrificing ourselves to protect Earth and humanity from a terrible threat. In truth, I do not know if this threat is genuine, or if our desperate attempt to stop it is anything other than futile. It is entirely possible that we have been deceived.

"But I accept that I cannot resolve this plight. Sometimes there arise forces and circumstances beyond our control, which dictate our fates. Nothing beneficial could have resulted from any attempt to mutiny against my commander, leaving me with no choice but to accept my fate.

"When I left Earth, I told you there was a very strong possibility that I would not be coming home. My fate has now been sealed, and there is no possibility that I will survive this.

"It breaks my heart to know that you will grow up without me. But you need to be strong. Learn all the things that death will deny me from ever knowing.

"I love you Karen. I love you more than anything else. And until I draw my final breath, my thoughts will be of you."

***

Mark's personal comm channel opened, and he knew that it was his brother before he uttered a single word.

"Mark," David said his voice barely above a whisper. "It's unbelievably devastating to me that you're about to die. I'm not going to try talking you out of this. I know that there would be no point in it.

"But there is something I have to ask you. You've seen something profound, something that must be divine or demonic. I know you have, or else you wouldn't be doing this. Please tell me what it is. I have to know!" There was desperation in his voice, as if he felt that his soul was at stake.

Mark was frustrated that his brother would bring this up, but had expected it nonetheless. He was laying down his life for his brother and the rest of humanity, and really didn't want to have to deal with talking about religious and theological issues in what could very well be the final minutes of his life. But he still owed his brother a response.

He opened his personal channel, and looked solemnly into the camera.

"David, these are the last words you will ever hear from me, so listen very carefully," Mark said. "The man who hijacked the *Aldrin* isn't a minion of your god or the devil. And neither are the beings that built the Bastion. There is nothing supernatural at work here. The extraterrestrials are as far beyond us as we are beyond amoebas, but they are not gods. It is true that a revelation has been made to me and my crew, but it is not in any way divine. This revelation was made by a pawn of the Bastion's builders. I suppose that I'm a pawn too. And the one who commandeered the *Aldrin* is a pawn as well. All of us are pawns. We've always been pawns. But even knowing that we're pawns isn't enough to free ourselves from being pawns. We have no choice but to play the game that the Bastion builders have set for us.

"And you'll be insulting my memory if you think I'm dying for your imaginary deity. And don't even think about offering me last rites. Nothing would piss me off more than if you were to do that."

Mark let out a deep sigh before continuing. "But I'm not going to waste my last words on yet another religious argument with you. What I want is to tell you how much you mean to me, and how you need to remember me. I want you to remember everything about me, the good and the bad. Remember all those times I stood up for you in school, even though I pushed you around at home. Remember how I helped you out with your schoolwork whenever you asked me to, even if I often called you an idiot for not understanding it. Remember when I was there for you when your girlfriend Lisa Baker broke your heart. And even though you've always denied it, I know that the heartbreak she caused you was the main reason you went into the priesthood. I know that you wanted to marry her, and you didn't think you'd ever be able to love another woman.

"And I want you to remember how condescending I've been towards you and your religious beliefs. That shouldn't be too hard for you to do. As long as you remember all of those things and everything else about me, a part of me will continue to live on after I'm gone. So please do that for me. I love you."

Mark took a deep breath, tried not to cry, and then resumed describing what Ning had showed him.

Chapter 32

Strapped into the commander's seat on the *Aldrin's* command deck, Ask was in complete bewilderment at the situation unfolding before him. The *Intrepid* was moving away from the Tabernacle and was on a collision course with the Cycler.

NASA must have been tracking the *Aldrin*, and valued the safety of their astronauts above all else. They should have ordered the *Intrepid* to move away from the Tabernacle as a precaution until the *Aldrin* was no longer a potential threat to them.

There was absolutely no reason for the crew to be doing this. It seemed impossible that the crew would suffer a mental breakdown to the point that they would feel compelled to make a suicidal attempt to destroy the *Aldrin*.

Unless...

This had to be the machinations of the *other*. It was the only possible explanation.

Ask felt his blood boil as he thought of his female counterpart. Legion had bestowed her with the same nanotechnology that they had given him, and she had blindly followed their will without question. Even after the catastrophe that nearly destroyed the human species, her faith in Legion had not been shaken in the least. And there had been no hesitation on her part when they ordered her to betray Ask and trap him in the frozen wastes of Antarctica.

Ask had scarcely devoted a single thought to her since he had awoken. As with Legion, there was nothing in the baselines' recorded history to indicate that she had ever taken an active role in guiding the development of civilization.

He had wondered if Legion had rewarded her unwavering loyalty to them. Perhaps they had given her their power after she had betrayed him, as they had instructed. It was infuriating for him to consider that, but he knew that it was a possibility.

If she was still alive and had been on Earth for the past seventy millennia, why had she abandoned Legion's guideline to lead baseline civilization on a continuous path of technological improvement? Nothing in the volumes of books he had read, the internet searches he had done, or the knowledge he had gained from the baselines' brains gave any indication of the technological leaps the guidelines demanded. Had Legion abandoned her?

And if she was among the *Intrepid*'s crew, she had failed to unlock the Tabernacle's power. So either Legion had not intended to give her their power, or the artifact was not the Tabernacle at all.

She must have been convinced that it was the Tabernacle, and was fearful that its power was intended for him and him alone. So in a desperate attempt to stop him from reaching the Tabernacle she must have revealed her secrets to the rest of the *Intrepid*'s crew, and convinced them to sacrifice themselves in order to destroy him.

Madness! All of it was madness!

And this might have sealed his fate. If he performed any propulsive maneuvers to avoid colliding with the *Intrepid*, he would burn up too much of the remaining propellant, and be unable to rendezvous with the Tabernacle. He would sail off into the void of space until his supplies were exhausted and he perished.

He had no choice but to flee the *Aldrin*. But there was scarcely enough time for him to get into a spacesuit before the Cycler and the *Intrepid* collided. Ask had to speak to the commander of the *Intrepid* and beg him to see reason while making his attempt to escape.

Ask put on a comm wristband and then activated the *Aldrin*'s communication system for the first time since he

347

had commandeered the vessel. The wristband would send his words through the *Aldrin*'s radio and to the *Intrepid*, and hopefully deter Mark de Rijk from destroying them both. It was desperate, but also the only way to avert the destruction of the *Aldrin* and *Intrepid*.

Ask then pushed himself out of the commander's seat and moved down the *Aldrin*'s corridor as quickly as he could, making his way to the airlock where the spacesuits were kept.

For the first time since he had awoken, Ask would speak as himself. Whenever Ask had imitated a baseline and interacted with other humans, it was always as a perfect mimic, masking his true persona. He spoke only when spoken to, and only as much as was needed for acceptable social etiquette. He had never spoken to any baseline with anything even remotely resembling his own nature, as he never felt there was any reason to do so.

A desperate plea for his life was more than sufficient justification to break his long silence. Some baselines would consider such an act to be dishonorable, even cowardly, and would rather die than beg for their lives. Ask considered such concepts to be laughable at best, for nothing was more important than the preservation of one's own life.

It might not matter anyway, for if the *other* had shared even part of her mind with de Rijk, it was unlikely that any utterance Ask was capable of making would dissuade the commander. But Ask still had to try. There was no other option available to him that had any possibility of changing his dire situation.

"Commander Mark de Rijk," Ask said, speaking for the first time in over seventy millennia with his powerful voice that had once moved the ancestors of all living humans. "You already know who I am, insofar as to what my female counterpart has revealed to you. Her corruption

348

of your mind is the only possible explanation for what you are doing. While I do not know the full extent of what she has disclosed to you, it is blindingly obvious that it is far from the truth. Whatever fragments of the truth she permits you to see, she does so only because it serves her own ends. And in that regard, she has succeeded, for she now bends you to her will, using you as her puppet."

Ask reached the airlock. There was barely enough time to get into a spacesuit, much less to depressurize the airlock. But if he did nothing, he would be sealing his own fate.

He continued to make his desperate plea to de Rijk as he donned the suit. Speaking was no more distracting for him than breathing was.

"She has likely told you that the Bastion is the Tabernacle of Legion that both she and I seek. She must have told you that I have nefarious intentions, and that I would commit malevolent actions against Earth if I were to obtain the power that Legion led us to believe is contained within the Tabernacle."

Ask pulled the bottom half of his suit on first, and then clutched a spare oxygen tank with his legs, knowing that he would likely need it shortly.

"I vow on my life that if this artifact is the Tabernacle, and it bestows me with its power, I will not use it to commit any hostile actions against you, your crew, or Earth. I merely wish to learn more of the beings behind all of this, just as you do.

"Why she would choose to deceive you on this and make you believe that condemning us all to death is something that completely eludes me. It could be that her millennia of isolation have driven her mad, and now that she sees that the power of the Tabernacle will not be hers, she has decided that dying is the only way she can hope to achieve tranquility.

"I implore you to consider the full implications of your actions. I have acknowledged the possibility that this alien artifact may not be the Tabernacle. I am prepared to surrender the *Aldrin* and myself to you in that eventuality. If you refuse to heed my words, you will be condemning your crew, yourself, and me to meaningless deaths. You must not do this!

"She would have you believe that she has broken the chains that kept you blinded from the truth. But I assure you that you remain shackled within the cave, the chains and the cave entirely of her making. Do not squander your life by bashing yourself against the jagged rocks of ignorance that line the cave walls to which she has chained you! I beseech you again to resist her siren's song and regain your willpower to overcome this senseless madness with which you have been afflicted!"

***

The first thing that struck Mark about the hijacker's voice was its familiarity. Ning had imparted the commander with so many memories of the centuries that she and the *Aldrin* hijacker had walked the Earth together, during which they had fought to bring order to a cruel, chaotic world. He knew of the passion they had held for each other, their commitment to Legion, and the horrors that all of them had committed.

It was somewhat of a surprise to Mark to hear the hijacker pleading like this. He had expected him to be too prideful to beg for his life in such a manner; that he would rather die than to beg for his life from someone as lowly as a baseline.

It was clear, however, that he was intelligent enough to know that he had no other chance of surviving than by making a desperate plea like this. Mark felt that he could at least respect the monster for swallowing his pride like that.

Mark found himself seriously considering what the

hijacker had said. How could he trust everything that Ning had revealed to him?

Yes, it was entirely possible that the Bastion was not the Tabernacle, just as the hijacker had said. Mark could respect the hijacker for his willingness to concede that possibility as well. But Mark felt that it was still too great of a risk to allow the hijacker to touch the artifact. That man had killed the *Aldrin* crew and likely a great many more people since he had awoken from his millennia-long stasis. This was someone who should never have the vast power that the Bastion and its alien builders wielded. Mark was not even sure if any single individual could be trusted with that kind of power.

The memories that Ning had shared with Mark were all too real and powerful to be dismissed by mere words. When Ning shared her mind with Mark, her memories of all the pain and horror the other had subjected her to were as vivid to Mark as if he had experienced them himself. And he had committed atrocities to so many others, not just to the *Aldrin* crew. His ruthless slaughter of scores of innocent people, his uncontrollable rage had nearly caused the extinction of the human species. Such a bloodthirsty monster could never be granted any chance of obtaining the power of the godlike beings that Ning called Legion.

He gazed out the window, his eyes locked on the approaching *Aldrin*. The Cycler was a big target, and he would have no trouble crashing into it. The bastard piloting it had made no transmission since his desperate plea for mercy, and had made no propulsive maneuvers. Collision between the two spacecraft was now inevitable, and there was just enough time for Mark to make one final transmission.

Ever since he began his career as an astronaut, friends, family, and strangers had called Mark a hero. He had never really considered himself worthy of being called a hero. He

351

was just an engineer that had been fortunate enough to double as a test pilot on many new spacecraft. He had saved the passengers of the lunar shuttle when he had made the emergency landing on the Moon, but he regarded that as simply him doing his job.

Now he had a chance to be a real hero as he prepared to sacrifice himself to defend humanity against a threat of unparalleled lethality.

"This is Commander Mark de Rijk of the *Intrepid*," he said into the communication console. "The *Aldrin* is about to rendezvous with the Bastion, and my crew's final attempt to activate the alien artifact and make contact with its builders seems to have been unsuccessful. Therefore, I have no choice but to proceed with the only remaining option for us, and ram the Cycler in order to kill the dangerous individual who commandeered that vessel. By the time you receive this transmission, I will be dead, and the *Intrepid* and *Aldrin* will have been destroyed. I will die knowing that we have saved humanity.

"My deepest regret is that my crew will also perish. While they will not die with me, they will only outlive me by a handful of hours. However, I will maintain hope that this sacrifice will finally awaken the Bastion, and that it will be compelled to save them. Perhaps that is nothing more than naïve, wishful thinking, but it is all I can do.

"I wish I could say that I'm fearlessly facing down death. But the truth is that I'm terrified. I'm terrified of dying. I always have been. Permanent cessation of consciousness is the most horrifying thing I can imagine. But death is something that inevitably befalls us all. What most people don't get is an opportunity to give their lives in order to save others. Dying so that others may live is truly the best way that anyone can die. And I'm going to perish saving more people than anyone ever has. I'll be saving everyone on Earth. My life is completely insignificant compared to the lives of all humanity. Therefore I do not regret what I am about to do.

"You'll probably never know the full extent of the danger that the *Aldrin* hijacker poses to Earth. I do not care to be remembered as a hero. I don't want statues or memorials erected in my honor. I only wish that you could know why this is being done, to know what I have learned. It saddens me to know that even after I send you the details of what I've learned, you likely won't believe it, and will instead think that I've had some psychological breakdown.

"And I especially regret getting not getting to learn more about the Bastion or the beings who built it. I hope that my crew lives so that they may discover more, and that anyone who hears this message continues the quest we began.

"This Mark de Rijk, commander of the *Intrepid*, signing off."

Mark let out a deep sigh after he finished talking. Then he transmitted the recording that he had made in which he had described everything he had learned from Ning. Words would never be able to do justice to the way the information had flowed into his brain, but Mark had done the best he could, and the people back on Earth deserved to know what happened here.

It was painful knowing that he would die without knowing what fate awaited his crew. But at least he would kill the bastard onboard the *Aldrin*, and humanity would be safe from his wrathful madness.

Mark looked at the massive Cycler that now filled his view, growing larger with each passing second as the two spacecraft rushed toward each other. Even if he wanted to turn away, it was now too late to make any difference: the impact between the *Intrepid* and *Aldrin* was now unavoidable.

He closed his eyes and took a deep, final breath.

***

The *Aldrin*'s alarms blared loudly, warning that a collision was imminent. Ask cursed himself for not having been prepared for this eventuality; his carelessness might end up costing him his life.

He had just begun to tighten the seals on the suit's gloves when the *Aldrin* suddenly and violently trembled, coupled with a sickening sound as the corridors shattered from the impact. The walls of the module crumpled before being ripped apart and Ask was hurled out into the black void of space.

He felt burning pain as pieces of shrapnel tore through his suit and his body. His suit alarm blared as it hemorrhaged oxygen from multiple punctures and the connections between suit components that he had not sealed prior to the *Aldrin*'s destruction.

He was stabbed by more excruciating pain as a large piece metal tore through his body and pulverized his liver and right kidney. No matter: they would regenerate, so long as he did not die from asphyxiation first, which became increasingly unlikely with each passing second. The stars spun around him as the venting oxygen caused him to spin uncontrollably.

His helmet display showed that he had already lost over half of his oxygen. It would not be long before the rest vented to space. But despite the severity of the situation, Ask refused to panic. To let fear overwhelm him would rob him of what little chance he had of surviving this.

Ask slowed his metabolic rate to conserve what precious little oxygen remained. He could also numb the horrendous agony from his injuries, but he chose not to. The pain gave him more reason to survive this.

He worked quickly to close the remaining seals on his suit components. With both hands, he gripped the metal shard that had impaled him, careful not to tear his gloves on the jagged edges. Then, ignoring the hideous pain, he pulled the fragment from his body, sending a burst of blood spheres spouting from him that quickly subsided as his wounds healed.

He wasted no time in repairing his suit using his patch kit. The damage was extensive, and he exhausted nearly all of the resin in the kit. He then connected the spare oxygen tank to his suit, narrowly saving himself from asphyxiation. The nanomachines would break down the shrapnel in his body, and he could already feel his body healing.

With the damage to his suit repaired, Ask used the MMU to stabilize himself. He was tumbling so rapidly that he ended up using most of the MMU's propellant just to kill his rotation.

Ask looked back and saw the devastation wrought by Mark de Rijk's suicide. Two crowning achievements of baseline spacecraft engineering had been reduced to a twisted mechanical graveyard, claiming the life of one of their best astronauts.

Crumpled, shattered radiators and modules from both of the ruined spacecraft continued to shred each other into smaller and smaller fragments. There were undulating, amorphous blobs of liquid hydrogen from the *Aldrin*, boiling off into wispy clouds. Pellets of deuterium and helium-three fuel had erupted from the *Intrepid*'s ruptured propellant tanks. Shattered fragments of the spacecraft began to spread outward in an ever-expanding cloud of debris.

Feeling empathy for the now-slain Mark de Rijk was something Ask could never do, not when the commander's death may very well have brought about his own. He reoriented himself again to look at the infinitely black artifact as he continued his rapid approach. He had no choice now but to place his faith in the belief that the object was the Tabernacle. If it were not, then he would be

355

doomed to die in just a few more hours.

It would be wasteful for him to use any of the propellant in the suit's maneuvering thrusters for deceleration; they now lacked enough propellant in them to bring his relative velocity with respect to the Tabernacle to zero.

The data from IE's robotic miners had indicated that any object that made physical contact with the Tabernacle immediately lost all of its momentum. Ask had to assume that the artifact continued to retain that property. It would be strange if the Tabernacle lost that property just because the baselines made physical contact with it, but he would not put that beyond Legion. He would not have been the least bit surprised if the Tabernacle had simply disintegrated when the baselines touched it. It would just be another symptom of Legion's madness; the same madness that had brought about this desperate fight for his own survival.

Ask was not motivated by vengeance. He never had been. But if given the opportunity to do so, he would not hesitate to make the *other* suffer for what she had done to him. If the Tabernacle bestowed him with its power, he intended to do just that. He might never be able to exact any form of vengeance on Legion, but the *other* was a different story. She would pay.

***

"Commander," Adam said in a desperate whisper. "Commander de Rijk, are you still there?"

No response came. They were too far to see the two spacecraft collide, but the silence told them all they needed to know.

"Jesus Christ," Oksana whispered.

"Well, this is it," Jed said drearily. "You thought you could appease the gods with a human sacrifice. And you managed to convince the commander of it. Now we'll see if your faith will be rewarded."

Ning kept her hands firmly planted on the Bastion's surface, but there still was no response. Maybe Mark had been right, that his sacrifice would appease Legion, and the rest of them would be saved.

'*Please*,' she said to the Tabernacle. '*Please help us. You've seen the sacrifices we're willing to make to safeguard your legacy. Now please help us.*'

Silence.

"Any luck?" asked Oksana.

Ning did not respond.

Jed chuckled grimly. "What did I tell you? We're all thoroughly fucked."

"Shut the living fuck up!" Adam screamed.

"Why should I cease my voice any sooner than the time when death will silence me forever? Many do not know when, where, or how they will die. There is almost a sense of tranquility to be had in knowing the specific aspects of one's own impending doom."

"Would you please just shut up?" Adam said, almost pleadingly.

"Why? Must you delude yourself into thinking there's even the slimmest of probabilities that we'll survive this? Well guess what: there isn't. We're going to die here. End of story. The only question is whether you want to wait until your oxygen runs out, or crack open your helmet and end it all right now.

"If you guys really wanted to live, you would have mutinied against the commander, taken control of the *Intrepid*, and gotten out of here like Mission Control ordered us to. But I knew that none of you had the guts to do that because of how blindly you were willing to follow the commander and this bitch. I did not bother to say or do anything that would incite a real mutiny because my efforts would have been entirely in vain. This bitch has us all

357

infected with her bugs, and she would have used them to incapacitate or kill me if I dared oppose her. She would have done the same to you too."

The mathematician glared at Ning "How about it?" said Jed. "Are you thinking about severing my neurons right now just to shut me up?"

Ning ignored Jed's fatalistic words. She didn't care how unsuccessful her previous attempts had been. She would keep trying until the oxygen in her suit's tanks was depleted.

Chapter 33

Ask could hear the voices of the surviving crewmembers of the *Intrepid* on his suit's radio, listening to their frantic cries. His helmet displayed the positions of four crewmembers. They were on the surface of the eternally dark object that had to be the Tabernacle, hoping and praying for some sort of salvation. The fools.

Listening to their voices, he was easily able to ascertain that the one called Ning was his counterpart. It was she who had convinced Commander Mark de Rijk to make a suicidal attempt to destroy him, and doomed all of them.

The commander must have had hope that the Tabernacle was observing them, and that by sacrificing himself, Legion would be prompted to save his crew. A foolish thing to do.

"Hear me, oh, ye who betrayed me," Ask said, his voice carrying the intensity of thunder, "and know that your attempt to destroy me has failed. Tell me, did you tremble in fear when you learned of my liberation from the state of living death to which you had condemned me? Do you tremble now, knowing that I shall reach the Tabernacle in spite of your failed attempt to end my life? Answer me, lest your fear has paralyzed you with silence!"

"You waste your breath," Ning snapped, "as well as your life. Is it not abundantly clear to you that this artifact is not the Tabernacle? Or that if it is, that it will not bestow us with its power? You have not only condemned us to die, but yourself as well!"

Ask laughed. "Your words are as futile in deterring me as mine were in averting your commander's suicide! Legion could be denying this to you as part of their game! Surely, you have contemplated this. Are you so foolish that, even now, you refuse to concede that they play a game of madness? Are you so blind that you cannot perceive that your actions stand in complete contrast to your words?

"If you truly believed that I could not harness the power of the Tabernacle, or that this artifact is not the Tabernacle at all, then why did you convince the commander to sacrifice himself in an attempt to stop me? Nay, you knew it was entirely possible that the Tabernacle's power was meant for me and me alone. Still you desperately attempted to stop me from reaching it! You only insult your own intelligence with your incessant lies!

"You know that Legion could have elected to terminate me long ago, as you yourself could have done! Yet they spared my life, and commanded you to preserve it, albeit in a state of living death…and you blindly obeyed! You knew full well that Legion intended for the Tabernacle to be mine all along. They have not spoken to you in all the time since you betrayed me, have they? You believed that their silence gave you permission to destroy me upon learning that I had awoken! You believed that there was no higher purpose than to obey the will of Legion, and yet now you have brought death upon yourself and these baselines because you feared that Legion intended to apotheosize me. Have your thoughts turned to rebellion, or have you gone so mad that you cannot perceive the hypocrisy of your actions?"

Ning gave no retort.

Ask laughed again. "It is just as I suspected. You fear me, for I speak in a voice that has long since fallen silent within your own mind: the voice of doubt and sanity. What you fear above all else is that I speak the truth."

"Shut up you fucking monster!" Adam screamed. "You're not getting anything! There's no fucking way that they would give everything to a monster like you! Ning told us everything about what you've done!"

"You poor fools," Ask said. "Did she share her mind

with you? Surely, she must have, for you otherwise would never be so foolhardy as to follow her to the trap into which you have fallen. Condemn me not as the harbinger of your deaths, for this was never my intention. She made you believe that my intentions are malicious. You were deceived.

"I was never so arrogant or foolhardy as she has been in her belief that this artifact is the Tabernacle. Moreover, even if it truly is the Tabernacle, I was never narcissistic enough to believe that its power was for me and me alone. On the contrary, I was prepared to accept the very real possibility that my voyage here was entirely in vain, much as yours has proven to be. And in that eventuality, I was willing to surrender myself to you! But now that both of our vessels have been destroyed, you have no hope of survival! And this is due entirely to her deception!

"Direct your anger towards the one who has manipulated you to serve her ends. What fragments of truth she has permitted you to see serve only to bend you to her will. You are but pawns to her! If you had refused to listen to her, your commander would not have sacrificed himself or your spacecraft. With my survival, the futility of this sacrifice is fully cemented.

"If this Bastion is the Tabernacle, then the death of your commander will have accomplished nothing. If it refuses to endow me with its power, or if it is not the Tabernacle at all, then striving to stop me accomplished nothing. Regardless of the outcome, the death of Mark de Rijk was meaningless. As shall yours.

"I do not promise that the Tabernacle shall apotheosize me, or that I will save your lives in the event that I am. But be thankful that in the final hours of your lives, I have provided you with more truth than she has. And be grateful that I have lifted the veil of ignorance that she pulled over your eyes."

361

"And what if you too are unable to wield its power?" Ning asked.

"Then I shall take solace in knowing that I will have dragged you into the oblivion of death alongside me!"

"Enough!" Adam cried, and propelled himself off the surface of the Tabernacle and toward Ask. "I've had enough of your bullshit!"

Ask's helmet display showed the baseline lifting off from the Tabernacle and toward him. Knowing his exact position, the astrobiologist altered his trajectory such that the two of them would collide head-on with each other.

Anger grew within Ask as he saw how unavoidable the collision was. This was exactly like the situation he had found himself in aboard the *Aldrin* just a short while ago. He had exhausted nearly all of the propellant in the MMU to stabilize himself in the wake of the *Aldrin*'s destruction. He only had enough remaining for two more propulsive burns, while the biologist surely had far more. If Ask were to alter his trajectory now, he would miss the Tabernacle entirely.

But Ask knew he could survive colliding with the baseline, while the biologist would surely be killed.

"What's the matter?" Adam taunted as he moved closer to Ask. "Can't move away from me?"

The biologist had expected that Ask had exhausted most, if not all, of the propellant in his MMU after fleeing from the *Aldrin*. And seeing him remain on his current trajectory all but confirmed this.

"Do you wish to hasten your death?" Ask said to Adam. "Because that is all you shall accomplish by attacking me."

"I'd do anything to shut you up."

"So be it."

Knowing she had no other choice, Ning pushed herself off the Tabernacle's surface, and came within fifty feet of

Adam. If she had remained at the Tabernacle, Adam would have quickly moved beyond the communication range of the nanomachines, and the ones inhabiting his body would fall dead. The *other* had enough kinetic energy to kill Adam when they collided with each other. Having functional nanomachines inside of him was the only chance the astrobiologist had of surviving. Maybe he would be able to latch onto the *other* and fight him, perhaps inflict serious damage to his spacesuit and kill him. Keeping Adam alive was her last remaining hope to prevent the *other* from reaching the Tabernacle.

Ask laughed upon seeing what Ning had done. "The extent of your cowardice is astonishing!" he mocked. "Even when your own death is all but inevitable, you still have others fight your battles for you."

"Shut the fuck up!" Adam screamed. He knew that Ning was following him so that her nanotechnology would prevent him from being killed by the coming impact. But he still would have done this even had she not followed. This monster simply could not be allowed to reach the Tabernacle. Adam knew he was as good as dead anyway; what did it matter if he died from a head-on collision with this bastard rather than asphyxiate in a few more hours?

The blow was so powerful that Adam felt his organs jostle and his brain rattle inside his skull. Even with the nanomachines in his body and knowing their capabilities, he was still astonished that he survived, much less remained conscious. He then began to kick furiously and punch at Ask with his right hand while gripping him with his left.

Ask grabbed Adam's right hand in his left, easily overpowering him with his superior strength, but Adam continued to kick as hard as he could. Ask sent his nanomachines probing through Adam's suit and into the astrobiologist's body. And then he felt them encounter the nanomachines of the other, and the futility in trying to fight them. This was yet another constraint that Legion had imposed on their nanotechnology: the nanomachines from different hosts always refused to fight each other.

Ning knew that she should grab onto them, to aid Adam in his desperate fight against the other. But her thoughts turned to what had happened the last time she had fought him directly, so many years ago, and both Ask and Adam sailed passed her.

Within seconds, they were beyond the communication range of Ning's nanomachines, and the ones within Adam's body fell dead. As soon as the defenses fell, Ask sent his own minions deep within Adam's brain. Paralyzing his muscle functions, Ask saw into the astrobiologist's mind just as he had with so many other baselines, seeing everything Ning had shared with him. It was just as he had suspected; she had revealed only fragments of the truth to him, coupled with outright lies in order to manipulate Adam and the others into making this suicidal stand. This poor baseline had never stood a chance to resist Ning's influence; such was the extent of her deception.

Ask could have killed Adam as easily and swiftly as so many other baselines he had vanquished. Every baseline he had ever killed had perished because they represented a threat to his life or wellbeing, or to further his own interests. But this astrobiologist had been neutralized as an immediate threat, and killing him would do serve no purpose in bringing him closer to the Tabernacle.

'You know that your life now hangs firmly in my hand, and how swiftly I could end it,' Ask said directly to Adam's mind. 'And yet I shall not do so. I shall instead grant you a gift.'

Ask opened his mind to Adam, showing him everything that Ning had not. Then he released the paralysis, but the fight was gone from Adam, and Ask

364

pushed him away.

"Adam!" Oksana screamed. "Are you okay?"

"I…I don't know," he whispered.

"I freed him from the siren's song under which you have all fallen," Ask declared. "Behold my mercy, and stand not against me lest you have been robbed of all cognitive faculties."

Ask continued to approach the Tabernacle, and neither Oksana nor Jed attempted to stop him. He stretched out his arms with his palms open wide, ready to accept whatever happened.

Slamming into the surface, he immediately lost all of his momentum, and ordered thousands of nanomachines to slip through the cells of his body and crawl to the outside of his suit. He felt some fly off into space, but others successfully made contact with the surface of the Bastion. So absorbed was he that he did not notice Ning had rejoined them on the surface.

The Tabernacle instantly became an inverse of itself. Whereas before it had been a hole in the fabric of space into which light fell, it was now a radiating source of blinding white light that seemed to fill the entire universe that proceeded to swallow Ask and the others.

Chapter 34

Ask found himself surrounded by a featureless white that seemed to stretch infinitely. There was gravity, and he was standing upright. But his spacesuit felt somewhat lighter than it would have on Earth.

He looked at the environmental sensor on the wrist of his spacesuit. It indicated that there was a breathable atmosphere present. This did not surprise him in the least. Ask removed his helmet, and took in a deep breath. The air tasted clean and pure.

"Welcome," said a voice. A voice was humble and nondescript, giving no indication of the power that spoke through it. And it was eerily familiar.

Ask turned to see a man that had suddenly appeared right before him. He wore a simple gray robe.

"I have been waiting a long time for you to arrive," the man continued in that unassuming voice.

It was a man whom Ask recognized, although he knew that this being was not a man at all. It was an avatar of Legion, and it had the very same appearance as the avatar he had seen and spoken to in the distant past. Even with recognition, Ask knew he still had to ask the daunting question that had brought him here.

"Are you the Tabernacle?" Ask said to the avatar in a calm, determined voice.

"I am."

***

Adam, Jed, Ning, and Oksana perceived Ask and the Tabernacle avatar speaking to each other, but they were not seeing with their eyes or hearing with their ears. It was as though the audiovisual information was being transmitted directly to their brains without having to pass through faulty sensory organs.

But they could not speak, move, or interact with anything. They were not even aware of their own bodies, if they still existed.

***

Ask felt his heart hammer. He had been waiting for this moment for thousands of years. As long last, he would get what he longed for, with Legion atoning for all of the suffering they had caused him.

"Will you give me the knowledge and power that I was promised?" he asked the Tabernacle, fighting to keep his voice steady.

"I cannot do so."

The Tabernacle's words instantly reignited the fire of rage within Ask, and it raged more fiercely than it ever had before. He fought to retain his stoicism, but this was too much. All of his efforts, all of the hope that he had invested in Legion; all of it was for nothing.

"Why do you do this?!" Ask screamed. "Why do you deceive and betray me?! Why do you play these insane games?! How far into the pit of madness have you fallen?!"

"Your anger and frustration stems from your own ignorance and incapability of perceiving the truth," said the Tabernacle in the same calm, bland voice.

Ask wanted to lash out at the Tabernacle avatar, to unleash the full fury of the storm that raged within him. But even in this state of indignation, he knew how futile such a gesture would be.

"What is it that I fail to comprehend?" Ask demanded, directing all of his energy into his voice. Wherever it was that the Tabernacle had brought him, he would fill it with as much of his voice as he could, for it was all he could do to express his enmity. "You commanded me to guide the human baselines on the path to civilization, and promised that if I did so, I would eventually find you and be given your power and wisdom. I obeyed every command you

367

gave me, only to have you reward my loyalty by destroying everything I did and imprisoning me in a state of living death. But even after all of the suffering that I was forced to endure, I was still compelled to reach you in the wake of my serendipitous resurrection. And now that I am finally here, you say that you cannot give me the very thing that I was promised. Explain to me how what you do is anything other than the workings of minds that have fallen into a state of complete and utter madness!"

"There is great purpose behind all that we do," said the Tabernacle. "You would know this to be true if you were to obtain that which you seek. And you confuse my own inability to provide you with that which you desire with a collective incapability shared by all of us."

Ask's rage abated. "Please elaborate," he said in a calmer voice.

"We fully intend to give you what you seek, but we cannot do so here. In order for Legion to bestow you with our gift, I must ferry you to the Empyrean."

"What is this Empyrean of which you speak?"

"It is the stronghold of Legion, and the source from which all their power in this universe emanates. If I bring you there, we will endow you with all that you seek."

Ask's anger dissipated further, but did not fade entirely. "I have no guarantee that you will honor your word," he said grimly, "for you have broken it before. And yet I am forced to concede that I have no choice in this matter. I never have."

"You grasp as much of the truth as one of your limited stature is capable of comprehending," said the Tabernacle.

Ask smiled thinly. "I believe that that is as close to commendation as you are capable of offering." He had now fully quelled his fury, returned to his stoic state, and stood as tall as one could before the presence of a god. "Very well. Please ferry me to the Empyrean."

"What of me?"

Ask knew the source of the voice immediately, and was not surprised in the least bit when he turned his head to the left and saw Ning standing right beside him. She wore her spacesuit, and held her helmet in her hands just as Ask did.

He knew what she had looked like from the footage and images of her and the rest of the *Intrepid* crew that had saturated social media. The façade looked nothing at all like her original appearance. Perhaps she had been like him, refusing to allow any baseline to see her true face once she had disappeared into the general population of their society.

Ask felt a brief resurgence of rage, and nearly lashed out at her, but he restrained himself. Legion was going to give him everything he sought, so there was no longer any reason to seek vengeance. He was aware that if they were to betray him again as they had done before, there was nothing that he could do to oppose them.

"I have done all that you commanded of me," Ning continued, "and never once did anything that was against your will. Are you truly going to toss me aside and reward only him? If that is your intention, I shall not object, for I have always trusted in your infinite wisdom."

"Your concerns are unwarranted," said the Tabernacle, "for we extend this offer to you as well."

Ning bowed her head. "Thank you. I cannot thank you enough for the generosity you have shown to a being as humble as I."

"Generosity is not a factor in any of our decision making processes. All that we do we do because it must be done. You shall see the truth of this once we reach the Empyrean."

Ning raised her head to look at the avatar directly in his eyes. "Of course," she said. "And I will gladly continue

369

to serve you to the very best of my capabilities."

Ask said nothing.

***

Whatever power the Tabernacle was holding over Adam, Oksana, and Jed was lifted when Ning agreed to the Tabernacle's offer. They all suddenly found themselves standing right alongside Ask and the Tabernacle.

Adam was momentarily discombobulated by his return to his familiar state of existence, but this passed quickly, and he removed his helmet.

"Adam!" Oksana cried.

He looked to see the physicist standing next to him, her own helmet having been removed.

"Are you all right?" she asked.

"Yeah, I think so," he grumbled, still shaky from his ordeal. Then he felt rage overtake him as he looked again at Ask and Ning standing before the Tabernacle avatar.

"You can't do this!" Adam yelled at the Tabernacle. "You cannot possibly give these two godlike powers after everything that they've done! They're monsters!"

Ning almost looked ashamed to see them, and Ask seemed to be indifferent. The Tabernacle's expression was completely unreadable.

"You may find their actions to be deplorable," said the Tabernacle, "but you cannot grasp the role that they play in our projects, for you have neither the authority nor capability to deny them the paths that they must follow.

"This is still bullshit!"

"Do not be so arrogant as to believe that your ignorance of our projects imparts you with wisdom or enlightenment. There is so much that you do not know. Our projects were initiated long before the first fusion reaction that birthed starlight, and will continue long after the last star has died. These two play vital roles in our endeavors, roles that are not yet complete. I must bring them to the

Empyrean of Legion in order for them to do what is required of them."

"You could have at least saved the commander!" Adam screamed. "You could have stopped the *Aldrin* and *Intrepid* from being destroyed!"

"No, I could not, for I had no permission to act."

"Permission? What permission? Whose permission?"

"I was required to remain dormant until the coming of this one," said the avatar, gesturing toward Ask. "Then and only then was I permitted to awaken and bring you within my body."

"Why the hell did you have to wait until then? You must have had some way of perceiving what happens around you."

"I am but the humblest of beings that comprise Legion. There are a myriad of protocols that we have deemed necessary in order for our projects to come to fruition. These are protocols that I must conform to, and I cannot rebel against them any more than you can cease to draw breath while continuing to live. I was only required to preserve the lives of these two, but I was free to choose whether or not to save your lives. So be grateful that I am being compassionate."

Silence befell them briefly, which was broken when Ask began to laugh.

"Did I not tell you that his sacrifice was rendered completely meaningless when I was approaching the Tabernacle?" he said. "Did it take until now for you to comprehend the veracity of my words?"

Adam sneered at Ask briefly, and then hung his head, wanting to cry. "Jesus Christ," he muttered. "The commander really did die for nothing."

"So what will you do with us?" Jed asked the Tabernacle.

"If you so desire, you may accompany us to the

371

Empyrean. I cannot provide any assurances that Legion will offer you the same capabilities that will be given to these two. Regardless of what transpires at the Empyrean, you shall see and learn a great many things on the voyage there."

"Like what?"

"There is no direct path to the Empyrean available to me. I must travel through a vast network of wormholes that spans the farthest reaches of the universe. We will traverse across a myriad of star systems and galaxies before we reach our final destination, billions of light-years from here. During the voyage, you will have the opportunity to see many star systems and civilizations.

"I will be your vessel and ferry you through the wormhole network. I shall provide you with all of your environmental and dietary needs for the duration of the voyage."

"What if we refuse?" said Adam.

"Refuse?" said Jed in astonishment. "You'd really turn down an opportunity to see the universe?"

"It's not that. I'd love very much to go on this odyssey. But I also want to be able to go home again." Adam looked back to the avatar. "Will you ferry us back to Earth if we request it?"

"I am not permitted to do so," said the Tabernacle.

"What? Why the hell not? You say that you have the ability to travel all across the universe. Taking us back home must be a fucking cakewalk for you!"

"You are correct that I could return you to your home planet by wielding only a tiny fraction of my power. But I am not permitted to do so, and this is due to the protocols I must follow. I cannot decide on the proper course of action Legion must take any more than a single blood cell in your body can solve the most trivial of mathematical equations. You cannot begin to grasp the enormity of our projects, or the care we must take in order for them to be successful. Should you refuse to accompany us, I shall honor your request, and you will be permitted to remain here."

"You'd leave us here to die?!"

"If that is what you desire."

"Jesus Christ. Your protocols are bullshit. You guys are fucking bureaucrats!"

"Your disapproval of our actions is fueled entirely by your own ignorance, and your undeveloped minds cannot even begin to fathom the reasons for our actions. I have given you a choice. So what do you desire?"

"Will you take as back to Earth at some point in the future?"

"It is possible. But I cannot say for certain. It is only upon our arrival at the Empyrean that your fate shall be determined."

"Can we at least contact Earth?" Adam asked. "Can we tell everyone what's happened? Let them know that we're safe?"

"No. I am prohibited from making direct contact with your home planet, and I cannot allow you to use my resources to do so either. Again, I offer you a choice: you may come with us if you so desire or you may stay here and perish just as you would have had I not brought you within my body."

Adam let out a long, deep sigh, slumping as though in defeat.

"I'll go," said Jed to the Tabernacle. He looked to Adam and Oksana. "This is what we really came here for. This is what it's all about, what it has always been about. This is the ultimate dream that people have had for generations. We're being given an opportunity to travel across the universe by an extraterrestrial intelligence. We'll see things no other human has ever seen before, learn things that no human has learned before.

"Yes, the commander's death was a tragic and unnecessary loss, but there's nothing we can do about that now. He's gone, and nothing can bring him back. But the most important thing to him was expanding mankind's knowledge about the universe. I always shared that value with him, and I know that you did too. So the best way that we can honor Commander de Rijk is by going on this journey that's being offered to us. This is exactly what he would have done if he was alive, and what he would have wanted us to do. Do you really want to turn this down?"

"Hell no," said Oksana. "I'm going too." She looked at Adam. "So what's it going to be for you?"

Adam sighed. "We have to choose between seeing the wonders of the universe or dying a pointless death millions of miles from Earth." He chuckled. "Not much of a choice now, is it? All right then. I'll go too."

The Tabernacle avatar nodded. "Very well."

The infinite whiteness dissolved, and they became bathed in the light of another star.

51587862R00233

Made in the USA
San Bernardino, CA
27 July 2017